SECOND CHANCES

by Dannye Williamsen

Published by:

Williamsen Publications

http://www.WilliamsenPublications.com,
http://www.DannyeWilliamsen.com

The sequel to *Second Chances: The Threads That Bind*

For my husband, John,
who has always been there for me,
no matter what the circumstances.
He is my best friend, and I have been
fortunate to have him in my life.

The Wolf: 1980

Chapter 1

His nose twitched slightly as he searched the air for clues. Otherwise Avatar stood motionless on the crest of the hill. The moon reflected off his coat, creating a silver haze that mingled with the early evening mist. Avatar turned his head ever so slightly trying to catch a breeze, anticipating smells of some kind. A sweet wafting of the night breezes should have carried the smells of at least a hundred animals, big and small, to his sensitive nose.

There was no breeze.

There were no smells.

Emptiness.

His ears stood taut as he listened to hear what he could not smell. It was almost deafening, but it was nothing. It was overwhelming in its nothingness. Total silence.

The wolf looked down over the land below him. It was filled with trees, trees that appeared to be dead. If it had been winter, no one passing by—neither human nor animal—would even have noticed the starkness. But, this was spring, and there were no animals, no birds, no insects. The air was oppressive. He raised his head and looked toward the horizon to see how far this devastation extended. He saw that its ghostly perimeter formed a circle about two miles in diameter.

A circle of death.

In its center was a cabin.

Differences in shade between the hollow shells of the trees, barely distinguishable to the eye, created concentric borders. These borders resembled the rings found after a tree was cut down—rings that indicated periods of growth and dormancy, growth and dormancy. Avatar stared at the cabin in the heart of this circle of death. He sensed that these ostensible borders represented dormant periods also—periods when death was not creeping further into the woods.

The wolf stepped into the circle, moving silently through the rings of death as he approached the cabin. The silence welled up around him. He could feel it brushing against him the way the underbrush would if it were there. The air joined with the silence, pressing down on him.

As the distance from the perimeter of this forsaken ground increased, Avatar sensed the spirit of another. He was not sure what it was. It was unlike any spirit he had ever encountered, and in his years of wandering, he had seen many. There were good spirits and bad, but the *very* good and the *very* bad were rare.

His nostrils flinched. He smelled something! The contrast of nothingness and this smell was overpowering.

"Ah! Another comes to join the fold!" Its words resounded in Avatar's mind. "The wolf becomes the lamb being led to slaughter." Then it laughed.

Avatar fell to the ground, his hindquarters trembling. A force unseen by the wolf pressed in around him beyond the silence and the heaviness of the air. His fear rose within. He felt his spirit starting to slip away. "I am not afraid," declared the wolf. He was not challenging the force. He was simply asserting his conviction that what happened in this place had no real power over him, "If it is time to give up this body, it is time."

His spirit was breaking its bond with his body, ready to take irreversible flight when suddenly it was seized as if a fist of iron wrenched it from the heavens, squeezing it with such power that it momentarily merged with this sinister force. For an instant the wolf's spirit entered the darkest recesses in the mind of this evil one. Such unspeakable horror resided there in calm anticipation that Avatar was more frightened by this than by any harm that might befall him. His fear, which had quickly reemerged when his life force was literally seized, was no longer for himself. He sensed the innocence of another, one who would not long escape this madman.

From deep within, the wolf howled, calling out to those like him. Their energy flowed into Avatar, surging through him, igniting sparks of life until every particle of his being was increased tenfold. The sparks grew into a flame and the flame into a fire which threatened to consume the dark spirit holding Avatar's life in its grasp. Then just as a hand touching a flame recoils under its threat, so did the dark spirit release the life force of Avatar.

As his spirit returned to his body, the wolf knew his earthly time was not yet over. He stood, feeling a strength in his limbs greater than they had ever known. He gazed at the cabin. The logs that graced the cabin walls were gray as ash. Avatar would not be surprised to see them crumble into a pile if even the slightest breeze rustled past. His gaze shifted to the window. The dark form of a man was outlined against the pale light in the cabin. Avatar was almost surprised it was a man. A monster of gargantuan proportions would have surprised him less. When their paths crossed again, he wondered, who would survive? Then he quickly turned and ran toward the perimeter. His mission had just begun.

Dark eyes filled with rage peered out the window of the cabin in the direction of the departing wolf. Particles of his dark energy reached out, beginning to rejoin the air around him. He was driven by a desire to see the wolf lying on the ground, nothing but an empty, misshapen shell. At the last second, he jerked back.

The wolf frightened him. Never before had he encountered anyone or anything that could resist him. He didn't understand what had happened. He had held the wolf's life force in his grasp. He felt it merging with his own, starting to lose its grip on the wolf's consciousness. Then suddenly it exploded with such force that he could no longer hold it!

What was this power greater than he?

He knew that it was time. He could not, *would* not, delay much longer.

"The Past is rarely the past. It weaves a thread through every thought, every breath, for generations to come."
- The Book of Metanoia

The Tangling of the Threads

Chapter 2

Day 1—Memphis

Fredrika loved her job. It was barely credible to her that only a few years ago she hadn't even known what commodities were. Now she was a respected technical research analyst for one of the largest commodity firms trading on the Chicago Board of Trade. Talk about synchronicity! The trail that brought her to this place in her life had been filled with fragile markers that she could have misread, failed to notice, or just ignored. She could never have planned this path for herself because she hadn't even known it existed. Even if she had, she would never have believed she could walk on it.

Before commodities, Fredrika was employed in the construction industry. She would never forget the panic that nearly overtook her the day she realized the construction company where she worked was folding. She had locked herself in her office and paced back and forth, silently mourning all her hard work that now would count for nothing. All the ups and downs of being a woman supervisor in construction and putting up with the antics of the construction crews for six years, not to mention the long hours that stretched far beyond a forty-hour week with no overtime pay. What difference had it made if she was suddenly going to be the victim of a recession? She had known what always died first in a recession. That's right. Construction. In a recession, the future was too bleak for people to even consider expansion. They preferred to hold tight. Consequently, they remodeled or redecorated, but they didn't build anything new.

The money was good in the building industry, and Fredrika had paid her dues, but seniority had no pull in a slump this deep. Memphis always seemed to be the last place to suffer the effects of a recession—maybe because it was a distribution center. After all, even if there weren't as many things moving, *somebody* had to distribute them. Anyway, by the time the first buds of this recession sprouted in Memphis, it was already in full bloom across the country, and it didn't look like that particular flower was going to wilt quickly.

Having discarded all the reasonable possibilities as being dead-ends, a casual comment from a friend saved Fredrika from initiating any plans that might later prove to be embarrassing. When her friend Sawyer revealed that his commodity broker mentioned an opening at his company, Fredrika had jumped at the opportunity. She knew matching her salary would be hard. Any job she took would, by necessity, be in a different industry, and she would be much further down on the food chain. Sometimes, she'd told herself, you just have to start over.

Her interview revealed, however, that the opening her friend Sawyer mentioned was a secretarial position in the brokerage division. Regardless of her potential financial woes, Fredrika was certain of one thing. For her, starting over did not mean typing letters until her fingers fell off and her mind's ability to think suffered irreparable damage. Disappointed, but not down for the count yet, Fredrika recalled seeing a second sign on the office door. It read: Technical Research Department.

"What's technical research?" she'd asked Mr. Stevens, the Director of the Brokerage Division and the man in need of a secretary.

"Well," he replied, sensing that this young woman would never consent to be his secretary, "the technical analysts study charts and use other technical information related to price fluctuations and then project future prices for the different commodities we trade, mainly on the Chicago Board of Trade."

"Hm-m-m." His words had sparked Fredrika's imagination, and she'd known this was what she wanted to do. No question. It didn't matter that she didn't have a clue what commodity trading involved. It didn't matter that it wasn't a perfect science. The idea of research coupled with the obvious challenge involved in projecting prices stirred up the ol' juices. Her mind was already racing down that path when she asked, "Is there anything open in that department?"

Within a few minutes, Mr. Stevens introduced her to Maury Stein, Director of Technical Research. After Stein explained in a little more detail the focus of his department, he inquired about her background. Fredrika explained that she had been a top level manager in the construction industry for six years, assuring him she was very detail-oriented. She sensed this would be an important consideration for any research position.

Reluctantly, it seemed to Fredrika, Stein said, "I do have a position. It's assistant to the grain analyst."

Her pulse raced. *Years* of coveting this position could not have engendered the passion already ablaze in her. If something piqued Fredrika's interest, her intensity level shot from cool to red-hot in less than 10 seconds, and this job had her rapt attention.

"However," Stein continued, "I have to tell you that we've tried to fill this position several times. The longest anyone lasted was two weeks."

"Why?" she asked. She didn't really care. She already knew she was going to take the offer regardless, but it seemed appropriate to inquire.

"Well, Hayden, the grain analyst, is a little temperamental. Actually—he can be very caustic at times. He's a nice guy. Really.

Still, it doesn't change the fact that he can be difficult to work with."

"I'll make it work *if it kills him!*" she declared.

Laughing at her boldness, Stein announced, "You're hired!"

"There is just one thing."

"What?" Maury Stein was not surprised she was proposing conditions. Her boldness almost assured it.

"I have to be guaranteed this is not a dead-end job. I want to be a technical analyst. I'm willing to pay my dues, but I *have* to know that being an analyst is a real possibility for me down the road."

Maury agreed. Rather than looking challenged by her audacity, a reaction she was quite used to in construction, he seemed intrigued. Months later a colleague confided Maury's comment to him about Fredrika that first day. "That woman won't be content to be an assistant for long. She'll probably have her dues paid up before the notices are even sent out!"

Over the next year she refused to be intimidated by Hayden's bullying or his antics, and they became good friends. Even though control was an important issue in her life, it didn't seem to matter that she couldn't control the markets because she *could* control her analysis of them. So she worked hard, charting and studying the markets. One day Maury came to Fredrika and asked, "What would you think about taking over the financial instruments markets?"

What did she think about it? She was elated. Her dream was coming true, and the timing couldn't have been better. As Hayden's assistant, the learning process had stalled out because she wasn't in a position to try her wings. All her trading was paper trading. No one else would ever knew what she projected or if it was accurate.

Even though Fredrika knew the financial instruments markets weren't very active at the time, it was a place to start. As it turned out, it was one of those fragile markers that could have been misread. Rather than being token markets given to a novice analyst, they turned out to be a gift from God. In a few short months, the markets no one gave much attention were suddenly the Holy Grail of markets.

Intensely dedicated, Fredrika's success as an analyst was phenomenal. The mystery of commodity analysis drew her into its folds like a cult, and her past in the construction industry was swept away. There was only the market. The one drawback was the pressure to always know the answers. It spawned a unique breed of people. People who spewed out on cue streams of information that would assign Abbott and Costello's "Who's on first and What's on second" routine to the status of kindergarten-level double talk. Unfortunately, it never seemed to stop. It pervaded every corner of their lives. Even after work at Élan's, the lounge on the first floor of the Clark Tower where everyone gathered for drinks and the free buffet, technical analysis was the only topic of conversation. Even weather, the old standby of conversation, lost out in the heat of passion when commodity traders were in the same room. Of course, Fredrika was as guilty of the passion as anyone else.

Within six months of becoming an analyst, Maury asked Fredrika to take over the responsibility of teaching the technical analysis training class in Chicago for all incoming account executives. "Are you sure?" she asked, afraid he would change his mind, but needing to actually hear him say he was confident she could do it.

"Why wouldn't I be? Of course, I think it's best if you go with me and observe this time. What do you think?"

Relieved, she replied, "I absolutely agree. You've been doing it for a long time. I know I'll pick up a lot of tips." Brown-nosing was not one of her strongest traits, but she could certainly step up to the challenge when necessary. Plus she *did* think it was best.

Fredrika was thrilled with this new development. Just the idea of it made her feel alive. It also scared the hell out of her. The boldness she exhibited when she interviewed for her job was just a front. In her heart she always felt she didn't know enough, that she was just one step ahead of the pack and frightened that one day they'd catch up with her, and it would all be over. She knew it wasn't a healthy attitude, but despite it, things always managed to work out.

Teaching was the first desire she remembered having as a child. Unfortunately, she hadn't been brave enough to pursue it as a career. So the chance to teach technical analysis was an opportunity she couldn't refuse. Once again, the belief that she couldn't possibly know enough served her well. It drove her to add more and more elements to each class she taught. Immediately after a session, she got busy planning improvements for the next class in six months. Tomorrow she would leave for Chicago to teach her third class since she had stepped in for Maury. Right now, however, she just needed a little quiet time.

Daydreaming was her favorite pastime when the markets were slow. It helped her balance the stress of calling the markets. It had always been the way she escaped the tensions in her life, no matter what caused them. As a child she sat alone on the front porch for countless hours dreaming of what her life was going to be like—all the while listening to the bees buzzing around the white-flowered bushes that grew next to the railing. Today she wasn't aware that in the quiet of her office in the Clark Tower, the buzzing lights were serving as a trigger, beckoning her to that same dreamlike state she experienced so often as a child. Her mind quickly slipped into a place somewhere between awareness and sleep.

"Freddie! Do you have a broadcast to send out over the wire?" The voice of her assistant, Joyce, blared over the intercom. Freddie jumped, banging her knee on the desk.

"No," she replied, rubbing her knee. "Just send out my prepared broadcast in the morning. After that, J. D. will cover for me until I get back." Clicking the intercom button again, Freddie asked, "By the way, Joyce, do you have those transparencies ready that I wanted to add to my class? If you do, I think I'll go ahead and leave."

"Sure," Joyce replied, a note of surprise in her voice. Freddie never left the office before 5 p.m. even though her markets closed much earlier in the afternoon. Even getting her to take a vacation had proved to be an impossible task.

Freddie caught the surprise in Joyce's response. She was a little surprised herself. Leaving early had not been her plan, but an urgent need to escape was driving her. Looking around her office, everything had a slightly unreal quality to it. She felt like she was either walking around in a dream or was stoned. She hadn't touched a joint in years, but she still remembered being high and the scary sensation on the downhill side of it. Scary because she had no control. She remembered floating like a balloon caught in the wind being thrust this way and that with great urgency and then suddenly being left to drift with no direction at all.

Riding down in the elevator from the thirtieth floor, Freddie shook off her stupor by reviewing her outline for the upcoming class. Although the elevator stopped several times, discharging and loading passengers, she never noticed. Concentration was her strong suit. When the elevator stopped at the lobby, Freddie stepped off and walked toward the garage elevators. She never took her eyes off her notes as she stepped into the open elevator, glancing up only to make sure she punched the button for the fifth floor.

Once on the fifth floor of the garage, Freddie allowed her attention to return to her surroundings as she approached her car—a white Buick Riviera with burgundy leather seats and wire wheels. To Freddie it was a perfect blend of elegance and sport, a quality she craved for her own—to be able to blend into any situation that arose with equal grace. The car purred quietly as it twisted around the spiral ramp to the parking lot. Choosing the lane closest to the building to avoid the traffic trying to exit at the stop light, Freddie noticed a man standing on the walk in front of the lobby doors. He looked with interest in her direction. It didn't matter to Freddie whether he was appraising her car or her. At that moment in her mind, she blended perfectly with her car. Smiling graciously *and* flirtatiously at him, she was in harmony with the universe. At least her universe.

Chapter 3

Day 2 — Chicago

The plane lifted off smoothly, and Freddie directed her attention out the window. She had no desire to get involved in a conversation with her seat mate, whom she had already dubbed "Mr. Personality," not because he was charming but quite the opposite. Despite his handsome features and dark, wavy hair, he was totally morose and obviously not prone toward conversation.

As the plane gained altitude, she was entranced by the view. From here the city looked undefiled. Skyscrapers reached toward the sky like beautiful, architecturally designed fingers, vying for the honor of pointing the way to somewhere. Even the less artistic styling of the buildings surrounding them fit into the drama supporting the majesty of the ten or so skyscrapers that spotted the skyline.

As the plane moved north, Freddie looked down at the houses and farms. From up here everyone was anonymous. You felt no one's sadness or malevolence or sickness. Not even their laughter or joy. It was simply what you could see with your eyes. Nothing more, nothing less. Freddie's thoughts drifted, the clouds passing by her window mesmerizing her. Her eyelids drooped, and sleep overtook her.

Soon the thin veils separating her dreams parted, and a hand as cold as ice touched her. She instinctively knew this was no dream, but she couldn't move. Fear paralyzed her. The coldness brushed the side of her face, moving slowly down her neck until it reached the bulge of her breast. Her heart pounded. She tried to scream, even to open her eyes, but not one muscle moved. She was in a void where there was only coldness—a coldness that reached into her chest like tendrils of ice and encircled her heart. She could almost feel her heart thumping against its icy surface. Her fear intensified, creating a tremendous force pressing outward against the silence of the vacuum.

A voice broke through, shattering the frigid stillness. "Miss, can I get you something to drink?"

Unable to speak, Freddie simply stared at the stewardess. The coldness retreated, leaving behind no trace of its presence, unless you counted the pounding of Freddie's heart and the reflection in her eyes of the fear that had engulfed her only moments earlier.

"Are you all right, Miss?" The stewardess frowned as a slight shiver passed through her. Infected by the unmistakable terror she saw in the passenger's eyes, she could not bring herself to traverse such a menacing mental field in order to console this woman. Instead, she fixed a ginger ale and passed it to her. She watched her gulp it down as if it were a life-saving tonic. Looking over her shoulder as she moved down the aisle, the stewardess was certain something was wrong. Very wrong.

Trembling, Freddie turned on the overhead light and grabbed the headphones from the pouch in front of her. She shoved them over her ears and twirled the radio knob on the console until the welcome sound of hard rock music filled her ears. She couldn't stand hard rock music. It grated on her nerves. Usually she automatically flipped to another channel or turned off the radio, but today she needed something to distract her. To keep her awake. She couldn't think of a better antidote to peaceful sleep than the banging, clanging, screeching sounds of hard rock. If drifting off to sleep meant having nightmares like the one she'd just had, then she would stay awake all the way to Chicago, maybe even all night.

Despite the racket resounding in her ears, Freddie's thoughts reached out in all directions, trying to find a rational explanation for what had happened. It must have been a dream, she reasoned, because there was no way it could have been real! Yet, strangely, she felt violated. When the coldness had moved down her neck to her breast, it held the familiarity of a lover's touch—an *unwelcome* lover.

Powerless to explain what had happened to her, she sighed and leaned forward to adjust the radio control knob. An incessant buzzing was escalating the discordant sounds already blaring over the air waves to a level beyond her tolerance threshold. After fiddling with the knob for a few minutes, she gave up and twisted it until the sound cut off with a click.

Staring out the window, she heard the captain announce their approach into Chicago. She took off the headphones and reached under the seat to get her purse. Raising up, she noticed for the first time that Mr. Personality's seat was empty. Since there were few places to go other than the lavatory on an airplane, she assumed that explained his absence.

He's been gone a long time, she thought, recalling that he wasn't there when the stewardess handed her the ginger ale. Just then the voice over the loudspeaker instructed everyone to put their seats in their "original, upright positions," a signal that landing was imminent. Mr. Personality was still not back. As the stewardess came down the aisle, looking from left to right to verify that everyone was complying with the instructions, Freddie reached out toward her.

"Miss, you might want to check the lavatory. The gentleman sitting next to me has been gone for quite a while."

Involving herself in the stewardess' job was not an indictment of the stewardess. It was just Freddie's way. If something needed to be handled, straightened, or fixed, Freddie always stepped forward. She viewed it as helping. Should someone have accused her of having control issues, she would have quoted the English poet, Alexander Pope—*Order is heaven's first law!*

"Pardon me?" the stewardess asked.

"The man who was sitting next to me—he hasn't returned. I thought you might want to check to see if he's still in the lavatory." Despite her earlier experience, Freddie had regained a modicum of control, and her voice was calm.

Looking quizzical, the stewardess replied, "I'm sorry, ma'am, but this seat has been empty since the flight took off. Perhaps you were just dreaming."

"Empty?" Freddie's calm was shattered by an indiscriminate rush of emotions, all trying to reach the surface at the same time. *First one there gets to be in charge!* Freddie struggled to hold back the onslaught as the stewardess hurried past, looking back as if whatever was wrong with Freddie was airborne and hot on her trail.

Freddie took deep breaths, trying to regulate her pounding heart. In a few minutes, she was breathing normally. "My God," she exclaimed under her breath. "I must be having psychotic episodes … no, that's not possible!"

Maybe it is, she thought.

"If I were psychotic, would I know I was psychotic?" she whispered. Realizing she was speaking aloud, she looked around to see if anyone was looking at her. *I'm not crazy. I'm perfectly sane,* she assured herself. As she rose to leave the plane, however, seeds of doubt crept in.

With her luggage in tow, Freddie hailed a cab outside Chicago's O'Hare Airport. After making sure that none of her luggage was left sitting on the curb, she hopped into the back seat.

"Union League Club on Jackson, please."

"Isn't that a men's club?" The cabbie turned around to look at Freddie.

"Well, yes, it is, and it isn't. Thanks to these enlightened times, they've opened the rooms to women. Of course, the smoking parlors are still off limits, but since I gave up smoking in my last life, it doesn't really bother me." Her quick wit usually made awkward situations manageable and frequently jumpstarted boring conversations. Often, however, her wittiness was simply designed to camouflage her fear, the womb from which her need for clever repartee originally emerged. Today it was mostly camouflage.

The cabbie chuckled and turned back to start the engine. Freddie leaned against the seatback and stared out the window at the Windy City with the watchful manner of a tourist. Her mind, however, was far from the sights of the city. When the cab slowed in front of the Union League Club, Freddie glanced at the meter.

"Thanks for *not* driving like the last cabbie I had in Chicago," she declared as she handed him the fare plus a generous tip.

"Don't you get caught sneaking into them smoking parlors, ya hear?" the cabbie called out as he pulled away from the curb.

Standing on the sidewalk looking up, she wondered why she hadn't insisted on staying somewhere else. Inside those walls, she felt like a pariah. Eyes were always following her, waiting for her to make a mistake and walk into one of the forbidden zones. The office always made lodging arrangements for her. Apparently, someone at the home office was one of the "good ol' boys" and had gotten a really good deal. If she objected, they would argue how sensible it was, being only a couple of blocks from the Chicago Board of Trade, which saved on cab fare. Of course, she hadn't made a fuss. She knew that despite all her success, it was still a man's world. Perhaps that was the very point they were trying to make by making reservations for her here.

Arranging her clothes in the closet, Freddie flicked her hand down each garment as she hung it up, hoping the wrinkles would disappear before she had to wear them. She put her last pair of shoes on the shelf, slid the garment bag onto the floor and shut the door. She looked slowly around the room. There was nothing left to distract her from her nagging thoughts except the room itself.

The room was rather plain. It did not appear to have changed since the late 1800s. Brown was the dominant color, which coincided with Freddie's vision of a man's smoking parlor and apropos, of course, for a men's club. Brown would be the obvious designer's choice for a smoking parlor. The smoky residue of all those cigars and cigarettes, settling on the brown leather sofas and the dark finish of the library style walls, would create a graded wash effect for an ambience of richness with an accompanying venerability. Unless, of course, in an antiseptic moment, you were coerced into giving the room the white glove treatment. A little elbow grease and voila! Just an old brown leather sofa and faded, but dark, paneled walls—with their spurious dignity discarded in the wash bucket.

Perhaps if there were a little more contrast in colors, she thought, *it would put me in a better mood.* She was still shaky, but the hour or so it took to get from the airport and settle in had clothed this morning's ordeal with a dream-like quality. Now, it seemed too absurd to be real. Maybe the excitement she'd felt last night about her teaching trip to Chicago wasn't excitement at all. Maybe it was apprehension. Initially she shrugged off the idea she could mistake apprehension for excitement. Freddie, however, was very aware of the ambiguous figures used by cognitive psychologists—the ones where an ugly, old hag becomes a beautiful young woman if observed from a slightly different vantage point. She knew the same concept applied to emotions.

Was there really a marked difference between the two emotions for her? Or were they just two ways of looking at the same thing? Her job, analyzing commodities, was certainly a mix of the excitement of being right and the fear of being wrong. Perhaps the two emotions had been in close company too long for her to recognize them as different emotions.

"But apprehension about what?" she wondered aloud. *Could last night's so-called excitement have really been a premonition about the nightmare on the plane?*

What a silly idea! she reproached herself. *Premonitions are dreams! Who gets warnings about future dreams?*

Okay, settle down, she chided herself before wondering, *Has anything else happened in my life that might be called weird or even odd?*

Freddie searched her memory for any qualifying event over the last several days. *The manic garage door.* No, that was just a coincidence. Last night she'd encountered an ornery garage door. It creaked and groaned and moved upward at a pace about one third its usual speed. "Come on! You can go faster than that!" Freddie had shouted at it, her impatience growing. The door jerked suddenly and flew upward until it rested parallel to the ceiling of the garage. Startled, Freddie had hummed the theme to The Twilight Zone. Thinking back on it now, though, it really wasn't that strange.

Searching for anything else that might fall into the category of weird, Freddie's thoughts naturally came to rest on her friend and neighbor, Jodi Minton. A remnant of the flower child era, Jodi could truly be called weird. Although she and Freddie were close friends, they were diametrically opposed on the surface. Jodi was blonde. Freddie was brunette. Jodi did anything on a dare. Freddie, on the other hand, was extremely conservative, rarely stepping outside her view of normal, societal limits.

Freddie swore to Jodi's face one day that her devil-may-care attitude was solely for its shock effect. Jodi had only smiled. Jodi loved upsetting people by refusing to meet their expectations or at least what she thought those were. Doing the opposite of what was expected or taking some simple act to an extreme was an addiction for her. Freddie suspected that without it, Jodi would simply dissolve into a wisp of smoke—the last vestige of of her character that wasn't irretrievably entangled with her obsession for extremes in some form.

Freddie knew that others wondered what drew the two of them together. The answer was found in the adage that opposites attract. It wasn't a very healthy truth, but Freddie privately acknowledged it. Even though Jodi's antics made her nervous, she secretly enjoyed the vicarious thrill of breaking through the conservative bindings that held her tightly in place. However, Freddie knew it went even deeper than that. The strength of the connection between her and Jodi was that they weren't actually that different from each other, despite appearances.

Freddie believed it was simply a quirk of environment that her own conservative side prevailed, whereas Jodi's conservative side was curbed by a more expressive and daring side. Freddie alleged it was the relative strength of Jodi's principal outlook that made her more susceptible to premonitions. In her naturally flamboyant fashion, Jodi's premonitions were full-blown, complete with minute details. They were so real that she often confused them with reality. This added even more layers to her kookiness.

Years earlier, Jodi had been fixing breakfast for her husband,

Carl, who has since pulled out of that race. He just couldn't maintain the necessary adrenaline flow required to keep up with his wife. One Sunday morning, about a year before he left, Jodi asked him if he had seen the headlines about Congressman Dodge.

"I read the paper, but I didn't see anything," Carl replied.

"How could you have missed it? It's on the front page!" Jodi grabbed the newspaper and thrust it toward him. He picked it up and turned the front section around so she could see it.

"And where on the front page would that be?"

Staring at the paper, Jodi said, "I saw it with my own eyes!" To convince him, she related the details of how Dodge was caught mishandling state funds to benefit his own business.

Used to the unexpected from Jodi, her husband simply shrugged. "Don't know what to tell you, babe," he said.

"Don't look at me like that, Carl! I am *not* crazy—at least not unless I want to be. I did not make this up!"

"Maybe you dreamed it." Carl didn't really care, but he thought he'd make one effort anyway to act like he did. It would help keep the peace.

The next Sunday morning Carl came into the kitchen, reading the newspaper as he walked.

"Anything interesting?" Jodi asked.

"You might say that," he replied as he dropped the paper face up on the table in front of her. There it was in big, bold print across the page: *Congressman Tries to Dodge Indictment.*

The subheading enlightened the reader further: *State funds find their way into congressman's coffins.* Dodge owned a mortuary. Apparently, the editor thought the play on words, especially the one between coffers and coffins, was too funny to pass up. Carl agreed.

Grabbing the paper, Jodi scanned the article, her eyes darting from side to side. It was exactly like she had described it. "Cool!" was all she could think to say as she grinned from ear to ear.

Carl sat down to eat breakfast, wondering what he had stepped into when he married Jodi. She could be a lot of fun, but her dark side worried him. It wasn't just the premonitions. This wasn't the first. It was all the other "way out there" episodes of hers.

Freddie always knew Carl was uneasy about Jodi, and that it had been the motivation for his departure. Jodi made her uneasy, too, but Freddie trusted herself to know when Jodi's attempts to go where no woman had gone before were completely out of control. Right now she could handle her. Maybe one day she wouldn't want to deal with the pressure of having a friend who was so unpredictable, but right now, it was manageable.

Her own experiences with the paranormal were never as vivid as Jodi's. Freddie tended to let the vision slip through her fingers like sand. Each grain sliding away from the others until there was no longer even a memory of the shape they once had when they clung to one another. She was not sure she wanted to know the future. The events of the last few hours were taking enough of a toll. What if the future held some incredibly horrific event? Did she want to know? Would it even help? She didn't think so. If she didn't know the future, there was always hope, even if it was only naiveté.

That was one thing about Jodi that endeared her to Freddie—a naiveté that was paired with an uncanny wisdom. One minute Jodi might be jumping up and down over finding a blue jay's feather, holding it to her chest as if it held the secrets of the universe. The next minute she was explaining the practical benefits gained from working through your fears. The childlike balance of naiveté and wisdom fascinated Freddie.

At this moment Freddie felt like a child, but a child who believed in monsters under the bed. A child afraid to open the closet. Determined to understand what happened to her on the plane, Freddie ran every event of the last twenty-four hours through her mind like celluloid on an 8mm projector reel. When it finished, she rewound the film and watched it again, looking for anything that could help her.

Earlier that morning when she arrived at the Memphis airport, it was misting rain. Parking her car in the garage, Freddie had thanked God that she shipped the handouts for the class ahead of time. Gathering up her suitcase, garment bag, and briefcase, she had walked toward the terminal. A faint buzzing noise made her shake her head, thinking her ears were plugged. When she noticed the fluorescent lighting, she'd assumed the buzzing came from the lights.

The departure level had been crowded. Cars were moving rapidly through the covered roadways in front of the terminal, leaping into position from lane to lane, their movements choreographed by some bizarre artist. Each door glowed with the lights from inside the terminal, and there was a single-mindedness by the participants in this peculiar performance to cease their movements exactly in front of the doors. The stretches of sidewalk between were laced with shadows and had only one occupant.

Reviewing this scene for the third time, Freddie was certain there had been a man standing in the shadows that morning, but she hadn't paid any attention to him. Why was she remembering him now?

The next scene was a kaleidoscope of colors and styles adorning the hundred or so passengers silently pushing their way to the gate. While she was among them, she had wondered why they pushed and shoved when they all had assigned seats. When she'd finally reached the boarding gate, she spent her time imagining the lives of those around her. What did they do for a living? Were they going to see loved ones or leaving loved ones behind? Seeing the families hugging and kissing had made her feel lonely and a little jealous.

In the midst of her people-watching, a commotion at the desk had caught her attention. Everyone's eyes were riveted toward a man in an expensive suit. He was cursing the agent at the gate because he couldn't exchange his ticket for a first class seat. His face was twisted into an ugly mask. She half expected his lips to curl under, revealing his fangs as he sprang for the throat of the gate agent.

Instead of being repulsed by such rude behavior, Freddie had been mesmerized. The man was so completely at one with his rage that no one dared intervene. The poor agent quickly realized that the usual platitudes she used with passengers were outside this man's radar. Unequipped to deal with him, she just stood silently as he raved on, unaware that her silence was fueling his rage.

Freddie had wondered what it felt like to let loose that way. To let all your disappointments and heartaches, all the slights by other people, just brew until they reached a boiling point. Then to open your mouth and spew hot liquid in the form of words all over anyone within reach. Burning them. Giving them a taste of what it was like to be you. Freddie knew this was something she could never do. Not because she didn't want to, but because it might destroy everything good left in her life.

As she mechanically sorted the handouts for tomorrow's class on the table in her hotel room, Freddie persisted in playing the scenes from that morning over and over in her mind. Without warning, her arm jerked, spilling several sheets onto the floor as the film in her head continued to roll. She recalled a man standing at the edge of the crowd at the terminal gate. He seemed familiar—well, more than familiar. Almost personal, like a family member or a distant relative.

She could swear he was the same man her memories beckoned from the shadows outside the terminal.

She remembered him looking directly at her. She gave him a weak smile, the kind you give someone when you feel like you've been put on the spot. He didn't smile back. He just looked straight into her eyes until she looked away, unsettled by his boldness. The infernal buzzing of the airport's fluorescent lighting had been grating on her nerves, and the man's unwavering stare hadn't helped. Her anxiety had risen as she moved slowly toward the boarding gate. She remembered whispering to herself: *Get it under control, Freddie!*

Keeping things under control was at the top of Freddie's priority list. If forced to describe herself in ten words or less, controller would be number one. Of course, that left nine words. Most of the other descriptive words that popped into her mind were words like empty—failure—lonely. Pretty depressing, but each reflected something missing in her life. She wasn't sure exactly what was missing because nothing had ever succeeded in obliterating those feelings. Not all these feelings had developed at the same time, but each produced the next with very little effort. As a result, she spent most of her time trying to orchestrate her life in an attempt to *not* feel empty, to *not* feel like a failure despite her success, and to *not* feel lonely. The more control she exerted over her life, however, the more emotionally cut off she became because she could never control the unpredictability of those around her. It was a vicious circle, one that was getting tiresome. Tonight she was worn out with the effort.

Still, the image of the mysterious man drew her attention back to her memory reel. She recalled the relief she had felt when she saw that the seat number on her boarding pass was 6A-Window. It meant she could pretend to look out the window and avoid dealing with chatty, prosaic conversations launched by passengers who were either too gregarious for their own good or starving for discourse of any kind. She hated small talk. She didn't hate people, but she did prefer observing them from a distance most of the time.

When nearly everyone was seated, the seat next to hers was still empty. *Good!* she'd sighed in relief, but no sooner had the feeling appeared than she saw him. Mr. Personality, Mr. Blank Stare himself, sat down in 6B.

Why me, Lord? Why do I always get the weirdoes? she'd muttered, not expecting an answer.

The replay of this morning's events stopped abruptly, and Freddie stooped to pick up the papers she'd dropped earlier. She was getting more and more tense the closer her memories came to that awful moment when something had breached her bulkhead. A cold breeze drifted past Freddie and left a shudder in its wake.

She had no answers for what had happened on the plane, other than being overworked and a little too emotional. Unfortunately, it was the only explanation that made any sense to her. She just needed to regain the excitement she had felt last night—*she refused to believe the feeling had been anything else*—and to forget about this crazy nightmare!

A loud, growling noise coming from her stomach reminded her she had rejected the snack on the plane and forgotten to eat breakfast. Freddie picked up the phone and called room service. Roast beef, vegetables, and a salad. *That should do it*, she thought, sitting down at the table in her room.

The handouts were now neatly stacked in groups, ready for the next day. After pulling out her lesson plan from her briefcase to review her class, Freddie pressed her fingertips against her forehead. She closed her eyes, drawing her brows tightly together. She hated these headaches. They never picked a good time to appear. *Maybe going downstairs to eat would have been a better idea,* she thought. Watching other people laughing and talking in a restaurant and imagining what they were thinking about and who they were always relaxed her. At the very least, it would distract her.

A thousand pins suddenly pricked her back, and nausea raced upward from her stomach to her throat. "Good grief!" she exclaimed. "What's wrong with me? I've never had jitters like this before." *A little edginess maybe,* she thought, *but not like this.* Despite her initial reaction, she knew instinctively the class wasn't the cause. It was something else. Most likely the last twenty-four hours. What did it all mean?

Overwhelmed, Freddie sat, holding her head in her hands as tears rolled down her face. All those feelings she kept so closely guarded rushed to the surface. She was tired of always being on guard, but control was the only solution she knew. Yet, she felt hopelessly enslaved by her need for it.

Gradually the familiar patterns of control won out, and the emotional outburst subsided. Taking her hands from her face, she tried to open her eyes, but they were burning so badly that she could only squint. Seeing the mascara all over her hands, she knew why and got up to look in the mirror. Picking up a tissue off the dresser, she bent toward the mirror to wipe away the smeared mascara, but instead froze with the tissue about three inches from her face.

Reflected in the mirror was a man standing near the edge of her room. She was glued to the spot, unable to move or even to make a sound. It was just like in her nightmares—she really had turned to stone! Her body was refusing to respond to the orders she mentally hurled at it. It refused to run from the man in the shadows, the man in seat 6B, Mr. Personality himself, the man who was now quietly staring at her.

Then she heard his voice in her head, but the room was deadly quiet. "It's time. You can't stop it!"

Freddie ran with all her might, but the exertion was only in her mind. Her body was still beyond her commands. Another sound intruded. This one seemed to be coming from somewhere inside her. Then she heard herself screaming at the top of her lungs, unable to stop. The man's reflection disappeared from the mirror.

A pounding at the door startled her, giving movement to muscles that refused to move only moments before. Freddie jerked around and ran across the room, frantically searching the room to see where Mr. Personality had gone. Maybe he went through to the adjoining room. Yanking open the hallway door, she saw two men, one standing behind the other. With a frightened gasp, Freddie fainted. The last thing she saw was a pair of shiny, black shoes.

She was lying face down in a dense fog. She kept trying to push herself up, but cold hands grasped her ankles and pulled her back down. Deeper and deeper. She couldn't breathe. The grayish white of the fog crawled into her throat, smothering her. She tried to scream, but it sounded more like the mewling of a baby.

No one will ever find me, she thought. Just at that moment those cold hands pulled her into a place filled with a strange light. Strange because it seemed wed to the shadows. Someone was standing on the other side of the space. She strained to see who it was, but the shadows protected him just as they protected the corners of a room. She couldn't even see him clearly enough to be certain it was a man.

Then it spoke. "It's time. You can't stop it."

Freddie recoiled, realizing where she had heard this before. Suddenly she was no longer in that unfamiliar place. She was lying face down on her hotel bed, and a stranger was asking her if she was all right.

"Yes," she answered hesitantly, shivering despite the warmth of the room. She turned over on her back just as he started to admonish her.

"You, young lady, need to sit up and get some of this food in your stomach. You know, stress is the biggest problem I have to deal with in this hotel. It's always the same. Too much work—too much worry—too little food. Then I get a phone call because some workaholic has fainted!"

Freddie assumed he was the hotel physician, although he looked like he belonged to another era. The pocket watch chain, swinging back and forth from a small pocket in his tweed vest, mesmerized her as he continued his ranting, seemingly oblivious of her.

"Just once I wish someone would really be sick. I thought it would be great fun to be the physician for a big city hotel, meeting famous people, rubbing shoulders with the movers and shakers. Instead, I get to put a damp cloth on the foreheads of a bunch of yuppie wannabes!"

"Excuse me?" Freddie broke through the trance she had slipped into.

"Oh," the doctor said as if he, too, had been in another dimension. "It's not your fault. You're just doing what you're destined to do." He closed his bag and stood up to leave. "Anyway, if you do need anything, let me know. Especially if it's something exciting," he added. Freddie just stared at him.

"I could use some excitement in my life," he mumbled as he shut the door behind him.

The memory of her dream, if it was a dream, washed over Freddie. The voice from the shadows had said the same thing as Mr. Personality. "It's time. You can't stop it." What did it mean? Was she losing her mind? No, that couldn't be. There *was* a man in her room. She saw him. Or did she? How did he get out of her room and into the hall so quickly? He was standing behind the room service clerk when she'd opened the door. Maybe he wasn't there at all. Maybe it had just been her imagination.

Perhaps the doctor was right. She was overworked, and it was making her vulnerable to mild hallucinations. Her mind was just releasing some tension, a way of protecting the circuits from overload, so to speak. *Maybe that's really what's wrong with schizophrenics,* she mused. *They're just releasing superfluous data to relieve the pressure in their minds, and no one really understands! Maybe I'm schizophrenic. Maybe...* Freddie knew her mind was running wild. She desperately needed sleep. Looking at the food tray, she decided eating might be a good thing, too.

Darian: His Pattern Begins
[1956-1980]

Chapter 4

The sun's rays highlighted the small boy's face as he tugged at the string hanging from the chenille bedspread. Fully dressed in new pants and shirt and wearing his coat and baseball cap, he was waiting. The warmth from the sun felt good to him, but it didn't dry the tracks on his cheeks. He leaned his head down and wiped his face slowly across the sleeve of his coat.

He didn't want to leave this place. As he looked around the room that had been the only home he could remember, an attendant appeared in the doorway. "Darian, it's time to go. Your new parents are downstairs, and they're very excited about taking you home with them!"

"I'm not going." Darian's voice was calm and clear. The resoluteness in it was not that of a four year old. Instead his voice possessed the gravity of one whose experiences over many years had molded a reliable perspective toward life and a conviction that if he were true to it, he would survive.

The attendant, Miss McKelroy, having worked in the orphanage for fifteen years, had heard this same cry hundreds of times. Sometimes it was said with conviction. Sometimes it came out between sobs. And sometimes it was accompanied by anger. No matter. It always broke her heart. She loved these children, these children who had done nothing wrong except draw a bad hand in life. She drew comfort from telling herself she was helping them find families who would love them and make them feel special. It was the one thing in life she was sure about—that they deserved to feel special.

"Darian, sweetie." She spoke firmly but gently because she couldn't bring herself to fuss at him. "We talked about this last night. You know I'll always be here. You can visit or call me anytime you want, but Mr. and Mrs. Beel want to love you, too."

She knelt down so she could look into his face. "Just imagine! You'll have your own room and all the other things little boys like. Most of all, Darian, you'll have two people in your life who will truly love you, two people who *chose* you out of all the others to be a part of their lives."

In fact she did believe that his adoption was the best thing, but she wasn't blind. She knew he was mad at her—that he believed she was betraying him by sending him away. There was no mistaking the look on his face. It seared her heart, leaving a mark like a branding iron on a steer. A mark that would never go away. A mark that one day should vindicate her, but it would fail. It was a mark that, instead of awakening memories of her compassion, would brand her as culpable.

The other children were not as loath to leave the orphanage as Darian, but then Darian was not like the other children. He had never tried to impress any of the potential parents who visited. He was perfectly happy to remain where he was. Miss McKelroy always treated him special, like he was her own child. Perhaps knowing he preferred to stay at the orphanage made *her* feel special. She, too, had no one else in her life, and everyone wants someone who makes them feel special. She wasn't sure who was suffering the most on this day of departure—her or Darian. Reaching down, she took his small hand and reluctantly led him toward the stairs to meet his new parents.

Darian paused to look through the balusters down to the foyer. The man standing below him was tall, perhaps six feet and four inches. His jet black hair was combed back on the sides and the top. The oil that held his hair in place reflected flashes of light from the chandelier that hung just below where Darian stood.

Staring down at the glossy top of the man's head summoned a special vision for the small boy of another day and another black, shiny surface. It was the day the preacher arrived at the orphanage to show off his new Cadillac. The broad, black hood was so polished it shimmered and competed with the sun, reflecting its light back into the heavens.

As he stood on the second floor landing, the memory of that day warmed Darian. Even now he was still curious to know if he could have seen himself in the shiny surface of that hood. Unfortunately, he never got the chance. Sitting on Miss McKelroy's hip as she talked to the preacher, Darian had been swinging his leg back and forth, coming perilously close to a head-on collision between his oxfords and the shiny new paint job on the preacher's Cadillac.

"Be careful!" the preacher man had shouted just as Darian leaned over Miss McKelroy's arm hoping to make a funny face at himself in the hood. Startled by the outburst, Darian had lurched backward, propelling his foot toward the car. With more zest than any of his sermons had contained in a long time, the preacher thrust out his hand to intercept the oxford.

Thwack! Screaming in pain, the preacher man had jumped around in a circle, his hand tucked into his armpit, bending and straightening over and over again. After the initial shock from the shout and the preacher's paroxysmal dance, Darian howled with laughter at such a funny sight.

Appalled at first that Darian had kicked the preacher, Miss

McKelroy immediately tried to defuse the situation by being overly solicitous toward the preacher, but the odds were against her. The ridiculous sight of the preacher hopping in circles and Darian's infectious laughter finally overruled all her social graces. She joined Darian, laughing so hard she made little snorting sounds, which nearly sent Darian into convulsions.

Now it was the preacher's turn to be appalled. With a snort of his own, which was most assuredly disgust, he had jerked open his car door and gotten into the driver's seat. Starting the motor, he cast them both a look that belied his calling and left the two of them standing on the curb, looking like escapees from a mental hospital too long off their meds.

Today was not the first time Darian had recalled this incident, but today was the first time the memory focused on the warmth of Miss McKelroy's laughter. The two of them laughing together. The laughter of friends. Darian pushed the thought out of his mind. *Things are not always as they seem.*

Before today, Darian's thoughts about the incident had centered not on the laughter, but on the overwhelming feeling of power and peace he experienced, even just thinking about it. He still didn't know why exactly. He just knew that at the moment the tables had turned on the preacher, he felt powerful—like no one could touch him. And even if someone had, he wouldn't have cared. That first evening he laid in bed, relishing the feeling, treasuring that small moment of triumph over those like the preacher who thought they were powerful, who were condescending, who felt sorry for him. Those who didn't know him and didn't really care. He had rolled this delicacy around in his mind, savoring all its nuances, every night since that day. It was his prize, his private triumph.

Strange, he thought, that this man standing below him on the

ground floor so strongly summoned the memory of his secret
treasure. The tall enigma looked up at Darian from the foot of the
stairs and smiled. His lips were thin. His face was angular with a
predaceous visage. Hungry but careful. The woman beside him
offered a timorous smile. Her lips stretched tightly over her teeth like
a balloon whose capacity has reached its limit. She appeared to be
teetering on the edge, not knowing whether to discharge or cling to
whatever it was that pervaded her world. When Miss McKelroy and
Darian reached the first floor, the woman knelt down and held out
her hand. Darian looked at her but made no move in her direction.
Eyebrows raised inquiringly, she looked at Miss McKelroy.

"He's just afraid to leave the only place he's ever known. All the
children go through the same thing. It may take time, but he'll adjust,
especially when it's just the three of you!"

Trying a little too hard to sound confident and cheerful, her
explanation sounded more like the faulty logic that leads someone to
buy a used car with a cracked block. Biting her lip, Miss McKelroy
placed the palm of her hand against Darian's back and gently pushed
him toward Ruth Beel. She expected him to register his disapproval
by obeying but dragging his feet in protest. Instead, Darian planted
his feet as firmly as if they were set in concrete.

Miss McKelroy bent down and whispered, "What's wrong,
Darian?"

"I'm not going." Darian didn't bother to whisper.

"But, Darian..." Miss McKelroy began just before Harry Beel
pushed past, nearly knocking her over. He bent down, put one hand
behind the boy's knees and the other on his back, and lifted him off
the floor.

"Now, young man, there'll be none of that! You will not be rude
to your Mother. Do you understand?" Before Darian had a chance to

reply, Harry Beel demanded, "Look at me when you answer!"

Recovering her balance, Miss McKelroy looked toward Darian, expecting to see a scared little boy. She saw instead a strangely calm Darian. He looked straight at Harry Beel for a few seconds before replying. "Yes."

"You will address me as *Sir* from now on and your Mother as *Ma'am*. Is that understood?"

Again, Darian looked him in the eye for at least three seconds before he replied, "Yes—Sir."

Confused by Darian's strange demeanor and shocked by the aggressive behavior of Mr. Beel, Miss McKelroy didn't know what to do. Truth be told, she didn't actually have the authority to do anything. She knew Darian probably deserved to be disciplined, but the lambasting she'd just witnessed seemed excessive.

The couple moved quickly toward the front door and down the walk. Miss McKelroy followed. Even though Darian's placement with the Beels was not her decision, she tasted the bitterness of bile in her throat as they drove away and her anxiety heightened. Darian turned to look at her through the window of the car. With the cold, unmoving countenance of a stone sculpture, he neither smiled nor waved. She felt a twinge of pain in her chest. The mark Darian left on her would be a long time healing.

In the back seat Darian ran his hand along the back of his leg, wincing as his fingers found the spot where Harry had been holding him.

"Stop wiggling back there and be quiet!" Harry shouted over his shoulder. "Can't you see I'm trying to hear the news on the radio? I won't tolerate insubordination, young man!"

Darian didn't know what insubordination was, but it sounded

worse than planting his feet and refusing to move. He could still feel the pressure of Harry's fingers slowly squeezing the fleshy part of his upper leg when he picked him up. At first it startled him, but as Harry scolded Darian, he had steadily tightened his grip until Darian thought he would be compelled to cry out from the pain. Instead he found himself staring trance-like at Harry, attempting to understand what was happening. Then something inside him snapped. In that instant he knew he would never cry out, even if Harry Beel took out a knife and started cutting off his fingers one by one. When Harry met Darian's gaze, his grip had loosened. Darian intuitively sensed an uneasiness in him. It wasn't something he could see—just something he felt.

Feelings were all Darian had that he could call his own. So he guarded them carefully, treasured them. Whenever an experience evoked a new feeling, he studied the experience and savored the feeling in his mind until he could determine where it belonged. Each feeling had a place and a purpose in his mind. It was like putting together a jigsaw puzzle. One day he would have all the pieces. Then his life would be different. Better.

This astonishing encounter with Harry Beel was another secret treasure to add to the feeling of power that had permeated the incident with the preacher. Darian's young mind was certain there was an important link between these two experiences for him.

When he was alone tonight, he planned to once again savor these moments. He would caress the feelings until they existed alongside every moment of his day like a safety railing to keep him from falling.

Chapter 5

*U*ndeniably a drill sergeant in another life, Darian's first-grade teacher barked out orders followed by threats of detention if she was met with insubordination. Convinced that Mrs. Gruen might be worse than Harry Beel when met with insubordination, Darian always strove to follow her orders, mostly because school was his only respite from the Beel house. Today, however, he especially did not want to stir up her ire. It was Festival Day. He had seen the rides being erected in the school yard, and he was particularly vigilant not to do anything that would cause him to miss the festivities.

When nap time came, Darian put his head down on his desk and daydreamed about the festival. This morning before class, he had watched the men set up the ride that looked like a spider with spaceships hanging from its legs. Imagining himself whirling through the air inside one of those spaceships sent a rush of excitement through him. He could feel the wind blowing his hair, catching his breath. Suddenly, laughter bubbled to the surface. Darian tried to stop it. It didn't sound exactly like laughter. More like a backward cough, but it didn't matter. It was too late.

"Darian Beel?"

"Yes, ma'am?" Darian raised his head to look at his teacher.

"Why are you not taking a nap?" she snapped.

"I—" Before he could finish, she cut him off.

"I don't want to hear any excuses. I warned you. I warned *all* of you. If you can't mind me, you will not attend the festival. Perhaps I should make an example of you, Mr. Beel."

Darian tried to explain. She simply waved her hand in the air and turned her back on him. "No excuses. Only babies make excuses."

Darian watched her walk away from him. Her arrogance angered him. Who was she to stop him from going to the festival?

"Hey!" he shouted.

She turned, intending to throttle this upstart for his rash behavior. He stared at her without blinking. The anger continued to rise in him, warming his body. Every cell was heating up to an explosive level. His eyes did not veer from her face. Like a tractor beam, his gaze held her transfixed in place. The other children started to squirm. The edgy silence was making them uncomfortable, and the diabolical expression on Darian's face was scaring them. It wasn't until they looked at Mrs. Gruen, however, that their screams blasted through the silence. The tightness in her face was gone. Her skin was slack and hanging awkwardly on her bones. She appeared to be standing only because some unseen force was holding her up.

Their screams startled Darian. Dazed, he looked around the room. The moment his gaze shifted, Mrs. Gruen's legs no longer supported her, crumpling as if made of gelatin, and she fell to the floor. Hearing the screams, two teachers ran into the room from the hallway. At first glance neither could see Mrs. Gruen and wondered aloud why she had left her class unattended. Struggling to sit up, her movement caught their attention. One of the teachers, Carla Tutor, ran toward her while the other attempted to distract the children enough to halt their screaming.

"Are you all right, Betty? What happened?" Carla knelt down and supported Betty Gruen with her arm.

"I'm not sure. I had just reprimanded one of the students. I was walking back toward the front of the room, and he shouted at me. I turned, and suddenly I couldn't move. I was literally paralyzed. I thought sure I was dying, maybe having a stroke." She rubbed her hand back and forth across her forehead. Carla could see that her hand was shaking. "Strange thing though. I knew I was still standing, and I don't know how because I wasn't able to exert any control over my body at all. Then, just like a puppet released by a puppeteer, I fell to the floor in a heap."

Tears crept from the corners of Betty Gruen's eyes. Not wanting to upset the children any further, Carla put her arm around Betty's back to help her up. "We need to get you to the doctor." Carla nodded her intention to Amy Purvis, the teacher who was trying to calm the children.

"Now children," Amy said, "we're going to take Mrs. Gruen to the nurse's station because she isn't feeling well. While we're gone—"

"It's his fault!" several of the children screamed before she could say anything else.

"What?" asked Amy, confused. Carla stopped in the doorway, puzzled by the outburst.

"He did it!" they all shouted, pointing their small, but savagely accusing fingers at Darian.

"No one did anything to her, children. She just fainted. That's all."

"No! He did it!" The children began screaming and crying all over again. Almost as one organism, they backed away from Darian, leaving him alone in the center of the room. Standing quietly beside his desk, even though he was still under the influence of the energy rush, Darian seemed an unlikely predator.

Other teachers were now standing in the doorway. The screaming had generated images of a catastrophe in progress in Room

123. Looking at Darian, one of them remarked, "Maybe we ought to take him with us. It might help settle the rest of the kids down." The others agreed. Mr. Scott, a second-grade teacher, took Darian by the arm and escorted him to the principal's office.

"Have a seat, young man. Someone will come for you shortly." With those words, Mr. Scott departed, closing the door to the hallway behind him.

Darian waited. No one came. He looked at the clock on the wall. He knew that two hours had gone by. The little hand had been on the 12 when they brought him here. Now it was past the 2. He could not remember where the big hand had been before, but he knew that when the big hand was on the 9 and the little hand was almost on the 3, school would be out. Right now the big hand was on the 6. The festival was over, and he had missed it.

Darian got up slowly and walked toward the door of the principal's office. He paused as he reached the door. There was a brief moment of indecision, and then it was gone. He opened the door and stepped out of the office. Turning, he walked toward the light at the end of the hallway.

The sun poured through the windows in the double doors, creating a blinding glare, but Darian didn't even notice. If anyone had seen his eyes at that moment, they would have testified that the little boy who eagerly anticipated the festival was no longer there. Something else had taken his place. Something sinister. Something filled with virulent, boiling hatred, the foul bubbles breaking the surface with greater intensity than ever before.

Even if it were possible to remove the cause of such heat, it no longer mattered. It had developed a life of its own. The new Darian walked through the doors of the school and did not stop until he reached his bedroom at home. In her ignorance Mrs. Gruen had callously nudged Darian along a path that would set the tone for his life. Unfortunately for Darian and those who crossed his path, it was not a compassionate one.

That day was the starting post for Darian's life. When he arrived home and went to his room, he sat down on the chenille bedspread, the only thing that reminded him of the orphanage in this awful place. He knew something was different. He was changing. Power was rushing through his veins, but he felt out of control. The voice inside him—the voice that had always been in his head, the voice that was his companion when he had none—spoke to him. It seemed much stronger, much louder.

"You must learn to control your power," it said. "Become one with the Power."

When Darian responded, he spoke aloud. It seemed perfectly natural because he never once considered the voice to be his own. "How?" he asked.

"Practice. Focus on little things first. When you master the little things, focus on bigger things until one day, you will be ready."

"How will I know when I'm ready?" Such a question revealed the trust Darian bestowed on this disembodied voice within him. He never thought to ask what the preparation was for. He simply obeyed.

"You will know. Now is not the time. When it is, you won't be able to stop it." A rush of excitement surged through Darian—one even more exciting than what had accompanied his fantasies about riding the spaceship tethered to a spider. In its aftermath, he became forever the humble servant of the fiendish master within him. He had crossed his Rubicon.

Darian's crossing occurred nearly two years after arriving at the Beels. Following the instructions of his Master to practice, his early labors were directed toward mastering *things*. The initial phase involved moving them at will, which was quite easy for him. Then his efforts focused on destroying these things without physically touching them. Some he crushed. Others actually disintegrated, leaving only a powdery residue to mark where they had been. Each success scored an emotional high for Darian from which he never fully descended.

From inanimate objects, he moved on to crawling insects. The joy he felt the first time he consciously manipulated the movements of a cockroach was unmatched. The cockroach struggled heartily to flee. Its slender legs and long feelers moved rapidly. Its yellowish brown body squirmed with the effort, but even the enduring cockroach could not prevail over Darian. Knowing he had the life of another creature in his hands, knowing he could quickly squash it, make it fly slowly through the air, or just toy with it at will was beyond any experience Darian could ever have imagined, even with a little boy's creative nature. It literally took his breath away.

In the heat of such malignant excitement, Darian moved on to larger living beings. Availability would have made dogs or cats a logical choice, but Darian declined. It wasn't that he felt any real compassion for them, but he figured their lives weren't much better than his. Dogs and cats didn't have any more freedom than he did. Besides, there wasn't much he could deny them that would particularly upset them. Their lives were pretty bland. They would probably thank him if he put them out of their misery, and he wanted his prey to suffer—most of all, to suffer loss of freedom, loss of choice. So instead he chose birds. Birds could fly. They could fly away from any place that didn't suit them. They could see the world, and no one could stop them. At least not until they met Darian.

Chapter 6

*E*ven though it was late April, the snow was still piled up on the window sill. Two birds sat there, calmly looking at the yard below. Unknown to them, they were being scrutinized by Darian. They sat perfectly still for a few minutes. Then they rustled their feathers in much the same way a person straightens his clothes when he stands up after sitting for a long time. Darian watched as they shifted their feet along the ledge, making little footprints in the snow.

For four winters, three springs, and three summers, Darian had watched the birds come and go. He had watched them fly high above the yard and then fly away, only to come back with string for a nest or food for their young. He watched them leave for the winter. That was when he hated them the most—when they were able to leave this place. But, his time was coming. He had practiced and practiced. Soon he would leave this place, too, and no one would be able to stop him, especially the Beels.

When Darian first arrived at the Beel house, he quickly learned that physical resistance was futile. The Beels had not adopted him to love. So far, love had only entered Darian's world once—Miss McKelroy. She was the only person he had ever cared about, but even she had not protected him from these people. Instead she had betrayed him.

At the Beels' there were no birthday parties, no trips to the zoo, no vacations to the beach. There was only the sterile, Victorian style house the Beels called home. From the street, it was uninviting. The grass was sparse, having starved from lack of care. The dirt canvas that was the front yard rose up in swirls at the slightest hint of a breeze, coating the windows. There were two windows on each side of the front door opening onto the porch. To any who peered in that direction from the street, the shadow cast by the porch and the coating of dirt on the windows gave the house a sleepy, indifferent appearance, which explained the barren yard, and effectively discouraged visitors.

Darian's room became his world. There was a time when he believed his world would expand beyond this room and this house. When he started to school, he had foolishly hoped to find lots of things to keep him away from home, away from the Beels. Darian learned early, however, that life was not kind, and that its brutality was not limited to the Beels.

The air was still cold on this April day because the snow still lay on the ground, but the sky was crystal clear. Watching the birds outside his window, he wondered what it was like to fly. What would it feel like to soar above the earth and look down on everything—to be untouchable? If only he could become the bird the same way he was learning to become one with the Power! *That's it!* The answer struck him with mind-shattering clarity. It was the next step to his freedom. A giant step. At last! His years of faithful practice had been observed and were being honored.

His mind whirled with the implications of his revelation. This far surpassed manipulating things or insects. If he literally became one with the bird, then he would have the knowledge of the bird. He would possess its skills. Would that mean he could adapt those skills to fit his own body? These were answers Darian didn't have yet, but he was certain about one thing: he had just graduated to a new level of endeavor that overshadowed anything he had accomplished in the past.

In a heightened state of anticipation, he returned his attention to the two birds who were still sitting on the window sill. Mimicking them, Darian sat perfectly still also. He closed his eyes and imagined one of the birds in his mind's eye. He saw its posture and its movements. He rose and stood beside his bed. He visualized standing on the window sill with the snow beneath his feet. He concentrated on feeling feathers take the place of his smooth skin. He shifted on his feet, held his arms down and pressed them tightly against his sides with his hands tucked around toward his backside. He moved his head to one side in a quick, jerky movement. Then he quickly repeated the movement. He shut out all sounds around him. He could actually feel the coolness of the snow under his feet. He was slipping into the world of the bird. He felt the transition beginning—the pull—

"DARIAN!" The irksome sound of Ruth Beel's voice destroyed Darian's concentration, and the connection with the bird was lost. Darian's face flushed with anger as he turned toward the door. Ruth burst into the room without bothering to knock. If it were possible to lock her out, he would, but locks were against the house rules.

"Ma'am?" Darian answered through clenched teeth. He found it easier to abide by the house rules on some things, such as how he was instructed to address the Beels, than to rock the boat, which only brought him to their attention more than was necessary.

"Your father needs help in his workshop. He sent me to get you." She stood in the doorway, waiting for Darian to heed her husband's orders. Darian cringed despite his best efforts not to react.

Harry's workshop was in the basement. Other than Harry and Ruth's bedroom, it was the only room in the house with a lock on it. Sometimes Harry frittered away months at his workbench, working on some stupid project. Last year he built a liquor cabinet with shelves spaced perfectly for his favorite whiskey. Recently he finished a stand to place next to his chair in the living room with slots for a shot glass and a glass of soda pop. It even had pockets for his cigarettes and his lighter. For Darian, these projects summed up the mentality of the miscreant who created them: stupid.

Harry often spent days at a time in the basement without even coming up to go to the bathroom. Once, during one of these intervals, Darian was in the backyard looking for insects for his practice sessions. He heard the tinkling sound of water and saw Harry pissing out the basement window into the concrete trough that ran alongside the back of the half-exposed basement. Darian didn't want to know how Harry managed if the call of nature involved more than pissing.

"DARIAN!" This time it was Harry shouting. "Get down here this minute!" He sounded slightly drunk. On a scale of one to ten, a raucous four was about right. Darian moved past Ruth, went to the basement door and stopped. Harry lurched up the stairs, grabbed Darian by the arm and jerked him down onto the steps.

Hearing the door lock behind him, Darian surveyed the room quickly as he was dragged down the stairs into the basement. Harry had started another project, but it was impossible to tell what it was. An empty whiskey bottle sat on the floor beside the sofa bed. Harry had obviously taken a snooze earlier. He was still in his underwear, the bed was opened out, and the sheets were rumpled.

"Get over here, boy! You need to be punished." Harry was pointing at the bed.

"What did I do?" Darian asked yet again, a question that had never been answered.

"You know what you did!" Harry shouted, reaching out toward Darian.

"I didn't do anything!" Darian screamed, his voice cracking from fear. No matter how often this happened, he was never able to control his terror.

"Who do you think you are, shouting at me?" Harry grabbed the boy by the shoulders. He pulled him so close that the eight-year-old boy was within six inches of his face, his feet barely touching the floor.

"You know what your punishment is," he snarled, releasing Darian. "Now, get to it."

Darian's experience at manipulating Mrs. Gruen had emerged from the intensity of his desire for revenge, but Darian had been too young then to realize the correlation. With Harry, Darian's terror of being molested had always eclipsed the rabid power of revenge, but today would be different.

Darian stood perfectly still. Rapidly moving images from the last four years created a strobe-like effect as they raced through his mind. Unspeakable horrors had taken place in this room behind that locked door. The worst of it was that the lock on the door was on the outside. It was designed to keep him in, not keep anybody out. After these sessions, Ruth seemed almost grateful to Darian. It was the only emotion, the only humanity, he ever received from her. Most of the time, she avoided him.

The sound of Miss McKelroy's voice floated through Darian's mind, telling him that the Beels chose to make him a part of their lives. He was a part of their lives all right. He was the target of their hatred, their anger, and worst of all, their perversity. Without warning, those very same emotions flooded through Darian with such ferocity that what little was left of the child in his psyche was as frightened of them as it was of Harry. The fear was short-lived, however, for the torrent of emotions drowned that little child. Every cell, every thought that could be called Darian was immersed in a white-hot rage, perhaps fueled by the lure of the giant step toward freedom he had experienced in his bedroom just minutes earlier.

Darian looked straight at Harry, who had sat down on the edge of the sofa bed, expecting Darian to comply. Harry had found it easy to force obedience from Darian in the beginning. He was barely over four years old at the time, even if he was a strangely moody four-year-old. After a couple of sessions of disciplining him, Darian was surprisingly compliant. Harry had never expected it to be so easy. Truth be told, it took a little of the fun out of it for him, but he figured he had to take what he could get. He never gave up hope that the boy would be a little more feisty, but the silence coming from him today didn't offer much promise that things were going to be any different this time. With a sigh of resignation, Harry looked up at Darian.

Despite the shadows of the basement, Darian's eyes glowed. For the first time, fear seized *Harry* in its grasp. He couldn't speak. His mouth moved in a contorted fashion, struggling to form words, but nothing emerged except garbled sounds. Darian held Harry's gaze in a vise-like grip. Then a laugh that was not that of a young boy gurgled to the surface. It rang with the venom of a shameless soul—a soul who would have dismissed Harry's perverse antics as being minor league. It was a laugh that made Harry's blood run cold.

"You pathetic old man!" Darian said with disgust as he spat in Harry's face. The spittle landed on the side of Harry's spider-veined nose and ran slowly down his cheek. Stunned, Harry did not move.

Darian's brows drew together in concentration. His hands formed small fists at his sides. Harry's spine arched backward, jerking his head behind his torso like the fall of a bullwhip. His mouth fell open as his eyes involuntarily rolled upward. Frozen in this grotesque position, he appeared forever caught in mid-seizure. The terror in his eyes was like a fire burning at the outermost edge of an Arctic storm—a temporary warmth remaining in what was fast becoming an icy wasteland.

A full minute later Darian's fists unclenched. His eyes relaxed. At the same moment, the body of Harry Beel fell limply back onto the bed. Looking down at him, Darian searched his eyes, which were fixed open, for any signs of life. There were none. No one was home anymore. A shadow of regret flitted across Darian's face. Then he saw the slight uplift of Harry's chest.

Good! He's still alive, he thought. Darian chuckled as he started up the stairs. Today was definitely a good day, the start of a better life for him. Looking over the railing toward the sofa bed where Harry was lying in a contorted heap, he thought, *Your punishment has just begun, Harry Beel, sir!* and gave a mock salute as he knocked on the basement door.

Chapter 7

Three years later

*T*here was no doubt in Darian's mind that he was special. Not just anyone could access the enlightenment the Master offered him. It would be akin to throwing pearls before swine to even approach most people with such coveted knowledge. They wouldn't understand its importance and most likely would dismiss it as ridiculous. However, he, Darian, had been chosen.

The life forces that had joined with his, despite their reluctance, had given him powers beyond anything he could have dreamed. Powers that were much greater than anything he imagined when he was still trying to become one with the birds perched on his window sill so long ago.

The first time he laid claim to someone else's life force was regrettably a faltering effort. At the time of the episode with Mrs. Gruen, he hadn't understood the significance of the energy surge he had felt. He had attributed it to his anger and concentrated on hurting her instead. As a result, he had released her life force back to her. It wasn't until his edifying experience with Harry that the Master guided him toward actually consuming another's life force, thus adding to his own power.

Darian had made sure when Harry Beel entered his permanent state of vegetation that Ruth understood he was responsible. Her fear of him now was palpable. Ruth was all too familiar with hatred, and the hardness of it was evident in Darian's eyes. Another sensation, however, exuded from his pores and literally filled the room, frightening her more than his hatred. As an emasculated victim of forces that were far less potent than this, she recognized power in all its sinister expressions.

Three years had passed since Harry ceased to function. Three years of Ruth preparing supper for Darian and serving him. Three years of retreating to the corner of the kitchen as he required, awaiting his needs. Sometimes Darian completely ignored her. Other nights he entertained himself by threatening her with colorful descriptions of the things he was planning for her.

Three years was enough for Ruth Beel. She finally made a choice. A choice that would drive Darian into intense experimentation and relentless practice to ensure that no one was ever able to follow in her footsteps again.

Supper began pretty much as it always did that evening, an evening that would haunt Darian with his failure for years to come. However, on this night when her transgressions would be paid in full, at least according to the tally sheet of a power *other* than Darian, Ruth Beel prepared a special treat for herself. Tonight she resolved not to let him torture her anymore. Her death would come as the result of her *own* hand, not his. It was time to draw down the curtain on this mockery that had been her life.

When Ruth was a young girl, she dreamed of a wonderful life. When she met Harry Beel, he was so handsome and debonair that all the other girls in her class at school were terribly jealous. Ruth wasn't the most beautiful of her classmates, but she was certainly the most shapely. At seventeen she could have posed for a pinup calendar and had men drooling over her in back rooms and other private places where they displayed their fantasies. Still, Ruth wasn't interested in modeling. It was 1947, and like many women at the time, she had been carefully trained to dream appropriately. So she daydreamed about being the wife of a handsome, successful man and entertaining his clients and colleagues in their beautiful home. She even imagined the whispers of the guests, "Everything is so lovely. I can't believe she arranged all this by herself!"

Harry had fit perfectly into her daydreams. So she believed her prayers had been answered. He was twenty-seven, older than she, and he was already regional director of a large firm that manufactured parts for farm equipment. Ruth envisioned herself the wife of the company's president by the time she was thirty. The very thought of it excited her so much that she failed to look beyond the surface to discover the true character of the man she was determined to marry. He never pressed her for sexual favors while they were dating or even after they were engaged. Thinking him chivalrous, Ruth had bragged on him to her friends, telling them how much he respected her and what a gentleman he turned out to be.

After the wedding, Ruth was terribly nervous—afraid, yet excited. She couldn't believe she was finally Mrs. Harry Beel. Her dreams were coming true! With Harry's permission, she made reservations at a prestigious hotel located in a nearby resort. It was only an hour's drive so they could spend their wedding night there, and Harry wouldn't have to miss work.

On the drive to the resort Harry was quite responsive to Ruth's excited chatter. Everything seemed so wonderful, and the resort didn't disappoint Ruth either. All she could say when they parked the car at the entrance for the valet was "Oh, Harry!"

Once in the room, Ruth unpacked her suitcase and hung up her clothes. She lovingly unfolded the negligee her best friends had chipped in to buy for her. It was very sexy, designed to show off her full breasts and tiny waist. As Ruth held it up for all her girlfriends to see, her friend, Judy had remarked that no man would be able to resist her in that. Ruth could hardly wait to see Harry's reaction.

Harry was still sitting in the chair with his back to her looking out the window when Ruth finished unpacking her clothes. Uncertain of what was proper behavior, she thought perhaps he expected her to unpack his suitcase as well. She pushed her negligee to one side and lifted his suitcase from the floor to set it on the bed.

"Stop!" Harry barked, rising halfway out of his chair. Startled, Ruth dropped the suitcase. It landed on the floor with a loud thud.

"What?!" she asked in alarm.

"Now, see what you've done! Don't touch that. I'll take care of it." Ruth nodded. Without an apology for scaring her or an explanation, Harry simply turned and sat back down in the chair.

Ruth picked up her negligee and went into the bathroom. Closing the door gently, she leaned against it as tears rolled down her cheeks. Something was terribly wrong, and she didn't know why. Had she done something wrong? Harry certainly wasn't acting like a man on his honeymoon—at least not the ones she had read about and seen in the movies. *Perhaps*, she thought, *my imagination is just running amok.* Within a few minutes, she convinced herself she was being silly. After all, things were only perfect in the movies and in books.

"I'll freshen up and put on my new negligee," she told her reflection in the mirror. "Once he sees me in this, everything will be all right. He's just nervous like me." Ruth made her first excuse for Harry that night, and it wouldn't be her last.

About fifteen minutes later, Ruth took a deep breath, grasped the bathroom door knob with determination, and stepped into the bedroom. Surprised, she stopped short of closing the bathroom door.

There were no lights on in the room, and the curtains were drawn. At first she was unable to see, but as the bathroom door, unhindered by a latch, swung open, the light coming through the bathroom window from the street lamp outside illuminated the bedroom with a soft glow. It was enough. Ruth gasped.

Harry stood stark naked beside the bed with his legs spread and his fists resting at his waist. If it could be said of a naked man, he held the stance of a swashbuckler. Ruth had never actually seen a man without clothes and certainly never imagined one as brazen with his nakedness. This from a man who had made no effort to touch her or have her touch him all the while they dated! Seeing him now brought to mind how many times she had wanted him to stroke the smooth skin of her breasts, to feel the tingle in response to his touch, but he had never even stroked them through her blouse.

"Come here!"

Ruth jumped. His voice cut through the moment like a knife. She hesitated, unsure of herself.

"I said, come here!" Harry looked at her sternly.

Ruth was trembling. Perhaps this was a love game. She had heard of such things. Being new at the game of love, she decided to play along. Trying to relax, she walked toward Harry, stopping about three feet from him. She didn't want to waste the effect of her sexy negligee. She could feel the fullness in her breasts, which was enhanced by the form fitting cups of the negligee.

Ruth trembled with excitement when Harry reached out with his right hand toward her left arm. She was already living the next move in this game, imagining Harry pulling her to him and pressing his lips to hers. Her mental reel shuddered to a halt when his hand grasped her arm and jerked her toward him with such force that her breath literally caught in her throat.

"When I say come here, I mean *come here*! I didn't say stop three feet away!" Harry's voice lacked the gentle caress Ruth had expected. It even lacked the staged quality that should have been there if he were playing a game. The malice in his voice was unmistakable.

Fear replacing her excitement, Ruth's trembling increased. Still holding her with his right hand, Harry had placed his left hand on her head and forced her to her knees. Ruth found herself facing his groin. She had never imagined that it would be so big. It pointed at her as if identifying her as the guilty party.

"Do it!" he shouted.

"Do what?" she cried. No one had prepared her for this—certainly not her mother.

"Don't try to play games with me. You know what to do. You thought you would distract me with that whore's garment you're wearing, but I'm not that easily fooled. You can't escape your punishment. Now get to it!"

Ruth was in shock. Unable to move or think. Harry grabbed the sides of her face, forcing her mouth open. Then he pressed himself into her mouth until she opened it further to stave off suffocation. Unable to comprehend what was happening to her, Ruth did nothing. Harry held her head, moving it back and forth until he felt a familiar throbbing. Ruth fainted either from fear or lack of oxygen, but her weight was supported because Harry still held her head in his hands. He thrust himself deep into her throat, quickly pulled back, and thrust again even deeper, releasing a flood of semen. Ruth awoke, choking. Finished with her for the moment, Harry shoved her head to the side, and she fell to the floor. Ruth's coughing subsided into sobs. Harry didn't seem to notice. Instead he walked into the bathroom and shut the door.

When he emerged a few minutes later, he instructed her to clean herself up. Ruth got up slowly and went into the bathroom. She locked the door very quietly. Thoughts of escaping through the window flitted through her mind. Maybe this was why her mother never talked about sex with her. She had regularly eavesdropped on her mother and her friends at their bridge parties and heard them remarking about "men's unusual appetites." At first she thought they were talking about food, but the giggling and the indiscernible undertones convinced her that it must have something to do with sex. That was the only thing that always elicited whispering. If this was sex, Ruth preferred romance. Still, she had married Harry and promised to love, honor, and obey him. If her mother could live with it, she certainly could. Looking in the mirror, she freshened up her face.

When she returned to the bedroom, Harry was in the bed, sleeping. She slipped in quietly beside him but chose to face the edge of the bed.

"Please, God, let it get better," she murmured as she closed her eyes. As she slept, Ruth dreamed again of her fantasies of a gentle, loving husband who appreciated her beautiful body and kissed her gently in places that set her to tingling all over.

She drifted slowly upward from her dream and realized that Harry was curled up behind her with his arms around her. His hands were massaging her breasts as he kissed her neck. At first she stiffened, but he continued to kiss her and run the tip of his tongue up and down her neck. Then he gently ran his tongue around the edge of her ear lobe. Every nerve in her body stood on end. She didn't know a person could feel this good. He pulled her closer to him until she felt his torso rub against her back. He kissed her ear and stretched to kiss the side of her neck. Ruth shuddered with excitement. He released her breast with his right hand, letting his fingers slide over her stomach and lightly brush her pubic hair. Then he gently straightened out her legs, pulling her even closer. She could feel his hardness against her.

Ruth's body was responding so strongly that she did not know how much longer she could keep from turning over to kiss his lips and throw her arms around him. At that moment he slid himself between her legs. A tremor passed through her, forcing a sigh of ecstasy from her lips. Her body responded. She could feel her wetness on him as he slid himself back and forth between her legs and knew he could not doubt how much she desired him. When he entered her, he would feel the welcoming wetness and the heat from the pulsating caresses that were already starting in anticipation of him.

Harry pulled back from her just a little. Ruth held her breath. At first he rubbed the wetness of her across her buttocks in an up and down motion. Then he pushed. Ruth was breathing rapidly, on the verge of a massive orgasm without benefit of penetration. Sensing that he was off the mark, she shifted herself into better alignment. Harry immediately placed his left hand, which was between her and the bed, on her groin to control her movements. Suddenly he shoved himself into her. Ruth screamed and lost consciousness for the second time. After a few seconds, she revived.

Although Ruth's virginity was still intact, she felt him inside her. The initial pain of such an unorthodox encounter had been excruciating, but it no longer hurt, and he was being very gentle. He was caressing her clitoris with his fingers. To her surprise, Ruth was aroused. Very quickly she reached the heights of sexual excitement. Harry held her upper body tightly against him as she moved in rhythm with the waves of arousal. As if in perfect harmony, they climaxed together.

At that moment, Ruth was not thinking of the perversity of what had happened that night. Perverse in its cruel nature rather than its actions. She could only deal with the ecstasy of the moment. With no other sexual experiences with which to compare it, everything seemed perfect to Ruth.

After that night, the nature of their sexual relationship never changed. Ruth begged Harry to make love in the traditional way so they could have a child. He refused. At first, Ruth assumed he just wanted to wait a while. After a few years, she ran out of excuses for him and admitted to herself that he didn't want children. This was Ruth's greatest sadness.

Harry's strange method of lovemaking no longer excited her. When he felt inclined to *punish* her as he had on their wedding night and at least twice a week since then, Ruth remained completely docile, refusing to struggle or appear affected at all. At first she thought her impassivity would deprive him of whatever thrill he was deriving from her so-called punishment. In time, she realized that her participation or lack of it had little to do with his experience. She was simply a prop.

One evening Ruth was watching a segment on the news about the local orphanage. The reporter was commiserating with the director about the difficulty of finding adoptive parents for children beyond the age of two. The director had agreed, adding that forty percent of the children in the orphanage had been there for at least three years.

"You do the math," he'd said. "That means that those forty percent have a slim chance of ever leaving here!"

"That's incredibly sad!" responded the reporter, turning toward the camera. "If some of you out there listening tonight could reach into your hearts and make a place for one of these children, you would change their lives and set an example for others to follow."

Ruth's mind whirred. Although Harry had refused to help her

create a child, did that really mean he didn't want children as she had assumed? What if she was wrong? What if it was something else? What if he was sterile? That thought brought her mind to a screeching halt. It had never occurred to her before, and now it seemed to be the perfect answer. He was sterile and too embarrassed to tell her. Of course! In that case, he shouldn't mind adopting a child. She determined to ask him at supper.

When Harry actually acted interested in the proposal to adopt a child, Ruth felt a little warmth toward Harry return. Maybe this would change things for them.

"Are you sure, Harry?" She hadn't wanted to get too excited if he was just going to change his mind.

A smile played around the corners of his mouth as he replied, "Of course, I'm sure. It has to be a boy, of course!"

Ruth smiled at Harry for the first time in years. "Whatever you want. Thank you, Harry. This will be so wonderful! You'll see! I'll call the orphanage tomorrow," she had replied with the same lilt her voice had had when she and Harry were engaged.

Harry's mood had changed once Ruth initiated the process of adoption. He didn't participate except to sign the necessary papers when called upon to do so and to insist very clearly when encountering any of the lawyers or orphanage officials that the child must be a boy. Ruth had chosen to see his insistence on a boy as a positive sign and to ignore what some might see as a mood. To her, compliance was better than his usual unresponsive moods.

When the big day arrived, Ruth had felt like a schoolgirl rather than a mother-to-be, but Harry continued to be nonchalant about the whole affair. When Ruth saw the young boy, Darian, coming down the stairs at the orphanage, she fell in love with him instantly. He did not respond as positively to her, and she'd looked questioningly at the attendant because she had no experience with children. She knew he was probably scared and didn't want to upset him. Then Harry stepped in. Ruth's chance for the all-important first impression was crushed.

The first year Darian spent in the Beel household, he was too young to start school. Ruth was glad. She had hoped it would give her an opportunity to spend time with him and experience the joys of motherhood. Things went well for a few weeks. Then one Saturday Ruth had decided to fix a special Sunday dinner to celebrate Darian's one month anniversary with them. It meant she had to go to the grocery for supplies. So she had asked Harry, who was working in his basement shop, to watch Darian.

"He can stay in the basement with you if you don't want to come up. I won't be gone more than thirty minutes."

"Yeah. Okay. Fine."

Taking Darian's hand, she walked down the stairs into the basement with him. "This is Daddy's workshop," she told Darian. "You're going to stay here while I'm gone to the store. We're having a party tomorrow. What do you think of that?" she asked, smiling at Darian.

"Okay," was all he'd said. He had not spoken unless spoken to since he had arrived.

"Come here, son. You and I will have a good time," Harry said. Ruth smiled and freed her hand from Darian's, feeling for the first time like a real family. Leaving Darian with Harry while she ran errands became routine.

About three months after Darian arrived, Harry had transferred to sales. Ruth was distressed. Another of her dreams slipped away. Harry was giving up his position as regional director, which meant he would never be president, and sales was not nearly as secure a position even though his net income would probably be higher. She dreaded his working out of the house, too, which was customary for all the salesmen. When she had asked why he changed jobs, the only answer she got was that he preferred it over the hassles of the office.

As time went by, her initial resentment about the job change had lessened. If she needed to run errands, she didn't have to worry about keeping Darian out too long. He could stay home with Harry. Plus, if the weather was bad, she didn't have to take the chance of his getting sick. If she'd had any friends to ask at the time, she would have told them she was starting to like having Harry around. Even her relationship with him improved. He still refused traditional lovemaking, but he had ceased to *punish* her as he called it. The last time he had punished her was about a month after Darian arrived. Ruth convinced herself he was changing because he was now a father.

That first year had passed quickly for Ruth. She was excited about celebrating the milestone as a family with a special dinner even though her relationship with Darian had not improved that much. He rarely spoke to her and only if she asked a question. He was very introverted, almost angry. She wondered what had happened to him at the orphanage to cause such distress.

Taking the layers of the celebration cake out of the oven, she had set about getting out the ingredients for the frosting. Opening the refrigerator, she remembered using the last egg for breakfast. A quick check of the sugar bowl told her she needed more sugar, too. Taking off her apron, she went to the foot of the stairs and yelled up to Harry, who was in his office.

"I have to go to the grocery. Keep an eye on Darian." Putting on her coat, she called out again, "On second thought, I may go by the fabric store, too, while I'm out to get fabric for his Halloween costume." Then she left.

A damp, windy day, it was not a perfect day for grocery shopping. There were only a few customers in the store, and Ruth was able to gather her groceries and check out within ten minutes. She ran to the car and put the sacks in the back seat. The fabric store was only about six blocks away. Anxious to buy the fabric and start on Darian's costume, she pushed the car over the speed limit. Ruth had a very unique costume planned. Maybe it would make him feel special even if he never actually said so. She was not really expecting a "thank you" or even a smile. He was such a remote little boy.

Pulling into the parking lot, Ruth parked the car and hurried toward the store, holding her head down against the wind. Grasping the door handle, she pulled. It didn't open. Raising her head, she saw the sign. *Closed for inventory.* Disappointed, she ran back to the car and headed home.

When Ruth returned home, she didn't have to struggle with her keys because she hadn't locked the front door. Entering the foyer, she started to call out to Harry that she was back but decided to put her packages down first. Entering the kitchen, she heard Harry's voice coming from the basement. Believing he had heard her come in, she naturally assumed he was calling out to her. She almost answered him but didn't. Instead, she stood very still and listened.

In a clear and angry tone, she heard him say, "You know what your punishment is. Now do it!"

Ruth froze. How many times had she heard those words? Her first reaction was automatic and self-directed. Then she quickly realized that he couldn't be talking to her. *Oh, my God!* she thought, *not Darian!*

She tiptoed to the basement door, which was ajar. Thankfully, she had not turned on the kitchen light which would have alerted Harry that she had returned. So, quickly, but quietly, she crept down the stairs until she could bend over and see into the basement. Harry's back was to her. She could see Darian on his knees in front of Harry.

"Harry!!" she screamed. "What in God's name are you doing?" Ruth ran and grabbed Darian and held him to her. Despite the tears running down his face, Darian did not make a sound. He just stood there limply with his arms at his side.

Harry turned to glare at Ruth with that look of retribution she had come to fear. It had been so long since she had seen it, she had almost forgotten the fear it once engendered. She froze for a minute too long. Harry grabbed her and pushed her to her knees. The floodgate opened. All the hopes and dreams she had nursed for the last year about becoming a real family were caught in the rush and jerked away from her, and she knew they were lost forever.

When Harry had finished with Ruth, he grabbed Darian, who had stood trancelike watching Harry abuse Ruth. Harry refused to let go of Ruth, however. He forced her to stay on her knees at his side while he punished his son.

Afterward, Harry gave Ruth an ultimatum—stop interfering with his punishment of his son or he would punish them both. Ruth knew she was weak, but she could not stand to go through that again. So on the days when he ordered her to lock the basement door from the outside so Darian could not escape his punishment, she was too afraid of him to resist. Harry punished her occasionally despite her efforts to obey his wishes. She assumed it was a reminder of sorts, and she accepted it as penance for her weakness and her shame.

After that day, Ruth was completely alone. Darian refused to have anything to do with her. It didn't matter to him that she was just as much a victim as he was. The only thing that mattered to him was that she had locked the door to the basement so that he could not escape.

The day Darian had turned the table on Harry could have been a blessed event for them both, but because Darian blamed Ruth nearly as much as Harry, it was not. Darian simply transferred his hatred to her and had tortured her constantly for the last three years.

Harry had long since died, of course. Darian had refused to allow Ruth to feed him more than just enough to survive. He wanted to watch him suffer, but there was hardly enough of Harry's life force left to make it a worthwhile effort. Not to be denied his retribution, Darian forced Ruth to perform fellatio on Harry shortly before he died and for a while afterward. The sound of Darian's laughter would echo off the basement walls as he shouted, "You know what your punishment is. Now do it!"

Eventually he made Ruth dig a hole in the backyard and dump Harry's body in it. When she tried to put a marker on the grave, he kicked it across the yard.

"Do you think I want a reminder that this piece of shit drew breath?" Ruth did not answer.

"Do you?" he shouted.

"No, Darian, I don't imagine you would."

Harry's death had not alleviated any of Ruth's suffering for she became Darian's primary plaything. His power was growing rapidly, and he forced her to do things for his own amusement with the sheer force of his mind. Once, he was able to hold her upside down with her feet on the ceiling for nearly thirty minutes. Ruth expected to have a stroke, but unfortunately, she survived.

Now, Ruth really was dying. It was no longer a distant hope. It was a reality. She had cancer. She had known for a long time but deliberately concealed it from Darian. She had gone to Dr. Howe in secret, pretending that she was shopping for groceries and other supplies. Last week the doctor told her that she could not possibly live for more than a couple of weeks. Despite his protests, she refused to be admitted to the hospital. Out of compassion, the doctor prescribed a powerful pain killer for her because he knew the pain would only get worse.

This morning Ruth awakened with a strange feeling. This would be her last morning. Smiling, she breathed a sigh of relief. At last her suffering would be over—her penance paid.

She pulled the bottle of pain killers from under the mattress. It was full. She had never taken any of them. The cancer had never been as painful for her as life was. On her last visit to the doctor, she asked him with feigned concern how many pills she could take without its being dangerous. It was all she could do to keep from laughing as he very thoughtfully answered her question. Surely he did not think she was serious! Which was more dangerous—pain killers or cancer? What difference would it make from which one death sprang?

No matter. Today these pills would release her from Darian's brutality and allow her to die by her own hand. At least she would have control over this one thing in her life. She would orchestrate *when* it came to an end!

The sun was setting. The lingering light was casting shadows around the kitchen. Sitting on the stool in the corner of the room, Ruth felt the pills starting to take effect. She leaned against the corner, allowing her head to drop forward. She was sure Darian wouldn't notice because she often fell asleep while he was eating his supper. She had learned to grab precious moments of peace long ago.

Ruth's mind began to drift, expanding beyond her body until she felt like a bird floating with the wind. She looked down and saw Darian, but she felt no fear. Then she saw herself, and she was filled with sorrow. She was just twenty-six years old when Darian came into their home. Now she was only thirty-three but looked like an old woman. From her new vantage point, she looked at Darian and realized how handsome he would be one day—proof that appearances are deceiving.

As Ruth floated, looking down on the scene in the kitchen, Darian suddenly leaped out of his chair, knocking it backwards. "Come back here!" he shouted.

At first Ruth didn't understand what was happening. She watched as he rushed to the stool in the corner and began to shake her.

"Where do you think you're going?" he kept screaming at her body.

Then Ruth understood and laughed as only a spirit freed of its earthly bonds can laugh. She was free! She had slipped away before he could take her life force from her. She had watched him steal the life force from all manner of living things and had vowed she would never become part of him. To that end, she had guarded her thoughts carefully and managed to hide her cancer from him. She was lucky he was so self-absorbed that he hadn't noticed the pallor and the thin, almost transparent look her skin had developed. She had been careful to apply makeup every day in hopes that he would think the discernible ravages of the cancer were merely his reward for being such a skilled tormentor.

Ruth could have taken the pills before going to bed and slipped away more easily, but she wanted to leave this world with at least one victory on her tally sheet. She had given up so much of herself to Harry, then to Darian, and finally to the cancer that she could not leave this world without at least one act of bravado—one time when she stood tall for something she wanted.

The last sight and sound that Ruth enjoyed on this plane was Darian screaming and shaking his clenched fists. "I'll find you, Ruth! You can't hide from me. I'll be so powerful one day that it won't matter where you are. I'll come for you! You belong to me!"

Chapter 8

Seven years later

Darian remained alone in the Beel house for seven years after Ruth departed. It wasn't as difficult as he thought it might be for an eleven-year-old. Harry's insurance had already been supporting him and Ruth for a long time. First with disability during Harry's "stroke" and then with life insurance once he died. No one had even questioned his death.

Darian had insisted his body remain at the house because he was unwilling to grant Harry even the slightest gesture of humanity. Afraid to thwart Darian, Ruth had called a doctor who still made house calls to come by the house and issue a death certificate. She told the doctor she would handle the funeral arrangements herself, which wasn't actually a lie. After all, she did dig his grave in the back yard. The insurance company was so delighted to close this account with a life insurance payout rather than years of disability payments that questions just seemed to fade into the background. The check was issued, and the file was closed.

Although Darian was only eight years old when Harry died, the nature of his thoughts were far different than the normal musings of a boy his age. He already knew money was a necessary commodity if life was to go on undisturbed for him. He'd informed Ruth there was no escape for her. So, unless she wanted to follow in Harry's footsteps, she would make certain everything was handled to ensure they could maintain their current situation. If Ruth had known the terror that lay ahead for her, her choices might have been different. As it was, she handled the financial issues with the insurance company without too much resistance because she, too, needed to eat.

When Ruth died, Darian was eleven. He notified no one. The only inquiry about Ruth was from a doctor's office. Curious about the reason for their call, Darian had pretended she was visiting her parents, who had actually died several years earlier, and expressed concern about his mother making the trip in her "condition." He assumed there was a condition. Why else would a doctor's office be calling? Besides, his rage at her departure had left him hungry for answers.

The nurse had only seen Ruth Beel in passing. She worked for Dr. Howe's partner and was just filling in for his regular nurse. Not familiar with Ruth's personal information, she did not realize that Ruth was only thirty-three. From their encounters, she had just assumed she was in her late forties at least. So, unaware of Darian's age, the nurse willingly responded to his concerns. "Son, it's probably a good thing she's visiting her parents now. She'll want to spend her last days with you, and as I'm sure you know, there aren't many of them left. This particular cancer is extremely venomous."

Although the nurse's bedside manner would not be especially comforting to most, it served Darian's need for information quite well. Hanging up the phone, a black rage erupted. How had he not known? Ruth had managed to rob both him and the cancer of their final pleasures. Losing was an experience he did not enjoy and determined not to repeat. Ruth's victory over him became his driving force. With renewed diligence, he had set out to obey the instructions from the master within to learn to control his own power.

Maintaining the status quo was incredibly easy for Darian. Ruth had no friends to ask questions or interfere. The doctor's office in a typical "out-of-sight, out-of-mind" mentality never called back. After all, repeat business from Ruth was certainly out of the question! Darian had never gone back to school after his showdown with Harry, and no one ever inquired. There was probably a collective sigh of relief from the school staff and an unspoken agreement to sweep it under the rug. It didn't matter to him. Darian didn't care what the outside world thought about him as long as it didn't interfere with his plans.

During the seven years following Ruth's demise, Darian practiced his control over living and inanimate objects with an ardor that could only be described as religious. Many fell by the wayside in his enthusiasm for his quest, but it was a consequence of no concern to him. His providence was more significant. He had a special destiny, and it was their fate to contribute to his.

Some theologians say that the number seven metaphysically represents a time of material completion. Perhaps this is true, for at the end of this seven years, Darian intuitively knew that the path he was on would take him no further on his quest.

In his musings, he hoped to hear from the Master, hoped he would show him the way. It was in his contemplations of his past achievements that an area of neglect was suddenly revealed to him. Strangely enough, he had never tried controlling the elements or anything beyond the earth. Sure, he had stolen the life forces of plants and animals and people. He had crushed and manipulated them all, but he had never attempted to control the wind, the rain, the sun, the moon, or the stars. He had limited himself to things he could touch. He never thought to reach toward the heavens, though it was certainly reasonable that he could only become omnipotent if he controlled the heavens as well.

Seizing upon this undeniable truth was a conscious shock for

Darian, and the infusion of energy was astonishing. His intention evolved. He no longer desired to simply learn how to use the power. He desired to become *one* with the Power itself, giving him dominion over everything and everyone. *Of course!* he thought, *none will be greater than me. Not even that mysterious God to whom so many bow their heads. All will be within my domain.*

Over the following seven years, Darian pursued this new revelation and worked diligently to control the heavens. He focused for days, trying to make it rain or to create a storm. In his arrogance, he even tried to keep the sun from rising. He failed miserably, but it never occurred to him to give up. He continued to increase his power through the abundance of transients nearby. He laughingly bestowed on himself a humanitarian award for his contribution to relieving the suffering of the homeless. In his distorted view, their lives finally counted for something.

Despite the steady diet of life forces and the phenomenal increase in his power, Darian was not able to control a single element of the heavens at the end of that time. Assessing his efforts, he determined that something was still missing. He didn't know what it was, but he could literally *feel* its absence. Being no closer to his destiny made him restless. It had been seventeen years since he first came to understand his power—thanks to Harry. But, he was twenty-five years old now. He needed to find the right path to achieve his destiny. And soon.

Perhaps, he told himself, *I need to leave the city and move to an isolated area, an area more suitable to my needs where I can better concentrate.* The sense of well-being this decision brought Darian caused him to quickly implement plans to find the perfect place.

His perfect place turned out to be a cabin located northwest of a small town named Sterling, about one hundred miles west of the Chicago suburbs. The cabin was surrounded by acres and acres of woods, and the woods were encircled by farmland, much of which was no longer being planted. There were no houses and no humans for miles, which suited Darian perfectly. The cabin was old and in bad need of repair. The owner had abandoned it eight years earlier to move into a retirement community in Chicago where he had recently died. Selling the Beel place, Darian bought the cabin from the estate executor for only the cost of the land.

Once settled into the more natural setting, Darian again focused on being able to control the elements. He replenished himself at first by stealing the life forces of the smallest animals that found their homes in the forest of trees surrounding the cabin. As his hunger grew, none of the animals escaped. Then the forest itself fell victim to his rapacious appetite. None were safe from his need to fuel his quest.

Fredrika: The Fear of Unraveling

Chapter 9

Day 3 — Chicago

Walking through the lobby of the Union League Club the next morning, Freddie was coaching herself to focus on the task at hand when she stopped suddenly to look into the large mirror placed above a small leather bench. The mystical gray surface of the mirror complemented the restrained style of the hotel, and in its shadowy surface, she saw the reflection of a stranger. A professional businesswoman, dressed in a two-piece suit, carrying a smart-looking briefcase, and looking very self-assured — definitely not someone to be taken lightly. The image evoked the same surprise it always did when she saw her reflection unexpectedly: *It can't possibly be me, but it must be.*

The surprised feeling didn't linger, however, because she had long ago accepted this contradiction between what she saw and how she felt. Just as she had accepted that she would never be "one of the gang." Not because she considered herself exceptional — quite the contrary. She considered herself unacceptable to others. A third wheel. Odd man out, and all the other phrases used to describe a person who has achieved none of the things that endow status in life.

Turning to her left as she exited the building, Freddie silently rehearsed her class presentation. The sounds of cars, horns blowing, and the shouts of "taxi!" by the scores of people lining the sidewalk were lost to her. She was driven by the dread she always felt before each class. What did the account executives expect from her? What if they knew much more than she did? What if she couldn't answer their questions? The fear of such embarrassment pushed her into near obsession over her class.

Reaching the Board of Trade, Freddie stopped on the sidewalk, ignoring the people pushing past her as they hurried toward their destinations. She took a deep, fortifying breath. As she started to exhale, she spotted him. Standing just inside the lobby doors was Mr. Personality. Freddie gasped, but with her lungs already filled to capacity, a coughing spasm ensued. Cupping her hand over her mouth, she lowered her head and tried to steady her breathing. When she raised her eyes, he was gone. Assuming that he was stalking her, she hurried into the building to intercept him but knew that it would be like looking for a needle in a haystack. Hundreds of people were always rushing to and fro in the Board of Trade Building during business hours.

She positioned herself as much out of the flow as possible and tried to visually inspect every corner of the entrance hall. There was no sign of him. Whether flesh and blood or smoke and shadows, she was certain she would recognize her stalker.

Okay, Ma'am, give us the details so we can draw a composite, remarked a sarcastic voice in her head. The truth was she would recognize him, but she could never describe him. Her image of him was more an impression without the details necessary for a drawing. *Well, Officer, he's sort of a shadowy guy. Seems to prefer gray, and it complements his personality perfectly,* remarked Freddie sardonically in her internal dialogue.

She would have to admit he was probably handsome, especially with that dark, wavy hair, but his features were slippery. When she tried to examine them closely in her mind, they simply slid out of view. She remembered trying to see a deer at the edge of the woods at twilight with her dad when she was a little girl. She couldn't see it at all until she directed her gaze to one side of it. Even then, the details were still out of focus. Her dad had said Mother Nature protected the deer by giving them the coloring to blend in with their surroundings, and even if you spotted them, you couldn't focus on them clearly enough to harm them. Perhaps that was the purpose behind Mr. Personality's dubious attributes—protection. *He's also very crafty, Officer, because he can appear and disappear at will!*

Freddie dropped her internal chattering and headed for the elevators. Within seconds she was completely surrounded by a throng of people. She dreaded this because when the elevator door opened, she unwillingly became part of a giant creature whose only goal in life appeared to be getting in and out of the elevator. On her last trip to Chicago, she had failed to shake herself loose from the forward-moving creature as it fled the elevator and was unsympathetically deposited outside the elevator twice before she reached her desired floor. Determined not to let it happen again, she pushed her way to the side wall, caught hold of the railing that encircled the elevator, and held on for dear life. After stopping on every floor, the elevator bell finally dinged for her floor. Freddie yelled, "Coming through!" and stuck her hand between the closing elevator doors just in time.

As the day wore on, her earlier concerns about her class fell to the wayside as they always did. The pressure to do her best and her love of teaching predictably produced a slam dunk—even if it was a pattern that Freddie was reluctant to count on. Her words flowed with incredible ease, explaining the most difficult notions for the brokers in ways they could understand. Because creating diagrams in her mind was the way she assimilated data, each new piece of information had to fit neatly in its place. This insistence resulted in a strongly logical approach to any concept, which the new brokers appreciated. Later they would be delighted to find her just as helpful with preparing customer presentations.

Her friend Jodi described this compulsion of Freddie's as "enabler extraordinaire." Freddie didn't deny that she seemed to shine when she was working to help someone else get ahead. All her creative abilities were released, reaping bounty aplenty for others. She loved helping others, but she often wondered why she wasn't happier. Why did doing the thing she enjoyed seem to keep her on the outside looking in? The idea that the wall of segregation was created by her fear of personal failure never occurred to her. Nor was she willing to acknowledge she avoided challenging this fear by always investing her energies in others and never in herself.

After class, some of the brokers in Freddie's class invited her to join them for dinner at The Trade, a restaurant favored by everyone for its steaks and desserts. She accepted. Returning to the hotel to change clothes, she signaled to the concierge. "Is The Trade restaurant close enough for me to walk?"

"It's not far, Ma'am. If you're up for it, I don't see why you couldn't walk," the concierge answered.

Perhaps a walk in the night air would clear her head. Today's class was very good, but her experiences yesterday, and this morning for that matter, were still casting a shadow over her spirits.

Dressed in loose, black slacks and a peach sweater, Freddie decided on a pair of soft leather shoes with rubber soles. She took one last look in the mirror to check her hair and makeup. The strands of gray in her hair shone brightly under the lights over the mirror. There were only a few, but at her age they were distinctive. She liked them.

At times like these, she saw the reflections of *two* women in the mirror. One was the level-headed, efficient woman she saw this morning. The other was a sensual woman to whom men were attracted, a woman who dreamed of romantic rendezvous and candlelight dinners. The level-headed one would never take the chance of acting on such capricious fantasies as these. Sadly, Freddie knew that even the sensual one had never been reckless enough to take that chance either—except in her dreams. *Maybe, that's because the only place my sensuality exists is in my fantasies!* she thought.

Stepping lightly out into the hall, Freddie was looking forward to spending the evening with her students who, in very short order, would be her colleagues. Checking the door to make sure it was locked, she started down the hall. She glimpsed a shadow moving around the corner at the far end of the hall. Her heart stopped for the length of one beat. Her nerves jangled the surface of her skin like hundreds of tiny ants crawling under her clothes, making her shudder. Looking at the stairwell door, she thought, *Maybe I should walk down. It's only three flights.*

While deliberating over the silliness of such an idea, Freddie saw the dark shadow of a large torso creeping out past the corner, growing larger by the second. She sprinted through the door into the stairwell and fairly flew down the three flights to the lobby. Bursting through the door at the bottom of the stairs, Freddie unceremoniously bumped into an old man. After assuring herself that he was not hurt, she leaned against the wall and placed her hand over her heart to ensure it remained in her chest. She didn't know if the heavy beating under her fingers was from fright or physical exertion.

While she tried to catch her breath and quiet the thumping sound in her ears, she looked around. Several men were sitting in the arm chairs scattered throughout the room adjoining the lobby. A few people were passing through on their way out, but no one looked familiar, and no one came out of the elevator while she was perusing the lobby.

Maybe he got to the ground floor first! Or maybe he arrived while I was steadying that poor old man I nearly knocked down. No, I don't think so. I would have heard the elevator ding, she thought as logic took over, only to quickly lose its footing. *Oh, God! Maybe he's waiting for me in my room! What if he's still there when I get back?*

Freddie's breath had deteriorated into short, gasping sounds. Her knees started to give way under the weight of this ominous thought. *Please, God,* she prayed, *give me strength. I cannot pass out in the lobby of this hotel.*

Taking charge of herself, she directed, *Take deeps breaths. That's it—nice, slow breaths. You can do it, Freddie. You know you always come through in a pinch!*

Addressing herself by name was not unusual, especially if she was trying to reason with herself. It separated her from the situation at hand. At least that was her take on it. Whatever it did, it worked. Her breathing slowed, and the color returned to her face. Looking around for a place to sit, Freddie spotted a soft-looking armchair and walked toward it. There was plenty of time to get to the restaurant even if she had to hail a taxi. Right now she needed to contemplate what had just happened.

Should I call the police? she wondered. *I can't. I don't have anything concrete to tell them. They would write off tonight as a hysterical female jumping at shadows. As for the rest of it, they'd probably claim I was mistaking a man who just had an appreciation for a shapely woman as dangerous. But, if that's true, what was he doing in my room last night? And how did he get out?*

Freddie strained her memory to see if she could clear up the details for a crisper picture of Mr. Personality, but it was still just shadows and feelings. If she saw him under less threatening circumstances, she might not even recognize him at all. She realized she couldn't call the police because eventually the incident on the plane would come to light. How would she explain his disappearing from an airplane in mid-flight? *No, they would have me in a mental hospital before nightfall!*

Freddie sighed. This was like being zapped into some science fiction movie. Tonight, ladies and gentlemen, for your enlightenment the Twilight Zone, starring Freddie Marsh as a confused young woman. A woman destined to live in a world forever spattered with hallucinations, ignited by a loosely rolled joint, its wisps of smoke flowing gently over the landscape of the real world—molding the shadowy forms that inhabit her evanescent world.

After a few minutes of aimless mental wandering, Freddie looked at her watch and realized she needed to hurry unless she wanted to take a taxi to the restaurant. During her walk to The Trade, Freddie "psyched herself out" as she described it, a fundamental factor for staying in control. Bathing herself in the feeling that everything was normal was exactly what she needed right now. She was no longer conscious of the mechanisms she used to accomplish this. Everything just clicked into place once she flipped the control switch. She did know, however, the source of her obsession with control. It was traceable to a single day that still seared her soul.

On the first day of school, her first-grade school teacher, Mrs. Grismore, talked for a *very* long time without a break. Freddie desperately needed to go to the bathroom. Nerves always seemed to put pressure on her bladder, and today was even worse because she couldn't go without permission.

Her teacher was a short woman with graying hair and a moustache on her lip, who had not smiled even once that day. Freddie waited until the pressure was hard to bear before she raised her hand. Mrs. Grismore ignored her. Finally, Freddie lowered her hand. The pressure escalated into pain. She crossed her legs and raised her hand again.

This time Mrs. Grismore responded. "Fredrika, I am trying to talk. What do you want?"

"I need to go to the bathroom!"

"Young lady, we took a break once this morning. You should have gone then."

"I did!"

"Well, you will just have to wait until lunch. It's only forty-five more minutes."

"But—"

"No buts, young lady. Now put your hand down and pay attention."

Freddie was panicked. She focused all her attention on holding back the flood, but in one brief, devastating moment, it was all over. She wet herself and her new blue and gray plaid skirt. She sat perfectly still, obviously in a state of shock. The acrid smell of urine drifted upward. An eternity passed. Freddie was sure she must be old and close to dying by now. Then the bell in the hall rang. As the others jumped up to form a line at the front of the room for lunch, Freddie just sat in her seat, staring out the window.

"Fredrika! What is the matter with you? A little while ago, you were jumping up and down to go to the restroom. Get up and come on."

Freddie tried to speak. Her mouth moved, but no words came out. Finally, a small voice that could barely be heard said, "I already went."

"What!?"

"I already went," she whispered.

"Stand up!" Mrs. Grismore barked. Freddie stood slowly. "Turn around." Even more slowly, Freddie turned around for everyone to see the dark circle on the back of her beautiful new skirt.

"Fredrika, I am ashamed of you. Why couldn't you have waited? Everyone else was able to wait."

Freddie's head was swimming. She could barely stand. Then the worst happened.

"Fredrika, I want you to stand in front of the radiator until your skirt dries. You will not go to lunch with the other children. You will stand in front of this radiator if it takes all afternoon for your skirt to dry. Perhaps that will teach you to control yourself."

A snicker erupted near the door, then another and another until all the kids were laughing. At that moment Freddie pledged to take her teacher's advice. She would learn to control herself. No one would ever see her lose control again.

Chapter 10

*A*fter walking for what seemed like hours, especially since the traditionally chilly spring breezes had picked up, Freddie finally saw the restaurant just across the street. The Trade was spelled out in bold, block letters. Underneath in italics, it read: *buy low, sell high*, an obvious attempt to appeal to all the brokers working nearby. *Of course,* she thought, *it could be owned by a burned-out broker—not an uncommon phenomenon.* Maybe the idea of hedging his retirement by buying a cheap old warehouse, fixing it up, and selling the food at sky-high prices seemed like sweet justice. Everyone thinks all brokers are rich, but Freddie knew it was usually just the wheeler-dealers, most especially those with no conscience when it came to their customers.

"Freddie!" a voice shouted from behind her. She turned to see one of the brokers stepping away from a taxi and waving at her. She waved back and waited until he caught up with her before she stepped off the curb to cross the intersection.

Ryan was a nice-looking man and probably Freddie's age. His dark brown hair with its soft curls gave his face a little boy quality, however. In class she had noticed he always looked straight into her eyes when asking a question, and as ludicrous as it sounded, it made Freddie feel special. She wondered as they walked across the street if he knew that it did, and if he did it on purpose, or if it was just the way he was.

Ryan placed his hand under her elbow as Freddie stepped up onto the curb. A warm, tingling sensation spread out from the spot where his hand was. She felt the blood pounding through her veins and heard the echo in her ears. She had a wild urge to throw her arms around him like she had seen in countless romance movies, but control won out because she knew fantasies were usually one-sided. She didn't even want to imagine how embarrassing that would be!

The dinner was fun. Everyone was talking and laughing, mostly about commodity trading, of course. No matter what subject was brought up, it wasn't long before it was being considered from the viewpoint of the marketplace. Even among these new brokers, there was an adherence to the unwritten law of all traders: Life is merely an extension of the Board of Trade.

Ryan sat next to Freddie. Once dinner was over, and only conversation and drinks remained, Ryan sat back and casually placed his hand on the back of her chair. The gesture left Freddie feeling strangely secure, and after the last few days, that was definitely an accomplishment.

"Can I walk you home? I mean, back to the hotel?" Ryan asked, pulling out her chair for her as everyone stood to leave.

"Are you staying there, too?" Freddie asked.

"I don't know. Which hotel are you in?"

Freddie laughed, realizing that he had no idea where "home" was.

"The Union League Club," she replied, a smile still lingering at the corners of her mouth.

"Me, too! That's great. Now you can't refuse me unless you insist on walking in front of me all the way back!"

"Didn't you take a taxi to the restaurant? I mean, aren't you afraid it will be too tiring for you to walk back?"

"What? Are you suggesting I'm not up to the task?"

Interrupting him, Freddie remarked, "I mean, on a full stomach and all, it would be even harder—"

"Keep this up, and I'll be drawing a line on the sidewalk and hiring someone to shout *ready, set, go* so I can race you back to the hotel!"

Freddie burst out laughing. Ryan was also as irresistible as a small boy. As they walked together, Ryan told her about himself. His excitement about his future radiated outward, engulfing Freddie. She felt safe and happy. Before she knew it, they were back at the hotel. Pushing through the front doors, she wondered why such carefree moments as these were so rare. She turned to thank him for walking her back to the hotel, but before she could speak, Ryan placed his hand on her arm and guided her across the lobby.

"Would you like a nightcap?" Ryan asked as they neared the bar.

"Sure!" Freddie heard herself saying.

The bar wasn't overflowing with people, but there were enough for a couple to be anonymous. Ryan chose a semi-circular booth in the corner away from walking traffic.

"Is this okay?" he asked as he ushered her into the booth. Freddie nodded as she sat down about a third of the way around. She liked his self-confidence. Nothing cocky or arrogant about it. He just seemed to be comfortable with himself. Ryan got in on the other end and slid around until he was next to her.

"Name your poison!"

Freddie looked at him with one eyebrow raised and a look of pained tolerance on her face.

"I'm sorry. I've just always wanted to say that! The truth is I'm a fan of Mickey Spillane and all the other corny detective novels from decades past. I'm a retro kind of guy. I hunger for the age when things were simpler, and sentences were always less than eight words long."

Freddie laughed at Ryan's verbal antics until the tears flowed freely down her cheeks. Ryan was laughing, too, a rich, mellow sound that warmed Freddie's soul. He impulsively put his arm around her and kissed her cheek. A surge of sexual energy passed through her. She stopped laughing and turned to face him. Their faces were only inches apart. Ryan was looking straight into her eyes. Again. She put her lips to his and felt him responding. Her mind and body were floating, and for a few moments she forgot where she was.

Ryan drew his head back and asked, "Would you like to go to my room?" Freddie didn't know what to say. Part of her desperately wanted to shout *YES!* but another part was holding her back. He didn't try to rush her. He simply looked at her.

"Can I get you folks something to drink?"

"What?!" The waiter's words jerked her back from the edge of a cliff. She just looked at the waiter in confusion for a moment. Then, shaking her head, she replied, "No, thank you. I just remembered I have a cliff to jump off of." The waiter retreated without a word. Obviously, she was not the first person the waiter had seen make the leap.

Ryan smiled and slid out of the booth, waiting for her to slide out. When she stood, he put his arm around her waist, kissed her lightly on the cheek, and whispered, "Don't worry. I always carry an extra parachute." Freddie smiled up at him. She wanted this night more than anything in the world right now.

Chapter 11

Day 4 — Chicago

*T*he sun peeked into the room the next morning, but it could only see bits and pieces of them. There was no way it could know what happened in that room during the night. A bit of sun touched Ryan's forehead and ran across his nose and the corner of his mouth. He did not open his eyes to greet it. Another slice of sunlight ran across Freddie's uncovered breast and her hand, which lay limply across her stomach. She did not move.

Gradually the sun hoisted itself farther up into the sky, and its rays shone onto her eyes. She blinked and began to stir. Her eyes were filled with sleep. Still groggy, she rubbed them as she sat up gently in bed. She absentmindedly flicked her hand to shoo away an insect that was buzzing around her head. Finally, Freddie opened her eyes and looked around. Her heart lurched. She couldn't catch her breath.

No!!! she screamed in her head, sinking rapidly into merciful unconsciousness.

The mattress moved as someone sat down beside her. Afraid to open her eyes, she wondered how long she had been unconscious. She felt the person bending over her. A scream was building from the depths of her soul.

"Are you going to sleep forever?" Ryan chided her. Freddie's eyes flew open, and she threw her arms around his neck. "Hey!" he cried. "Maybe I should have awakened you *before* I got dressed!"

Freddie laughed, almost able to forget what she had seen earlier that morning. Ryan looked at her inquisitively.

"What?" she asked.

"You have a strange look in your eyes. Is something wrong?"

"No, I'm all right. I was just having a bad dream. That's all."

"Well then, get up sleepy-head. We have class in two hours."

Freddie slipped out of bed. Realizing that she would have to go back to her room to get cleaned up for the day filled her with dread. As she put on her clothes from the night before, she asked, "Would you mind walking me back to my room?"

"Sure. Can't get enough of me, eh?" Ryan's laughter lifted her spirits. She was feeling better already.

To keep from laughing every time she saw that lopsided grin which seemed to have taken up permanent residence on his face, Freddie avoided looking at Ryan that morning in class. Despite the amusing distraction, Freddie was enriched by the interest the brokers showed as she talked about Character of the Market Analysis, a method for measuring the quality of a given move in price. Their rapt attention fired up her pedagogue gene, and with enthusiasm, she explained how the rate of change, or the momentum index, was determined, which led her to a discussion of the variations in momentum indicators. The rest of the session focused on various indexes, volume and open interest, contrary opinion, and structural theories, which included two of her favorite topics—cyclic analysis and the Elliott Wave Theory.

In wrapping-up the latter, she summarized, "As I initially said, the underlying principle of the Elliott Wave Principle is that two forces are constantly at work—one building up and the other tearing down. Stated as such, it doesn't reveal its drawback. In practice, however, a problem arises in the interpretation of wave extent or of when one force becomes dominant over the other. Therefore, it is suggested that this approach be used in conjunction with other tools of analysis when making a market decision."

When Freddie concluded, everyone was sitting silently with stern expressions on their faces. "Lighten up, guys! It's not that bad. That's why I gave you so many tools to use." She looked at their overwhelmed faces. "Okay, guys. Let's take a minute to review what the point of all this is.

"The market prices—those things you will use to make a living and your clients will use to establish personal wealth—are a result of supply and demand. This makes it very volatile, but objective. The *value* of a commodity does not change as rapidly as the price. If there is an increase in desirability for the commodity, the price of it will far exceed its intrinsic value. In reverse, a lack of desirability causes the price to sink below its intrinsic value. However, just like with a rubber band, the limits of elasticity will cause the price to eventually move back toward the value.

"Technical analysis is the study of the fluctuations of *price*. Fundamental analysis, on the other hand, is the study of the less violent movements in the fluctuations of *value*, followed by the attempt to relate the results of that study to a particular price level.

"Analyzing price is obviously the more objective approach. If you ask people for the value of a commodity, you will likely receive several different answers, any of which may be true due to the subjective interpretation of fundamental factors, such as weather, reports, and other such events. However, if you ask people for the price, you will receive only one answer. So, doesn't it make sense that the analysis of one established result—*price*—creates less variation than the attempt to relate the analyses of several subjective results—

value—to a price level?

"Are you with me?" Heads nodded.

"Despite the tendency of fundamental traders—who should more accurately be called event traders—to disparage technical analysis, it's quite a reliable method. With the changes that are occurring with computers, it is becoming increasingly obvious that the processing of data is going to escalate in speed and complexity. This should only enhance your ability to use these tools.

"But, it is important for you to remember that the method is only as reliable as the person using the tools. Also, despite the objective nature of technical analysis, a master of technical trading recognizes that it is just as much an art as a science. It is one thing to have the charts and the indicators in front of you. It is quite another to open yourself up to the energy and the momentum of a commodity, to view it as a viable entity. That's when you really connect. That's when you soar!"

Seeing their smiles, she said, "That's enough woo-woo for this session. I hope you've all enjoyed the class. Hopefully, I have recruited a few future technical analysts! If you have any questions, you know you can call me any time." Her comments were followed by loud applause as she turned to gather up her course materials. Expecting them to leave, she was startled by the silence in the room and turned around to face the class.

"Did I forget something?" she asked.

"Miss Marsh?" A young man named Brian was standing with a package in his hand.

"Call me Freddie."

"Freddie, we've really enjoyed your class. It's the best one we've had. So we all pitched in to get you something so you would know how we feel." He started toward the front of the room.

"That isn't necessary," Freddie said.

"We think it is," said Brian. He handed her the package. Freddie accepted it and tore off the wrapping, revealing a shiny brass plate with bamboo styled edging. In its center was an engraving.

To Freddie Marsh

"The mediocre teacher tells. The good teacher explains.
The superior teacher demonstrates. The great teacher inspires."

— *William Arthur Ward*—

Freddie Marsh is our inspiration!

The class of 1980

Freddie read the words to herself. She could not possibly have read them aloud. She looked up at the class, and as if they understood her inability to speak and sought to ease her discomfort, they gathered around and began to all talk at once.

Chapter 12

$\mathcal{A}$fter class, Freddie sought solitude in a booth in the back corner of a small Italian restaurant near the Board of Trade. She wanted to savor what had just happened. Surrounded by wine racks tucked into every conceivable corner of the room and the sweet fragrance of the flowers cascading from the shelves of the old cupboards scattered around the room, Freddie listened to the soothing melodies of the Italian love songs playing on the sound system. Closing her eyes, it was easy to imagine being at a seaside cafe in Italy with the Italian waiters speaking in their quaint rendition of English to their American customers. She could almost feel the sea breeze blowing through the veranda of the sidewalk café and smell the sea. Gulls flew over the sandy beach, their rasping calls filling her ears.

In her dream world, she turned her attention away from the beach and saw the cadenced movement of a young man coming toward her. His dark hair, lightly tanned skin, and his muscular arms and torso effortlessly summoned wanton thoughts. Enjoying the pleasures engendered by such mental wanderings as he approached her, she was startled out of her rapture by déjà vu. He was very familiar—too familiar. The rhythm of her breathing shifted into short, quick gasps for air. In her fantasy world, she escaped from its frightening reality by closing her eyes to shut it out.

In desperation, her mind leapt back into the physical reality of the Italian restaurant, firmly situated in downtown Chicago. Disoriented, Freddie still managed to scrutinize the restaurant like a frightened animal who smells its natural predator approaching.

Realizing it had only been a daydream, a deep sigh escaped her lungs, which had been holding on to her last intake of breath as if it were her final one.

The little child in her who was afraid of monsters under the bed now had another thing to worry about. The monsters were invading her mind. She felt frightened and alone. She had no idea how to handle the waking nightmares or the events of the last few days. With the intensity of an addict, she craved a warm, safe place to crawl into where nothing and no one could harm her.

Her need to run and hide worked against her as she once again began losing her grasp on reality. The people in the restaurant were becoming distant as if the camera behind her eyes was deliberately pulling away from the scene before it clicked the lenses shut to reveal only blackness. Something enticed her mind to follow the only pinpoint of light, and it carried Freddie back in time toward the safety of her mother's womb.

Instead of feeling safe and warm, however, her tension was escalating. Darkness swirled around her. Snatches of light revealed she was not alone. *There!* She saw the tiny fingers of a baby moving past her in the swirl. Then two hands appeared and disappeared. Freddie convinced herself that it was herself she saw, safe in the warmth of her mother's womb. Before the tension could ease, she saw three tiny sets of fingers pass before her.

Three hands?! The now familiar clutch of fear resurfaced. *Who was this?* In answer, the light swelled to reveal a baby rolling gently over to face her. He, and it was a he, looked straight at her. The scorn on his face was inconsistent with an innocent child's expressions.

"Who are you?!" Freddie screamed.

Her verbal assault drove the terrifying vision away, but it left her sitting in a restaurant with everyone staring at her. The scream, unlike the rest of her waking nightmare, had not confined itself to the vast regions of her mind. Feeling sick, Freddie grabbed a ten dollar bill out of her purse and threw it on the table before rushing past the waiter and out into the street. She was a full block away before she slowed her pace.

I've got to do something, she thought, or *I'm going to lose my mind!*

Chapter 13

Day 5—Memphis

$\mathcal{F}$reddie hoped returning home to Memphis would restore her life to normal. Unpacking her bags to the distant drone of the television, she carefully removed her dresses from the garment bag. Hanging them in the closet, she noted grimly that they looked like she had slept in them. She would have to send them to the dry cleaners unless she could steam out the wrinkles by hanging them in the bathroom with the shower running.

She opened the wrapping paper around the brass plate her students had given her. Picking it up, she once again read the inscription. Carrying it into the living room, she made room to display it on one of her bookshelves.

Looking around the room, Freddie sighed. Everything around her seemed normal. She could hear the familiar voices from the television that kept the house from being too quiet. Intense silence was a natural part of one's life if you were single unless you took steps to alleviate it, hence the television, which ran whether she was in the room with it or not. Looking around at the familiar surroundings, she questioned whether her adventures of the last few days were even real. No one was popping in or out of her presence now. There was no sign of Mr. Personality in the real world or the dream world. Of course, she hadn't had the courage to actually sleep yet.

Perhaps all of this was just nerves. *Don't be ridiculous!* she thought. *If this were just nerves, you would be a neurotic porcupine by now, Freddie Marsh, because every nerve you own would be standing on end!* No, this was not nerves. Besides, anxiety usually strikes its first blow *before*, not during or after an event. Perhaps she was having a full scale nervous breakdown. If that was true, it would explain the seemingly unprovoked jitters. Of course, it didn't explain why she felt perfectly fine now. It also didn't explain her headaches or her increased sensitivity to the buzzing of fluorescent lighting.

Maybe I have a tumor— the voices from the television broke into her reverie as if in answer to her query. "Let your fingers do the walking," proclaimed the familiar Yellow Pages slogan.

"Maybe what I need to do is look in the Yellow Pages for a shrink!" Just saying it aloud vented some of her fear, the fear that she was indeed losing her mind. *Okay. I will. I'll pick out a shrink tomorrow.*

The doorbell chimed softly. Freddie's first instinct was to ignore it. She was just too tired to deal with anyone right now. Unfortunately, whoever it was did not intend to go away quietly. On the third ring, her curiosity overrode her pressing need to be alone, and even for Freddie, curiosity was difficult to control.

Pulling the door of the guest bathroom closed as she hurried down the hall, Freddie realized that all the deadbolts were still in place on the front door because she had come in through the garage. She grabbed the key from the ledge on the side of the grandmother clock in the foyer as she passed. After a quick glance downward, she made a mental note to rewind the clock. All the weights were sitting at the base of the inner chamber like abandoned souls.

Freddie could hear someone shuffling their feet on the porch. "Just a minute," she shouted through the door as if the visitor couldn't hear her unlatching and unlocking. Although an intruder would never make it through all the defenses this entry held, it was likely her protection measures would ironically seal her fate if Freddie ever needed to escape the house.

"Who is it?" she asked before unlocking the final hurdle, the door knob. There was no answer. Her heart raced in response to the adrenalin now rushing through her system. Panic seeped into her pores.

"It's me!" a voice said with such matter-of-factness that for a brief moment, Freddie wanted to strangle her. It was Jodi, her capricious friend. As soon as Freddie opened the door, Jodi dropped an object in the direction of Freddie's left hand. It missed its target and hit the concrete with a harsh, ringing sound and bounced once before landing near the edge of the porch. Jodi bent down to retrieve it and placed it in Freddie's hand.

"Sorry! I won't bother you. I just thought I better return your house key while you were home." Without taking a breath, she hopped off the porch and headed down the sidewalk. Freddie had her mouth open to respond, but her friend's sudden departure startled her into silence.

"Hey! Give me a call when your company leaves, and we'll visit. Okay?" Jodi hollered over her shoulder.

"What?"

"Your company. When you're alone, let me know. I can come back later to get the scoop." Jodi said with a conspiratorial grin on her face.

"I don't have c-company!" Afraid to look behind her, Freddie leaped onto the porch, slamming the door quickly. A chill literally ran down the length of her spine.

Jodi laughed. "You don't have to hide your boyfriends from me. I promise not to tell a soul." Jodi was geared up to give Freddie a run for her money. No way was Freddie pulling the wool over her eyes. Then she saw the wild, frightened look in her friend's eyes. "Hey! What's going on?"

That one question uttered in complete sincerity crumbled Freddie's carefully constructed wall, built to separate reality from the madness she feared was overtaking her. The remaining fragments dissolved into tears as Jodi put her arm around Freddie and led her to the curb. Freddie turned sideways on the curb because she was afraid to turn her back on the monster—whoever he was. Jodi watched her friend, aware that her skittish behavior was unnatural, and wondered what was causing such an extreme reaction.

Jodi decided to approach the situation head-on. "Should I call the police?"

"N-n-no," Freddie replied hesitantly.

Sitting quietly on the curb was not Jodi's style. She was itching for a fight. She would beat the hell out of that guy if he had hurt her friend. She was very familiar with the reluctance of abused women to confront their attackers, and Freddie's reactions seemed to fit the pattern. However, Jodi was having trouble imagining how a relationship could have escalated to violence so quickly. After all, she hadn't known Freddie even had a boyfriend. Determined to rise to the challenge and settle the score regardless, she stood up, but Freddie pulled her back to the curb. She landed with a soft thud. After a few minutes, Freddie regained her composure but wasn't willing to go back into the house.

"Well!? Out with it!" declared Jodi. "We cannot sit on this curb forever, you know, and you won't let me go in the house to see who's there. So?"

Freddie reluctantly told her what had been happening over the last few days. Everything. Even about the icy hand on her breast. She hurried through it, expecting Jodi to burst out laughing at any moment. When she finished relating the incident in the Italian restaurant, Jodi exclaimed, "My God! No wonder you look like hell!"

"Thanks a lot!"

"You're welcome, but what does all this—weird though it is—have to do with the man I saw in your house? Who is he?"

"There is no one in my house, Jodi. The only explanation I can give you is that it must have been Mr. Personality himself."

"Oh, shit!" Jodi jumped up from the curb and ran toward the house before Freddie could stop her. It was just the natural way of things for Jodi—full steam ahead. She disappeared inside. Afraid for her friend, Freddie followed cautiously. It was absolutely the last place she wanted to go.

Jodi didn't know what she expected when she rushed into Freddie's house. Of course she heard what Freddie told her about Mr. Personality's adroitness at appearing and disappearing at will, but—well, she didn't really believe it. After all, she had seen this guy herself, and she was pretty sure she could tell the difference between the ghostly countenance of either an actual spirit or Freddie's imagination and the visage of a flesh-and-blood, and as she had noted, quite handsome man. He had been standing only ten feet behind Freddie when she saw him. There was no way she had been looking at a ghost.

Quickly assessing that he was not in her line of sight when she stepped out of the front hall into the great room, Jodi hurried to check out the back exits. The chain lock was still fastened on the kitchen door, and the safety bar was locked in place on the patio door. Impossible to accomplish those things while exiting. *Perhaps he's hiding in the bedroom.* Grabbing the biggest knife she could find in the knife block on the kitchen counter, Jodi hurried toward the hallway, passing Freddie, who was still standing on the front door threshold, on the way.

Reaching the first bedroom, she stopped cautiously in the doorway, keeping one eye trained on the other doors. A quick glance told her he wasn't in this room. There was no place to hide, not even the closet. She had seen the inside of that closet, and there was no way Freddie could cram another book in there, much less a whole person. Turning, she headed down the hall. She pushed open the bathroom door and peered in. No one there.

That left only one bedroom because the second bedroom was piled high with all the antiques and other treasures that Freddie had discovered. She planned to use them when she started remodeling her house. Right now, they were in storage in the extra bedroom. The furniture was very carefully arranged with no wasted floor space. The closet door was blocked with an armoire. Jodi's attention turned to the remaining room. Stepping gingerly into the doorway with the knife raised to shoulder height, she looked around the room. No need to look in the closet. Freddie's suitcase was leaning against the door. As Jodi walked back down the hall toward the front foyer, she saw Freddie still standing in the doorway.

"All the doors were locked. Weren't they?"

"Yeah, but—"

"I thought you believed me."

"Well, I do, but it would be easier to believe if I hadn't seen him with my own eyes!"

"No, it would be easier to believe if you had seen him *disappear* with your own eyes."

"Yeah, well, I didn't know I was seeing a ghost at the time. Maybe if I had, I would have looked a little closer. But, he didn't look like a—

well, he didn't look like he wasn't a person." Jodi sat down on the arm of the sofa.

"Jodi, what am I going to do? I don't know what's happening, and I'm scared. These kinds of things don't fit well into my world."

"What kinds of things—ghosts?"

"Ghosts and anything that isn't tangible or logical."

"This from an analyst of the most obscure subject matter on the planet! What, pray tell, is logical about what you do for a living? I would think you would be more tolerant of things plucked out of thin air!"

"Now wait a minute!"

"And not only that, but some of those guys you work with are more scary than any ghost," remarked Jodi, sliding off the sofa arm onto the cushion. "Besides, what if the only evil intent of this ghost is to get in your pants? I mean, he already copped a feel on the airplane."

"Jodi! That's disgusting!"

"I don't know. He looked pretty good to me!" Seeing that Freddie was not responding to her attempt to lighten the tension, she asked, "Want to stay with me tonight?"

"I don't think it matters where I am. He seems to be able to find me regardless. At least he hasn't had any trouble so far." Freddie stood looking into the back yard for a few minutes. "You know, he looks so familiar, but how can that possibly be? I've racked my brain trying to key in on where I've seen him before, but I always come up empty. I've even been going over people I met at the convention we had in Chicago year before last. Of course there were so many people there that it would be impossible to remember everyone I saw. I keep expecting this guy to be some misguided trader who lost everything, including his mind, and is hell-bent on getting revenge because I recommended that he sell T-Bills."

Smiling, Freddie added in a brief burst of levity, "Of course, I'm never wrong so that can't be it unless he waited too long to act on my recommendation and, in his anguish, blames me for his losses."

Jodi was glad to see the break in Freddie's mood and continued the banter. "He must have lost more than his mind. It seems he also lost his ability to hold himself together. Hey! Perhaps you're being visited by the Ghost of Recommendations Past. That means that soon you'll get to meet the Ghost of Recommendations Present and Recommendations Yet to Come. Tell me—how vague have you been in your advice lately? Is there a chance you've fashioned your words to reassure buyers and sellers alike? Maybe you've been employing the centuries old technique of double-talk. That might make your next visits *pretty* scary!" Jodi broke off because she realized she had gone too far, a common offense for her.

Despite her affection for Jodi's imagination, Freddie wanted to wring her neck. "You're a lot of help!"

"I've got it!" Jodi shouted as she jumped off the sofa, nearly knocking Freddie backwards. "Sorry."

"What have you got?" Freddie asked, stepping to the opposite side of the ottoman.

"My aunt! That's who we need to see." Jodi grinned with the assurance that she had just solved the current riddle of her universe.

"You think your aunt knows Mr. Personality?" Freddie asked sweetly.

"Of course not!" Jodi declared, choosing to ignore the sarcasm being thrust at her. "Remember me telling you that my mother's family is Chickasaw Indian?" Freddie nodded. She knew Jodi was very proud of her Indian heritage, and her strong features gave evidence of it despite her blonde hair.

"Well, my aunt Miya is special. She married my grandmother's brother, but she comes from a long line of medicine men and women on both sides of her family."

"And?" Freddie had no idea where Jodi was headed, which was not that unusual.

"*And*, she can talk with the spirits! We could go see her. I know she would help us figure out what's happening." The more Jodi talked, the more excited she became—jumping up and down like a kid.

Freddie looked at her without expression. Jodi's eyes were opened wide, her mouth twisted to one side, and her face looked strained as she waited for a response. Freddie exploded into gales of laughter. Tears rolled down her cheeks as she dropped down on the sofa. It felt good. Just like earlier with Ryan, laughter was a great way to vent the tensions she was feeling.

"Sure! Laugh at me, will you? I was just trying to help." The look on Jodi's face teetered somewhere between outrage and laughter.

Wiping her eyes, Freddie replied, "I'm sorry, Jodi. It's just that sometimes the balls you hit are so far to the left that it startles me. This one is such a leap from twentieth century logic that it struck my funny bone."

"She really can, you know."

"Can what? Talk to spirits?" Jodi nodded. "Oh, come on! You don't really believe that. Do you?"

"Yeah, I do. I've seen her do some pretty miraculous things."

"Well..." Freddie hesitated. She didn't want to hurt Jodi's feelings. "If I see any signs that this—this *ghost* means to harm me, I'll think about talking to your aunt. Okay?"

"Any *signs*? What's it going to take—being run down by a Mack truck?"

Freddie smiled. "Besides, I thought you didn't really believe he was a ghost."

"Well, maybe I don't, and maybe I do, but it never hurts to find out for sure."

Darian: Expanding His Quest

Chapter 14

Sterling, Il—three years later

$\mathcal{D}$espite his repeated failures since moving to the country, Darian constantly reminded himself he could already control every manner of life on the planet as well as any objects created by that life. So it was a reasonable assumption that the next step in his evolution was control of the heavens. If everything that lay beneath the heavens was under his purview, what other step could there be? He believed it was only a matter of time until he experienced a quantum leap. This belief had always been enough to sustain him until the day the wolf walked out of the forest. That day marked the end of one cycle and the beginning of another, very significant one for Darian.

Sitting in his armchair that day, lost in thought, Darian had sensed the approach of a strong spirit. A wolf. *Ah!* he'd thought, *Another comes to join the fold!* His anger had found yet another target.

Pressing his life force around the wolf, he had felt the darker energy of the wolf's fear as his life force was pulled from him even though he had not fought for his life. Disappointed that the wolf had not had the strength of spirit he'd desired, Darian had lashed out in anger. At last he had gotten a response. The wolf howled. Then something had happened. Energy flowed into the wolf. It had surged through him, igniting sparks of life until every particle of his being was increased tenfold. The sparks had grown into a flame and the flame into a fire that had threatened to consume Darian. He recoiled.

Once back in his body, Darian had walked to the window, his

eyes filled with rage as he peered out the window of the cabin in the direction of the departing wolf. Particles of his dark energy had reached out, beginning to rejoin the air around him. He was driven by a desire to see the wolf lying on the ground, nothing but an empty, misshapen shell. At the last second, he had jerked back.

The wolf frightened him. Never before had he encountered anyone or anything that could resist him. He didn't understand what had happened. He had held the wolf's life force in his grasp. He had felt it merging with his own, starting to lose its grip on the wolf's consciousness. Then suddenly it had exploded with such force that he could no longer hold it!

What was this power greater than him?

At that moment he had known it was time. He could not, *would* not, delay much longer.

For the next month Darian did little else but sit in his cabin and think. How could there possibly be a force on this planet that he could not subdue? *How could this be?* Such an anomaly only clarified for Darian that something was indeed missing.

If absorption of life forces was the key, he would already have achieved his goal. If concentration was the key, the last three years alone in this cabin should have taken him to the ultimate experience he yearned for. So, if a mere wolf could connect with a power that nearly defeated him after all his efforts, then some element had to be missing. Some piece of the necessary whole. That element could not be within him because he had placed himself completely on this altar. There was nothing else to give. The Master had told him years ago that he would know when he was ready. Sitting here, knowing that he had sacrificed everything, he understood that it was time to reach out somehow—to find the key that would deliver his destiny to him.

One morning Darian awoke with an idea so compelling that he was stymied as to why he hadn't thought of it before. *This was it!* he thought. His parents. He had been abandoned, but it did not mean his parents were dead. He needed to locate them. For this, he would have to return to the orphanage.

In his distorted view of the world, Darian found it a reasonable conclusion that he could not ascend to his ultimate place in the universe if the life forces of those who created him were not joined with his. Was he not the product of their union? He was proof that the whole was greater than the sum of its contributing parts. But yet, imagine what would happen if the whole were increased by the life forces of the parts from which it sprang. It would be like multiplying himself by himself—undeniably increasing the potential, the power.

Immediately gathering up what he needed, he made the trip to Peoria, Illinois, which was only about a hundred miles south of Sterling. Parking the car across the street from the orphanage, Darian turned off the motor and stepped out of the car. He stood in the street and looked at the building. Since the first night he had been "punished" by Harry in the basement, he had sworn to himself never to let his thoughts wander back here for any reason. As he looked at it now, despite the evil that had long since taken command of Darian, he still felt the sweetness of a few memories scurry past his senses. The boyhood memories were too faint and too few, however, to have much impact on Darian the man.

With renewed determination, he strode up the front walk. Pushing through the entrance, he walked to the office of the administrator. He still remembered where it was. He quickly turned the knob, not bothering to knock. Behind the desk sat an older woman. Judging from the gray in her hair, she was at least in her fifties. She was bent over the desk with pen in hand working on a ledger when she heard the door open. Removing her reading glasses, she looked up to greet her ill-mannered visitor.

"May I help—" Her words broke off. "My God! It's you." She hurried around the desk and flung her arms around him, hugging him tightly. Darian made no move at all. He wasn't merely taken aback by her friendliness; he was shocked by the intimacy—shocked by the actual touch of another person.

She released her grip on him and held him at arm's length. "I can't believe you're here after all these years! You're just a larger version of how you looked then. What have you been doing with yourself?"

Darian just stared at this woman without replying. Misjudging his silence, she asked, "Darian, don't you remember me? I was an attendant when you were here—Miss McKelroy." She snickered. "Of course, you were just a little boy. Why would you remember me?"

Her effusive greeting had disquieted Darian, but of course he remembered her. He hadn't expected her to remember him, though, much less be glad to see him.

"Here, sit down, Darian. You look tired. Tell me all about yourself. I tried to contact you after you were adopted, but Mr. Beel told me it would be upsetting to you. Might keep you from adapting to your new life. Since it was against the rules for me to make contact with one of our charges after their adoption, I was forced to agree. If my supervisor had found out, I would have been fired on the spot!"

Darian's carefully constructed belief system was threatened by her statements. *If Miss McKelroy really had cared—maybe things weren't the way they seemed—if he had known.* Finally he spoke. "You tried to contact me?"

"Of course. Did you think I would just forget you?" she asked as she sat down behind her desk.

Her words sparked a foreign emotion in Darian that welled up and further threatened his control. At first, he was fascinated by its unfamiliarity and tempted to give in to its allure, but the connection was broken by her next question.

"What brings you back to the orphanage after all these years, Darian?"

The answer to her question brought his attention back into familiar territory. He was once again focused on his quest. No sympathies or misty-eyed notions could penetrate his resolve. Still, it didn't mean he couldn't use them to achieve his purpose. So, he approached her meekly, hoping to use her obvious fondness for him to get the information he needed.

"I want to find out who my parents are."

"Darian, I'm so sorry, but the state laws prevent me from disclosing that information to you," she responded sadly.

Clenching his teeth, Darian strove to control the rage that sometimes activated his power before he was ready. He inhaled deeply before speaking. "Miss McKelroy, the Beels are dead. I have no family left. I would at least like to know where I came from. Perhaps even find a new family." Darian could be very good at manipulation if necessary.

"But, Darian—"

He interrupted her before she could refuse again. "Did you ever get married and have a family?"

Startled by his question, she replied, "Actually, yes. I left the orphanage to get married about two years after you left. I became Mrs. Frank Tierney. We had a son named Joel." She hesitated, shifting her eyes to some random spot on the wall behind Darian. "They were both killed in a horrible accident when my son was nine. About eight years ago I returned to the orphanage when the job of administrator opened up."

"Then you should understand how I feel. I lost my real family without ever knowing them. Now I've lost my adoptive family." Continuing to play on her sympathies, Darian added, "I just want to feel that I'm connected to someone in this world...that I'm not alone out here." He deliberately tugged on his bottom lip with his teeth like a small boy fighting back tears.

Miss McKelroy's greatest qualification for working at the orphanage, whether as an attendant or administrator, was her genuine concern for the children. Unfortunately, it could well be her undoing. She walked over to one of the tall file cabinets lined up in the nook at the side of the room. Originally a closet, the doors had been removed, leaving plenty of space for file cabinets. She preferred keeping the files here rather than in the basement—out of the way of burst pipes or failed sump pumps.

Reaching into one of the drawers, she paused and turned toward Darian. "It's not really a good idea for you to contact your parents, Darian."

"What do you mean? Why shouldn't I contact them?" His rage bubbled to the surface, again causing his face to twitch. Having turned back to shut the drawer, Miss McKelroy didn't notice.

"Sometimes children are placed in an orphanage because the families die or can't support them—"

Who does she think she is, trying to tell me what I can and can't do?

"—but sometimes they just don't want them. If that was the case, it would be better if you don't know who they are."

Realizing the implications of her words and actions, Darian's rage spewed forth.

"DO YOU REALLY THINK I CARE WHETHER THEY WANTED ME OR NOT? I DON'T NEED THEIR LOVE, he shouted. Then, as if it explained everything, he added, "THE POWER IS ALL I NEED!"

The timbre of his voice had shifted. It was the same voice Ruth had heard come forth from Darian when Harry suffered his "stroke." Malevolence flowed from the words and left an acid trail in its wake. Involuntarily, Miss McKelroy threw her forearms up in a defensive gesture. Her show of weakness only inflamed Darian. With a flick of his hand, he drew the first particles of her life force from her body.

Laughing when he saw the look of terror on her face, he said, "Now you know what I've been doing all these years. Nothing is going to stand in my way, Miss McKelroy, least of all you."

As her body fell limply to the floor, Darian stepped over it and opened the file cabinet drawer she had just closed. Flicking through the files, he finally saw the name Darian Beel. Opening the folder, he was filled with a sense of triumph when he saw the names of his parents. That is, until a notation in the right hand column caught his eye: [Deceased]. They were both dead. Clenching his fists in anger, he crushed the sides of the folder and flung it to the floor where it landed on Miss McKelroy.

He slammed the drawer shut and stepped over the body of the only person who had ever shown him kindness as if she were insignificant. Just then, a fragment of information nudged his awareness and stopped him in his tracks. Reaching down, he grabbed up the folder from the dead woman's chest and opened it. There it was. His anger had almost caused him to ignore it. A smile slowly transformed his face from one etched with rage to the charming countenance of a very handsome young man.

Pleased that his journey hadn't been for naught, Darian strode back to his car. In a few hours he arrived at his cabin, still savoring this new knowledge. Except for rare moments, he never gave much thought to his feelings about anything. He simply focused on his quest. Besides, since his primary emotion for most of his life had been varying degrees of rage, it was difficult for him to imagine any other. So it was natural that rage was the feeling he had always associated with any thoughts of his family. Until now.

Discovering that his parents were dead should have infuriated Darian because it threw a wrench into his plans of melding their life forces with his to take him to the next level, and it also robbed him of the pleasure of ending their existence himself. Instead, he was now experiencing unfamiliar emotions as a result of his newly discovered information. It had never occurred to him that his parents had had other children. Such a slap in the face—their choosing to abandon him—should also have ignited his rage. Instead, he was intrigued by the idea of having a sibling.

It's got to be the part that's missing! He was sure of it because this was no ordinary sibling. This was his twin—one who began life with him. Darian could barely contain his excitement. Joining his twin's life force with his own would surely make him complete. He would be coming full circle to the point of his creation. It was an appropriate beginning for what he was destined to become.

The question of how to approach his twin dominated Darian's thoughts for several days. There were many things to consider before embarking on this journey. What if his twin was as powerful as he was? What if his twin didn't understand the power the way he did? After all, he had dedicated his life to his quest. It was possible that his twin had never even discovered the power within. All these considerations generated even more questions.

Trying to judge the reactions of a person with essentially the same genetic makeup as himself was more difficult than he thought it would be. He knew, of course, that he had chosen the best path for his life, but what if he had mistakenly chosen the wrong path and not encountered the Master within? Would someone have been able to convince *him* that his path was wrong and theirs was right?

Trying to imagine himself waffling like a politician was ludicrous. He was a man of strong convictions, and he believed this would be true no matter what path he had chosen. This was what worried him the most. If his twin objected to his plan and was as powerful as he, there would most certainly be a clash of wills.

Unwilling to just assume his twin would be agreeable to his plans, Darian chose an unconventional method of assessing the situation. Long ago, he had learned to control the particles that constituted his own life force. He had certainly had plenty of practice reaching out and absorbing the particles that made up the essence of life for those animals and people unfortunate enough to cross his path. This exercise had taught him not only how to disassemble but also how to *reassemble* enough of his own life force at will to create a holographic-like image of himself.

Unlike a hologram, however, this image wasn't passive. He could actually experience sights and sounds as if he were there in the flesh. After all, it wasn't a synthetic representation. It was his pure essence teleported by the medium through which the power moved. It was the perfect way to explore the world of his twin. Eventually, he would share with his twin what the Master had shared with him.

When it's time, you can't stop it! Surely the power behind these words would strike the same chord within his twin as they had in him.

Chapter 15

*D*arian needed information and the only place in his experience that stored information was a library, and the closest town of any size was Sterling, Illinois. Leaving the cabin, he drove into town. He had no idea where the library was located. He had driven through the town only once when he first arrived in the area. Since then he had bought supplies and groceries in the small towns west of Sterling.

Coming into town from the north, he passed various retail businesses and came to a stop at a traffic light. On his left was the Community General Hospital, according to the sign. All he could see ahead of him was residential. While he waited for the light to change, he pondered whether to continue on this road or turn onto LeFevre. Whichever way he went, he needed to find a pay phone so he could look up the address of the library.

He decided at the last minute to turn left onto LeFevre Road. After innumerable starts and stops, the road came to an end at Freeport Road. A restaurant named Klocke's stood on his right and a cemetery on his left. Past Klocke's, he spied business establishments at the end of the street. Turning, he found his way to Route 2 where he spotted a pay phone at a gas station.

Within minutes he knew the address of the library: 102 W. 4th St. The gas station attendant told Darian that Route 2 becomes 4th St. only a couple of blocks down.

"Just stay on it. Once you pass the split in the road, it's one-way, but make sure you stay in the right lane so you can go straight. 4th St.

sorta ends at the parking lot for the library and then picks up again on the other side. If you get in the left lane, you have to turn left, and you'll wind up on the other side of the river in Rock Falls!"

Darian followed the instructions and found the library easily. It was an old, but stately building, sharing its spot in the universe with Behren's Funeral Home. The character of the library's architecture was actually enhanced by the contrast between the two buildings as they quietly functioned side by side. The building reminded Darian of the school he had attended in Peoria for a brief, but memorable time.

Parking in the east parking lot, Darian followed the sidewalk around the building to the south entrance. Above the door were engraved the words "Carnegie Library." A white sheet of paper was unceremoniously taped to a pane of glass in the door announcing "Not an entrance. Use the ramp door." Large evergreens grew on each side of the steps, and Darian couldn't see where the ramp door was. He didn't remember seeing an entrance on the parking lot side. Then he caught sight of people emerging from the west end of the building carrying books. Stepping out from the cover of the evergreens, Darian spied a very long ramp leading to a double set of doors.

Entering the library, he hesitated for a moment to get his bearings. He centered his focus on a desk with a large sign that read "Information." The woman behind the counter was probably in her twenties with dark brown hair that fell loosely around her shoulders. Certainly not the old maid vision Darian had expected from his memories of the school's library years ago. He supposed things had changed in the last twenty years. As he drew nearer, she looked up at him and smiled.

"May I help you, sir?" she asked in a low, sultry voice. Darian wondered if she spoke in such low tones when she wasn't in the library's chambers.

"I was wondering if you could help me locate someone," Darian replied, not bothering to lower his voice.

"Are you wanting information on a historical figure?"

"No. I'm trying to locate a relative I've never met. A cousin. I found out about him when I was going through some old papers that belonged to my parents. He seems to be my only living relative so I thought I'd try to find him."

The young woman smiled warmly at Darian. "It's so sad when our families pass away and we're left alone. You feel so disconnected. I'm an only child, and both my parents were killed in a car wreck out on Route 2 last year. So I understand how you must feel."

On impulse, Darian replied, "I'm sorry you lost your parents." It was the first time in more than two decades that Darian had felt even a thread of compassion for another living being, but something about this woman fascinated him. The encounter captured his attention so completely he was staring at her with an intensity that was causing her to blush.

To break the uncomfortable pause, she asked, "Do you have his first and last names?"

"Huh?" Darian was startled out of his preoccupation by her question, having temporarily forgotten why he came to the library. The response this woman activated in him was not one with which he was familiar. He tried to integrate the experience into some familiar schema—a schema that could provide him with a reasonable expectation of what should happen next, but he didn't have much success. It wasn't like Darian had much of a social history. His knowledge of social situations and people was minimal and primarily negative. None of his schemas included such emotions as human compassion.

Recovering quickly, he answered, "Oh. Yes, I do."

"Good. Then we can probably locate him through one of the databases we have access to. We may be a small library, but our Head Librarian is a real nutcase for technology. She pesters the city fathers relentlessly about being progressive. She says if they can continue to support every program Sterling High School dreams up on one hand, they can't, on the other hand, deny the taxpayers of Sterling access to the best resources available. You should hear her when she gets going. Pretty impressive and effective!

"But, you didn't come here to listen to me rave. Let's see what we can find out for you. Are you familiar with computers at all?"

Darian's awareness of the burst of technology into the layman's world was virtually zero. He had had no interest in the activities of the world. Even now his only interest was in finding his twin. His lack of knowledge about worldly activities had never concerned him. However, if that lack of knowledge meant appearing inadequate in the presence of another, his ego was likely to respond with the only easily accessible emotion in its repertoire—rage.

Until the day he struck down Harry, Darian had felt the world was unfair, and he hadn't felt powerful enough to protect himself against those in command. Harry's excesses had driven him over a threshold from which there was no return, a threshold that enabled him to test his power against one who claimed to be in control. In that case, Harry. Unfortunately for Harry, Darian was victorious.

Since that day, whenever even a taste of inferiority tickled his palate, his rage would burst forth, reeking vengeance on anyone caught in the blast. Today, however, some alien part of himself sensed that this woman was not pointing out his inadequacies. So he simply answered her question.

"No, I've never used a computer."

"I'm not surprised. They're just starting to make computers that aren't as big as this room. They're pretty expensive, but thanks to Miss Stark, we have one. She subscribes to a database service so we're able to gather information that's more recent than some of our hard copy reference books."

Placing her hand on his left elbow for a brief moment, she said, "Follow me. We'll go to the computer terminal, and I'll try to help you find your cousin. First, though, I need to drop this book off at the desk in the Reference Room."

Darian followed without protest. The young woman continued to make small talk as they walked, but Darian didn't hear what she was saying. He was looking at her face, her smile, her hair, her eyes. New experiences holding any fascination for Darian was rare unless they were directly related to his quest. He never allowed himself the serendipity that accompanied most encounters. He preferred to orchestrate all events except the most mundane. It was inevitable that one day chemistry—sexual chemistry—would step to the forefront and catch Darian off guard.

"What's your name?" Darian asked, wanting to know more about her.

"Oh! I'm sorry." She automatically raised her hand to her left lapel. "Well, no wonder! My name tag is missing! You probably think I'm terribly rude."

"No," insisted Darian, "I just want to know your name."

"It's Angela. Angela Downing. What's yours?"

"What?"

"Your name?"

"Darian."

"Just Darian? No last name?"

Hesitating, Darian replied, "Marsh. Darian Marsh." He used his parents' last name. Giving her the name Beel seemed like the wrong thing to do. Of course, the name Marsh kept his traceable identity a secret, but it was more than that. He didn't want to mention that awful name in her presence, the name that conjured up memories of Harry and Ruth.

Suddenly Darian was face to face with a huge statue of an Indian woman. She stood regally next to a large column. While Angela returned the book to the Reference Desk, he leaned over to read the article taped to the wall. It identified the statue as Sacagawea. He speculated why a statue had been erected for this woman. She must have possessed power of some kind to have been commemorated in this way. He speculated about the kind of power she must have held.

"Ready?" Angela asked Darian. "Thanks, Marilyn," she added, waving her hand to the woman just arriving at the Reference Desk. She led Darian through a narrow doorway into a strange room. It was dimly lit, and the floor was made from glass tiles. The stacks were close together, but you could see through to the floor below where there were even more stacks.

Angela weaved her way through the room. "Here we are," she said as she stepped out into a larger, more airy room. There was no one else in sight. Darian was glad, although he wasn't certain why. "The terminal's over here," she said, pointing toward the corner of a desk just barely visible behind one of the stacks of books. "Miss Stark doesn't allow anyone except library personnel to use the computer so no one will bother us." She laughed, "We only get one or two people a week who actually want us to look anything up anyway. What's the chance of both of them coming in at the same time?"

Darian spontaneously laughed with her. It was a strange feeling. It wasn't bad, but it scared him a little. As Angela sat down in front of the computer and started the process of logging in, Darian's mind assessed his situation. He wondered what these strange feelings were that had emerged since he met Angela. His natural wariness prompted him to conclude they were distractions. If they were designed to deter him from his path, he couldn't let that happen.

Looking at Angela, he wondered if she was deliberately trying to sidetrack him with her sweetness. Darian knew there were forces out there that sought only to disrupt the natural order of things. Most of his life had been spent attuning his energies to receive only the true reality. He had not expected to be so easily tempted by such enemies.

Interrupting his thoughts, Angela said, "Okay. Tell me your cousin's name, and together we'll find him if it takes all afternoon." She smiled at Darian and nodded her head as if to reassure him that everything would be all right.

No, he told himself, reconsidering his initial assessment, *this doesn't make sense. If she wanted to distract me from my path, she would try to keep me from finding my twin.* Confused, Darian seriously considered the possibility she was simply trying to help. He had trusted only one other person in his life, and that had not turned out well. Inexplicably, he decided to trust Angela. Besides, if he was wrong, the remedy was certainly within his grasp.

"His name is Fredrik Marsh," he said. He watched her type in F-r-e-d-r-i-c-k. "No c," he said.

"What?"

"No c. The note I saw didn't have a c in Fredrik." He wished he had brought the folder with him. Maybe there was something else in there that would have been helpful.

Darian watched as Angela continually typed in information on the keyboard. Periodically, the screen changed. Finally, he asked,

"What are you doing?"

"Well, the database service has several directories I can search through. Some are national while others are regional. You know, like states." Pausing, she asked, "You said you've never used a computer before, but have you been around them at all?"

"No." He felt the old, familiar emotions trying to rise to the surface. He could feel the heat of them on his face.

"Don't be embarrassed!" she said, noticing the tightening of the muscles in his jaw. "It's not like many people have access to them unless they work in some fancy office. I did read an article the other day that predicted there'd be a computer in every home in twenty years. Can you imagine? I mean why would you need one at home?"

Her easy chatter, as she worked on the computer, relaxed Darian, and his anger crept back into its lair.

"I've got it!" she cried. "I found a list of people with the last name Marsh and the first initial F." Darian frowned. Noticing, she added, "That's just in case the information you have is wrong about how to spell the first name."

Looking back at the list, she remarked, "Of course, this list covers the whole country. It would make it easier if you knew what part of the country he lives in."

Darian closed his eyes, trying to concentrate on what he had seen in the folder. Why hadn't he brought it with him or looked at it more closely? After seeing that his parents were dead, he hadn't paid much attention. The notation about his twin was just penciled in on the top corner of the page. He hadn't really expected to find anything else in his file about his sibling. All he could remember was the name Hohenwald. It knew it was a city, but he couldn't remember whether it was Texas or Tennessee. The abbreviations were close, and he had been too focused on his new discovery to pay much attention to peripheral information. He told Angela what he could remember.

"Hohenwald? That's funny! Imagine telling people you were born in a *hole in the wall*!" Laughing again, she added in that same mellifluous tone, "That should narrow it down some. Hmm…it seems that Hohenwald is in Tennessee.

"Now I just need to narrow down this list some more. You know, people don't usually move very far from where they grew up. So let's include Mississippi and Alabama as well."

She scooted her chair over a little. "Pull your chair in closer, Darian, so you can see the screen without getting a crick in your neck." Darian scooted his chair to the left just far enough that he wasn't touching her.

"It shouldn't take more than a few minutes," she explained, shifting her chair's position again until their knees were touching.

Darian was finding it difficult to concentrate. Actually, even swallowing was becoming harder. He cleared his throat and coughed lightly. "There's a water fountain around the corner there if you need a drink," she told him, pointing toward the far side of the room.

"Yeah, I think I do," he replied, pushing his chair back.

"Ah! That narrows it down some," she declared. "While you're gone, I'll plug into some other databases and get more information on some of these names."

Darian left her to her search and walked around the corner to the water fountain. He was feeling anxious, and except for his encounter with the wolf, fear was another unfamiliar emotion. All the feelings that had coursed through him since he entered the library were unfamiliar enough to set off alarm bells and give rise to anger. Could she really just be trying to help him? No one in the world except Miss

McKelroy had ever supported him for even the briefest of moments, and as he had discovered, trusting *her* had been a mistake. Now was not the time to slip up. His destiny was at stake.

Darian knew nothing about the addictive nature of sexual chemistry, but nonetheless, it guided his decision to restrain his anger. He would be very careful, however, and make sure she had no opportunity to double-cross him. There would be no more Ruths, no more Miss McKelroys. Grounded by his decision, he returned to join Angela at the computer.

"Tell me, Darian. Do you know how old your cousin is?"

"Twenty-eight," he said. "As a matter of fact, if what I heard is true, we have the same birth day. April 6."

"That helps a lot," she replied. She continued to modify her search and check other databases. Darian sat quietly, unwilling to initiate conversation.

After about twenty minutes, Angela spoke. "I think I've narrowed it down some, at least for Tennessee. There are two possibilities. One lives in Knoxville. He's 28 and teaches at a secondary school in Johnson City." She scrolled down the screen. "Wait! Didn't you say that he was your only living relative?"

"Yes," replied Darian.

"Well, that eliminates him. His parents live in a suburb of Chattanooga. That only leaves one in Tennessee the right age. If he's not the one, we'll check Mississippi." She turned to Darian and smiled. "I'm so glad you came in today. This is fun, and I hardly ever get to use the computer," she said, turning back to the screen.

Darian said nothing. He could think of nothing to say.

"Okay. The next one lives in Memphis. He's a commodity analyst. Wait a minute!" Angela looked closely at the screen. "Look at this. He is a she. Her name is Fredrika with an *a* after it. That's different! Oh well," she said, starting to change her search parameters to Mississippi. "But wait," She scrolled further down the screen. "Darian, is it possible that your cousin is actually a woman? If not, this is Twilight Zone material. She's 28 years old, and her birthday is April 6."

"Uh—" Darian started to reply.

"That's not all! She was born in Hohenwald, Tennessee!" She turned to look at Darian. "I think we have our target. Don't you? That's just too many coincidences for me. Are you sure you just didn't notice the *a* at the end of the name?"

Confused by the turn of events, Darian muttered, "It's possible." Still unable to accept the idea that his twin was female, he asked, "What about her parents?"

Angela turned back to the screen. "They're dead," she replied in a tone of finality. For her it was now a closed case.

Stunned by this information, Darian was silent. Mistaking his silence for skepticism, Angela said, "I might be able to get more personal information on her if you promise not to tell anybody where you got it." She glanced over her shoulder toward the door.

"What are you talking about?" Darian was curious.

"Well, there's a guy who comes in here a lot. He moved here from Chicago last year. He's a real computer genius. What he's doing here I don't know, but he's shown me some things about getting into government databases. That's how I was able to get some of the more personal information on Fredrika, but I don't know enough to go any further. He'll be in here later tonight to finish something he's working on. I bet he would be willing to find out a lot more about her. Whadd'ya think?"

Darian was nearly overwhelmed by the energy Angela was expending toward his needs. Usually he was forced to figure out the best way to force others to bend to his wishes. This was like a free ride. It wasn't going to require anything from him to have his twin served to him on a platter. *Unbelievable!*

"I think that's great!" he replied to Angela, returning her smile.

He noticed a little color come into her cheeks before she replied. "I'll go ahead and check out the rest of these. If anybody else comes up, I'll have him check them out, too, but I think Fredrika is our girl! Listen, I'll be in tomorrow by noon. Come by any time after that, and I'll let you know what he found. Okay?" she asked, letting her gaze linger on his eyes for just a moment longer than necessary.

"Okay." Darian rose quickly and stepped back for Angela to pass. Another first. An act of courtesy he had never accorded anyone. They walked together back toward the main check-out desk. As he reached the exit door, Darian gave in to an impulse to turn and look back. Angela waved. For a moment Darian simply looked at her. Then he hesitantly raised his arm and waved back.

Later that evening Darian willed his thoughts to focus on his twin Fredrika, if indeed she was his twin. *Perhaps she'll recognize me. Even though she's a woman, we may still look enough alike that she would recognize me.* The prospect of meeting her excited Darian, although it was difficult to be sure of the reason. It was possible, of course, that the idea of having a sibling, a twin, was just exciting to him, but the reality probably had more to do with the progression of his quest.

Chapter 16

*T*he next day at twelve-thirty, Darian entered the library to see what new information Angela had for him. Walking toward the information desk, he scanned the room but didn't see Angela anywhere. An older woman was sitting at the desk, one who met his earlier expectations of a librarian.

"Is Angela here?" he asked.

"No. May I help you with something?" The older woman got up from the desk and approached the front counter.

"I need to speak with Angela," Darian demanded.

"Well, then, you'll have to come back another time because she isn't here," the woman remarked as she turned and walked back toward her desk.

Darian's temper was in the countdown stage. *Who did this woman think she was?* "When will she be here?" Darian asked in a loud voice.

"Sh-h-h!" the woman admonished, placing her finger on her lips. "This is a library, sir, and I would appreciate your remembering that!" The old woman obviously had no idea that chastising Darian was like striking a match under him. She didn't seem to notice his face was beet red as she continued, "She just didn't show up. I have no idea where she is."

With his teeth clamped together, Darian asked, "Do you know how I can reach her?"

With the ignorance of an insect being eyed by a toad, she retorted just before turning to sit back down at her desk, "We do not give out home phone numbers, young man! You will just have to come back tomorrow." With that she opened the book she had been reading.

Darian stood there, struggling to contain the rage threatening to erupt. Already at full boil, it was taking tremendous effort on his part to keep it from spilling over. Visions of his first-grade teacher leapt into his mind. The tone. The voice. He could almost believe it *was* Mrs. Gruen sitting mockingly in front of him, her body turned ever so slightly to one side in dismissal.

"Hi!" a voice behind him called out and touched his arm. Darian whirled around so fast that he nearly knocked Angela down. "What's wrong?" she asked.

Darian didn't answer her at first because he was so focused on controlling his rage. No one was more surprised than he when calm began descending on him the moment he focused on Angela. "Nothing," he replied. Pointing toward the old woman, he added, "Except—well, she's a nasty old woman!"

Angela laughed and took his arm, leading him away from the front desk. Leaning in toward him, she whispered, "She's always like that. Don't know why. Some of the other girls say it's because she's an old maid, but I'm not sure that's it. I think she's just lonely."

The conciliatory twist Angela put on his attitude toward the old woman surprised Darian. He watched her as she took off her coat and tossed it onto the nearest table before pulling out her notebook.

"Wait until you see what I've got for you!" she exclaimed.

With his attention refocused on his reason for being here, Darian asked, "Were you able to get her address?"

"A lot more than that! Look," she said, sitting down at the table and pulling a chair over next to hers. She motioned for Darian to sit down. "Here. I wrote it all out for you. I not only have her name, address, and phone number, I know where she works, her birth date, and the kind of car she drives. We even found out that she teaches classes in Chicago a few times a year at the home office of her employer. Plus, her parents are dead. My friend confirmed that for me. Oh, and by the way, we went ahead and double checked all the southern states. She was the only one whose birth date and age matched.

"Perfect!" declared Darian as he perused the list of information. Looking up, he saw that Angela was smiling at him, but there was a tentative look on her face.

"Is something wrong?" he asked.

Whispering, she asked, "Remember I told you my friend was a computer genius?" Darian nodded. "Well, he's able to get into computer systems he shouldn't be able to get into. I don't know how. He says it has something to do with networks and phone lines. He lost me after the first sentence or two. Anyway, the point is, he decided to check her out from *start to finish* as he called it."

"Why?" Darian asked, intrigued not only by such a subversive approach but also by the reason for the man's interest.

"Oh. I just think he enjoys breaking into places he's not supposed to be." Angela paused as she leaned back in her chair to see if there was anyone within earshot.

"What did he find?"

"Well, he uncovered the death records of her parents as well as her birth record. She was born right here in Illinois! Her parents apparently moved to Hohenwald, Tennessee, not long after, which confirms what you said. So even though she wasn't born there, she lived there as a child. The real find, however, was when he discovered she's a twin!"

Darian was now on full alert. If Angela knew too much, she left him no choice. She would have to be eliminated. He felt a twinge in his chest at the thought of killing her. Strangely, it was joined by a sense of intense satisfaction at the thought of taking her life force inside him. If Darian had been a normal man, he would probably have recognized this feeling as sexual satisfaction. However, his only experience in that realm was as a victim of perversity where the only satisfaction belonged to the pursuer.

Angela continued her report on their findings. "Out of curiosity my friend checked newspaper files in Peoria for April 6, 1952, for her birth announcement, hoping to find other relatives mentioned. That's when he found it—an announcement for twins born to the Marshes. For some reason he couldn't locate the other twin's birth certificate, but he did discover that the other child was put up for adoption. Apparently, the other twin had respiratory problems at birth. No diagnosis was listed. Just that there was a problem.

"The case was marked as a *charity case*. So we figured the parents didn't have the money to deal with the medical bills that might be involved for the boy."

"Boy?" Darian, of course, knew the twin was a boy because he was the twin. However, his response to Angela was not just to maintain his position of ignorance about his "cousin," it also masked his confusion about the reason he had been put up for adoption. He didn't remember being sick. This new information startled him.

"Yeah, they were fraternal twins. It looked like the state took him over. You know, an orphanage or maybe he was adopted. We couldn't get any more information. My friend says it's impossible to track down state orphanage records. Not only is it rare to find an orphanage that would have the money to put their records on computer, but since the records are supposed to be sealed, there's not much motivation to preserve the information and none whatsoever to relay it over the phone."

Whispering, she added, "I just hope they don't check the phone records too closely this month at the library!"

Despite his reactions to what Angela was telling him, Darian couldn't help being absorbed by watching Angela as she continued to talk. No one had ever been so eager to talk to him before.

"I think it's so sad that you might have another cousin, and we have no way of finding out. If he was adopted, he wouldn't have the last name of Marsh, which makes it a lost cause trying to find him. Hey, maybe Fredrika knows something about him! Whadd'ya think?"

A sigh escaped Darian's lips. Her genuine concern for him was affecting him, despite his best efforts to remain focused. Why was she so interested in him? The only interest anyone had ever shown in him before was designed to destroy him in some way, a thought which renewed his determination to remain cautious.

"Maybe," he replied hesitantly.

Shaking her head affirmatively as if he was in full agreement with her assessment, she said, "Listen. I've gotta go, or I'll get fired. Then where would you be when you need more information?" She laughed as she grabbed her coat and hurried toward the door marked "Employees Only."

Darian picked up the notebook paper she left behind for him and left. He had what he needed.

Chapter 17

Day 1

*H*aving received the information he needed from Angela, Darian was tempted to visit his twin in the flesh. Only the knowledge that he would be at a disadvantage deterred him. He knew nothing about her except that she shared the beginnings of life with him. He was hopeful she shared his spirit, but that was yet to be seen. Did she have the power within her? Was she aware of it or was it just lying dormant and untended?

Showing up unannounced might result in her calling the police, drawing unwanted attention to him. Darian preferred that she willingly merge her life force with his. This time would not be like the life forces he had seized in the past, for he had only been interested in the energy they afforded him. This time his interest was not about fuel. It was about a rejoining of the essence that began twenty-eight years ago. The essence that created them both. Even though he knew they had simply shared their mother's womb as fraternal twins do, he believed they had shared more than this. It was no accident that had brought him to the awareness that she existed. The Master had led him to her, and it must be because she, too, possessed the power.

Darian had no doubts, of course, that his life was the primary one. After all, he had dedicated nearly his entire life to the Master. It would be up to him to bring her along until she was willing to merge with him. There was no other way. It was destiny.

The principal concern now was how to proceed. Erring on the

side of caution seemed the best approach. He now knew where Fredrika lived and worked. Maintaining surveillance on her without arousing any suspicion was a simple matter. Projecting his consciousness without assembling an image was actually the easiest way for him to travel. He had been practicing this every day while living at the cabin, reaching out into the woods to spot his prey. For long distance travel, the main requirement would be to have a destination.

Having decided on a course of action, Darian returned to his cabin to begin what could well be the last leg of his journey that began over two decades earlier. The cabin that had been Darian's refuge for the past three years served as shelter from the wind and the cold, but he had made no effort to make it comfortable or aesthetically pleasing. It boasted an overstuffed chair, an end table, a small dining table with a single straight-back chair (he'd used the others for firewood), a bed with a pine headboard, and a chest of drawers. These were all furnishings left behind by the previous owner—things cast aside because they wouldn't complement his new place at the retirement community.

Darian didn't care. It was all he needed. The lumps in the mattress were visible through the faded blue sheets and the blanket, which at one time had sported brilliantly red roses. Now the blanket was so fuzzy from use that the roses appeared to be bleeding slowly into the white background. There were no pictures on the walls, no signs of connection with anyone or anything.

Sitting down in the overstuffed chair with its worn upholstery, Darian contemplated what it would take to project himself to a place so far away. He'd discovered his ability to teleport himself to another place while at the Beels' house after Ruth's death. Until now, however, there'd been no need to use it except to feed his power and, of course, for his own enjoyment. When he was at the Beels, he'd only ventured about a mile away and spied on activities in town. Since moving to the cabin, he had enjoyed taunting the animals in the woods as well as an occasional camper or hiker. Of course, the animals always sensed his presence and became skittish immediately. People, on the other hand, usually had to be motivated. He was forced to touch them or move objects to get any enjoyment from the experience. He admired animals more than people. At least they used their natural instincts.

Darian reminded himself the issue at hand today was whether he could teleport himself from Northwest Illinois to Memphis, Tennessee, and back successfully. It was just under six hundred miles by road, and he had never traveled there before.

Taking a deep breath, he declared aloud, "Learning to do this is part of my destiny." He used the affirmation to adjust his emotional rudder and bring him back on course with his quest.

All dissenting thoughts released from his mind, Darian leaned back against the soft stuffing in the chair. Gradually, he allowed just the thought of Fredrika's office to appear in his mind. He homed in on the location Angela provided for him: Poplar Ave. in the Clark Tower on the 30th floor. He imagined himself being there. In less than a minute, Darian was hurtling through space. There were no signposts. No markers. He was in a giant vortex filled with sparkling glitter that whirled around and around.

Astonished, Darian realized, *I'm the glitter! These are my particles!* Never before had he been in the transitional state long enough to see it like this. He was absolutely overwhelmed. Even reduced to his most elemental form, he was perfection, and perfection was beauty.

The whirling slowed. Darian sensed the presence of shapes— possibly people. He'd made the decision before he left his body behind to maintain a disassembled state, invisible to the naked eye, because he didn't know enough about Fredrika to judge how she would react to a ghostly image. So he remained still, listening. On this plane of expression, nothing was denied him. He could hear not only spoken words, but also the thoughts of those around him.

Wait! A voice was speaking from the intercom at the desk in front of him. The voice asked Joyce—apparently the woman sitting at the desk—something about a class in Chicago. Didn't Angela say that Fredrika taught a class in Chicago? He focused his attention and listened. The woman named Joyce was thinking that hell must be freezing over for Freddie to be leaving work early for Chicago or anywhere else!

Shifting his gaze toward the closed door, Darian knew with certainty that Fredrika was behind it. He hesitated. *Strange*, he thought, *excitement I expected—I'm always excited before I encounter my prey—but what's with this hesitation? It feels like...like fear.* Puzzled, he lingered for another minute outside her door. Finally, the intoxicating effects from the excitement of victory outweighed the fear of defeat, and he passed through the door into Freddie's office.

He was stunned. *I can't believe it. She's...she's absolutely beautiful!*

Darian's sense of beauty was not comparative, and his partiality would be evident to anyone except himself. His idea of beauty started and ended with his vision of himself. Since he'd never bestowed value on any one outside himself, it was only natural that his perceptions of such abstract concepts as beauty and goodness used himself as the baseline. Suddenly, however, something more urgent than this mirror reflection of his concept of beauty was overriding his concentration. He was reentering the vortex. He tried to focus, to stop the pull back toward the cabin and his body, but he couldn't.

The wind flitted in and out among the hollow trunks of the trees surrounding the cabin like a child skipping through the woods. The wind was unaffected by the silence of death for it knew itself to be beyond the reach of any power on the earth. The stronger the wind blew, the darker the sky became. Storm clouds threatened to pour rain down on everything, for they were not fussy about who received their gifts.

Inside the cabin, Darian remained in the overstuffed chair. His expression denied his presence. His eyes were vacant. His face slack. His arms lay limply on the arms of the chair. He was as lifeless as the chair he sat on. Then, inexplicably, the fingers on his right hand twitched. Anyone watching would swear they had just seen life pumped back into a dead man. His limp form filled up with life like a balloon expanding as someone blows air into it. Darian had returned. His form was vital again. The eyes were no longer vacant. Instead, they looked at the world around them in confusion.

A clap of thunder, followed closely by a flash of lightning, startled Darian, bringing him out of his altered state. He looked around the room. Everything was secure. Traveling such a long distance and staying too long had put his body at risk because he couldn't readily defend it from intruders.

He wondered, *What would happen if my body were destroyed while my life force was absent? Would I continue to exist on a finer plane, one where bodies were not needed?* Darian couldn't answer that question. A part of him longed for that existence but knew it wasn't time yet. He still had battles to win here to ensure his power.

The current battle—if it turned out to be a battle—was presenting him with unexpected problems. Seeing Fredrika had ripped a huge tear in the fabric of his world. The resemblance between them was uncanny. He had no doubt now that she was indeed his twin, but having seen his own features reflected back to himself in the form of this stranger had disrupted his thinking. A gnawing fear was growing steadily. A war against her would be like waging war against himself in a slightly different form. What if she was stronger than he was?

Darian's rate of breathing accelerated. His heart pounded. The beating of it in his ears was so loud he expected his head to explode within seconds. The rolling thunder outside the cabin only exacerbated the pounding in his head. The last time fear had managed to control him this way was in Harry's workshop.

Effortlessly, the memory of that day enraged Darian. His heart continued to pound and his breaths were still coming in rapid bursts, but he was no longer a victim of his emotions. Anger won the day for him as always. The anger fed on the energy that powered his fear, growing bigger and bigger until every particle of Darian's being was transformed once again into a destructive weapon. His anger was well-developed—too well-developed for him to see that fear had always been the actual source of its power.

The transformation was successful. The conscious fear receded, filling up the dark corners, watching and waiting. Darian exhaled in relief. Everything was back to normal.

He pushed himself up from the chair. He was a little unsteady on his feet—a side effect from disassembling and reassembling into his physical body, a hitch he needed to resolve. Walking across the room to the kitchen sink, he picked up a glass off the countertop. Turning the faucet slowly with his left hand and watching the water stream into the glass, he thought about his next move. Of one thing he was certain. He could not allow Fredrika to threaten his destiny. Faltering would be his downfall. Maintaining a constant vigil was key.

Projecting such a long distance had taken more energy than he expected. He was accustomed to the shorter jaunts of the past whose side effects had always been minimal—a mild headache maybe, but with his energy preserves remaining close to their original level. Obviously, projecting to a distant place was different. The only other time he had felt this drained was the first time he succeeded in breaking down the bonds which held him in his body.

So, he decided to forego visiting Fredrika again—at least until tomorrow. *Rest and practice should increase my tolerance. Soon I'll be able to travel more often and stay longer.*

Confident with his decision, Darian stretched out across the bed to take a nap. He pulled the rose blanket across his legs because the storm was cooling off the cabin. He quickly slipped into that realm often called daydreams, but which cross easily, if untended, into the dreams of deep sleep.

Darian walked across a great hall. Large tiles covered the floor and sparkled from the light of the cut-glass globes hanging from the ceiling. The globes were uniformly spaced, creating small circles of light that overlapped each other like hundreds of tiny spotlights shining on stage waiting for the actors to perform their roles. He squinted to see past the glare of the lights to the end of the hall, but he couldn't focus on anything. The play of the lights was too distracting. Quickly he turned to look behind him. It was the same.

"Where am I?" he shouted. No one answered. He hurried on.

"It must go somewhere," he mumbled. He walked until his legs ached. He felt the itch of irritation. Somebody was obviously playing a trick on him. His blood pressure rose. The warmth that accompanied it was like an old friend, and he welcomed it with open arms. Just as it began to envelop him in its familiar shroud, he heard a voice. A voice calling his name. He spun around to see who else was in this place.

At that moment his whole body jerked with a spasm that woke

him up, dragging him out of the great hall and returning him to his cabin in the woods. Waking up didn't dissolve Darian's anger. Anger had consumed so much of him over the years it would be hard to locate a part of him, conscious or unconscious, that was not infested by it.

He sat up, throwing his legs over the side of the bed. Bright flashes of light leapt through the windows of the cabin and created a strobe effect on his groggy state of mind. He struggled to regain his sense of balance. Closing his eyes, he managed to shed the sedative effects from his nap, but the uneasiness remained.

He didn't recall ever dreaming about anything except his quest. His dreams had taken many forms, of course, because the last two decades had not been static, but they were usually about the next stage he was trying to achieve. They dealt with how he could achieve his mastery. He had never doubted his dreams. They were his true and constant companions. His dreams always affirmed him. Until now. Now it felt like there was a traitor in his midst. Only he didn't know how to find it.

Darian started to pace across the cabin. Because of its size, he could walk the entire width in less than twenty paces. Passing by the front window, he sensed movement in the woods beyond the cabin. He stopped and focused all his attention in the direction of the movement. Within seconds he confirmed the presence of a pack of wild dogs meandering around the outskirts of the devastation surrounding the cabin. They were sniffing and growling, uncertain about the emptiness in the midst of the woods. Darian doubted they sensed his presence yet.

The prospect of taking all the dogs at once excited Darian— enough that he forgot all about his dream. Three animals at a time was his record. Not because he had tried more and failed. It was just rare to find more than that roaming together in these woods. Today—well, today he considered this a gift from the Master. A gift to replenish his energy. Ravaging the entire pack of dogs, seven in all, would renew his spirit. He was so invigorated by this opportunity that he didn't even notice that the languor resulting from his jaunt to spy on Freddie had already vanished.

With hardly a thought, he willfully reached out into the woods toward the dogs. He spread the particles of his essence out like a net thrown to capture an escaping animal. He didn't want a single cur to escape.

Sensing his presence, some of the dogs began to growl. Others howled. Accustomed to facing their enemies, the dogs were turning in circles, seeking a clear vision of what was upon them. They could feel its smothering presence but were still not able to see it. In a protective gesture, each dog backed up until his rear nudged the familiar fur of another dog. Gradually they formed a defensive pattern resembling spokes in a wheel, covering all possible approaches. Growls were intermixed with whimpering. Fear was setting in fast for the dogs.

Darian was ecstatic. All concern about his abilities were vanquished. Once again he was the most powerful. With the utterance of a single thought, he drew their life forces from their bodies. Not one at a time. No. That wouldn't reflect his true power. He drew them all in at one time and quickly returned to the cabin, leaving their bodies to return to the soil in their own good time. They were of no use to him.

Reentering his body, Darian was thrown into a state of exhilaration. The infusion of so many life forces made his nerve endings tingle. It was orgasmic. His body felt buoyant, but he wasn't able to move or control any of his functions. Slowly the rush subsided, and he regained control. He was aware of a strange sense of satisfaction. He had nothing with which to compare it. The feelings scared him a little while it was happening, but at the same time it felt so good he hadn't wanted it to end. And now—well, he felt good. *Really* good. He sat in his chair for a long time with his eyes closed, savoring the feeling.

Chapter 18

Day 2

Darian woke before the sun. His mind was whirring. He was anxious to communicate with Freddie, but observing her still seemed the best approach. Consciously, there was no sign of the fear he experienced last night. Regardless, it still guided his thoughts and actions and was responsible for his decision to use his holographic-like image rather than appear in person the first time he revealed himself to Freddie.

For most people, their emotions regularly give way to other emotions—an act that helps make them cognizant of being governed by their emotions. Darian didn't have this advantage. With rare exception, his anger was a constant state, change occurring only in its degree. The occasions when other emotions took center stage were infrequent enough to set off alarm bells, but not so he could free himself of being controlled by such emotions. Rather, the bells acted as a warning of an impending threat to him. Being threatened by anything for *any* reason unfailingly aroused his anger and returned it to its rightful place, ready to destroy any transgressor in view. Such a pattern made his encounters with Freddie particularly vulnerable to disaster.

In his pre-dawn strategy session, Darian had decided to monitor Freddie at home this morning. If he decided to show himself, she would be alone. No complications. Before the journey, however, he wanted to make sure his body was nourished. Such a precaution might be the key to an easier recovery when he returned to his body after the jaunt.

Darian liked that word—jaunt. He had heard the word for the first time when he was still in school and liked the sound of it. Later he had looked it up and discovered that it was a "short trip, especially for pleasure." The first time he managed to literally leave his physical body, he knew that *jaunt* was the perfect word for the experience.

Looking out the front window, Darian saw that the storm of the previous night had passed over. In the east, the sky was already azure. Only a few cloud puffs remained. The wind had blown the rest away. The sun had barely cleared the horizon, but the bare branches invited its light into the darkest recesses of the woods to awaken any life it could find there. With single-mindedness, Darian concentrated on the sun. The light reached further and further as the sun rose higher in the sky. He was the sole spectator—at least in these woods. When the sun climbed into full view, leaving the earth behind, Darian turned away from the window. Once again the sun had arisen, oblivious to his desires.

He went to the refrigerator and pulled out bacon, eggs, bread, butter, and jelly. Eating hearty was a habit he had formed when he was about nine years old. At first he hadn't thought much about his increased hunger. Later he realized his quest took a great deal of energy. His body was simply demanding to be refueled. Even though his goals were more non-physical in nature, his efforts to achieve them had a physiological impact on him. For his body to survive his unusual actions, it was necessary to have sufficient energy reserves.

Placing three strips of bacon on one side in an iron skillet, Darian took three eggs out of the carton, cracking each one open and letting it fall into the skillet. Using the edge of the spatula, he made sure the egg whites stayed separate from the bacon until they began to cook.

Then he removed the spatula.

Pulling out three slices of bread, he refastened the bag and returned the bread, the bacon, and the egg carton to the refrigerator. Dipping a knife into the butter, he rubbed it across the first slice of bread in a deliberate manner, leaving a half inch butter-free border. After stopping to flip the bacon, he turned on the broiler in the oven and returned to buttering the bread. In a few minutes he tossed the bread onto the oven shelf. He wasn't worried about spill-over, thanks to the butter-free border.

Darian paused to scoop the bacon grease over the eggs in the skillet and remove the bacon. Then he put away the butter and wiped off the counter. He liked things to be neat. How they looked wasn't important, but everything should be in its proper place.

The clear, gelatinous material of the eggs changed to white, and the yolks were covered by a white veil. He scooped the eggs out of the skillet onto his plate beside the bacon. Opening the oven, he carefully reached in and grabbed each piece of toast by its corner, careful not to touch the hot shelf. Placing his plate on the table, Darian sat down to eat his breakfast. After eating, he cleaned up his dishes and put them away.

Darian's initial excitement when he awoke this morning had transformed into unwavering determination. He would do what he had to do to convince Freddie, as her assistant called her, to become one with his quest.

Sitting down in the overstuffed chair, he stretched his arms out on the faded upholstery. He placed both feet on the floor in a comfortable position, spaced about a foot apart, and let his head rest on the back of the chair. Even for short jaunts it was easier on his body if he positioned it in a balanced position. Otherwise his body would shift and fall to one side or his head might wind up hanging forward on his chest.

Before he learned how to keep this from happening, he would sometimes return and find himself in the middle of a muscle spasm. It not only caught him off guard, but re-entering his body with his energy reserves low made it nearly impossible to control himself under the onslaught of such unexpected pain. The only saving grace was if his jaunt involved more than just traveling and observing. If it involved consuming the life force of another, the additional life force replenished his energies, making it easier to withstand the physical discomfort.

Closing his eyes, Darian once again released all thoughts except those involving Freddie. He focused more on his sense of Freddie than on the woman he actually saw yesterday. He enjoyed the special benefit he derived from being able to hear her thoughts. It felt like he was a part of her mind. It gave him a sense of her no one else could imagine. It was certainly more personal and more revealing than just meeting a person. It was more enlightening than having them verbally tell you about themselves because there are always secrets people refuse to share.

Before Darian had time to focus on a place, he was hurtling through the space of the vortex. He saw the glitter of his particles flying around like debris caught in a whirlwind. Concerned that he needed to focus on a destination and not just a person, Darian was frightened he might be trapped in this place. Almost before he had time to think about it, however, the whirling slowed and Darian arrived in a parking garage outside an airport terminal.

Perplexed, he wondered where the hell he was. He hadn't been thinking about an airport. Where was Freddie? Then he remembered. Freddie was scheduled to go to Chicago today. Had his unconscious knowledge led him here? If so, he was both comforted and unnerved.

Comforted that the Master was guiding him, but a little unnerved that he, Darian, was not in conscious control of himself.

Directing his attention to his surroundings, he saw Freddie walking through the garage, headed toward the terminal. Darian chuckled. He could hear her thoughts. She was sensing his presence but attributing it to the buzzing fluorescent lights! *That's funny!* he thought. *But still, if she's sensitive enough to detect my presence like this,* he thought, *surely she is part of me.* So far so good.

He followed her through the terminal to the gate. Hundreds of people were milling around, and Freddie took her place among them, placing her suitcase on the floor beside her. She surveyed the room.

Perhaps she's searching for me, Darian thought. Encouraged, he revealed himself to her despite his original plan. He wasn't particularly worried about being in the midst of a crowded airport. He was in no danger from any of them. However, he didn't want to draw attention or create a riot. So he only reassembled enough to create an impression. No one else would even notice him. If she was searching, she might be able to see him.

He came into view, so to speak, at the edge of the crowd where it was less conspicuous. Almost immediately he saw Freddie looking at him. She smiled. In his semi-assembled state, he didn't have control over such subtle movements as smiling and waving. So he simply stood as he was. She turned away.

Distressed that he hadn't been able to respond, Darian allowed himself to flow back into the amorphous state in which he usually traveled and waited. When Freddie reached the ticket agent checking the boarding passes, he heard her confirm Freddie's seat location. Darian flowed ahead of her onto the plane.

This time he reassembled just enough that he could have more control over his movements. He was surprised Freddie saw him earlier because no one else seemed to notice. Even now, those who were entering the plane to find their seats weren't reacting in any way to his image.

Reassembling in the seat next to her, he felt his excitement rising when Freddie spotted him. Then he heard her remark to herself, *Why me, Lord? Why do I always get the weirdoes?*

Anger swelled. Even in this disembodied state, his anger was an ever present companion. Normally he wouldn't care what anyone else thought of him, but for some reason, her calling him a *weirdo* punched all those buttons that had governed his entire life.

Darian was losing his concentration again. Eagerness had already spurred him to abandon his plan to merely observe. Now his anger was impeding his desire to communicate with Freddie. He tried refocusing his thoughts, but he couldn't let go of his desire to crush her, to show her how powerful he was and how pitiful she was.

His angry thoughts reached out, carrying his particles with them. The particles of his life force brushed against the side of her face. They moved down her neck until they enveloped her breast. He felt her heart pounding. He felt her desire to scream in sheer terror. *Take her now!* he told himself. *Drain her until she is no more.*

He reached in and touched her pounding heart. He held it within his grasp. He felt its pulsating rhythm resounding through every corner of his consciousness. An unbidden memory flashed through his mind. Without warning his anger retreated and so did he, returning to his disassembled state. Gone from Freddie's sight.

Darian stayed only a minute or two longer. Long enough to hear the stewardess ask her if she needed a drink and to watch her tremble as she put on a pair of headphones. The last thought he heard was Freddie trying to convince herself he was just a dream.

Back in the cabin, adjusting to his body, Darian experienced minimal discomfort. Even though it was the longest trip he'd ever taken, he seemed none the worse for it. A good omen.

He remained in his chair, reviewing his jaunt and deciding his next move. He remembered how angry he had been when he encircled her heart. He wanted to squeeze it until it burst, releasing her life force to him. Then something very familiar had intruded. Sort of like a flashback, but he couldn't quite bring the memory into focus.

A low rumbling from his stomach interrupted his thoughts. Realizing it was well past lunch time, he rose to fix a sandwich. The only thing in the refrigerator was salami. He thought about opening a can of tuna fish, but decided it was too much trouble and set about making a sandwich.

Wrapping a paper towel around the bottom half of his salami and mayonnaise sandwich, he picked up the glass of milk on the counter and walked out to sit on the front porch of the cabin. It wasn't really a porch, at least not the kind that held a swing or several chairs. It was more like a stoop. Darian plopped down on the top step of the stairs leading to the yard.

No one else would consider sitting on these steps to enjoy their lunch. There was absolutely no scenery to admire. The terrain looked more like a long forgotten planet where cosmic storms had ravaged the land, and all life had given way to dust. Darian didn't see it that way. He didn't actually notice it at all. Unless they were intrusive, his surroundings were never an issue. He chose this cabin *because* it was isolated, and it was even more so now. With the destruction Darian had inflicted on the woods and the animals for at least a half-mile in every direction, the cabin resembled a bull's eye in a very large target of death.

Unaffected by the view, Darian reviewed the last couple of days.

His first jaunt was cut short by his surprise at Freddie's beauty. He admonished himself that he hadn't anticipated it. She *was* his twin after all. But, the most important lesson he learned from his first trip was that he must remain alert. Otherwise...well, otherwise all would be lost.

Suddenly he remembered the dream he'd had just before the pack of wild dogs entered his lair. The frustration he'd felt when he couldn't find an end to the great hall was reawakened, followed by the memory of the voice calling his name.

"Who was that?" he asked aloud as if there were someone there who could answer his inquiry. The voice was familiar, but now he couldn't recapture the sound.

The sun moved lower in the sky. Darian finished his sandwich and set his glass down on the porch. What was he going to do about Freddie? Her being aware of his presence seemed like a good sign even when he wasn't fully reassembled. Having never encountered another traveler, it was only conjecture, but he reasoned that perhaps the buzzing she heard was her life force, her own particles of energy, vibrating in response to an inevitable and compelling attraction between their particles, straining to be reunited.

Darian smiled, a gesture that transformed his visage into one of innocence—the look of the "boy next door." Surely, he thought, the only reason Freddie was that sensitive to him was because she *was* part of him, had shared the beginnings of life with him. The earlier anger he'd felt about her reactions to his appearance dissipated, and he easily rationalized her actions.

She was probably overwhelmed by my power...and frightened. It may take a little time, but she'll come around.

Such rationalizations were unprecedented. Darian had never looked at the world from another's viewpoint. Even considering the possibility that a viewpoint other than his own had value would have been outrageous before today. Darian didn't notice this subtle shift though because his thoughts had already moved on to what he would do when he saw her again tonight.

Normally his first thought would center on pinpointing Freddie's location before teleporting, but today's experience had shown him that wasn't necessary. He had teleported to the airport, despite his assumption that Freddie was at home. Obviously, this was a valuable lesson. Before today, he had always been acutely aware of his prey's location because his prey was always in the vicinity of his cabin. He had just assumed that focusing on the location was important. Now he realized that the time spent passively observing Freddie—something he had never done in the past with other prey—had given him a sense of her. He had bonded with her in some way he didn't understand, but he didn't need to understand it. All he needed to know was that he could always find her.

Armed with this knowledge, Darian once again entered the vortex and found himself in Freddie's hotel room. She was crying. As Darian emerged from the vortex, he heard thoughts flitting around in her mind about failure and loneliness. The moment he reassembled, however, she spotted him, and her mind flushed away all the thoughts it was nursing.

Feeling a rush of excitement, Darian was anxious to reassure her there was no need to be afraid of failure or loneliness. When they were joined, she would never have those feelings again. This was the second time a new, though not fully formed, emotion had emerged in Darian. This time it was compassion although Freddie obviously did not recognize it as such. Responding to his own feelings of excitement and urgency, he said, "It's time. You can't stop it!"

Freddie screamed. Almost immediately, there was a pounding on the door. Befuddled by her reaction and the pounding, Darian partially disassembled as she ran across the room. He glided through the wall into the hallway to see who was there. Freddie opened the door. Looking past her concerned visitor and directly at Darian, she fainted.

Perhaps I should take advantage of her being unconscious, he thought. Maybe he could reach her more easily. Not wanting to waste time, he reached out to her and surrounded her with his life force. He struggled to keep a hold on her and was determined to remain until she lost some of her fighting spirit. Perhaps then he could talk to her. Finally, she weakened.

Once again, he started with the message the Master had given to him, "It's time. You can't stop it."

Like a rubber band springing back to its original shape after being stretched, Freddie wrenched away from him. Shaken, Darian was unable to linger any longer. The glitter of his energy quickly entered the vortex, whisking him away.

Chapter 19

Day 3

*E*xhausted with his efforts in Freddie's hotel room and frustrated by her reaction to him, Darian considered devising an alternate plan. Observation didn't seem to be working out that well—mostly because he kept losing his resolve. Perhaps his own eagerness to advance in his quest was his problem. He was trying to move too fast. Despite this reassessment, however, he couldn't come up with a better plan than to passively observe until he found the best time to approach Freddie again.

It did occur to him that he might be expecting too much from her. Just because *he* knew how important his quest was didn't mean she would understand. Although, he suspected she might be the only person who would. *She certainly has strength of spirit*, he thought. A smile flitted across his mouth.

On the morning of the third day, his jaunt landed him in the lobby of the Chicago Board of Trade. He spotted Freddie on the sidewalk at the same moment she saw him, and his appearance obviously upset her. He desperately wanted to communicate with her but held tight to his plan. Looking at all the people milling about, Darian realized that observing her here was a waste of time. All her thoughts would be focused on her work with little time for personal reflection. If he was to understand her, he had to be privy to her private contemplations. Disappointed, he opted to try again in the morning—perhaps before she woke.

Chapter 20

Day 4

*T*he next morning Darian found Freddie in someone else's room. Apparently that someone else was the man in bed beside her. Just as Darian's elusive image started to take shape, she awoke.

Unfortunately, she fainted. Again.

In his frustration, he was tempted to approach her as he had the first night she was in Chicago. It seemed the only way he could reach her was when she was unconscious! He watched Freddie for a few minutes more, but she remained out of it. Tired of this ridiculous game, he determined his only option was to wait until she returned to Memphis. Surely in the privacy of her home, his odds of approaching her without fear of interruption or of her escaping would improve.

For Darian the pressure for moving ahead in his quest increased proportionately to his frustration over Freddie. Nearly seventy-two hours and four jaunts ago, Darian had judged that Freddie deserved a chance to adjust to the idea of being part of his quest. Now it seemed like it might take longer than he expected, and his patience, along with his compassion, was wearing a bit thin. Both were relatively new emotions and unaccustomed to the trials that tested them.

Darian believed it was imperative for him to share with Freddie what the Master shared with him. If he couldn't make her understand the importance of her role, he wasn't sure what to do. Back in his cabin, he searched for answers, implored the Master to guide him. Nothing came to him. Was he wrong about his twin? Maybe she meant nothing to his quest. Maybe he should just treat her like everyone else—take her life force and move on—but something kept him from taking this path. He just couldn't give up yet. Tomorrow he would try again.

Chapter 21

Day 5

Darian's connection with Freddie was so focused now that a single, directed thought could teleport him to wherever she was. Very quickly he emerged in the living room of an unfamiliar house. He assumed it was Freddie's. Everything was very neat, which instantly appealed to him. Playing it safe, he did not reassemble as he moved through the kitchen and the dining room and back into the living room. Darian was taken aback that he felt at home here. It wasn't like his cabin. For one thing, she had much more furniture than he had, and there were pictures on the walls. Everything, however, seemed to have a special place and, most important, was in its place!

Thoughts he recognized as Freddie's broke through his own thoughts. Her thoughts were erratic. She was even contemplating a shrink. His resolve *not* to appear to her weakened. She was breaking down. She had no place to run. Perhaps now she would listen. He started to reassemble.

The sound of the doorbell interrupted his plan. Almost fully reassembled, he paused, choosing to remain in the living room until Freddie answered the door. At first she didn't respond, and the doorbell sounded again. He could hear her considering whether to ignore it or not. Then he heard her coming down the hall and a door close in the hallway as she moved toward the front door. He moved out of Freddie's line of vision in the living room.

When she finally unfastened the host of locks and bolts, Darian moved into the foyer behind her. He wanted to see who the intruder was. Freddie called the woman Jodi.

Good! She's leaving, he thought, as the woman handed Freddie a key. His thoughts were so focused on what he wanted to tell Freddie it took him a minute to become aware of the conversation taking place between the two women. Jodi had obviously seen him standing behind Freddie. *How can that be?* Freddie suddenly leapt out the door and slammed it behind her.

Shocked by the turn of events, Darian immediately disassembled and focused his thoughts on his cabin. After his return, his mind whirled around with the same intensity the particles holding his very life within them had whirled in the vortex. The last few days had been very confusing for him, the prospects of success dimming. He was so sure the appointed time had arrived, but the reactions he'd gotten from Freddie so far made it impossible to deal with her. How could he communicate what she needed to know if she continually ran from him — literally and figuratively?

Darian braced himself for the possibility he might never be able to communicate with her and, even worse, the possibility that her power was greater than his. The very thought sent a shudder through him.

Chapter 22

Day 6

Darian had a restless night. The nightmares housing his fears about his quest haunted him. This morning he had no drive to do anything. He sat in his chair, staring at nothing. He was not aware of the changes that had occurred in him over the last week. The emergence of compassion for Angela's loss of her parents, his attempt to make excuses for Freddie's initial reactions to him—none of these actions were usual for him, and yet he had failed to notice them.

Abandonment by his parents to an orphanage at birth contributed to Darian's sinister view of the world. Other children more often became apathetic when faced with unsatisfied needs, but Darian had learned to be a survivor. Leaving the orphanage when he did and moving in with the Beels only confirmed for him that his approach to life was correct. Affection might have made a difference, but there was none to be had for Darian.

At a time in his life when he should have been learning to respect those in authority, such as teachers and parents, and to recognize and accept the diversity forever present in life, he landed in an alien world. Those he should have been able to respect abused and rejected him. Because he was different from his peers, he was cast out. He had been given no acceptable reason to accommodate such a world.

Without friends or allies as well as being a victim of horrible perversity, Darian never acquainted himself with a need for intimacy. Instead he determined to never again be on the receiving end of abuse or rejection. To do that, it was necessary to manipulate the world around him, especially if it threatened him—as his first-grade teacher and later Harry Beel had discovered.

It wasn't until Ruth escaped him that Darian considered his relationship with the world in terms other than dealing with immediate threats to himself. That was when he had started to plan, to formulate goals. His ultimate goal, however, had not yet been achieved even though he was nearing the end of his third decade. Until recently, this had never bothered him. Instantaneous success was never his goal—only eventual victory. So it was fitting that his ultimate goal had encompassed the whole of his life so far.

Despite his progress in his quest, Darian never advanced beyond the clutches of his anger and was not mindful of a need to do so. He'd had no practice expressing the gentler emotions. Just as the structures connecting cell bodies in the brain die when no information passes through them or muscles wither when not used, these emotions were so rarely used it was difficult for them to express. When they did, Darian didn't recognize them or know how to act upon them.

For the rest of the day Darian's thoughts were centered on the differences between himself and Freddie. She couldn't possibly know what it was like to be abandoned. After all, their parents chose to keep her, to love her. She had no idea what life was really like because she had never ventured outside the box, never rattled the cage of authority. She had always been protected because she played their game.

Well, he thought, *it's time she learned that her world is an illusion. Who does she think she is—rejecting me without cause?* He was offering her a priceless gift, and she had snubbed every attempt he made to talk to her. *What she needs is a wake-up call!* Darian still wasn't ready to destroy her, but he wanted to wake her up from her Pied-Piper existence. She needed to know she was vulnerable—that life didn't always give you what you wanted. You had to take it.

"Destroying someone close to her should be enough of a pinprick to burst her illusions of safety," he declared aloud, slamming his fist down on the chair arm.

Reflecting, he only recalled seeing her interact with three people: the man in bed with her in Chicago, the woman at work, and the woman named Jodi. Darian ruled out the man in Chicago because Freddie wasn't in Chicago any longer. He wanted her pain to be up close and personal. He wasn't certain about her relationship with the woman named Jodi, but he *was* sure she would notice if her co-worker, her assistant, was killed. His decision was made.

Chapter 23

Day 7

*M*onday morning, Darian wasted no time before focusing on Clark Tower, the office building where Freddie worked. When he emerged from the vortex, he was in the reception area outside Freddie's office. He moved quickly, still disassembled, downward through the building until he reached the ground level. Then he traveled toward the north side of the building where he entered the parking garage.

Although he hadn't wasted much time observing the woman named Joyce that first day, it was long enough to get a sense of her as he had with Freddie. Trailing her scent, it was only seconds before his life force was thrust into the third level of the garage. He saw Joyce walking toward the elevators. She was alone. It was still too early for the usual rush of people.

Darian eavesdropped on her thoughts. Joyce was dreading the increased work load that invariably accompanied Freddie's return to work, which was why she planned to get a head start this morning. She reminisced about the relaxed pace wile Freddie was in Chicago last week.

Joyce snorted. "When Freddie's here, time seems to slow down so Freddie can squeeze in more things she wants to get done," she said aloud.

She immediately admonished herself as she walked toward the elevator. Her boss was pretty hands-on. Freddie didn't just throw things on her desk and walk away. She always divided the work up between them. It was just that Freddie was a workaholic, and trying to keep up with her was more than most people could handle.

Whenever Freddie taught in Chicago, the only time she was ever out of the office, Joyce wound up feeling guilty—like she was goofing off.

Oh well! Time to get back in the saddle, Joyce! she told herself.

That's where you're wrong, Joyce.

"Who's there?" Joyce's voice squeaked. She knew she hadn't spoken aloud. Being a woman alone in a parking garage was scary enough by itself. Hearing someone call you by name and not being able to see anyone was worse, especially when they seemed to be hearing your thoughts. Her throat tightened, making it difficult to utter anything in a normal tone of voice.

What's the matter, Joyce?

Looking around the garage, she searched for the source of the voice, refusing to believe she wasn't hearing it with her ears. "Who are you? What do you want?" she demanded. Although she appeared to be in control, it was only a façade. Her gut was in knots as she hurried through the garage, heading for the stairs. If she could just get to the stairs, she would run like hell for the street level.

I don't think you can outrun me, Joyce. the voice whispered. *Besides, there's no one on the street level either.*

Losing all semblance of control, Joyce turned and ran back toward the elevators, praying that one of them would open. As she entered the small waiting area in front of the elevator doors, one of them slid open. She raced toward it, ready to hit the close-door button just as soon as she got inside. Throwing herself at the open elevator, she reached out with both hands to grab the frames of the elevator doors and dropped her purse at her feet just inside the opening.

A man who looked vaguely familiar stood inside. She didn't know him but was grateful for the presence of anyone, even a stranger. She glanced over her shoulder to see if she was being followed as she stepped inside, letting the doors glide shut.

There's no one there, Joyce, because I'm right here.

She whirled around. "What do you want? I don't have any money." Joyce knew this went way beyond robbery, but her mind wasn't able to rationally accept that the man standing before her could not only read her mind but thrust his own thoughts into it.

I want you, Joyce.

She started to shake. Visions of being raped amid a flood of other images and emotions coursed through her mind. Darian interrupted the onslaught.

No! I don't want your body. Even in her mind the disgust in his voice was obvious. *Your life force is all I want. Your body is of no use to me.*

Confused, the only words that emerged were "What are you talking about?" Her legs were barely able to hold her up. She knew it was pointless to try to run when and if the elevator doors opened. Besides, it hadn't helped her before.

She suspected the sheer volume of adrenalin coursing through her body was causing her to hallucinate. This man didn't seem real. He was more surreal—almost like she could run her hand right through him. "I don't understand," she added in a lame attempt to inject reason into this freakish situation.

It's not necessary that you understand.

In desperation, Joyce begged. "Why me?" Her voice quivered, and tears rolled down her cheeks. "I haven't done anything to you."

Darian looked at her. He had reassembled as much as possible without a flesh and bone body when he entered the elevator. He wanted to make sure Joyce could see him. He reached out now with the image of his hand and let it brush her hair. Joyce's legs gave up the battle, and she began to fall. Darian's life force reached out and supported her.

You're not important, Joyce. You're just a pawn in a larger game. The only reason you matter is because Freddie cares about you. You're someone she'll miss. She has to understand that her life is not perfect, that her safety and the safety of those around her is only an illusion. He paused, still looking down into her face. Unable to do anything but stare back at him, Joyce wondered in the midst of her terror if evil had always been so handsome.

Don't worry. It doesn't hurt, he told her but unable to hide the contempt he felt for such weakness.

The last words she uttered were a cry for help. "God! Help me! Please, please don't do this!" No one heard her. It wouldn't have mattered if they had.

Darian observed the look of terror that remained on Joyce's face as she lay on the red carpet of the elevator. It was always the same—the look of terror that emerged on their faces when they realized they couldn't resist him. Eyes opened wide; mouth open in a silent scream; terror written in every line of their faces.

There was a certain satisfaction for Darian in this evidence of his power over them. Yet, it mystified him, too. He knew that when he first began consuming a victim's spirit, he or she could sense the nature of his quest as they merged with him. That was the part he didn't understand. Armed with such knowledge, why would they continue to resist, knowing they were sacrificing themselves for something so wonderful?

Glancing at Joyce once more, he knew her look of terror would serve a greater purpose. Even if Freddie didn't see it herself, he was sure she would hear about it. With his work done, Darian returned to his   cabin.

Chapter 24

*I*t was still early when Darian arrived back in his body. He sat still for a few minutes to recover, but it didn't take very long. His nervous system had quickly learned to make the adjustments needed to regulate the energy levels required for revitalization of his body after his travels. Those levels depended on the amount of energy he had absorbed or released while absent. During the jaunts, his body's vital functions were temporarily slowed, similar to the levels achieved by yogis. There was just enough life force functioning to retain vitality. Even if someone happened across his body during this time, their first guess would be that he was dead.

For scientists attempting to perfect suspended animation, their main concerns had always dealt with deterioration in the central nervous system and whether memory and mental faculties embedded there remained intact. These things were of no concern to Darian. He wasn't gone from his body long enough for deterioration of his central nervous system to take place. Besides, enough of his essence remained with his body to prevent physiological detriment. What Darian knew from experience that the scientists didn't was that his memories could not be extricated from his life force. They weren't permanently linked to his brain and therefore subject to deterioration or destruction. When the particles of energy flowed from his body, they contained within them the fundamentals of who he was—and that, without a doubt, included his memories.

Today he was steeped in those memories. Pulling the overstuffed armchair across the floor, he left marks stretching out behind it from the center of the living room to the window. He sat down and propped his feet on the window sill. As he rested his elbows on the arms of the chair and clasped his hands together in his lap, flashes of his past paraded through his mind in a bizarre spectacle.

Flash—Miss McKelroy kissing him good night—*flash*—the two of them laughing at the preacher—*flash*—being handed off to the Beels by Miss McKelroy—*flash*—Harry in his basement workshop (Darian shuddered involuntarily)—*flash*—Miss Gruen—*flash*—Harry—*flash*—Ruth—*flash*—Miss McKelroy on the floor.

The memories moved quickly. Suddenly, they slowed as *flash*—Angela came into view. Darian remembered the time he spent with her. He remembered her face, her eyes, her hair. Strange things started happening in his body as his thoughts lingered on her. He closed his eyes to shut out the feelings.

Flash—the image of Freddie filled his mind, and the old, familiar feelings flowed through him. He was growing tired of this game. If Joyce's death didn't make a difference—if Freddie didn't respond to him—

Abruptly, Darian's thoughts slipped away from Freddie to Angela so swiftly that he didn't even realize there had been a shift. Picturing Angela in his mind, he felt the same way he had when she touched his knee the other day—confused.

Replaying in his mind the two encounters he'd had with Angela, Darian noticed a change that most teenage boys find quite common, but which Darian had never experienced. He wasn't ignorant of the way in which men and animals procreated, but he had never felt those urgings. He had always saved his energies for focusing on his quest. Before now, wasting his energies for anything other than improving or using his power was too big a risk as far as Darian was concerned. But he was so close now. Surely...

He sat quietly, observing the changes in his body, his mind becoming the puppet of his hormones as he thought about seeing Angela again. Unaware of the subtle manipulation of his thoughts by his hormones, he congratulated himself on his decision to stay away from Freddie for a few days to give her time to mull over his destructive potential. *Waiting,* he told himself, *might stoke her fear enough that I can easily overcome her and make her listen.* The instant his hormones got their way by eliminating the obstacle that stood between them and gratification, they turned his thoughts to musing about Angela.

After a few minutes Darian got up, left the chair by the window, and walked toward the kitchen. Fixing a quick snack, he decided to take a nap and then go into town shortly before noon to arrive at the library just as Angela did.

A couple of hours later, Darian woke to a flood of sunlight filling the cabin, its brilliance washing away any signs of the occupant's perverse plans. Darian stood before the bathroom sink after taking a shower. The old medicine cabinet on the wall boasted a mirror that had obviously reflected many faces in its time. Darian's face was not so different from the others and was better looking than most.

The mirror reflected large, dark eyes set in a handsome face. Thick, dark hair parted on the side that curved gently back over the ears. Thanks to a natural wave, his hair appeared to be styled rather than the product of Darian's barbering skills. He found it simple to cut. He just held it out from his head in locks and cut them all the same length. Even when it was too long, it never looked shaggy. It obediently fell into place.

Darian had grown into quite a handsome man. Today Darian gazed into the mirror, trying to see his physical self as others did. Joyce had thought him handsome—evil, but handsome. Of course, he paid no attention to her assessment of his character because he knew it wasn't true. However, he didn't really doubt her evaluation of his beauty. He knew it was true. It just made him wonder what it was like to be her or anyone else gazing upon the perfection of his face. It had never mattered to him before how others felt or what they thought. It was inconsequential. So gazing at himself in this way now made him uncomfortable. With a brusque movement of his hand, he opened the medicine cabinet to retrieve his toothpaste, and he finished the remainder of his toiletries without closing the cabinet's mirrored door.

As eleven o'clock approached, Darian locked up and got into the car that was a "gift" from Harry Beel's estate to drive to Sterling. It wasn't Harry's car, of course. Keeping something that was a hand-me-down from Harry was out of the question. Instead, Darian had used some of the money he received when he sold the Beel house in Peoria to buy a used car.

The car was a Pontiac, blue with gray interior and only 30,000 miles on it. He had rarely needed a car in Peoria. There were plenty of stores within walking distance of the house, but now that he had a nice-looking car, he enjoyed riding in it. When he bought the car, he had asked the dealer to deliver it to the Beel's house for him. He used the excuse that he had to go out of town and instructed the dealer to leave the keys in the wooden planter on the front porch—a remnant of Ruth's attempt at gardening. He assured the salesman that no one would steal the car. The truth was that Darian had never learned to drive. So he spent hours sitting in the car, practicing going forward and reverse without ever leaving the driveway. It wasn't long before he mastered the fundamentals, but he didn't waste time getting a license. To Darian, such rules didn't apply to him.

Cruising along the lonesome country roads outside Sterling and accelerating until he nearly lost control on the loose gravel excited him. He usually waited until the last second before backing off the gas pedal. Today, however, Darian didn't push the envelope. Instead he cruised along at a reasonable speed, his thoughts focused on planning a strategy for dealing with Angela.

Dealing with people in the flesh was not a familiar exercise for him. When he met Angela the first time, it was in the flesh, but his thoughts had been focused on Freddie—well, mostly. Now he was solely focused on Angela—thanks to the centering power of his physiological uprising. His focus was unsullied by emotions related to caring or love. It was simply responding to a need, and Darian saw not only the probable cause but a way to fill that need.

Driving down LeFevre Road, Darian realized that the intersecting streets were numbered. Passing 3rd Ave., then 4th, he turned south on 5th Ave. rather than driving all the way across town as he had before.

When he reached 4th Street, the one-way route to the library, it was still too early to meet with Angela. So he cruised around the one-way loop forming the spinal column of this town.

He watched the people walking along the sidewalks. Some were obviously on their way to a particular place while others were just strolling, peering into storefront windows and talking to each other. As he waited at the traffic light at 3rd St. and Locust, he noticed a large group of people milling around on the sidewalk in the next block. Curious, he bent his head down to read the sign above the establishment. It presented a funny-looking little man dressed in green and sported the name Kelly's. It was either a place to eat or a bar. Perhaps both.

The light changed, and Darian made a left turn onto 3rd St. He slowed for a teen-ager who ran across the street and went into a tiny café called Maid-Rite. He noticed the mural painted on the side of the building across the alley. He had seen several murals on other buildings, but they sparked no interest in him. Deciding to circle back to 4th St., he turned on 2nd Ave. At the next block, the light turned red. A man and woman holding hands emerged from the Sterling Daily Gazette building and crossed the street in front of his car. The woman's smiling face was tilted upward toward her companion's. Darian could sense how powerful the man felt by watching his body language. Sneering, Darian thought, *He has no idea what real power feels like!*

After driving around a while longer, Darian pulled into the parking lot beside the library. Getting out of his car, the comfortable vision of his reflection in the curve of the window caught his eye. Reaching up, he let his right hand pass over his hair gently, admiring its perfection. Then he turned and started toward the building.

"Hey!" someone shouted.

Darian turned to see Angela, running across the parking lot toward him.

"What are you doing here?" she asked. "I figured I'd never see you again."

"I..." Darian hesitated. He was caught off guard by her sudden appearance as well as her outspoken greeting.

"Hey, don't mind me. Nosy is my middle name," she laughed. "After all, the library *is* a public place!" Her laughter rang out across the parking lot. Darian had never known anyone who laughed as much as this woman.

"I'm just glad to see you again," she said, slipping her arm inside his when she caught up with him. The same stirrings that had been haunting him since the first moment he met her arose. Right now he had no choice but to hold them in check, but what harm could come from walking with her, he thought, letting his free hand fall gently over hers.

"Actually I was looking for you," Darian remarked.

"Really?" Angela's voice sounded hopeful.

"Yeah. I've been thinking about you and thought maybe we could go to dinner. Since I don't know where you live, I thought I'd catch up with you at the library."

Angela couldn't believe it. Here was this drop-dead good-looking guy asking her out. It had to be a dream. Determined not to appear too excited, she calmly asked, "Tonight?"

Darian couldn't tell if she was interested or not. Since his experience with asking a woman out on a date was non-existent, he let his instincts lead the way. "Yeah, if that's okay with you."

"Yes, it's great!" she exclaimed, forgetting her resolve to appear nonchalant. "What time do you want to pick me up? I can get off early. I have a lot of time coming from last week. I worked late every night helping out when they took inventory of the new book shipments." Suddenly she became aware she was rambling and quickly closed her mouth, tucking her lips between her teeth as if someone had zipped and locked them.

The flood of positive emotion from Angela intrigued Darian. Ordinarily his conversations with others were sterile at best. If there were any emotions involved, they were more likely to be negative. He was enjoying this. He thought about the man and woman who'd crossed in front of his car earlier. Now he understood what the man felt. It didn't compare to *real* power, the kind of power Darian had nourished all these years, but he had to admit that it was certainly intoxicating!

"What time can you get off work?"

"I can leave at 5 o'clock. Of course, I'll have to go home and change clothes. Where do you want to go?" Angela asked.

Since Darian had never eaten anywhere in town, he turned the question back to her. "What do you suggest?"

"It depends on what you like. If you're into home cooking, we should go to Sal's Place. It's not fancy, but the food's good."

Darian could tell by the way Angela's mouth drew slightly to one side when she finished speaking that Sal's Place was not what she had in mind. "Where would you really like to go?" he asked. "We'll go wherever you want."

Without missing a beat, she replied, "There's a new place in Rock Falls called Donovan's. It just opened up, and everyone says it's the place to go. There's even a bar and a small dance floor. A friend of mine said they have a live band tonight." Her hands were clasped in front of her like a child begging for a special present.

Darian smiled. "That's where we'll go then!"

Angela squealed and clapped her hands together. In a rush of excitement, she leaned over and kissed Darian on the cheek. Heat flooded through him like water being released from behind a flood gate. A mad torrent, racing to lay claim to every surface it could reach. Taking a deep breath, he asked her where she lived. He said he'd pick her up at six o'clock and started back to his car.

"See you later!" shouted Angela across the parking lot. Darian turned and waved back at her.

Chapter 25

Getting in his car, Darian realized he had six hours to kill. Driving back to the cabin was an option, but not one he favored. He had never explored Sterling. Who knows? He might discover something interesting. Besides, he needed to locate Angela's house and the restaurant.

Pulling out onto Locust, he made the mistake of staying in the outside lane as it wound around the downtown and found himself crossing the Rock River into Rock Falls. Just past Wheelox Furniture, he saw a billboard advertising "Donovan's—the liveliest spot in town!" It instructed all interested parties to drive straight ahead one mile and turn right. Within a few minutes he was in front of the restaurant.

A lot of people were coming and going, laughing and talking. It was still the lunch hour. *Why not?* he thought, *I have to eat lunch somewhere.*

As he entered the restaurant, a young woman with menus in her hand approached and welcomed him to Donovan's. "Are you expecting someone or are you dining alone?" she asked, her eyes searching the entry behind him.

"No," he replied. "I'm alone." Smiling, she laid all of the menus except one on the reception desk and led him to a small table pressed up against the wall with a single chair on each side.

As Darian pulled out his chair, she asked, "Could I get you something to drink?"

Glancing at her name tag, Darian replied in a soft tone, "That would be great, Robyn. I'd like some iced tea."

"I'll bring it right back to you." She smiled cheerfully at him, hesitating a moment before she turned away.

Darian was warming up to this new feeling of power. Of course, he would never trade his natural powers for it, but it definitely had its own charm. Within a minute, Robyn returned with his iced tea.

Leaning over him to set the glass on his right side, she asked, "Is there anything else you'd like before your waitress gets here?" This was not her normal way of greeting and seating a customer, but this man intrigued her. Of course, he was very good-looking, but there was something else—something strangely compelling about him.

"A menu?" Darian asked.

Embarrassed, Robyn realized she had carried his menu away with her when she went after his drink. Her face turning red, she apologized. "I don't know where my head is today! I'll get you one right away." She hurried away.

Darian smiled. Every moment was taking him closer to being hooked on the mysterious relationship existing between men and women. The inexplicable dominion he had over Angela and Robyn without even trying fascinated him. They knew nothing of him. Yet, they were drawn to him like an insect to a light, unaware the light masked the electrical force of his true nature. He congratulated himself on choosing to eat lunch here. It would be great training for his date with Angela.

The waitress moved up from the table behind Darian after picking up her tip just as Robyn reappeared with the menu. Hastily placing the menu on the table in front of Darian, Robyn returned to the front desk. Realizing her customer would not be ready to order, the waitress stepped forward to tell him she would come back in a few minutes to take his order.

Enjoying all the possibilities before him, Darian spoke quickly. "Maybe you could suggest something to me. I've never eaten here before." The waitress stared at him, a queer look on her face.

"Is something wrong, Mary?" he asked, taking advantage of her name tag to create a feeling of intimacy between them.

Startled, Mary assured him nothing was wrong. She'd seen a lot of handsome men pass through the restaurants and bars where she had worked before, but this guy... For some reason, she was uneasy. Shaking her head slightly, Mary started the litany of standard suggestions for Darian.

Darian opened his menu as she talked. "Do you mean this?" he asked, pointing at the item on the menu fancifully called Donovan's Reef.

"No, this one is the filet mignon," she replied, reaching across the menu to point at the correct item. As she did, her hand brushed against Darian's. Her sharp intake of breath alerted him.

This game excited him, especially since he was finding himself to be a natural player. Exploiting the opportunity, he took her hand in both of his and said, "What a lovely ring! Are you married?"

Jolted by the emotions she was experiencing, Mary laughed nervously and said, "No. Besides, that's the wrong finger. Well, it's the right finger. Just the wrong hand." Darian made note of this for future reference.

"Well, it's lovely anyway!" He released his grip on her hand, but she didn't immediately remove it. "I think I'll take your suggestion of the filet mignon." Realizing that her hand was still in his, she quickly retrieved it. Flustered, she took his order.

While eating lunch, Darian savored his experiences so far today. As he cut a piece of the filet mignon, he caught the sudden movement of the chair on the other side of his table. Robyn was pulling the chair out to sit down.

"Robyn," he asked in a tone that implied concern, "is something wrong?"

"Oh, no. I just had a break, and wanted to ask you if you live around here. I mean, I've never seen you before, and I've lived here all my life. And, trust me, the town's not big enough to miss knowing too many people!"

"Actually, I live outside of town in the country." Darian did not want to be any more specific than this.

"Oh. Do you plan to stay around here?" Robyn's voice made it obvious the answer she wanted.

This is like stalking prey, Darian thought as he smiled at Robyn. "I don't have any immediate plans to leave." Then he couldn't resist putting her on the spot. "Why?"

Robyn was embarrassed. She was aware she had been terribly transparent, but she wasn't quite ready to give up her pretense of simple neighborliness. "Nothing. I just like getting to know new people. When you live in a place like this, it gets really boring if you don't reach out when you can." Aware of how silly she sounded, Robyn got up, hoping to appear nonchalant. "Well, I've got to get back to work. Maybe we'll see you again?"

"I'm certain of it," Darian replied. With a pleased expression, Robyn turned with a quick wave of her hand and headed back toward the front desk.

Two hours passed. The other customers had long since gone back to work or wherever. Only one other couple remained in this part of the dining room. Darian decided he better leave if he was going to find Angela's house. Besides, leaving a decent interval before returning for another meal might be wise. He waved his hand in the air to get Mary's attention. She had failed to return to the table as often as he thought she might. Curious, he wanted to talk to her one more time before he left.

Stepping aside as the last couple in her section walked through the doorway, Mary hesitated before heading toward Darian's table. "Yes? Do you need something else?"

"Well, I need two things. I need to know where to pay my check."

"I can take it, or you can pay at the register near the exit," interrupted Mary quickly. A little too quickly, thought Darian.

"Okay. The other thing is that I need to locate an address. Do you know where 1024 Avenue D is located?" Darian looked directly at her, holding her gaze for only a few seconds before she dropped her eyes toward the table. He might have interpreted her action as a rejection of him, but his senses picked up a strong vibration of fear, an emotion with which he was very familiar in other people. She was definitely afraid of him!

Excited, Darian pushed farther. "Do you have a map to help me locate it?" he asked before she could answer him. He saw her twitch. Although he wasn't sure what was happening or why, her fear stoked his excitement.

Mary nodded and left to get a map. After a few minutes, Darian wondered if she would return, but to his delight, she walked in and placed the map on his table. It was already opened up and folded back so that a certain segment of town was visible. Darian saw a small red circle drawn around the words *Avenue D.*

Stepping back, she said, "You can have the map. That address has to be in Sterling because in Rock Falls, Avenue D ends at 10th St."

Darian didn't intend to let her get away this easily. "Thanks for marking the street for me, but the problem is that I don't know exactly where I am now. I was just driving around and followed the directions on a billboard to find this place. Can you show me where we are now?"

The line of Mary's jaw tensed, but she smiled at Darian with her best customer service smile. She reached to pick up the map, planning to spread it on the adjacent table to mark the restaurant's location. Anticipating her action, Darian unfolded the map and spread it out. He saw Mary jerk her hand back.

Things are starting to get interesting, he thought. He was tempted to reach out—just a little—just enough to read her thoughts but chose not to ruin the excitement of the chase.

Twisting the map so she couldn't read it from where she was, he asked, "Now, where are we located?" He had allowed just enough of the map to lap over the edge of the table so he could anchor it with his forearms. Not realizing this, she reached out and caught the edge of the map to turn it around in a last ditch effort to keep her distance. It didn't budge.

"Are we near this area?" he asked, pointing west of the red circle, knowing full well that Rock Falls was south of Sterling.

Easing forward, Mary leaned over an invisible fence she had erected to separate the two of them and pointed toward their location but quickly withdrew her hand. Darian could smell her perfume but was not close enough to physically touch her.

"Show me again. I didn't catch it. Here, mark it if you will." Since he wasn't going to release the map, she would have to come closer to mark the spot.

Mary took a deep, but silent, breath. She was frightened of this man. She couldn't explain it. She just knew there was something sinister lurking under that handsome face and the innocent tones. She had long ago learned to trust her feelings. Her mother called it a gift, and she had warned Mary never to ignore those little signals her gift offered her.

Right now, however, she didn't know how to respond. She couldn't just walk away. Her boss would call her on the carpet for being rude to a customer, and she couldn't risk losing this job. She would just have to be careful.

Stepping closer to the table, she reached across to draw a circle around their location with her pen. Suddenly, she felt Darian's arm snake around her waist. She froze leaving the circle looking like the letter C. All sorts of emotions rose within her—fear, excitement, longing. She was drowning in the torrent of mixed emotions. Her connection with her surroundings started to fade.

"Is something wrong, Mary? You don't look like you feel well. Here," Darian stood without releasing his grip on her waist and sat her down in his chair. Before she could recover her senses, he quickly pulled up a chair from the next table and sat down. Making sure that he was touching her, he began to stroke her hair as one would do with a sick child. Mary trembled uncontrollably.

"It's all right, Mary," he told her soothingly. "No one's going to harm you," With a rapid change in manner, he barked, "Look at me!" Shivers rippled through Mary, but she was not able to deny his command. She turned her face toward him.

Darian smiled at her as if they were sweethearts and everything was perfectly normal. She could only stare. Glancing quickly around the room and seeing no one, he very carefully released part of his life force. He wanted her to feel him, to know how powerful he *really* was.

Invisible to the naked eye, tiny particles began to stream from him. He directed them toward her throat. As they began to glide along the side of her neck, he saw her flinch, but he managed to hold her gaze. He allowed his precious particles to flow down through the collar of her blouse until he could feel the swell of her breasts and the rapid beating of her heart. He encircled both breasts, letting his energy dance back and forth lightly over her nipples. He sensed her excitement growing as well as her fear.

His own excitement caused him to release even more of his life force. Being this close, he wasn't concerned. His body would never be deprived of enough vitality to disturb his posture. His energy continued to flow over her torso until it reached an area he had never before explored. Although it was true that he had forced Ruth to perform fellatio on Harry's dead body, he had never witnessed or experienced sexual intercourse between a man and a woman.

The particles floated gently through Mary's pubic hair entering that unfamiliar region. He felt the heat rising in his groin and glanced downward. Looking back at Mary, he saw tears running down her face even though she was still transfixed. He was not able to pull his life force back. He felt the particles racing headlong against the walls within her. His body began to tremble as he felt something strange, something wet. A warm liquid had started to flow inside her. His particles exploded in all directions like a giant pinball machine gone amok.

Suddenly he was back in his body, and the feeling of wetness was still with him. At first he thought it was the lingering sensation of Mary, but he quickly realized he had just experienced a new and electrifying event in his life.

The quiet sounds of Mary sobbing caught his attention just as he heard Robyn's voice from across the room. "Is something wrong?" she asked, walking toward them.

"I don't know," Darian replied. "She was light-headed, and I let her sit down, but now she seems to be hysterical about something. I hate to do this, but could you take care of her? I really have to go."

"Sure. No problem." Robyn smiled sweetly at Darian and sat down next to Mary, putting her arm around her shoulders. "Are you all right?" she asked. Not waiting to hear Mary's reply, Darian grabbed the map off the table, dropped money on the table and left.

It didn't take long to find Angela's street. All the houses on the street looked like they were built forty or more years ago. Looking at the addresses painted on the curb—980, 984—he realized that Angela's house was in the next block. Finally he spotted 1024 Avenue D.

The style of the house had taken its lead from the English countryside. The walls were stucco and had been painted beige in the distant past. Small cracks meandered across the surface. Ivy wound upward, wrapping its tendrils around the dark brown trim of the window casements.

Darian slowed to get a good view of the house, but he didn't stop. Turning left at the end of the block, he noticed that no houses faced the side street. He saw an opening that looked like a driveway, however. Approaching, he realized it was an alley. Making a sharp left turn, he pulled into it. It ran behind all the houses on the two parallel streets, giving them a second entrance. It was obviously the route used by the garbage collector because garbage cans were lined up like sentries all the way down the alley.

Darian drove slowly, trying to determine which house was Angela's. He figured it wouldn't be too hard to spot. These houses were built before tract housing; so each one was distinctly different from its neighbor. Angela's house had a one-car garage in the back. There was a space for pull-off parking just outside the garage door. So Darian pulled into the space.

He wanted to know more about Angela. He wasn't sure why. It

just felt important. Glancing at the house, he realized the porch door was ajar. This was enough for him. Getting out of the car, he studied the other houses as he walked toward the gate. He saw no one, but he wasn't worried. He didn't exactly look like a burglar.

Reaching over the small gate, he quickly unlatched it. It swung open by itself. Taking care to latch the gate back, he walked up to the porch and walked in as if he belonged. *If anyone's watching, that should ease their suspicions*, he thought.

Once inside, he wasn't worried because no one could see what was going on inside. It wasn't a screened porch. It was sectioned into windows with glass louvers that rolled outward, more for ventilation than visibility. Besides, the house extended toward the back property line on one side, giving the porch protection from prying eyes. At the moment, all the louvers were closed, and it was impossible to see through them unless the sun hit them just right. Even then, you only saw shadows.

Lawn furniture adorned the porch, but like the house, it came from a different era. A metal glider capable of seating at least three people and two metal rockers had been recently painted and adorned with plastic cushions in a bright orange and green design. Darian sat down on the glider, letting it slowly rock back and forth. He was getting the *feel* of the place the same way he did with a person.

Wanting to see the inside, he started to disassemble. Then he noticed one of the windows opening onto the porch was cranked out about half an inch. After inspecting it, Darian put his fingers under the edge of the window toward the center and pulled. With a soft clunking sound, it gave into the pressure and opened easily. Lifting his right leg, he stepped through the open window. Once inside he cranked the window shut.

Looking around, Darian realized he was in the dining room. In front of him was a very old pedestal dining table with four straight back chairs. A matching buffet and hutch engulfed one wall. It was easy to imagine this furniture being in the house since the carpenter finished the last brush stroke on the finish. There were four plates, four wine glasses, and four water glasses lined up on the top two shelves of the hutch, On the bottom shelf were two stacks of smaller plates and four cups stacked in twos. Obviously, Angela didn't have much company.

Above his head, a shelf extended all the way around the room. It was only about one foot from the ceiling, but Angela had it filled with various knickknacks. At least one plant decorated each wall with its branches hanging loosely over the edge of the shelf. The plant above the hutch had curled its vines gently through the decorative molding on the hutch and was straining to reach the ornate knobs adorning its doors.

Darian moved through an archway into the living room. A sofa and chair were upholstered in a multi-colored, tapestry-like material of golds, reds, and greens, deeper shades than their bright cousins on the porch. A glass-door bookcase stood against the wall closest to the dining room.

Curious, Darian squatted down to see what was in the bookcase. Among the hardcover books, he saw *Moby Dick, The Adventures of Tom Sawyer,* and *Gone With The Wind.* The bottom shelf was filled with stacks of paperbacks. He opened the glass door and took out a couple of books. They had titles like *Lost in Passion* and *Forever Shamed.* Putting these back, he pulled out several more. They all sported pictures of muscular men without shirts or with their shirts unbuttoned, holding or kissing women dressed in a myriad of different ways. Some of the women looked like someone had tried to tear their clothes off. Others were dressed in long dresses with fancy hairdos.

No doubt about Angela's interests. This should make things easier, thought Darian, viewing life as always in terms of conquest.

Replacing the books, he continued through the house, stepping first into a small hallway. He saw three doors. The first opened into Angela's bedroom. Her bed was made, and everything was neatly arranged, which appealed to him. A silky, peach-colored comforter was spread across the four-poster bed. Over the bed on the wall hung a watercolor of irises in subtle shades of peach and rose with accents in green and gray. There was only one chair, decorated with a peach slipcover, positioned in front of the window.

A small stool sat in front of an early 20th century dresser with two drawers on each side, and a shelf that extended between them about six inches from the top. Angela's cosmetics and perfume were neatly arranged on the shelf. A wooden frame attached to the dresser base supported a round mirror. The frame only extended halfway around the mirror, leaving the upper potion bare. Stepping in front of the mirror, Darian looked at himself. *Handsome indeed,* he thought. A self-satisfied smile appeared on his face as he realized what an asset it was.

Turning, Darian left the room. Opening the next door, he discovered a small bathroom. Everything was white except for the peach accents which Angela had added to the room—the peach curtain around the base of the free-standing sink and the window and shower curtains.

Darian started to shut the door but stopped when he noticed the medicine cabinet. He opened it and saw a bottle of aspirin, some vitamins, toothpaste, and a small box. Opening the box, he pulled out a circular object. It felt like rubber, but it was hard around the edges and flimsy in the middle. After looking at it for a few minutes, he placed it back in the box and set it on the shelf.

At the end of the hall, a swinging door opened into the kitchen. The extension on the back of the house was part of the kitchen, making it big enough to have a work table in the middle of the room. A large window in the side wall overlooked the yard next door. Darian opened the refrigerator. It held a few cold drinks, a loaf of bread, a package of sliced ham, a jar of pickles, a small jar of mayonnaise, and a sickly-looking tomato. Opening the freezer compartment revealed chicken pot pies, frozen pizza, and Rocky Road ice cream.

Walking slowly back through the house, Darian noticed a large book on the floor, leaning against the side of the sofa. Picking it up, he sat down and flipped it open. It was filled with pictures, neatly glued to the black pages of the book with a caption printed on a thin strip of paper and glued beside each picture.

Darian started at the beginning. There were lots of baby pictures, all labeled *Angela* with different dates and locations. He spent the next thirty minutes browsing through her family history. He knew her parents were dead, but he discovered she also had an uncle named Tom in Wyoming. Finally he put the scrapbook back where he found it.

Looking at the clock on the end table, he realized it was five o'clock. This time he went through the back door instead of the window, remembering to lock it. Looking around as he stepped off the porch, he saw no one. He casually walked to his car and drove away.

Chapter 26

*T*he sun was dipping lower in the sky when Darian left Angela's house the first time. By the time he returned, the partially overcast sky made it dusky enough to use his headlights. As he turned onto Avenue D, he looked at his watch. It was three minutes before six o'clock. Five minutes earlier he had driven down the alley to see what kind of car Angela drove. Unfortunately, it was inside the garage. Slowing his car as he approached her house, he saw Angela running out the front door, heading toward the curb. She opened the passenger door and jumped in.

"Hi!" she said as she fastened her seat belt.

Seeing her run across the yard, Darian assumed something was wrong. His first thought was that somehow she knew he had been in her house, but her tone of voice dispelled these concerns. "Are you running from something?" he asked, still wondering what her rush was.

"Oh! No. It's just against the law to park on this side of the street. I forgot to tell you. You see, there's an alley in the back of the house. They expect us to park there. I guess they assume all our visitors are psychic!" She laughed, turning sideways in the seat until she was nearly facing him. "You're looking good!"

"I look just like I did this afternoon," Darian replied.

"Well, you were looking good then, too!" Angela was obviously excited. Whether it was because of him or because he was taking her to Donovan's didn't matter to Darian. Either way, he would use it to his advantage.

"Are we still going to Donovan's?" she asked.

"Isn't that where you wanted to go?"

"Absolutely! I hear it's wonderful! A friend of mine interviewed for a job there. I haven't talked to her in a while; so I don't know if she got it. Maybe she'll be there tonight." Angela secretly hoped so. She wanted to show Darian off. That was one of the main reasons she suggested going there. Darian listened but didn't mention that he had gone there for lunch.

Arriving at the restaurant early by dinner and dancing standards, they still had a difficult time finding a place to park. Angela slipped her hand around Darian's upper arm as they walked toward the restaurant, a gesture that surprised him. When she stepped to one side as they approached the entrance, Darian quickly took the hint and opened the door for her.

Robyn wasn't in the lobby to greet them when they entered. Instead, an older woman with snowy white hair, styled in a youthful cut, welcomed them and asked for his last name. She wrote the name Marsh on her pad and informed them there would be a short wait. "Would you care to wait in the bar? We have a live band performing—the Style Seekers."

"Oh! Let's!" cried Angela, tugging at Darian's arm with a wistful look on her face.

"Sure. Okay."

"We'll announce your name when your table is ready. It will be at least fifteen to twenty minutes."

Taking Darian's hand, Angela led the way. "Isn't this great?" she asked, looking back at him over her shoulder.

"What?' he asked, genuinely at a loss.

"The bar and the band, silly!" She giggled and squeezed his hand. "Here. This looks like a great table. It's right on the edge of the dance floor so we can see everything."

All the tables in the bar area were high with armchair bar stools. Turning the seat toward her, Angela stepped on the rail encircling the legs and hoisted herself onto the stool. She let the seat swivel to its natural position facing the table. Before Darian had a chance to sit down, she reached over and grabbed the seat of his chair, pulling it closer to hers. Without commenting, Darian sat down.

"This band is really cool. Don't you think?"

"Yeah," Darian answered, not knowing what else to say. He was not a music aficionado, regardless of the genre. Of course music wasn't foreign to him, but he never paid it enough attention to consider what was good and what was bad. It just was.

"Want to dance?"

"Uh..." Yet another thing that Darian knew nothing about. A feeling of discomfort crept through him, a state that tended to be unhealthy—for somebody.

"Two left feet?"

"What?" he asked.

"Two left feet. That means you don't think you dance very well."

"That's it exactly. Two left feet." Darian was relieved to have an excuse, but Angela was not to be thwarted. Her excitement about this night was not going to let something as insignificant as two left feet get in the way. Jumping off the bar stool, she grabbed Darian's hands and began pulling him toward the dance floor.

"Come on. I'll teach you. It's really very simple, and the dance floor is so crowded no one will even notice you!"

Darian was not convinced by her plea.

"Ple-e-ese!" Angela ceased pulling on him and moved in closer until her face was just below his. She was looking up at him like a little girl begging her daddy for a piggy-back ride. Without warning, she kissed him quickly on the lips. Before Darian could react, she pulled away again, urging him to follow her onto the dance floor.

Darian slipped off the stool and followed her. Smiling, Angela turned and threaded her way through the crowd until she found a spot near the wall but close to the band. She took Darian's hands and placed them on her waist. Placing her hands on his upper arms, she said, "Now, watch my feet. It's a really simple step. Once you learn it, you just do it over and over. Then, if you want, you can personalize it with a few steps of your own."

For three or four minutes Angela demonstrated the steps, encouraging Darian to try. Darian watched her feet as she stepped to the right and then tapped her left foot next to the right before stepping back to the left and repeating the process in reverse. He watched as she added in some quick movements to break the monotony. It looked rather idiotic to him, but looking around the room, Darian saw that apparently no one else shared his opinion. If this was part of the game men and women played, he thought, then he would master it.

"Okay, I have it," he told Angela after watching her for a few more minutes.

"You do?" Angela's surprise made her jump to the conclusion that Darian just wanted her to stop pushing him to dance. The music slowed down and stopped. The song was over. Some of the couples were moving off the dance floor. Angela turned and walked toward the table as the band struck up another song.

"What's the matter? I thought you wanted to dance!"

Stopping and turning toward him, she replied, "Oh! I do. I just thought...nothing."

"Is there something wrong?"

"Of course not. I thought you were embarrassed."

"Should I be?"

"No, but you haven't even tried to do the steps. I thought you were upset that I dragged you out here."

Knowing full well that no one could drag him anywhere against his will, Darian replied, "I watched your feet just like you told me to, but then the song ended."

Angela laughed. "You're an unusual guy, Darian!" Grabbing his arm, she said, "Let's dance." Expecting him to be awkward, she was amazed. It wasn't just that he'd committed the steps to memory. It was the fluidity of his movements. Perhaps the lack of any effort in the past made it easier for Darian to learn. *Maybe it's just beginner's luck,* she thought, *but he certainly got the hang of the rhythm and the steps quickly.* As she danced with him, she couldn't help thinking that he looked like a professional dancer—at one with the dance.

Angela would have understood if she had known more about him than just being a casual acquaintance. To dance well, there has to be an intimate relationship between the mind and the body. They have to work in concert with each other to express the rhythm and message of the music. For Darian who had been self-absorbed all his life, nothing else mattered in this world *except his* mind and *his* body. It was a very simple thing for him to absorb the music and use himself as an instrument of expression. This *particular* expression had just never occurred to him before.

Within minutes, Angela joined the others on the dance floor watching Darian move to the music. He had his eyes closed and was unaware that he was dancing alone until the music stopped and everyone applauded.

Looking around, Darian asked, "What's everyone clapping for?"

"You," Angela replied simply. Then she turned and walked back toward the table. Darian followed. Once she maneuvered herself onto the bar stool, she stared at the table top for a few minutes, running her fingernail along the incisal edges of her front teeth. Finally she looked up. "Are you making fun of me?"

"I haven't said a word," Darian replied, confused by the direction the conversation was taking.

"No. I mean by pretending that you couldn't dance."

"I've never danced before in my life."

Unwilling to believe such a statement, Angela cried, "This is not funny, Darian! I felt really stupid. There I was trying to teach you to dance, and you probably taught John Travolta!"

"John who?"

"Stop it! You know who I'm talking about, but it doesn't matter. I don't like being made fun of!"

Darian could see that. Despite the angry tone in her voice, her eyes were getting red, and her chin quivered in anticipation of a tearful outburst. Part of him was irritated by her aggressive behavior, but his instincts warned him it was just part of the mating ritual so he let it pass.

"Listen, Angela," Darian said, leaning across the table and taking her left hand, "I have never danced before. Honest. I just watched your feet and did what you did." Seeing that she was warming up, he added, "Maybe you're a better teacher than you thought."

"But, all that fancy stuff—I mean, it seems impossible that anyone could be that good the first time."

"I just personalized it like you suggested." Darian could see that she was pleased. "Besides, you said I was an unusual guy."

"You certainly are," Angela said, placing her right hand over his, "and I think I like it!"

"Marsh! Table ready for Marsh, party of two," announced a voice over the intercom. Darian and Angela slipped off their stools and wound their way through the tables to the front lobby where Robyn was waiting to seat them.

When Robyn saw Darian emerge from the bar, she moistened her lips, smiled brightly, and walked toward him. Angela stepped through the doorway and reached for Darian's hand. A frown passed rapidly across Robyn's face, and her beckoning smile changed into a perfunctory greeting.

"Well, hello, Robyn. It's nice to see you again!" Darian had not missed the sudden shift in her manner.

She merely smiled in answer. "Follow me, please," she said as she headed toward one of the several dining rooms off the main hall.

While Darian and Angela were eating, he saw Robyn stealing glances at his table every time she seated someone in the same dining area. He pretended not to notice.

"Darian, I'm really glad you asked me out tonight." Angela hesitated. She'd wanted to ask him this next question all evening but was unable to work up the nerve until now. Not until she saw Robyn looking at him for the umpteenth time. "How do you know Robyn?"

Darian looked at Angela and grinned. "Why?" he asked.

"I just...I just wondered." She felt really foolish. "She keeps looking at you like she knows you," she said, trying to save face but not succeeding.

"I met her here," replied Darian without any further explanation.

"Oh! I didn't realize you had been here before. Why didn't you tell me?"

"It didn't come up. Besides, I've only been here once before." He didn't think it necessary to mention that it was earlier today.

The waitress came up to the table. "Are you ready for dessert?"

"Could we?" Angela asked Darian.

"Of course."

"I want the Shamrock Surprise!"

"The what?" asked Darian.

The waitress answered for Angela. "It's a spice cake, filled with nuts and raisins and topped with a thick cream cheese icing tinted green." Turning back to Angela, she inquired, "Would you like a scoop of ice cream on the side? It comes with it, but some people prefer to leave it off."

"Yes, I want the ice cream. Thank you."

"You, sir?"

"Nothing, thank you." The waitress picked up their plates and left the table.

"Trying to make me look like a pig, eh?" Angela was smiling at him. "Tricked me into ordering, and then you fink out. How underhanded of you! Don't be expecting any sympathies from me when you see how good it looks." She reached across the table and tapped him on the nose. "You can't have any of mine!"

Darian laughed easily in response to her banter. "We'll see about that!"

Interacting with women wasn't all that difficult, he thought. Of course, the women he had encountered today were obviously attracted to him, and responding to them only enhanced the interactions. Nonetheless, Darian was pleased with his adeptness at manipulating their feelings. This newfound perspective of power continued to intrigue him. The intoxicating effects of being able to control these women so easily was more long lasting and interesting than his past exploits of simply seizing the life force from his prey. True, Angela and Robyn weren't terrified of him the way Joyce had been—although Mary probably was—but they were still caught in his web, a web housing a force far more foreboding than the humble spider.

As they rose to leave, Darian looked across the small dining room. Robyn had been bussing a table near the exit, but now she was staring directly at him. It was difficult for him to discern the emotion that was so evident on her face. Was it hurt? Perhaps the look of the betrayed? Or maybe it was plain and simple anger. Darian smiled at her and winked. Embarrassed by her own unconcealed expression, she quickly turned and resumed clearing the table. With his hand on Angela's back, Darian steered her around tables to exit the dining room. Without a second thought, he deliberately planned his path to walk past Robyn.

Having cleared the maze of tables, Darian released his hold on Angela, who continued walking toward the dining room exit. As he approached Robyn, he reached out and put his fingertips under her chin, pulling her head up. When she looked at him, he pursed his lips in a kissing gesture. She made no response except for the pain of her jealousy which was very clearly written across her face, even for Darian. He walked away without the slightest hesitation.

When he and Angela reached his car, Darian pretended to be counting his money before putting it in his pocket. "Hey! The cashier gave me too much change. I'd better take it back."

"That's really nice of you." Angela added this to her lengthening list of things she liked about him. "Wait, I'll walk back with you."

"No. It won't take a minute. I'll be right back. Besides, I meant to go to the restroom before we left." He opened her car door, and she sat down on the front seat. Before he shut the door, he handed her the keys. "Turn on the radio to keep you company until I get back."

"A poor substitute," she said as she took the keys.

Walking back into the restaurant, he asked the cashier where he could find Robyn.

"She's on break in the employee lounge. Would you like me to get her for you?"

"Do you think it would be all right if I went back there? We're friends, and I just need to tell her something real quick."

"Well, I guess so. I don't see why it would hurt anything. Go down the hall past the restrooms. You'll see a door with no sign on it. That's the employee lounge."

Darian followed her instructions. Opening the door, he looked quickly around the room. No one was there except Robyn. She was sitting at a table with her head bent forward and resting on her arms. She didn't bother to raise her head when he entered, assuming it was just a co-worker on break.

Locking the door behind him, Darian walked quietly across the room until he stood behind her. He gently placed his hands on her shoulders. She jumped, intending to rise out of the chair, but he held her firmly in place.

"It's only me, Robyn," he said.

"What are you doing here?" She tried to sound angry, but only sounded hurt.

"I came to see you."

"Yeah, right! What happened to your girlfriend?" she asked, not bothering to disguise her attitude.

"She's waiting in the car." Darian caught hold of her arm and pulled her up out of the chair, turning her toward him. He pulled her close to him until he could feel the roundness of her breasts against his chest. He slowly bent down and kissed her on the neck.

Robyn trembled but not from fright. The excitement of knowing that Darian was here, kissing her neck and caressing her while his date twiddled her thumbs in the car—well, it was one hell of an aphrodisiac. She knew she would let him have her here and now if he wanted her.

Darian, however, had no intention of carrying it that far, at least not now. He just wanted to keep her securely entangled in his web. He kissed her passionately on the mouth, holding her face in his hands, mimicking one of the illustrations he had seen on the paperbacks in Angela's house. Then he stepped back from her with his hands on her shoulder. "I have to go now. Would you like to see me again?"

"Yes," she answered quickly, afraid he would change his mind if she hesitated.

"I'll be in touch." He turned and left the room. Robyn sank back onto the chair, still trembling.

Getting into the car, Darian said, "Sorry it took so long." Looking at the clock on the dashboard, he added, "I'd better be getting you home."

Okay." Angela sounded disappointed.

Darian drove past her house and turned the corner. He pulled the car into the alley parking behind Angela's house.

"How did you know which one was mine?"

"I counted the number of houses to the corner when we drove past." He certainly wasn't going to divulge his earlier investigative excursion.

She got out of the car quickly without waiting for assistance. Walking around the car, she stopped at the gate. Turning to face Darian who had followed her, she said, "I really had a good time tonight. Do you think maybe we could go out again sometime?"

Darian was somewhat taken aback. He had intended to go in with her, but it was obvious she was stalling him for some reason. "Sure we can. I had a good time, too, Angela." He opened the gate, still thinking he would just follow her in.

"Well, good night." She stood on tiptoe and quickly kissed him on the mouth before hurrying down the sidewalk to the porch.

Darian just stood there staring after her. When she reached the porch, she turned and called out, "Darian!"

"Yeah?" he responded, still confused by the turn of events.

"I *really* like you!" Then she hurried into the house and shut the door.

Getting back into his car, Darian thought, *It must be part of the game.* He knew she was attracted to him. She even admitted it. *This must be why it holds such interest for people,* he thought. *Not everyone plays the game the same.* He smiled, thinking that this game was more intriguing by the minute. The game took hold of him the way craps and blackjack take hold of the gambler. The only difference was that in this game, the odds were definitely in his favor.

With nothing else to do, he drove away in the direction of Donovan's. Parking at the edge of the parking lot, Darian waited. The restaurant closed at nine o'clock on week nights, according to the marquee in front. The bar stayed open until ten, but he noticed there were only a few cars left in the parking lot.

It was ten minutes after nine when the front door of the restaurant opened and Robyn walked out. He watched her as she walked toward the opposite side of the lot. Starting his car, he drove toward her. She saw his headlights and instinctively moved to the left side of the aisle without turning around. He pulled up beside her, totally ready to master this game.

"You said you wanted to see me again," he said.

She looked up. Seeing who it was, she asked, "Are you serious?"

Crossing his eyes, he asked, "Do I look serious?" She laughed. "Get in."

"What about my car?"

"Where do you live?"

"An apartment a few blocks from here, but my roommate's home tonight. I could just leave my car, though, and we could go in your car."

"Okay." Darian wasn't quite sure where they were going, but so far in this game, he was finding it advantageous at times to let his prey lead him before showing his hand. He followed her to her apartment. After locking her car, she ran over and jumped in the front seat of Darian's car.

"Where would you like to go?" he asked.

"Well, it's kind of late, at least for this town. Did you just want to go somewhere we could talk and get to know each other?"

"Um-m-m..."

"Some place private?" Robyn asked, hoping to sweeten the pie.

"Yeah, that sounds good." At that moment he knew instinctively that she would do whatever he wanted her to do.

Crossing The Line

Chapter 27

Day 7 — Memphis

$\mathcal{M}$onday morning started early for Freddie as it always did. She was at her desk by 6:30 a.m., trying to catch up from her trip. Head bent over her desk working on her charting, an unusual noise brought her to full alert. Getting up, she looked out into the hall but saw no one. *Just my imagination working overtime,* she thought, which was not surprising after the events of her trip to Chicago.

She wished Joyce had come in early. She always got a lot more accomplished when the two of them worked together. Of course, she knew it wasn't fair to inflict her workaholism on Joyce.

Still, Freddie enjoyed this quiet time before others started to file in around 7 a.m., trying to get settled in before the New York markets opened at 7:30 central time. From the 30th floor of the Clark Tower, Freddie looked out over the city and imagined herself as being safe and secure in an ivory tower. The sounds of sirens and horns blowing had no meaning for her even though there was an unusual number of sirens this morning, but of course, it was Monday. The gates were open again, and people were mindlessly rushing into work, still in a daze, trying to make the transition from the weekend to the work week. Their mindless daze probably explained the need for so many sirens.

At 7:10, Maury Stein stepped into Freddie's office and closed the door. "Freddie, there's something I need to tell you."

For a brief moment Freddie stiffened, thinking he was going to fire her. Perhaps word had gotten back somehow about her and Ryan. Maybe the good ol' boys at the Union League Club had notified him she was a nutcase and didn't want her in their establishment anymore. Then she saw how pained he looked. She didn't think firing her would cause him that much pain, so she relaxed even though she was still curious. "What is it?"

"It's about Joyce," he said quietly. Freddie waited as Maury stood, wringing his hands, a motion she always thought too melodramatic for real life. Hesitantly, he said, "She's dead, Freddie."

"WHAT?!" Freddie jumped up from her chair, slamming it into the window behind her. All the usual things went through her head—a car wreck, a mugging. "How?" she demanded.

"It's kind of strange. The paramedics aren't really sure. She was found outside the elevators in the parking garage."

"Well? Was she knifed? Strangled? Did she have a heart attack? They have to have some idea!" Freddie was starting to hyperventilate. *Okay, don't overload. Don't lose it,* she thought. *Get yourself under control.*

Placing her hands on the desktop to steady herself, she listened as Maury told her what he had seen and heard. Joyce was found, lying on the floor of the elevator in the parking garage, by one of the brokers. The broker nearly fainted from shock when he saw her face. A grotesque look of terror was frozen on her otherwise lifeless face, and her skin was a strange grey color. The broker had also told Maury that his skin still crawled every time he thought about the look on her face.

Tears crept from the corners of Maury's eyes as he struggled to tell Freddie what had happened. Freddie's control broke. Maury walked around her desk and put his arm around her for a minute. Sensing she needed to be alone, he left. She wept in silence for nearly thirty minutes. Finally, she wiped her face off and retouched her makeup. Taking deep breaths, she opened her door and prepared to make her broadcast. Regardless of what gruesome event had taken place in their world, she knew the markets would continue to trade as if nothing had happened.

The day was finally over. Freddie was on her way home, but she was still traumatized. She couldn't settle her nerves about Joyce's death. No one seemed to know exactly what happened. *Life is becoming way too bizarre these days,* she thought. *Maybe the end times are coming early.* At this point, even the ridiculous prophecies of the doomsayers were beginning to seem reasonable to her. *Maybe the world is just a huge electrical circuit, and it's starting to short itself out. That would explain a lot!* she thought, desperate for any explanation.

As she drove, her mind was miles away from the traffic zipping in and out around her. A red glow in front of her snapped her back to the present. The car ahead of her was stopping. She slammed on the brakes, sliding to within a few feet of the stopped car. She saw the driver looking at her in his rear view mirror and saw his fist raised in the air. She ignored him and placed her hand on her chest in an attempt to coax it into slowing its pace. She couldn't tell if its frantic rhythm was because of the close call or the events over the last few days.

A psychiatrist sounds good right now, she thought but knew immediately it was not an option. Anyone, especially a psychiatrist, on the listening end of her story would just assume she was nuts! *Except...*she thought for a minute. *Maybe it wouldn't hurt to talk to Jodi's aunt. At least she can't have me committed.* It was decided. Tomorrow she would leave work early. She'd ask Jodi to take her. She knew her friend wouldn't refuse her.

Chapter 28

Day 8

$\mathcal{D}$arian opened his eyes and stretched his arms before clasping his hands behind his head. It was morning, but he didn't get up. He just lay there, staring at the ceiling of the cabin. Last night in the back seat of his car, parked at a lovers' lane, was the first time he had ever experienced sexual intercourse. It wasn't unlike when he'd consumed that entire pack of wild dogs the other day and afterwards returned quickly to his body. The impact of that much energy had generated a strange combination of excitement and fear. Last night was an echo of that experience.

Robyn, too, had experienced a wild mixture of feelings. Darian recalled that when she first cried out, he thought she was afraid. Yet, she held on to him so tightly that he'd have had to struggle to wrench himself loose. His own chaotic burst of emotions soon followed. Once the rush of emotions subsided, a lingering satisfaction settled over them both. Robyn was snuggling up close to him and kissing his chest.

Darian enjoyed not only the tremendous charge he experienced, but also the crazed obsession Robyn had exhibited. However, once the rush was over, he had no desire to continue even though he could tell she would have welcomed it.

Today he planned to enjoy another encounter, but not with Robyn. Her roommate created too many complications. Angela, however, was a different story. Her sudden coyness challenged him. It kept him from just filing this new experience away and moving on.

Thoughts of Freddie slipped into Darian's mind. He mused about what her reaction had been when she heard about Joyce. *Perhaps now she'll understand that I could do to her what I did to Joyce if I'd wanted to. Maybe she'll realize I'm trying to communicate with her.* He wondered why she wasn't like all the other women he'd met lately. The sight of him seemed to terrify Freddie. If she were anyone else, her terror wouldn't be a problem. If she would just cooperate, he thought, it would be so much easier.

Should he contact her again? Without being aware what was driving his decision, he concluded she needed time to digest what had happened. In truth, his attention was being sidetracked by this tantalizing new sexual adventure in power. As he'd told himself last night, *Power is power. The circumstances don't matter.*

Darian's experiences in the world were too narrow for him to know that centering his focus on random sexual experiences would drain away his own life force, distracting him with its cunning ability to excite and tease until it was too late—until he was in its clutches and the power he thought he had was gone, along with his quest.

Looking For Answers

Chapter 29

Day 8

*T*he house itself was ordinary-looking on the outside. It sat on one of maybe five streets that could jokingly be called a suburb of a small community in northern Mississippi. Freddie wasn't even sure if the town had a name. A short picket fence that had not seen a coat of paint in a long time was nestled around the edges of the front yard. Wild flowers were growing everywhere, extending their colors through the slats in the fence, giving it a charming appeal despite its otherwise derelict appearance.

There was no sidewalk—just a path worn smoothly into the ground from the passing of many feet over the years, winding its way from the gate to the porch steps. Looking at it, Freddie wondered if it was all planned. It was too perfectly wild.

Excited, Jodi walked ahead of Freddie, calling out, "Hello-o! We're here!"

A woman stepped out onto the porch. Freddie had expected an old woman, wrinkled and perhaps hunched over. Instead, the woman in front of her was strikingly beautiful. Her skin was a chestnut brown. There were wrinkles, but they were hardly noticeable. Her hair wasn't white. It was black with many streaks of white interspersed and pulled tightly into a bun at the nape of her neck. She stood tall and straight and looked more like a woman in her late thirties than a woman in her mid-fifties.

"Aunt Miya," cried Jodi as she rushed over to hug her, "this is Freddie, my best friend."

Aunt Miya nodded and extended her hand to Freddie. "You can call me Miya. I'm so glad to have you both here. Come inside and have something cool to drink." She turned and went inside.

Entering the house was like stepping back in time for Freddie. Jodi's aunt had retained all the decorations, tools, and furnishings she could from her heritage. Jodi was quick to point out that her aunt had created many of the crafts hanging on the wall herself.

Turning to Jodi, Miya asked if she had had a chance to visit the cabin she inherited from her grandparents by way of Miya. "Nope. It's on my calendar though!"

Freddie listened politely as Miya asked Jodi a lot of catch-up questions about her life. She even gave in to Jodi's insistence that she tell Freddie about their family history. Knowing that the telling was more for Jodi than Freddie, Miya gave a very shortened version.

Finally she turned to Freddie with a look of concern. "My child, I understand that strange things are happening to you. Do you want to tell me about them?"

Freddie shifted her weight in her chair. "It seems kind of silly in the light of day."

"Although the light can destroy evil, my child, there are times when the *light of day* is evil's best protection. You can convince yourself in the light of day that your imagination was the cause of your experiences, and your pride prevents you from examining it too closely. Thus, evil wins both the day and the night."

Feeling as if she had been suddenly immersed in an ice cold pool of water, Freddie's shoulders jerked in reaction. Without thinking, Jodi remarked, "Someone just walked over your grave." Realizing the bad form of her comment too late, Jodi said, "I'm sorry, Freddie. I wasn't thinking."

Lowering her voice, Jodi mumbled to herself, "Graves and ghosts. You are really stupid sometimes, Jodi!"

Freddie sat silently for a few minutes, staring at her hands, trying to sort out her thoughts. How could she explain the series of events recently? Lost in a maze of thoughts, it took a minute before she realized that once again she was looking at three hands, not two—this time in her lap. With a sharp intake of breath, she leaped out of the chair, squealing loudly and violently brushing her lap as if it were covered in ants. Jodi jumped up and reached for Freddie, but she jerked away and continued to slap at something mysterious on her lap.

"What is it?" Jodi shouted to be heard above Freddie's cries of terror. Miya took Freddie firmly by the shoulders. Freddie tried to pull away, but Miya's hold on her was strong.

"Look at me, child! Look at me!" She shook Freddie to get her attention. Then a stronger and unfamiliar voice declared, "I said, look at me!"

Startled, Freddie stopped her struggling. She and Jodi both stared at Miya. Although Miya was looking right into her eyes, Freddie wasn't sure who was talking. The last command had sounded like a man. The shock of it sobered Freddie enough that she temporarily forgot her terror.

The voice continued as Miya's lips moved in perfect synchrony. "Good," it said, obviously referring to Freddie being calm. "You cannot give into this evil, Freddie. You cannot lose control. It is closer than you think."

"How do I stop it?" Freddie asked in a small voice.

"It is time. You cannot stop it." Freddie's blood nearly curdled in her veins. Those were the same words Mr. Personality had used in her hotel room. Fear was building in her. She could feel its coldness moving through her body. She wondered if perhaps she was going to die. Right here. Tonight. In this very room. At least then it would be over.

Her curiosity, however, could not resist one last question. "Why me?" Her muddled brain was attempting in its typically methodical way to answer the question for her when a different emotion rose within her. Anger. It began as a warm feeling in her head, then her face. Her heart began to pound, and her hands clenched into fists.

"NO! I will not give in!" she shouted even before the voice speaking through Miya could answer. *Who does Mr. Personality think he is? He can't just dance in out of nowhere and take over my life or even take my life!*

Miya had not stirred. The male voice said, "Know this well. We live in the shadows we cast, and a turn of the head can change what we see and know with our five senses."

Miya's gaze shifted suddenly, and with a small sigh, her hands fell from Freddie's shoulders. She appeared to be recovering from a hypnotic trance.

Oblivious to her aunt's condition, Jodi asked, "What does that mean, Aunt Miya?"

"What does what mean?" her aunt asked in confusion.

"What you just told Freddie about living in shadows and things changing with a turn of the head."

"I'm sorry, sweetie, but the last thing I remember is grabbing Freddie by the shoulders to quiet her."

Jodi cast a meaningful glance at Freddie as if to say *I told you so* before turning back to her aunt. "Your voice changed, Aunt Miya. You sounded like a man. You warned Freddie about an evil that was coming and that she couldn't stop it. Then you said the part about the shadows and stuff."

Freddie broke in. She spoke quietly. "You said, 'Know this well. We live in the shadows we cast, and a turn of the head can change what we see and know with our five senses.' Then you let go of me."

Miya sat without speaking. Turning her head, she let her gaze move slowly around the walls of the room, taking in the artifacts remaining of her people. Jodi couldn't sit still any longer. "What is it?" she asked urgently. "This is making me nervous."

"It should," replied Miya. "It should."

Jodi jumped up and started pacing back and forth across the room. "All these cryptic remarks are driving me insane! Get to the point. Where did the voice come from, and what the hell are you all talking about?" She was shouting.

"Sit down, Jodi." Her aunt patted the seat next to where she had seated herself. "You, too, Freddie, and I will tell you both a story." Miya settled back against the sofa and began her story.

"Many, many years ago, long before the white man came to this land, there was a great Indian who was chief of his people. He was a kind and strong man. He had only two children, unusual for such a great chief, but his wife, daughter, and son were very special to him. His people believed that the Great Spirit favored him and his family. The Chief's people were well-treated and happy.

"One day a man entered the village. He was not known to any of the villagers, but in the giving spirit of their people, they welcomed him. They fed him and gave him new clothes. As they sat around the fires, they told stories of their great chief, of his goodness and his kindness toward his people.

"The man seemed interested, which encouraged the villagers to talk. They seldom saw strangers so they had few opportunities to tell these stories that reinforced their belief that the Great Spirit favored their Chief above all others. They were understandably proud. When the man asked to meet the Chief, he was told that their chief was out with a hunting party and would return in a few days. As the evening wore on, the villagers began leaving the camp fires for the comfort of their own hearths for the night. A place was provided for the stranger to sleep. So, little thought was given to him as they each wandered off to their sleeping quarters.

"When the sun was coming up over the horizon, there was a great wail that arose within the camp. The sleeping villagers awoke and rushed from their huts to discover their Chief outside his hut on his knees, wailing and tearing at his flesh.

"*What is wrong?* they asked. In the midst of his anguished cries, the Chief threw back the skin covering the entrance to his hut, The villagers gasped. The Chief's wife and children were lying on their mats. Their eyes were open, and their faces held a look of terror forever preserved in death. Their skin was grey, and there was no substance remaining in their forms. The villagers fell on their knees, crying in pain."

Freddie gasped, her hand rushing to cover her mouth. Miya continued, "Standing up, the Chief held the covering back for all to see. *Who is the cause of this?* he asked, looking at his people. Those nearest the hut sucked in their breath as one. Lying next to the mat of the son were the new clothes which had been given to the stranger. The villagers told their Chief of the stranger. Although many braves were sent to find him, he was nowhere to be found.

"The villagers did not know what to do. The Chief could not be consoled. He no longer laughed. He would not eat. He would only sit and stare into the distance. His sadness was like a dark shadow over the village. The moon went through its cycle, and nothing changed.

"One morning the village awoke, and the Chief was no longer there. Scouts were sent out to search for him because they feared the great sadness had killed him. A single scout saw him from a great distance, saw him walking into the forest. He never came out.

"Over the years medicine men have passed on stories about what happened to this great Chief. They say the spirits told them the Chief walked into the forest where he was led to a great grey wolf, who had suffered the same kind of loss. The wolf stood alone on a rock outcropping howling. As the Chief watched him, he embraced his pain, and he, too, began to howl. As they howled in unison, the tremendous energy generated by their pain intermingled. No longer feeling an attachment to this earthly plane, their life forces joined and became one. From that day on, being neither man nor beast and yet being both, they have sought out the spirit of evil to destroy it.

"As time passed, the medicine men tell us, they recruited others to serve their cause. Their warriors are called Avatar because they are an embodiment of the spirit of the Great Chief and the Wolf. These warriors are most often embodied in the forms of wolves." Miya paused. She seemed concerned about something.

In her usually blunt way, Jodi asked, "What has this got to do with anything?"

"The voice you say you heard speaking through me...what you say it said...the only time I ever heard those words before was from my grandfather, the one who told me of the Avatar. He said the spirit of the Great Chief rarely chooses to speak *through* a human, using the voice from his earthly time, unless an evil is approaching the intensity of the one who stole the lives of his family."

Miya flicked her hand in dismissal toward the door. Freddie turned and saw a young man standing there. He looked at her and then turned and walked away. "My son," said Miya. Turning back toward Freddie, she said, "Child, I think it is time for you to tell me everything that has happened so far."

Freddie hesitated for a second. She had no way of knowing if the story Miya told them had anything at all to do with her. Although the look of terror on Joyce's face that Maury described sounded a lot like those on the faces of the Chief's family, Freddie was reasonably sure Maury had exaggerated. Freddie hadn't seen any wolves either, but the bottom line was that she couldn't deny she needed help. So, over the next thirty minutes, Freddie recounted in as much detail as possible everything that had happened, including the vision of the third hand in her lap earlier.

Chapter 30

$\mathcal{F}$reddie sat alone on the sofa in her den, her knees pulled up to her chin and her head resting on them. Her arms were wrapped so tightly around her legs, that if she turned loose, it would be easy to imagine seeing her arms and legs flop wildly around until all her limbs regained their proper positions—like one of those toy snakes tightly folded into a can and released with a flurry when the cap was removed.

The sun had set some time ago, but she didn't bother to turn on the lamp. The night sky was filled with clouds, masking the light of the moon. Shadows were creeping out from the edges of the room, but the backyard light at her neighbor's house kept the den from succumbing to complete darkness.

Freddie had been sitting with her eyes closed for so long, it no longer felt like she was in her den. Her mind wandered lazily. Recent events had so overwhelmed her that control was difficult to maintain. It was easier to just give in and let her mind wander aimlessly through the craziness. An inertia gradually took over, a heaviness making her unable to move until finally she didn't even want to.

Freddie had experienced the inertia before. She recognized it as simple depression, a normal reaction to stressful events. She was absolutely certain the last few days qualified as stressful by anyone's standards! What she feared, however, was that hopelessness would take over her life again if she didn't regain control.

In her late teens and early adulthood, she suffered from depression so badly that she literally created a means of stepping out of life. She developed headaches so severe her doctor had insisted on a hospital stay to run neurological tests. He suspected a brain tumor. Deep down inside, beyond the depression, Freddie knew there wasn't one. She knew that this pain, although real, was of her own creation. College scared her. Life scared her. As a teenager, she had written poems that in today's over-analyzed world would have been a red flag for a potential suicide—like this verse from a poem written when she was fifteen. *Death is the only way this fear will end / It's such a sweet sound to my ear / because gone will be the trials of life. / Then I'll have nothing to fear.*

Freddie had actually made a suicide attempt once, but something strong within her kept her from taking it far enough to be successful. Of course, at the time she viewed it as just another failure. She knew now it was only her fear of the unknown that drove her to such extremes, but that was exactly what was scaring her now—the unknown.

After Miya listened to the things Freddie had seen, she had told her some things Freddie wasn't sure she wanted to hear. Miya said that a great war between Good and Evil had been going on since the beginning of time. She explained that Life itself is the struggle between these two opposites, that we shift from side to side, positive to negative in trivial events every day, and the impact isn't necessarily significant. However, Miya warned, this time, the evil stalking Freddie was not only significant, it was intense and dangerous. She cautioned Freddie she could not survive against such an evil adversary unless she turned to the Great Spirit for help.

How did I get caught in this struggle? Freddie had no idea what was going on or why it was happening to her. She'd never been religious. Oh, she believed that there was a Power greater than herself responsible for the creation of life as she knew it. She just couldn't buy the idea that life could be boiled down to good versus evil, despite Miya's attempts to explain the universality of the conflict.

Was life just a cruel game? It reminded her of a movie she saw once that was all about a game pitting people against the system with death being the downside. To live, you had to win the battle against the system, the evil pursuer. She'd hated the movie, and she hated this, but there was obviously no button to press for opting out.

Whatever this thing was, in her heart she knew it wasn't going away.

The time is now. At least that's what all the ghostly apparitions in her life were saying. For what it was worth, Freddie was pretty sure she wasn't insane. It didn't explain what was going on, but it went a long way toward calming her. At least the complete chaos surrounding her was not of her own making.

She did need to make a decision about what path she was going to take. Not only had Miya made it clear, but her own instincts told her she needed help—help that went beyond what was available from anyone she knew. She began flicking through options in her mind. Her old self struggled to get back into operation. If she could just organize everything in her mind, she might be able to beat this *thing*, whatever it was.

Okay, she thought. *What are my options?* First, she could consider Miya's suggestion—meditation—but Freddie had shrugged this off when Miya recommended it. The first thought that came into her mind was sitting cross-legged on the floor chanting monosyllables and expecting something to magically happen. Freddie was a doer. Her kinesthetic side made her feel safer, more in control. Meditation seemed too "airy-fairy" to her.

Thinking back over all these events in the comfort of her sofa, Freddie couldn't shake the feeling that Mr. Personality seemed familiar somehow. But how could that be? Her parents kept popping up in her head. Did he remind her of them? *Too weird*, she decided, shrugging it off.

Frowning as she tried to get his features clear in her mind, she realized she had never seen him clearly even though he was in the same room. There were always shadows or just a general sense of vagueness about him. It reminded her of an impressionistic painting. From a distance your eyes fill in the missing refinements, not only with lines but with your own experiences. You see what you expect to see. That was the beauty of impressionism to Freddie. It was more personal than any other style of painting, but if you moved in too close, you couldn't pick out the features of the people in the painting or even begin to describe what they might look like.

This described her experience with Mr. Personality. But even so, he seemed familiar. Was she just imposing her experiences, filling in the missing spaces, or was he familiar for a reason? Freddie sensed that the answer to this question could be the key to discovering who he was.

Still sitting on the sofa, she emerged from her reverie enough to realize that the sun had set. "My God, what time is it?" Flicking on the lamp, she looked at the clock. It was eight-thirty. She'd been sitting there for an hour and a half! It seemed like only a few minutes had passed. Reaching for the phone, Freddie dialed Jodi's number.

"Hello?"

"Hey! It's me."

"What's going on?"

"Nothing much. I've been thinking about everything—about what your aunt said and what happened at her house." She paused.

"And?" Jodi used the same tactic on Freddie that Freddie often used on her to get her to open up and talk about her feelings. Freddie recognized the ploy.

"And nothing. I must have fallen asleep. I woke up on the sofa with cramps in my legs from sitting in a fetal position for so long."

"Well, what were you thinking about *before* you fell asleep?" Jodi could be as persistent as Freddie.

"I told you what I was thinking about."

"Okay. What did you think about the things you thought about?"

Freddie couldn't help but laugh at her friend. "You are a nosy witch!"

"Me??! You weasel everything out of me, and you call me a nosy witch?"

"Okay. Okay. I was thinking about the things Miya said."

"You said that already." Jodi remarked.

"Well, I'm having a little trouble taking some of the things she said seriously. I mean, come on, a man merging with a wolf? How crazy is that?"

"I learned a long time ago not to question her stories. I know it sounds a bit crazy," conceded Jodi, "but what do you call what you've been seeing?"

"Point taken," replied Freddie.

"Okay. So you find it a little hard to believe that a man merged with a wolf. How do you explain the voice we heard speaking through Aunt Miya?"

"Well..."

"Okay then. Go ahead. Explain Mr. Personality to me." Jodi's voice was edged with sarcasm.

"I can't," said Freddie, a whisper of defeat in her voice.

"Are you just going to ignore everything she said?" asked Jodi, sounding frustrated with her friend. Freddie was usually so take-charge that it troubled her to see Freddie giving in to this...this.. whatever it was.

"No, but what am I expected to do? Miya said I needed to learn to meditate, to get in touch with God. Then what? Is God going to fight this battle, if it is a battle, for me? For heaven's sake, Jodi, put yourself in my place. What would you do?"

"Well, I happen to think she's right about life being a battle between good and evil. I mean, think about it. Just about every situation you can imagine comes down to a choice between what we see as right and wrong, good and evil, God and the Devil. I never thought much about it before, and I didn't really expect to see evil in the form of a person, but why is that so incredulous? We grew up with stories of the boogeyman, and the churches preach about the Devil. What are these things if not evil personified?"

"I can't believe that all life amounts to is good versus evil. In the grand scheme of things, that puts life on the level of a B movie!"

In a tone more serious than usual, Jodi replied, "I don't know what to tell you, Freddie. I don't have the answers, but I do know one thing. This situation isn't going away, and I feel in my heart this is a crossroads for you and perhaps for others you don't even know."

Listening to Jodi voice the same conclusions she had come to earlier, Freddie sighed. "I'll call you later. You're right. I do have to make a decision about where to go from here." Hanging up, she resumed her position on the sofa.

Chapter 31

Day 9

$\mathcal{F}$reddie awoke with her head on the arm of the sofa. Despite sleeping the night in such an awkward position, she was incredibly rested. She sat up and stretched her arms above her head, clasping her hands together and interlacing her fingers. Feeling her muscles relax, she stood and went to the kitchen.

Coffee sounded great to Freddie right now. With her new, stainless steel coffee brewer, the coffee she made at home finally tasted like it did at a restaurant. Gone was the aftertaste that made her think it had been lightly seasoned with melted plastic. Freddie was so engrossed in making the coffee that her problems had failed to find their way to the surface. This was the first morning in nearly a week she had awakened without being afraid to open her eyes. She actually felt good.

Freddie sat down at the breakfast room table. Placing her elbows on the table, she held her coffee cup within inches of her nose so she could smell it. She could see the sun struggling to rise above the tree line. What a beautiful day!

As she sipped her coffee, the first fragments of the problems that had besieged her thoughts yesterday surfaced. Strangely, the numbing fright that had held her immobile then had dissipated. She was almost peaceful. She couldn't explain how, but during the night, she had apparently made a decision. Looking at the clock, Freddie realized she was going to be late for work if she didn't hurry.

She arrived at the office earlier than usual despite her late start. Freddie wanted to catch up with Maury before he was waylaid by a client or another analyst. The office felt abandoned. Joyce's personal belongings were gone, and the desk top had been cleared. Freddie was unable to suppress a shudder, thinking about what had happened.

Going into her office, Freddie saw that there were a lot of papers on her desk. Most were neatly stacked as she had left them, but there were some new stacks she didn't recognize. Then she realized that someone had cleared out Joyce's desk and placed the contents on her desk. Putting her purse in the bottom drawer of her desk, she heard the front door to the office open. She looked down through the common area to see that Maury had arrived.

Everything is in Divine Order, she thought. *He came in early, too!* Raising her arm to get his attention, Freddie called out, "Maury, can I talk with you a minute?"

"Sure," he said as he passed her office door. "Just let me put my things away." In a few minutes, he returned.

"What do you need?" he asked, leaning against the door frame.

"Maury, I want to take a leave of absence." Freddie unwittingly clenched her hands. It was a nervous habit that appeared when she was afraid of the outcome of a situation.

"Why?" Maury asked, frowning. He wasn't insensitive to what Freddie might be feeling after Joyce's death, but Hayden was pressuring him for vacation time, and he was already short an analyst. His prime metals analyst had succumbed to the offer of more money from another firm, and now Freddie was wanting a leave of absence?

"I've got some serious personal problems, Maury, and they're affecting my ability to concentrate. You know I've never asked for time off or for anything else, but with the way my life is going at the moment, I can't call the markets in a responsible way. It could be a bigger problem for me to be here than if I were gone for a while."

Maury looked at her for a minute. "Are you sure this isn't just because of what happened to Joyce? I know you worked together, and I know you liked her."

Freddie interrupted him. "It didn't help my state of mind any, but it's not the problem right now. I just need the time." Freddie realized she wasn't sure that Joyce wasn't part of the problem, especially since talking to Miya.

"How long?" Maury was thinking he could call Freddie's markets while she was gone. It would give him a chance to prove he hadn't lost his touch. Calling such high profile markets as the financial instruments could be a kick, too.

"Three months," replied Freddie.

"*Three* months?!" said Maury, shaken out of his fantasies and looking at her as if she were crazy. "Three months?" he repeated. Maury wasn't sure he wanted to put himself on the line again calling markets for three months, at least not something as volatile as the financial instruments had become.

"I know it seems like a long time, and I know it's a lot to ask, but I promise not to ask you for any more favors for the next three years. I'll teach every class in Chicago until the day I die, and I'll do all kinds of PR for the department."

Maury didn't answer. He stared into her eyes for a long time. She managed to hold perfectly still.

"Okay," he said. "Somehow, I feel this isn't a choice of whether I give you a leave of absence. It feels more like a choice of whether you take a leave of absence or just leave. Am I right?" Maybe Maury knew her better than she thought.

"You're right. I didn't realize it until you said it, but it's true. I have to go. What I'm really asking you is…can I come back?" Freddie knew there was no turning back now.

Maury nodded. "Your place will be waiting for you when you return. When are you leaving?"

"At the end of the day today." Freddie reached out and shook hands with Maury. "Thanks, Maury. I'll never forget this."

Maury grinned and nodded his head affirmatively, trying to lighten the mood. "You better not!" Freddie wondered if she'd been misjudging Maury all this time. Turning to leave, Maury said, "Don't forget to leave me your desk charts and anything that will keep me from looking like an idiot!"

Freddie laughed. "Yeah, right! Don't worry. I'll even write the broadcast for tomorrow."

"Good. That's good." Maury pulled the office door closed, wondering if he would survive the next three months. He had given up full time analysis for management, and in this business, it doesn't take long to be out of step. He said a silent prayer as he walked down the hall to his office.

Freddie sat down at her desk and picked up the phone. There were details she needed to handle before the day was over. The markets wouldn't be much of a distraction because they were currently moving like their feet were mired in molasses. It resembled the markets in 1979 when she began "calling them" for the company. When they exploded in the spring of that year, she fought to keep them and keep them she had. She became the analyst for the premier markets. Freddie knew how enviable her position was and only hoped the markets were still hers when she got back!

The phone was ringing for the fourth time. Ordinarily Freddie would have hung up, but knowing Jodi, she'd just let it ring. There was absolutely no telling what Jodi was doing. So it was best to give her time to untangle herself from whatever project was currently claiming her attention.

"You got me!" Breathless, Jodi answered the phone as unconventionally as she did everything else.

"What if I don't want you?" Freddie remarked, trying to disguise her voice.

"Huh?"

"You mean I actually managed to make you speechless?"

Jodi laughed. "Not really. I was just trying to imagine someone not wanting me."

"You idiot. You're absolutely hopeless!" Both women laughed

because they never took the other's jabs seriously. In a more sober tone, Freddie asked, "How do you feel about my using your cabin for a short respite? Say, two or three months."

"Two or three months? Should I charge rent?"

"I hope not." Freddie laughed.

"What's going on? What about your job?"

"I took a leave of absence. I'm going to find out what is going on in my life if I have to tear it apart from stem to stern."

Jodi's cabin sat in the middle of twenty acres of woods. There was even a small lake, but it wasn't really that far from civilization, just twenty miles over the Mississippi line. It had belonged to her grandparents, Miya's parents. A few months earlier Miya had moved into the house where they had visited her. Freddie didn't know why Miya had made the move, but it was a perfect solution for her right now.

"How are you going to go about tearing apart your life out in the boonies?" asked Jodi.

Freddie knew Jodi was poking fun at her while seriously wanting an answer to her question. "I plan to meditate on the problem, and I need a quiet place to do it."

"You really believe you'll find answers in meditation?"

"No. I plan to do some research, too, but I thought it wouldn't hurt to explore all my options. Besides, your cabin's close enough to civilization that I still have reasonable access to information."

"Well, it's okay with me, but I have to admit that I'm really curious about what's going on myself. Do you mind if I help?" Before Freddie could answer, Jodi continued, "By the way, I spoke to Aunt Miya this morning. She's more agitated than I can ever remember her being."

"Did she have a vision?" Jodi had told her that Miya was known to have them, and she was anxious for any information that might clarify her own thoughts.

"No. She says the visions are for you. She seems to think the

Great Chief will communicate with you at some point. I told her that was all you needed—another *spirit* appearing."

"Boy! I can go along with that!"

Changing the subject, Jodi said, "You said *information.* What kind of information are you looking for?"

"I need to find out more about my family. I need to know where I came from, who my ancestors were, anything I can come up with."

"Why? What makes you think it has something to do with your heritage?"

"Nothing specific. It's just that Mr. Personality seems so familiar."

"Oh, yeah?" Jodi was surprised. Although Freddie had mentioned his looking familiar the night Jodi had seen him in the foyer, it never occurred to her that he might be linked to her family. This gave everything a new twist and not a particularly nice one. Why would one of her relatives be involved in something like this? "Didn't you tell me that all your parents' relatives were dead?"

"As far as I know."

"Well, if they're all dead..." Jodi's voice trailed off into silence as she realized that she didn't like the direction this logic was taking.

Freddie spoke up. "If they're all dead, and they are somehow connected to Mr. P., then I'm in deep shit. If they're not all dead, and one of them is connected to this whatever it is, then perhaps I can resolve the problem."

"I'm not sure I would want to find my relatives if they were connected to this," Jodi remarked. "Regardless, it sounds like a huge project. Look, you know I can help. I can get information out of anyone about anything."

"I know and don't think it hasn't crossed my mind. I was rather hoping you would stay with me at the cabin, at least for a little while." Freddie hated asking for this kind of commitment from Jodi. She had always taken care of her own problems, but she really needed a friend right now.

Jodi was not only a friend but very flexible. She had been on disability for several years now. Her "craziness" had finally erupted at work one day when she discovered her boss was giving her commissions to his "secretary." It was the icing on the cake, and she blew. Her boss had been screwing over Jodi all along, but she had finally reached her limit. She knocked the computer off her desk along with everything else in reach. In reaction, the company insisted on a psychiatric examination. She was officially tagged as manic-depressive.

It was true that Jodi sometimes did crazy things that might qualify as "manic" to a stranger. To someone who knew her, however, it was just another attempt to get attention and to be the kid she never got to be. It was also true that she could get depressed but no more than Freddie had in her own life.

Besides, if your life isn't working, and you aren't getting any pleasure out of it, why not create a little excitement? Of course, to the conservative psychiatric community, an act such as "letting my hair down, holding my arms out and turning in circles until I'm dizzy" might seem a strange thing for a grown woman to do. To Jodi, it was just a way to break up the monotony.

The diagnosis, however, provided her with an income and plenty of free time. Wiser than the psychiatrists she was forced to see regularly, she left her alcoholic husband shortly after that because she knew things could never get better with him in her life. Since then, she'd used her time to get involved in all kinds of volunteer work, and she was having a ball! Most important to Freddie right now was that Jodi didn't have to punch a time clock.

Chapter 32

Day 11

$\mathcal{N}$ot going to work yesterday felt very strange to Freddie. Her life was so predictable that any break in the routine of work and sleep required an adjustment period. Consequently, vacations weren't that enjoyable. By the time she learned to relax, it was time to go home. If she took a month's vacation, she might be able to squeeze two weeks' worth out of it.

The first year she was an analyst, Freddie went to Disney World. Every day she was on the telephone until 3:00 p.m. following the markets. Then she spent a couple of hours updating her charts, which she had taken along, naturally. Then if there was anything left of the day, she would go out to a restaurant for dinner and walk around. To this day, her memories of Disney World were limited to a hotel room and a couple of restaurants. Of course, her current trip wasn't a vacation so she would still be working. Only this time, it wasn't about profit and loss. It could well be about life and death.

Her luggage was open on the bed. She had packed comfortable clothes—jeans, slacks, T-shirts, a few blouses, a light jacket, and a few pairs of shoes, including some hiking boots in case she decided to strike out for a walk around the property. Looking around, Freddie decided she had packed all the clothes she'd need. She placed the case for her personal IBM Selectric II typewriter beside the bed. It was brand-new on the market. Freddie had promised herself she'd wait until all the bugs were worked out of things before she invested in them, but she never did. She stuffed legal pads, pens, pencils, paper clips, a small stapler, several manila folders, some stationery and envelopes in her briefcase. If she ran out, she could always drive back into town. Closing her briefcase, she took one last look around.

Glancing at her watch, Freddie noted she had at least an hour before Jodi arrived. They were taking both cars. Freddie could go on ahead, but she told Jodi she was concerned about getting lost. The truth was that Freddie wasn't ready to be alone in a cabin in the middle of the woods. Gathering up her luggage, she carried it to the garage so she would be ready when Jodi arrived.

Placing the last piece of luggage on the back floorboard of her car, Freddie decided to watch television while she was waiting. It might stave off dwelling on unpleasant possibilities. There was nothing on, however, except the usual morning cornucopia of talk shows. After flipping through several channels, Freddie just let it rest on the last. One was as good as another. After a few minutes of watching the corny antics of the host, Freddie's mind slipped into neutral, and she dozed off.

In her dream, she was walking down a path in the woods. Trees hugged the path in a tight embrace. Their leaves were just beginning to fall, and the path was strewn with splashes of orange, red, and yellow. She stopped and looked behind her. The colorful path turned about 500 feet behind her. She saw nothing but trees. In front of her, the path gently curved to the left.

Having no idea where she was, Freddie continued in the direction she was going. Her pace increased as her anxiety grew. She had seen nothing to tell her what lay ahead. Finally, she was able to see a little further around the curve and spotted a sign beside the path. She quickened her pace, only slowing when she could read the words.

END—2 miles.

Thank goodness, she thought. *At least I'll be out of these woods, and two miles isn't so far.* After a while, another sign appeared.

BEGINNING—1 mile.

That's odd. How does something begin where it ends? She knew she had walked at least a mile, which meant that the end of this path should be about a mile from where she was.

At the end of the next mile, Freddie spotted another sign. She could tell that the path did not end despite the large word printed on the sign—END. As she approached, she realized there was another sign immediately behind it. Stepping to one side, she saw in big letters the word BEGINNING.

This doesn't make any sense. The only way this could be true is if the path is a circle. Obviously, if the path was a circle, following it was ludicrous. She walked a few steps to see if the path continued on past the curve. Standing still for a few minutes, she decided that she had no choice but to continue. She had no idea where she was, and the trees were so thick with underbrush, she would never be able to push her way through them.

After a while Freddie rounded a curve and realized she had indeed come full circle. Losing her well-honed reserve, she plopped down in the middle of the path and began to cry. She had no answers, no Plan B. Totally miserable, she pulled her legs up close to her body, wrapping her arms around her knees, a now familiar position, closed her eyes and wept.

When she could cry no more, she simply sat where she was. There was no reason to get up. A tingling sensation traveling up her spine warned her that she was not alone. Her head jerked up, looking in all directions. Standing about ten feet from her was a wolf. Freddie was terrified. Her heart thumped in her chest, and her mind raced around in an effort to develop a plan for escape. If she ran, she would be the loser for sure. She didn't think she could climb a tree fast enough to escape his reach. If she sat still, perhaps he would tire of her and go away. Not the best plan, but the only one she had. Remembering what she had read about dogs, she looked him right in the eye, trying not to break contact first.

For a moment, neither moved. Her eyes started to water. Then the wolf walked slowly toward her. The light filtering through the trees flickered off the wolf's back. His fur sparkled like the little silver icicles Freddie used to hang on the Christmas tree when she was a girl. Fascinated and scared at the same time, Freddie didn't move. She couldn't move.

The words *you know the answer* popped into her head. *Where did that come from?* she wondered. It was a masculine voice, and none of the voices in her head, except Mr. Personality, had ever been male! Again she heard the words. Freddie knew she must be on the edge of flipping out. Yet, as crazy as it sounded, Freddie believed the wolf was talking to her. She saw subtle expressions flit across his face, in his eyes. Expressions that hinted at interaction on his part.

Then the voice spoke again. *The answer is within you. You will have to search hard to uncover it, but you have no choice. It is time, and you cannot stop it from happening. You can change the outcome, however, if you try. Remember, you are not alone.*

All the while the voice spoke, Freddie never broke eye contact with the wolf. Somehow he was speaking to her. His message that she was not alone filled her with courage.

Suddenly a harsh buzzer sounded, causing Freddie to jerk awake. The dream or vision or whatever it was faded as she hurried to answer the door. Seeing Jodi standing on the porch, obviously packed and ready to go, Freddie was tempted to share her dream with her. Instead, she decided to give herself time to think it through on the drive.

When Freddie finally pulled up in front of the cabin, she was glad, but a little nervous. The drive down the country roads with tree branches hanging over to form a canopy had reminded her of her dream except that she was driving a car.

"Well, it's still standing! That's a good sign." Jodi hollered at Freddie as she got out of her car. "Come on. Let's check it out and then bring in the luggage. I could use a cup of coffee!"

A little while later, Jodi was stoking the fire with a poker. The weather here in the South at this time of year could be cool, but it didn't normally warrant a fire. She just always liked having one. "There! Perfect. Am I the best fire-builder you ever saw or what?"

Laughing, Freddie responded, "I can't resist voting for the *or what*!" Jodi grabbed the pillow on the chair closest to the hearth and flung it. Freddie tried to dodge, but Jodi was too quick. The pillow struck its target. "Thank God nothing dangerous was within reach!"

"That's right, and you would be well-advised to scan the surroundings before you toss another of your smart-aleck remarks in my direction. I'm at the top of the game when it comes to lightning-fast retaliation!"

Jodi curled the fingers on her right hand, blew on her fingertips, and rubbed them on her shirt in a boasting gesture. Then she plopped down on the sofa and threw her feet up onto the ottoman. Freddie followed suit.

"Do we start right away, or are we going to take the night off?" Jodi was only half joking. She knew she'd have a clearer head in the morning.

Freddie stared at the flames in the fireplace. "I'm not sure there is such a thing as taking time off from this. Right before you got to the house this morning, I fell asleep watching one of those monotonous talk shows."

"So, what else is new?" Jodi interjected.

Ignoring her comment, Freddie continued. "I had a dream, a really strange dream. I don't know if it means anything or not. I mean, are dreams just your imagination at work or does an inroad open up when you're asleep through which the Universe communicates what your conscious mind holds at bay during your waking hours?"

"Whoa! This is way too philosophical for me—at least until I've had my caffeine hit."

"I'm serious, Jodi!"

"Okay. I was just trying to lighten the mood." Jodi shifted her weight so she could turn sideways and give Freddie her full attention.

Freddie described her dream. When she got to the part about the wolf, she hesitated, knowing where Jodi would go with this. Regardless, she decided, she had to tell the whole story. As expected, Jodi dropped her feet to the floor and perched herself on the edge of the sofa cushion.

"Whoa! Remember the wolf Aunt Miya told us about? The one who merged with the Great Chief?" Freddie nodded. "Do you suppose it's related?"

Freddie glanced back toward the fireplace, hoping to find an answer in the hypnotic flames as their colors shifted from red to orange to gold to yellow. "I have no idea," she said finally. "I mean, if this is just an ordinary dream, it's probably just a conglomeration of everything I've heard recently, including the story Miya told."

"What if it isn't just an ordinary dream? What if it's a vision?"

"If it's a vision, I can't give you an informed answer because visions are outside the realm of logic."

Speaking in a patronizing tone, Jodi replied, "Well, letting go of logic and rational thinking for a moment—I know this will be difficult, but try." She raised her eyebrows, cutting off any smart remarks Freddie might be planning. "If visions are meant to impart knowledge to you that it's impossible to receive any other way, don't you think it might be wise to examine this a little further? I mean, try to understand what the things in the vision mean. Like, what about the screwy road signs and going in a circle, not to mention the talking wolf."

Freddie didn't answer right away, and Jodi was wise enough to let the silence abide. Freddie struggled to determine how you investigate something as intangible as a dream. Of course, those who doubted the validity of what she did for a living—analyzing price charts with no regard for tangible "causes," such as crop reports and so on—contended that her profession was more soothsayer than analyst. Freddie knew they were wrong. Charts *were* tangible evidence of real activity, and the predictable patterns had proven themselves over and over again.

Of course, even with the charts, an intuitiveness was required to call the markets well, an intuitiveness that separated the "men from the boys." Yet, it was no more than was required in any style of investment trading. This dream or vision was different though. There was absolutely nothing tangible to prove it had even occurred. There was no record. It was totally a memory, one she was starting to question.

"Hello-o-o." Jodi cocked her head, waiting for Freddie to come back to the present.

"I was just thinking about what you said. I don't know where to begin." Freddie stood and walked to the refrigerator. Opening the door, she reached in and pulled out a bottle of Brit Free, a new non-alcoholic wine she had brought from home. She kept the label turned away from Jodi as she poured them both a glass. She knew Jodi would harass her if she knew. Besides she wanted to see if Jodi even noticed.

Seeing Jodi get up, she quickly put the bottle back in the refrigerator and said, "That's okay. I've got it. I'll bring it to you."

"Cool! At least I'm getting a butler out of all this, not to mention free wine!" Freddie grinned, knowing that Jodi would eventually see the bottle and then there would be hell to pay. Taking her glass, Jodi sipped the wine and settled back against the arm of the sofa. "Well, what are you going to do?"

Freddie sipped her wine slowly. Biting the corner of her bottom lip, she said, "I suppose I need to consider everything as evidence even though I can't touch it, see it, or smell it. I have to accept that everything involved with this investigation, not just the dream, is totally atypical. If I don't, I won't make any headway. In the morning I'll start trying to sort everything out."

Freddie raised her glass of faux wine. Jodi raised hers until the rims of the two glasses touched and waited for her friend to speak.

"Here's to discovery and resolution!" declared Freddie. *I hope that toasting with fake wine isn't a bad omen,* she thought as they each drank to the toast.

Freddie settled back on the sofa to watch the dancing flames. Two hours later when the last ember blinked out, both women were lightly snoring. Freddie was curled into a fetal position with her head on the arm of the sofa. She had fallen asleep before Jodi, who was stretched out with her feet on the ottoman. Lying beside her on the sofa, label side up, was the bottle of Brit Free.

Chapter 33

Day 12—Mississippi

Jodi announced she was taking a long hike to clear the cobwebs in her head. "Maybe the antidepressants will kick in," she remarked. Jodi's banter concerning her medications always amused Freddie. Although the subject wasn't comedic material, the way Jodi dealt with it was.

"Come out on the porch," Jodi told Freddie. "I want you to know which way I'm going."

"Are you planning to get lost?"

"Not if I can help it, but you never know. If the antidepressants kick in, I might have a burst of enthusiasm and wind up in the next county!"

"Okay. At least I'll know which way to point when I call in the local sheriff," Freddie laughed.

"I'm serious,"

Frowning, Freddie asked, "Serious about what—your meds or getting lost?" Freddie joked, but she was a bit concerned. it wasn't like Jodi to be so cautious. "What's wrong?"

"Nothing's wrong. I just think we should keep tabs on each other. I mean, duh, we *are* in the middle of nowhere here, and there are other evils lurking in the world besides Mr. Personality, you know."

Jodi started across the clearing. She had almost reached the path leading into the woods when she turned and hollered back to Freddie. "By the way, the neighbors who live farther up the road have a large dog who wanders everywhere. He's a friendly mutt, but a very large mutt. He won't hurt you, but please don't feed him!"

"Why?"

"Because Miya said you'll never get rid of him if you do," she hollered as she disappeared from sight.

Freddie went back into the cabin to start figuring out why her life was coming unraveled. Sitting at the desk in front of the window, she decided that a list of all the *facts* surrounding recent events was where she should start. In her usual orderly manner, she began by numbering the lines one through ten. Then she printed the word FACTS across the top of the page. She stared at the sheet for a few minutes. She didn't know what to write down.

This is great, she thought. *I can't even make a simple list.* Looking at the headline for her list, she took her pen and put quotation marks around the word FACTS. *I can deal with that,* she thought. Putting it in quotes made her feel better about writing down the things going through her mind. The last thing she could attest to was their status as true facts.

Still unable to organize her thoughts or perhaps bring them into the light of day, she decided to try word association and just write down whatever came to her mind. Then she would sort them out.

Okay. First word. Mr. Personality. She scribbled words that she associated with Mr. Personality: fear, vague, shadows, bully, Joyce. Freddie stopped, letting her eyes rest on the last word. Joyce. This was the first time she had explicitly associated Joyce's death with Mr. Personality. *Why would her death be related to Mr. Personality?* she asked herself. It was bizarre for one thing, and that certainly established a common denominator. Before she had left work, Freddie was not able to find anyone who knew the cause of Joyce's death. Reaching for her day book, she made a note to make some calls tomorrow to see if a cause of death had been determined.

Turning back to her list, Freddie frowned. As much as she hated to admit it, her close relationship with Joyce meant she had to consider that Joyce's death was somehow connected to the craziness invading her own life. The idea was totally weird, but she had promised herself to consider every possibility. She had to if she was ever going to make sense of any of this.

Second word. Evil. The associations flowed. Good vs. evil, then Miya's Great Chief and the wolf. Freddie stopped writing. Reading back over the two words and their associations, the one gnawing question she had was Why me? How in the world was she connected to any of this? She had no connection with Miya's or Jodi's heritage. Supposedly one of her great grandparents was Native American, but she doubted that qualified her to participate in their traditions. Or their ghost stories.

Freddie remembered telling Jodi that Mr. Personality looked familiar to her. That has to be the key, she thought, but she had already thought of everyone she knew and had come up with nothing. He must be kin to me in some way. Family resemblance could explain why he looks familiar.

Freddie laid her pen down. She felt she had turned a corner. It wasn't much, but at least there was something to focus on that might help her unlock this mystery. She determined to tackle it in the same orderly fashion she used to approach her normal life. Strange, she thought, normal seemed remote at the moment, but still, being able to apply her familiar and comfortable approach to this cockamamie situation was affirming.

Slipping into problem-solving mode meant that coffee was required. Freddie always brewed a pot of coffee when she was starting a task at home. Even at work, she made sure she had a fresh cup of coffee when she started work on a project. Although Joyce had been convinced she was into the caffeine rush, Freddie believed it was more conditioning than anything else. Whatever it was, it was as automatic as breathing for her.

Reaching into the cabinet to get a filter, she wished she had thought to bring her new coffeemaker with her. The one on the kitchen counter looked pretty old. No telling when Miya had bought it. Probably why she left it behind. It would probably take forever to brew. She finished preparing the coffee and wandered over to the front window to wait for it to brew. There was no point in getting started until she had coffee in hand.

Looking across the yard, Freddie saw a light flash at the edge of the woods. She focused her attention on the area expecting to see Jodi emerge at any moment. After a few minutes, she turned to check on the coffeemaker. It was still dripping. Out of the corner of her eye, she caught a glimpse of another flash of white. She couldn't tell if she was seeing a light, a reflection, or maybe just a quick glimpse of something white, like a person's shirt. She stared at the area where the flash had been, hoping to get it into focus, but she saw nothing. Was she just imagining things? After standing at the window for ten minutes trying to catch sight of it again, she suddenly remembered her coffee.

"Damn! I bet it's lukewarm now!" She hurried across the kitchen to check it out. Sticking her finger into the pot to prove her point, she poured a cupful and plopped it in the microwave. "Thank God their idea of roughing it includes electrical appliances." She laughed, opening a closely guarded gate just enough to start her giggling. Almost immediately she felt a welcome release of tension.

Sobering up, Freddie grabbed her coffee and returned to the desk to figure out where she had seen Mr. Personality before. She listed all the places she had worked as well as any place where she'd been actively involved, labeling the columns as clubs, school, church, and— Freddie hesitated. She had started to write family, but active involvement was not a phrase she associated with family. She had never really known her parents' families. Now that she thought about it, she wasn't even sure why. It had just never come up. *Perhaps that's where I should start,* she thought.

"Okay. Let me see." Sitting up straight in her chair, pen and paper in hand, Freddie was prepared to grab this bull by the horns. "First, we need to analyze what we know about Mr. Personality." Shifting to the use of plural pronouns and talking aloud were quirks of Freddie's problem-solving mode.

Freddie continued, "If we can establish some sort of profile, then maybe we can determine where we need to look in order to find him." She read aloud as she wrote. "One. He always says the same thing: *It's time. You can't stop it.* Two. He's obviously not flesh and blood since no one can see him but me." She thought about the stewardess and the hotel manager, who obviously both thought she was nuts.

"Wait a minute! Jodi saw him. Why was she able to see him?" Freddie frowned as she strained to come up with a logical answer. "Maybe the connection is not just with me. Maybe it involves Jodi, too!" That felt good. At least she wouldn't be alone in this. Then she remembered that Jodi had only seen him that one time, and that had been in *her* house, not Jodi's. Her temporary relief vanished.

"Okay. Forget it. We're back to square one," she said, erasing part of number two. "Two. He's not flesh and blood, but he can make himself visible to whomever he chooses, or maybe it depends on certain conditions whether others can see him," she wrote. *Maybe he is flesh and blood though. Maybe he just projects his image like the holographic images they use on the Star Trek series.* "Okay, okay, okay!" Freddie submitted to the will of her invisible audience. "I know that stuff is only possible in the movies, but something is going on, and I'm open to suggestions." No one answered.

Freddie's concentration was broken when she saw something move across the yard at the edge of the woods. She jumped to her feet, her heart racing, expecting to see Mr. Personality materialize in front of her eyes. A large, scraggly dog emerged, followed by Jodi. Freddie sighed with relief and threw up her hand to wave. Jodi waved back as she reached down to pet the dog.

"I thought you said not to encourage him," Freddie yelled as she stepped out onto the porch.

"Obviously, it doesn't take much to encourage him," Jodi replied. The dog was trotting along behind her as if he had just returned home with his master. "I can't help it if he's too dumb to know where he lives."

"He looks pretty smart to me. He's certainly got your number."

"Look, just because you're all rested doesn't give you a license to pick on a poor girl who has been trekking all over this side of God's green earth and is tired and weary and consequently without her normal, cutting-edge faculties with which she could cut you into tiny pieces before you even put two words together!"

"Well, being tired and weary hasn't impaired *your* ability to put two words together! Of course, it is unfortunate you still can't put two words together that make sense."

"I give! I give! I'm too tired to do battle." Jodi threw up her hands in mock surrender. "But, don't think the war is over!" she called out over her shoulder as she ran into the house ahead of her.

Freddie laughed. "Any time. Any place!"

After Jodi showered and changed clothes, she came back into the main room where Freddie was still laboring over her lists. "What have you come up with?"

"Not much. I tried to make a list of the facts, quote-unquote."

"And?"

"And I think Joyce's death is connected to all this." Freddie's voice cracked with emotion. The thought of Joyce being killed because of her made her want to throw up and then beat the crap out of somebody.

"Why?"

"Well, I'm going to check to make sure, but last I heard, they didn't know what killed her. She didn't have heart trouble that I knew about. I'm pretty sure she would have told me. Besides, she was only 20 years old!"

Hesitating, Freddie continued, "Maury told me her skin was a grey color. Plus, he said she looked terrified." Pausing, she bit her lip. "How did Miya describe the family of the chief?" she asked, but she knew the answer.

Jodi stared at Freddie, who could almost see her mentally stepping back in time as she repeated what Miya had said. "Their eyes were open, and their faces held a look of terror forever preserved in death. Their skin was grey, and there was no substance remaining in their forms." Jodi spoke in a hushed tone. "My God, do you think...?!"

"I don't know what else to think at the moment. I intend to make a few calls and see if someone can give me some information that makes better sense."

Jodi moved across the room and sat down on the sofa. Her heart was pounding, and her breath was coming in short gasps. It felt like the capacity of her lungs had decreased, and she was teetering on the verge of oxygen deprivation. Her pulse increased. She could only stare at the floor.

"Jodi!" Freddie shouted her name, afraid that somehow this craziness had infected her, too.

Jodi looked up. The light in her eyes was muted as if she was looking through a fog. She was not focusing properly. "What's wrong with you?" Freddie asked anxiously.

"I...I don't know. Suddenly it all got too real for me. I guess I've been thinking about this as an adventure, sort of a fantasy extravaganza, a chance to be part of some cool, psychic thing. It never really hit home until you pointed out the similarities between my aunt's story and Joyce's death. The idea that it might actually be happening now in the 20th century—I mean, when it was speculation or some legend, that was one thing, but this is frightening!"

"I know. On one hand it seems too incredible to be true, and on the other hand, I know I saw what I saw. For that matter, you even saw it. That's another thing. No one but you seems to be able to see him other than me. Why do you think that is?"

"Now you're really scaring me!" Jodi rose from the sofa. "I need a drink. This is getting way too intense for me." She went to the hutch against the wall, opened the door, and reached in. She brought out an unopened bottle of wine. "This one has alcohol in it, thanks to Aunt Miya," she said, glancing over her shoulder at Freddie. "Do you think you can handle it?" Freddie nodded. She was as strung out as Jodi.

Handing Freddie a wine glass with a couple of ice cubes in it, Jodi poured the warm wine into their glasses. "Do you think my being able to see him means that he's after me, too?" Jodi shivered and swilled her wine as if it had life-saving properties. Not to diminish her concern for her friend, but Jodi preferred that Freddie have the sole honor of being on his list.

"I don't know, but I think if he was, you'd have seen him at some time other than with me. Don't you?"

She hadn't thought of that. Relief flowed sweetly over Jodi, a feeling enhanced by the chugalugging of her wine. "Maybe it's because I'm sensitive to psychic influences, and you can't rule out that we are very close. That would only make it stronger."

Freddie sipped on her wine. Despite the possible connections her list-making had unearthed, she still didn't know where to go from here. If she just had a clear goal, one that wasn't encumbered with so many unknowns, one where she had obvious choices, she'd be hell on wheels. But this—this craziness was trying to take her down avenues she'd never taken before, and there *were* no clear-cut choices. She felt powerless and totally inadequate for the task at hand.

Control was important. Normally she avoided circumstances that even hinted at the possibility of her not being in charge of a situation. Now she was being hurled into the unknown with such intensity, she expected to drown in its depths. The way she felt right now, she wasn't sure she could reach the top in time to absorb the invigorating sweetness of being in control again before it was too late.

Chapter 34

*T*he water ran rapidly over the rocks, throwing its white-gloved hands up in the air in applause with every encounter. The fast-moving stream moved quickly through the woods, meandering to and fro. The tree branches hung protectively over the stream as it curved through the woods. On its banks was a perfect hiding place, a place where fishermen could set up camp and escape from civilization because the eye could not follow the stream's path. If another fisherman was around the bend, it would be as if he were on another stream in some other place. As the stream flowed on its way this day, it passed few fishermen. The woods were quiet. Most vacationers had left. Only the locals remained, except for one camp.

Charlie and Cleland sat on canvas camp stools. Cleland poked the campfire with a stick. "Whatcha trying to do?" asked Charlie brusquely.

"I'm trying to get the firewood to catch," replied Cleland. Reaching behind him, he picked up a bottle of bourbon. Putting it between his legs, he unscrewed the lid with one hand, still poking at the fire with the other. He held the bottle to his lips, guzzling down at least a double shot.

"Hey! Instead of drinking that, why don't you put it on the fire? Maybe then you could get it to catch!" Charlie laughed raucously, followed by a loud, snorting sound.

"Maybe I'll just throw you in. Shit makes great fuel!" Cleland flipped a hot ember in Charlie's direction.

"Damn, Cleland, I was just kidding! You don't have to get all worked up!"

"You're the one that started it. You're always starting things."

Just like when they were kids, the steady tossing of words back and forth in an attempt to one-up the other continued.

"That's not true!" Charlie declared. "The cat wasn't my idea!"

"What cat?" asked Cleland.

"You remember Frank Pierson's cat. The one that was always sitting on our fence, the one we used for target practice? Anyway, remember how mad you got when Frank's mother came down and told Mom she'd seen us doing it? She said we were monsters and should be put in juvenile detention, and you told her to go to hell. Mom punished us because you cursed at Mrs. Pierson. That was when you decided to send the bitch's cat to hell instead. I'll never forget the smell of burning fur, and geez Louise, could that cat screech!"

With a smile of satisfaction, Cleland nodded. "I'd forgotten about that, but it was a long time ago."

"Not me," said Charlie. "I thought that was the bravest thing I'd ever seen. I never told you, but at that moment, you were my hero."

Cleland cocked his head, looking at Charlie in disbelief. "Don't screw with me!" he demanded, thinking Charlie was making fun of him.

"I'm serious. I knew then that you and I'd always be together. We were two halves of the same pie—we saw life different than everybody else—and I was right. We've always been together, haven't we?"

"Well, yeah, but I didn't know you felt that way. I just figured you hung around 'cause we were brothers."

"Yeah, sure, like that would make a difference!" Charlie snorted. "You don't know me as well as I know you, Cleland. We are a lot alike. The same blood flows through our veins, but there's still a huge difference between us."

"Yeah? Like what?" Cleland asked, taking another swig of bourbon and wiping his mouth on his sleeve.

"You do what you do because you're angry. You're trying to get revenge on the world."

Cleland interrupted. "The world deserves it. Who do they think they are? They keep the best of everything for themselves, and every time I try—"

"I know, I know, but that's *not* why I do it."

"You don't think the world deserves to have its butt kicked?" Cleland inquired defensively.

"Probably, but I do it because I like it. It feels good. Even if the world was handed to me on a silver platter, I'd still fuck over people every chance I got. I'm powerful because I can do things other people can't do or won't do."

Cleland didn't respond. He just stared at the campfire. Finally Charlie said, "Remember that man we tied up in Little Rock? We gagged and blindfolded him and then forced him to listen to his daughter screaming while we took turns raping her?" Cleland nodded.

"What were you feeling?" Charlie asked. Cleland just looked at him. "Okay, I'll tell you what you were feeling. You felt a tremendous rage ripping you apart. When you raped that girl, it was like payback for all those faceless people out there who rape you every day, who make you feel small and unimportant. Knowing her father was forced to listen and was unable to do anything about it was your reward. It was sweet revenge."

"Exactly! See, we're not really that different."

"Yeah we are, Cleland. I didn't feel any of those things. I tied up the man and raped the daughter because I had the power to do it. That's what gives me the right. They had no choice. It was what I wanted.

"I could just as easily have persuaded the father and the daughter to have sex with each other. I don't need to be violent. You know why? Because I have the power to do anything I want and to get others to do anything I want them to do. Now, *that's* a high!"

Still staring at Charlie, Cleland asked, "If that's true, how come you're always violent?"

"I'm not," Charlie replied quietly.

"What the hell are you talkin' about? I can't think of a single time that we haven't killed or raped or beaten somebody!" The pride in Cleland's voice was unmistakable.

"We're not always together, Cleland. When we settle down somewhere for a while, I usually find a woman I want to control. Then I spend time with her away from you. Usually I bring my little fun to a close just before your rage gets out of control, and we have to move on."

There was a crackling sound in the woods on the other side of the stream. Both brothers jerked their heads in the direction of the sound. They were on full alert. They had just settled into this camp after hitchhiking and literally hiking from Byhalia, Mississippi.

Crap! thought Cleland. *We should have killed that damn kid.* But they didn't. Cleland wanted him to live. It wasn't a moment of compassion—just the opposite. Cleland wanted him to suffer in silence forever. What man is going to admit he was raped by two men and was too afraid to resist when they forced him to orally satisfy them too? Of course, Cleland gave him a choice. He could act like he was enjoying it or take his chances and run. Cleland waving his gun around probably helped the boy make the right decision.

Still, it seemed a little soon for the sheriff to have found their trail. They'd been passing through town when it happened, so no one knew them. All the same, they weren't taking any chances. Cleland and Charlie sat perfectly still. Then Charlie raised his hand, pointing across the stream. Cleland saw it then. It was a girl jogging. Apparently they were close to a trail. After she disappeared, they quickly moved their meager camp farther back from the stream.

Settling back into their conversation, Cleland said, "I thought we were a team, Charlie. I didn't think we had any secrets from each other." He sounded like a spurned lover.

"We are a team, Cleland. I won't ever leave you. You started me on this path in life, big brother, and I'll always be grateful to you."

Charlie paused. "Let me explain it this way. You know how much you like bourbon?" Cleland nodded.

"You know how much you like it when we drink together and get rowdy and kick ass? I'm talking mean, sloppy drunk?" Cleland again nodded.

"Well, I like it, too, but I know you like to be by yourself sometimes. Just you and the bourbon and no distractions." Charlie looked at his brother. He had seen Cleland curl up by himself too many times, content to have nothing but a bottle for company. Thinking how peaceful those times were for him, Cleland nodded.

"That's how it is for me, too, Cleland. Only I don't want to be alone with a bottle. I want to be alone with my power. I want to experience it in my own way. I want to relish it and feel its inebriating effects."

Charlie felt sorry for his brother. He knew Cleland understood the need to be alone with his bottle, but he knew that his brother could never comprehend the power Charlie possessed. Out of brotherly love, perhaps the only love he had ever felt, Charlie changed the subject. "Want to go for a walk?"

"Sure!" Cleland stood, and the two brothers waded across the stream. After climbing up the shallow bank, Charlie started down the trail in the direction the jogger had gone.

"Where ya goin'?" asked Cleland.

Grinning, Charlie answered, "It's time for a little payback!"

Hitting their palms together in a triumphant high-five, Cleland shouted, "All right!"

They followed the jogging trail. It crossed the stream at a narrow point and then veered away from it after about a mile. Charlie kept expecting to find a parking area where they might find a lonely jogger. Maybe even the one they'd seen earlier. After a while, he decided to turn around.

"Let's head back the way we came. See if we missed anything. Maybe we ought to get off the trail and stay closer to the stream."

Looking at the leaf strewn path, Cleland said, "It doesn't really look like anyone's been here lately. Wonder where that girl we saw went?"

Charlie was wondering the same thing. "I wasn't paying close attention. Maybe there was a cabin off the path somewhere."

After walking for ten minutes, they cut through the woods in the direction of the stream. They couldn't get lost following the stream, and maybe they'd discover another trail they missed.

A dog barked. Cleland grabbed Charlie's arm. "Listen!" Both men stopped. "There! Did you hear that dog barking?" Cleland asked excitedly.

"Yeah! Maybe it belongs to somebody. Let's head in that direction."

They turned, heading away from the stream, and crossed over the jogging trail. The dog barked again. Cleland and Charlie adjusted their direction to match the sound. Within a few minutes, they discovered a small trail. It wasn't one you'd notice if you were on the main jogging trail unless you were looking for it. It only claimed the distinction of being a trail for those who knew it existed.

Charlie knew that Cleland's adrenalin was flowing. He wasn't doing anything in particular, but Charlie had noticed years ago when they were kids that the tops of Cleland's ears turned red when his excitement was mounting. It was a fact that had served Charlie well. If he saw the signs of Cleland's rage mounting and the timing was wrong, he was able to distract him. Cleland never suspected, and Charlie never told him because he didn't want to hurt his feelings.

"Let's be quiet until we find out where this goes," Charlie said.

"Okay." Cleland was grinning from ear to ear. Charlie headed up the trail. It was only a few minutes before the underbrush started thinning out.

"There must be a clearing up ahead. We need to be careful, but I want to get close enough to see what the situation is." Charlie moved forward, stepping off the trail and side-stepping through the trees. He stopped and squatted down. Cleland slipped up behind him, peering through the less daunting underbrush.

"A cabin," Charlie noted.

"Yeah," agreed Cleland enthusiastically.

"If we follow the woods around the clearing, we can come up on the back side of the cabin. Maybe we can see how many people are in there. If we decide to go in, we need to know what to expect."

"Sure!" Cleland was quick to agree. Like a kid who'd been promised free passes for all the rides at the amusement park, Cleland was totally focused on the cabin.

They circled the cabin, choosing the direction opposite from the driveway. Charlie kept glancing around to see if the dog they'd heard was anywhere around, but he didn't see him. Crouching to make sure they weren't seen, Charlie tried to see in the windows as they moved across the front of the cabin. But it was too far, and there was enough sunlight reflecting off the glass to protect those inside from prying eyes. He wasn't concerned though. Once they were on the back side of the cabin, the glare would be gone. The woods encroached on the cabin in the rear. So they could get closer without being seen.

Inside the cabin Freddie walked across the kitchen with her wine glass in hand. A movement caught her eye. Already unnerved by the white flashes earlier, she jerked so hard that her wine sloshed over the edge of her glass, spilling onto her shoe.

"What is it?" Jodi asked.

Putting her glass down, Freddie peered out the window toward the woods. "I swear I saw someone!" she replied. Jodi jumped up and ran to Freddie's side. Together they stared at the woods, trying to isolate anything that didn't belong.

"Are you sure?" asked Jodi.

"It sure looked like it. Earlier, while you were gone, I thought I saw someone, but maybe the sunlight was glinting off a leaf or something. I kept expecting you to walk out of the woods. You did show up in a little while so I didn't think anything else about it. Now, though, the sun isn't shining on the backyard, you're here, and my instincts are telling me that I just saw something move."

"Maybe it was an animal," Jodi offered in a shaky voice.

Freddie was hoping that was true as much as Jodi was. After a few more minutes, Freddie turned from the window. "It must have been my imagination working overtime!"

"I certainly hope so!" Jodi declared, following Freddie back to the living room area.

Outside, Charlie watched as a woman stepped up to the kitchen window. He stood perfectly still, wondering if she had seen them or was just looking out the window. Another woman joined her. It was the jogger. *That's all right,* he thought. *We can wait as long as it takes.* When the women disappeared from the window, Charlie motioned Cleland to step farther back into the undergrowth before continuing around the clearing.

There was a back door near the far edge of the cabin, and the woods were close enough on that side to make it from the woods to the door without being seen. Charlie glanced at Cleland. His ears were bright red. Charlie grinned.

Placing her fingertips on her forehead, Freddie pressed hard, directing them upward toward her hairline and then down, allowing the palms of her hands to embrace her cheeks. She paused for a moment before running her fingers along the sides of her nose and over her mouth until her palms cradled the curve of her neck. A moan escaped her lips.

"I'm going to take a shower," she announced with a deep sigh. "Maybe it'll clear my head."

"Good idea. Maybe I need to take another one!" Jodi replied with a half-hearted laugh.

Freddie had been in the shower for ten minutes when Jodi heard the squeak of the faucet as the water was turned off. She had been sitting on the chair with her eyes closed, sipping her wine, and trying to relax. She heard the sultry tones of the saxophone tape Freddie put in when she got out of the shower.

"Freddie!" Jodi called out, planning to ask if she wanted a glass of wine. Freddie didn't answer. *She probably can't hear over the music,* Jodi thought. That was okay. She would just relax and wait until Freddie came back.

In a little while, hearing the floor board creak behind her, Jodi said, "Freddie?"

Before she could turn around, a large hand covered her mouth and jerked her backwards until she was no longer resting on the chair, and her shoulder blades were being pressed against its back. Jodi kicked her legs trying to regain a foothold so she could defend herself. Then she felt the knife being pressed into her side and froze.

"Whoa, missy, unless you want to die and miss all the fun!" Cleland laughed softly in her ear. Jodi felt goose bumps popping up all over her body. Bile rose in her throat. "Just be calm. Not all the guests are here yet!"

Jodi was desperate to warn Freddie, but she could still hear the saxophone tape playing. If she screamed, Freddie might hear her, but it would hardly matter since the brute behind her would surely slice her open before she drew her next breath.

Chapter 35

*A*fter Freddie emerged from the bathroom and turned on the tape player, she threw on her clothes and walked to the bedroom window. Standing in the middle of the front yard was a wolf. It looked just like the one in her dream. She closed her eyes and shook her head, expecting it to dissipate as quickly as Mr. Personality. When she opened her eyes, it was still there.

If it speaks, I'm checking myself into Bolivar, Freddie thought. Bolivar was for many years the home of a regional mental hospital. In the South it was the same as a New Yorker being taken to Bellevue. Turning from the window, she started brushing her hair.

Freddie. The voice sounded in Freddie's head just as clearly as if someone were in the room with her. She whirled in a circle, expecting to see someone else in the bedroom.

I am here, Freddie. Look out the window. She looked out the window at the wolf. *You're not crazy. I'm as real as you,* he assured her.

Who are you? Freddie thought.

I am Avatar. Freddie jumped back from the window, her eyes widening in fright as she recognized the name from Miya's story. *Don't be frightened. I am here to help you.* The wolf walked closer to the window so that she could see him clearly.

For some reason Freddie felt as natural carrying on this mental conversation with the wolf as she did talking with Jodi. *There's something in his eyes*, she thought. Suddenly, the hair stood up on her neck. She tensed.

Two evil men have entered the cabin, Freddie. Their intent is to torture and kill you and your friend.

What can I do? Freddie felt the panic rising in her chest. She was starting to hyperventilate.

You have the power to stop them, Freddie. You only have to let go of the control you have so carefully held in place all these years.

I can't! Freddie was frightened. Her instincts said the wolf was telling her the truth about the men. The hair on her neck never stood up unless something adverse was at hand.

If I let go, I don't know what will happen. Before, I—I— Freddie stuttered. She was confused as well as frightened, unable to follow a thought all the way through.

FREDDIE! The wolf literally shouted her name in her mind. It startled her so badly, her fear lost its grip on her for just a moment. *What happened before doesn't matter. You're in a different place in a different time. You've been waiting many years for this day. You must let go and let your true strength emerge. Do it now or your friend will die!*

What Avatar said was bizarre, but she had nothing to lose, except another friend, and she couldn't stand the thought of that. *What do I do?* she asked the wolf.

Simply allow your mind to lead you. You have all the forces of good behind you. That is why I am here—to guide you. Don't embrace your body. Embrace your soul, the part of you that wanders through the Universe when you allow it out of its cage. Become one with all that it represents. It will protect your body and those you love.

Although she had no idea why, she seemed to understand what Avatar was telling her to do. Taking a deep breath, she released it slowly. Slipping her feet out of her loafers, she tiptoed to the door. Sensing something behind her, she looked back over her shoulder but saw nothing. She eased the door open just as Charlie turned to search for her. Stepping out of the bedroom, she spoke quietly and firmly. "Let my friend go."

Charlie was more surprised by her demeanor than her demand. "I don't think so, little girl." Charlie expected this to be an enjoyable conquest. The woman had spirit, something he rarely encountered. Usually their victims were so frightened, there was no challenge in it, and it took some of the enjoyment out of it for him. As confident as he was with his power, he still enjoyed matching wits with pretenders to the throne. *Maybe today will be the day*, he thought.

Freddie watched him without a sign of fear. She felt a different rhythm flowing through the circuits of her mind. She had always known, even though she'd tried not to think about it, that she could do things others couldn't, but she had never trusted herself enough to explore the possibilities. The strange conversation with the wolf had infused her with the courage to let the walls fall down. Maybe it was the other-worldliness of it. She didn't know, but she felt free, unencumbered by worries and doubts. She was stronger than she had ever been. She had no idea what she would have to do to save her friend, but having a plan was no longer important. Trusting herself was all that mattered.

"I said let her go." Freddie moved into the room. In the background she heard a faint sound like insects swarming.

Cleland was cackling with pure ecstasy. *This is the best yet*, he thought. *We'll show little miss know-it-all who's in charge!*

"Get her, Charlie!" Cleland yelled as Charlie took a step in Freddie's direction.

Freddie raised her forearm, pulling it toward her middle until her hand, positioned in a loose fist, was just below her waist.

"Look, Charlie. She's gonna Kung Fu you!"

Charlie ignored Cleland. Something about this woman was making him uncomfortable. Instead of moving toward her, he took a step backward. Her eyes locked on his. He saw no fear. Her voice had revealed no cowardice. Her face was relaxed, and her eyes clear.

This was a first for Charlie. *Everyone* showed fear. They might try to hide it, but he could always see it. There would be a telltale tightening around the mouth or a slight twitching of the eyes. Even when some managed to control the obvious physical manifestations of fear, they were never able to hide what was in their heart. Their eyes were like visual megaphones, blaring out their fear for Charlie to see. But not this time. This one was different. There were no signs at all. Charlie took another step backward. His mind encountered a feeling that was new to him, one he had only witnessed: Charlie was afraid.

He became aware of movement. His eyes fixed on Freddie's arm as she turned her hand palm side down and raised her elbow. Everything was happening in slow motion for Charlie. Looking into her eyes, he knew that today was indeed the day for payback, but not quite the way he'd planned. He wanted to scream at Cleland, to warn him, but it was too late.

At the rim of his vision, he saw her arm as she flung it outward and upward. Charlie felt himself being hurled through the air, literally knocked breathless by the force. The bones in his back cracked loudly as he slammed against the sloped ceiling of the cabin. He felt the jagged end of one of his ribs puncture his right lung.

Ironically, the fear that consumed Charlie was the greatest high he'd ever experienced. He smiled. In the next moment his heart was penetrated by the end of yet another shattered bone. As his spirit left his body, which was now falling to the cabin floor beneath him, Charlie thought, *This was the best yet!*

Cleland had not seen Freddie as she prepared to make her move on Charlie. He was too busy staring at Charlie. He had never seen him back off from anyone before, least of all a woman. "Hey!" he shouted. "Quit joking around!" but his voice had trailed off as he saw Charlie's body fly across the room.

"Charlie!!" he screamed as he saw the light leave his brother's eyes. He recognized it. He had reveled in it with countless others because it had been his sweet revenge, but not Charlie. It couldn't be happening to Charlie.

He turned to face Freddie, pulling Jodi half out of the chair by her shoulders. His rage was feeding on his fear. He tightened his grip on Jodi, holding the knife so tightly against her throat that blood droplets were falling on his left arm gripping her chest.

"Hey, bitch!" he shouted. "You can kiss your friend goodbye. Nobody kills my brother and gets away with it!"

Before the sound of his words had left the air, Freddie raised her hand into the air and slowly drew her fingers toward her palm in a choking motion. Cleland felt an incredible pressure on his windpipe. The knife clattered to the floor as he grabbed his throat with his right hand. His attention shifted from Jodi to an urgent need for air. He relaxed his grip on her, but she didn't move. Jodi was just as afraid as Cleland, but the focus of her fear was no longer Cleland.

Freddie continued to hold her right fist in the air as she raised her left arm. She reached out as if grabbing someone by the collar and then moved her arm sideways. Jodi felt herself being picked up and removed from Cleland's grasp. He was too busy trying to breathe to object.

As soon as Jodi touched down on the sofa, there was a startling bellow. Freddie had released her hold on Cleland's windpipe, and his continued efforts to suck in air were rewarded with a tremendous rush of oxygen, nearly choking him. Jodi jerked around to face Freddie and Cleland and froze. The knife that had fallen to the floor only seconds before was now rising by itself with the handle end up. Jodi didn't know if Cleland couldn't move or was too scared to move. His eyes were stretched wide, his pupils dilated. The tip of the knife tilted upward until the blade was horizontal to the floor.

"L-L-Look, la-lady," Cleland stammered. The sound of his voice startled Jodi, and she jumped away from the sound. Cleland backed away from the knife. It was following him. He backed into the countertop and grabbed the edge with both hands.

"We didn't mean no harm!" Cleland eased his right hand along the edge of the countertop until he felt his hand bump against his hip. He eased forward gently so that he could slip his hand behind him. He paused. Freddie hadn't moved. She was looking straight into his eyes. That was good. At least she wasn't watching his hands.

Cleland took a deep breath. He knew he would only have one chance. He grabbed for the pistol stuck in the back of his jeans and lunged sideways at the same time. He was going to shoot the bitch where she stood.

Cleland was so intent on his plan that it wasn't until he hit the floor without firing a shot that he realized the knife was protruding from his chest. He stared at it in disbelief. Looking up at Freddie, all he could say was "Why?" Then he died, as clueless as he had been in life.

Even though the threat had passed, both women were perfectly still. Freddie was still staring at Cleland lying on the floor. Jodi was staring at Freddie as if she were an alien.

"Are you all right?" asked Freddie finally, turning toward Jodi.

"I don't know," replied Jodi.

"What's wrong?" asked Freddie, walking toward her. Jodi unconsciously began scooting away from her toward the far end of the sofa. Freddie did not seem to notice her friend's reaction.

"Who are you?" Jodi cried out.

"What are you talking about? Are you sure you're okay?"

"No, I'm not sure! How did you do that? It's not like it's something they teach in a martial arts class." Freddie suddenly understood. Jodi was afraid of her.

"Jodi! I'm not going to hurt you. I was only trying to save our lives. They were going to torture and kill us for god's sake!"

"Did you recognize them? Were they escaped convicts or something?" Jodi thought perhaps Freddie had seen their pictures in the newspaper. Although that still didn't explain what she had just seen.

"No," Freddie hesitated. "I was told."

"You were told? By who? The Easter bunny?" Despite her friend's apparent fear of her, Freddie was glad to hear the smart-aleck attitude return.

"Of course not." Smiling sheepishly, Freddie continued, "By a wolf."

"Oh, right! You had another vision, and this time he conveniently told you who these guys were. Freddie, for god's sake, tell me what's going on! You come in here acting like a cross between E.T. and Steven Segal, and you expect me to be satisfied with a vision as an explanation?!"

"Look, Jodi, first of all, I didn't have a vision. When I got out of the shower, I walked over to the bedroom window, and I saw a wolf. Right there in the front yard. A real wolf. And well…he spoke to me."

"Wait a minute! He spoke to you?"

"Telepathically, of course."

"Oh, of course." Jodi rolled her eyes toward the ceiling. "What could I have been thinking?"

"Do you want to hear this or not?" Freddie snapped.

"Go ahead."

"When I saw him, I thought it was just a daydream, maybe because of the dream I had earlier. So I walked away from the window. Then I heard a voice in my head just as clearly as I can hear you. He told me who he was and that he was here to help me."

Jodi glanced sideways in disbelief.

"Jodi, I know you think I'm crazy, but it did happen. I didn't believe it myself at first." Then she added, "Jodi, he said his name was Avatar."

"You mean like the wolf Aunt Miya told us about?" Jodi's interest was piqued. The events of a few minutes ago temporarily forgotten.

"Yes. He warned me about these two men. He said that they would kill us both if I didn't do something."

"Did *he* give you the power?" Jodi's earlier skepticism had dissipated somewhat.

"No." Freddie was afraid to continue, afraid of Jodi's reaction. Jodi said nothing. She just looked at Freddie, waiting. "He said I had to let go of my need to control. To control, well, myself. He said I had to let my true self emerge." She paused. "He said if I didn't, you would die. I just couldn't let that happen." Her voice trailed off.

Not wanting to let Freddie see her cry, Jodi substituted an attitude. "Well, Superwoman, what else did he tell you other than you can leap tall buildings in a single bound? Or did you already know that?"

Freddie knew that the attitude was how Jodi hid her feelings, but she also knew her friend was not satisfied with her explanation of what happened.

"Avatar said I had all the forces of good behind me and that he was here to guide me. Jodi, I don't really know what happened. I trusted what he said, and the next thing I knew I was doing what you saw."

"Are you sure you've never done this before?"

"Nothing like this. I had some bizarre experiences when I was young, which has a lot to do with why I'm such a control freak."

"What do you mean by bizarre experiences? Have you killed anyone else?" The moment the words escaped her lips, Jodi regretted it. "I didn't mean...I meant...well, I just wondered," she finished lamely.

"It's okay," Freddie replied. "No, I haven't killed anyone before, but I did cause accidents."

"Accidents?"

"Well, you know how when you're a kid, you get upset about something and you wish silly things?" Jodi shook her head in confusion. "Did you ever get mad at another kid and wish something bad would happen to them?"

"Well yeah."

"Well, the things I wished happened."

Frowning, Jodi asked, "Are you sure it was you? It was probably just a coincidence."

Knowing that wasn't so, Freddie continued. "I wished Grady Turner would fall on his face in the mud because he said I looked like a boy wearing a dress. He did. About ten feet from where I was standing." Freddie gave her an abridged version because she didn't want to make herself seem too weird.

"That could definitely have been a coincidence."

Shaking her head, Freddie said, "We were in geography class, and Mrs. Wiseman took us across the hall to another classroom. They had just completed a 10' by 10' replica of the Mississippi Delta. They used actual plants to simulate trees. They'd hauled in mud to create the delta and the bed of the river. It was pretty incredible. Grady tripped on his shoe lace and sort of catapulted himself face down in the middle of the display. He landed somewhere around Vicksburg, Mississippi," she said solemnly.

Jodi was laughing hysterically. Freddie had never thought of it as funny before, but Jodi's reaction made her realize that it really was hilarious. Caught in the throes of laughter, neither woman seemed to notice the two dead men still lying on the floor across the room.

Chapter 36

*A*fter the police left and the ambulance took the two men away, Jodi announced she was going back to Memphis for a few days. She told Freddie she needed to ground herself after the scare she'd been through and headed to the bedroom to pack.

"Go ahead. I may go back myself in the morning," Freddie told her. Jodi was relieved Freddie's feelings weren't hurt. Freddie, however, knew Jodi was still uncertain how to deal with her and with what had happened. For that matter, so was Freddie.

While Jodi packed her things, Freddie stood at the window and stared at the woods. She was trying to sort out her own feelings. It was hard to believe what she'd done with her mind. Of course, she had told the police a slightly different story. As far as they were concerned, she had simply taken the two men by surprise. After discovering the two were already wanted by the law all over the South, the inconsistencies in her story, like all the broken bones in Charlie's body, were ignored. Case closed.

She still couldn't believe she'd killed those men. She'd always thought killing was not in her nature. *Of course, it was a life and death situation. Anyone else would have done the same thing,* she thought. She turned from the window and began to straighten up the living room. A nagging doubt as to whether she should have killed them kept trying to surface until finally the old Freddie, the one in control, emerged and set things right.

"Well, I'm ready! Call me later if you decide to come home. You're welcome to stay here, of course." Jodi had stacked all her bags at the front door. Now she was trying to pick them all up at once to take to her car.

"Hang on! I'll help you. You can't carry all of those in one trip!"

Freddie grabbed a couple of bags and held the door while Jodi wriggled through with the others. "Got any place else you want to go?" asked Freddie. "It's a shame to waste all these packed clothes. You could go on vacation for at least two weeks and only have to unpack half of them!" Freddie was desperately trying to erase the stigma of today's event from their relationship.

Jodi chuckled. "You just can't give a girl a break, can you?" She threw the bags into the back of her car. Leaning on the driver's door, she and Freddie gazed at each other for a minute. Neither spoke. Jodi broke the silence. "Hey! I'm serious. Be sure to call me when you get back. I want to know you're all right!"

Freddie smiled, recalling lines from a poem she'd written about Jodi: *It doesn't matter where I'm led; You're always there for me, my friend.*

"We'll go to Smokey Ridge and eat barbecue until we burst! My treat."

"Hey, now you're talking! Juice cooks the best hickory-smoked barbecue I've ever tasted, bar none."

Jodi giggled.

"What?"

"Remember that girl who used to call him Grease all the time instead of Juice?"

Freddie nodded, laughing. Juice was a nickname given to Jerry Welch, the owner of Smokey Ridge, because of his last name. "Yeah, I guess calling a guy who owns a barbecue joint Grease made more sense to her than Juice!"

Still smiling, Jodi said, "I better go. Take care."

Freddie headed back toward the cabin after Jodi's car disappeared from sight. Just as she reached the porch, she stopped. Turning quickly, she saw the wolf walk out of the woods.

"You were right," Freddie said aloud as if talking to a wolf was normal. "I did have the power within me to stop them."

Power, replied Avatar, *is an ambiguous thing. It can be the strength you need to overcome negativity. Yet, it can also become the negativity within you. You have much to learn about power.*

If you allow the power to work through you, it will always choose the right path and the best outcome. If you attempt to control the power, to direct its path, a less desirable path will always be selected by your human will.

Freddie was shaken by his words. "Are you saying that I shouldn't have killed those men?"

It is not for me to judge, Avatar replied. *I am simply trying to guide you toward an understanding of your power, to teach you how to not become attached to outcomes. You must be willing to set aside your anger or any other emotion and allow the natural outcome to emerge.*

"I don't understand. You told me to stop them. What else was I supposed to do?" Freddie was upset. She worried she had made the wrong choices.

It has nothing to do with what you were supposed to do, replied Avatar. *It has everything to do with your relationship to your actions. Ask yourself what you felt when it was happening. Were you angry, vengeful, excited? Who were you at that moment? Do you know why you were there at that moment expressing in that way?*

"I don't think I can answer those questions," replied Freddie.

I know, but if you are to become what you are meant to be, you must search for the answers.

Freddie was silent. Her mind ground to a halt. Shutdown was a common occurrence when she was overwhelmed. The strength she'd had earlier was fading. She was frightened and bewildered.

Avatar moved closer to her until his muzzle nudged her hand. *I will come with you back to the city. You are not alone.*

Tears of gratitude rolled down her cheeks.

Chapter 37

Day 12

The shadows of the night still lingered in the room, but Darian could see well enough to make out the features of Angela's face. She was lying next to him, breathing softly. Occasionally she stirred, but for the most part, she was perfectly still. After dropping her off on Monday night, he had returned unannounced Tuesday evening. Angela let him in, and he had been here ever since.

Angela was not asleep. She knew Darian was awake, but she wasn't ready to officially open her eyes and talk to him. She had to go back to work today. Her three days accrued time off were now used up. She had hoped Darian would try to talk her out of going back today, but he didn't say anything last night when she brought it up. The last three days were unlike anything Angela had ever experienced. Darian had barely let her out of bed.

Of course, what Angela called love-making was something else entirely for Darian. For him it was exploration. Exploration of a new frontier where his feeling of power was accompanied by a tremendous feeling of satisfaction, which he did not yet understand. The responses he received from Robyn and Angela made more sense to him than the terror his prey experienced when he absorbed their life force. Perhaps he could learn something here that would help him in his approach to Freddie.

Angela stirred. Stretching her arms above her head, she yawned. "Good morning. Have you been awake long?"

"No," Darian replied.

"Well, I've got to get ready for work. I promised I would come in early today since I've been off for three days. Can you find everything you need? You're welcome to stay here, you know."

"I'll think about it. I have some business to take care of."

Disappointed by his indifference, Angela slid out of bed. She put on her robe as she walked out the door on her way to the bathroom. She turned on the shower as soon as she reached the bathroom so the water would get warm. Standing in front of the sink, she looked in the mirror and grinned. She felt like she had been transported into one of her romance novels. Chuckling, she thought, *I'd put the last three days up against any of them!*

Opening the door of the medicine cabinet, she gasped. She couldn't believe her eyes. How could she have forgotten? *This can't be happening!* She plopped down on the toilet seat lid as the beginning strains of panic washed over her.

Knock. Knock. "Can I come in?"

"Just a minute." She shoved the diaphragm back into the medicine cabinet and rushed to get in the shower. She did not want Darian to see her face right now. "Okay," she called out.

Darian opened the door and came in. He noticed that Angela was not her usual chatty self. After using the toilet, Darian left, and Angela burst into tears.

She managed to get dressed and maintain her composure long enough to get out of the house. Watching her drive off, Darian wondered why she had been so quiet this morning, but the thought was quickly replaced by a desire to check on Freddie.

Sitting down on the slip-covered chair in the bedroom, Darian made note of how relaxed he was feeling and then directed his mind to focus on Freddie. Within seconds, he was thrust into the now familiar vortex. He never knew where he would find himself anymore. So it was good he chose to never reassemble straight away when his jaunt ended.

He immediately spotted Freddie. She was in a bedroom, but not one Darian recognized. The interior looked like a log cabin. He watched as she headed for the door and then looked over her shoulder like someone was there. *She still senses me,* Darian thought. *That's good!*

Darian was so focused on Freddie he failed to tune in to anything else. Following her into the next room, he was surprised by what he saw. There were two men, and one had Freddie's friend by the throat.

The next words out of Freddie's mouth shocked Darian. She calmly ordered them to release her friend. Up until now he'd seen no evidence of her having any power at all, except for the power to resist talking to him!

The next few minutes unraveled in slow motion for Darian, who was still disassembled. Normally, such unexpected events caused his concentration to falter, sending him roaring back through the vortex to his body, but this was so unexpected and so frightening for Darian that it had the opposite effect. His thought processes froze. He could not have returned to his body even if he had wanted to.

First, his attention riveted on the man Freddie slammed against the ceiling. As the man's spirit left his body, she made no move to absorb his life force. Darian heard a strange sentiment from the man's spirit echoing through the air around him — *This was the best yet!* Darian continued to watch as Freddie killed the second man, also without moving from the spot where she stood.

Then it was over. Darian's thoughts rushed in all directions. He was shocked by Freddie's power but also confused that she made no effort to consume the precious life forces they offered. *Why?* Before he could ponder the answer, he realized his energy was waning, and he was growing weary. For some reason he could not discern, his energy level was diminishing more quickly than usual.

Darian returned through the vortex to Angela's bedroom. He wasted no time driving back to his cabin. Contemplating the possibility of Freddie having powers similar to his was quite different than witnessing them. For the first time in his life, Darian might have to face an opponent who was his equal in strength. How skilled was she? Her performance today was just a form of simple telekinesis, but perhaps she had other, more advanced skills.

Sitting in his overstuffed chair at the cabin, Darian was heartened by a critical point in the evaluation of her skill—she had allowed the life forces of the two men to escape. If she had not learned to replenish her energies, she could never compete with him. Another vital point was her recklessness. She permitted a witness to live. Her friend, Jodi. The world would certainly wreak its own vengeance on Freddie if he did not get to her first.

Chapter 38

Day 13

*U*nable to reconcile what he had seen yesterday with his earlier encounters, Darian awoke this morning, determined to revisit his twin. If Freddie had the power to destroy others and was willing to use them, there was no reason she shouldn't talk to him. They couldn't be that much different.

Focusing once again, he emerged from the vortex—this time finding himself in Freddie's kitchen. She had obviously returned home. Infused by his recent success with women, Darian decided to let his charm infect her. While in the kitchen he practiced smiling the way he had with Robyn and Angela and Mary. He was becoming quite flexible in his reassembled state, despite the lack of flesh and bone.

Wait! What's that? Growling? Darian's attention jerked away from working on his approach to Freddie and focused on the animal present. As it growled and bared its teeth at Darian, a familiar sensation niggled at his mind. Then the realization hit him with the intensity of an adrenalin rush. It was the same wolf who had defied him in the woods!

How can that be? Forgetting about his desire to confront Freddie, Darian practically lunged into the vortex, wondering if he'd just escaped a trap.

He couldn't think straight. He'd never expected to encounter the very wolf who had sparked his rush to reach the ultimate level of his power—who had propelled him into his quest for Freddie. Obviously Freddie knew the wolf. *Had she orchestrated the incident when the wolf had come into the woods? Perhaps the wolf was simply bait.* Darian wondered if he had just been lucky that day.

Needing to plan his next move against Freddie but distracted by his frustrations, Darian's anger rose up swiftly, igniting a desire for the physical contact that accompanied his recent sexual adventures. His desire, however, was not sexual. He intended to carry this new experience to its definitive conclusion. Like everything else in his life, sex could ultimately have only one purpose—to serve his quest.

Of course, simply relieving his victims of their life forces was much faster than sex, but having learned his lessons well from Harry Beel, the perversity of this unique method stimulated Darian. During the sex act, his victims truly gave themselves to him; they wouldn't suspect the finality of the gesture, of course, but the deceit itself would be titillating for Darian. What he didn't admit to himself was that the act would temporarily assuage his frustrations about Freddie.

His mind now focused, Darian drove into town. He wasn't fastened on a particular victim. Any woman would do. Convincing her to be with him was not an obstacle. With the windows down, he cruised slowly along the main streets of Sterling. He was looking for a woman alone. A lot of women were coming out of the buildings, but none were alone. As Darian slowed to pull into a parking space, he saw a woman in the telephone booth at the corner of 2nd Ave. and 4th St. He changed course and turned left off the one-way street to enter the parking lot adjacent to the phone booth. He drove through the lot and parked as close to the phone booth as he could. Getting out of his car just as the woman started down the sidewalk, he was surprised and pleased to see that it was Robyn.

It must be a sign, he thought. *This is going to be easy.* "Robyn! What a delight to see you again!"

Startled, Robyn turned toward the voice. Seeing that it was Darian, she grinned and waved. She couldn't believe her luck. "Hi! What are you doing here?"

"Oh, just goofing off. I was wondering what there is to do in this town, and then I saw you! Do you have any plans?" he asked.

"No," she replied eagerly.

"What do you think about going for a little drive?" Darian didn't want to waste time playing games. He had business to conduct. Either she was interested or she wasn't. She was.

"Sure!" Although Robyn was not usually this promiscuous, she had not been able to forget the reckless abandon of their tryst in the car last Monday night. It had haunted her all week. She wasn't a greenhorn, however. She knew it had been purely a physical act, but the raw honesty of the encounter had excited her beyond any romantic experiences she'd ever had. The bottom line was she was not going to pass up an opportunity to experience that kind of thrill again.

Feeling no need to be creative, Darian drove to the same lovers' lane they visited before. It was off the road about a mile. It had once been a picnic area, but now only lovers came here.

"Isn't this the coolest place? It's so private, especially during the day," Robyn remarked. Darian agreed but for a different reason.

Getting out of the car, Darian motioned her to get out, too. Waiting at the front of the car, he took her hand and led her to a picnic table. Standing beside the table, he began unbuttoning her blouse. Robyn didn't protest. He very quickly removed all her clothes and spread them out on the table. Then he lifted her up, placing her on top of her clothes, letting her legs dangle off the end of the table.

Then he began what would become a ritual over the next day or two: an affirmation and renewing of his power.

Just as Robyn reached her zenith, Darian began drawing her into him. For the first few seconds, she was not aware what was happening. Her thoughts revealed to Darian she was still in the throes of an orgasm. Then with frightening clarity, she sensed what was in Darian's mind. Terror erupted. Her life force had not completely released its hold on her body, and she began to flail and moan, but it was too late. She was no match for Darian.

The last thought Darian heard was *Why?* He didn't bother to answer. He remained where he was for a couple of minutes to steady himself. Then he calmly reached over to the where his pants were neatly folded and put them on. He scooped Robyn up and laid her on the seat attached to the picnic table while he gathered up her clothes. He laid them on top of her. Picking her up again, he walked into the woods. About ten yards in he spotted a shallow ravine, apparently the path taken by the rain water from higher ground. He lowered her body to the ground, straightened his clothes and returned to his car.

Chapter 39

Day 13

*F*reddie's trepidation about her return to Memphis had nothing to do with the city. She knew now that her surroundings were inconsequential to her feelings. The cabin certainly hadn't offered the peace and serenity she sought. Sitting on the sofa in her den, she let her hand glide across Avatar's head, who lay beside her. She didn't know how much help he could be, but it was comforting to have him here. At least she had someone to talk with.

Just imagine, she thought, *at one time I was worried people would think I was crazy because I was seeing people who didn't exist. Now I'm seeking companionship with a wolf!*

Does it matter what others think of you?

Startled by the intrusion of the voice in her mind, Freddie said, "What?"

Does it matter —"

"I heard what you said," Freddie interrupted. She felt more comfortable carrying on her end of the conversation aloud. "I just didn't realize you could hear everything I was thinking. I'm not sure I like that."

I can't always. Sometimes, however, you open up your thoughts to the Universe, and then I can hear them.

"I wasn't talking to the Universe then," she replied, not quite knowing what that meant. "I was talking to myself."

Perhaps you thought you were, but you must have desired some assurance that you weren't crazy, or I couldn't have heard it. When you seek answers or assurances, your thoughts radiate out into the Universe in search of those answers, Avatar told Freddie. *Then they return with solutions or ideas that direct your path, and sometimes they even draw others to you.*

"I would say that's nonsense, but in light of everything else that's happened recently, I'm not as sure of reality as I once was."

That's the first step, said her new companion. *You must be willing to let go of reality as you know it. You are going to face frightening things in the days to come, and you must be able to accept their reality.*

Avatar got up and crossed the room to lie down on a rug. He directed his attention outside the patio doors like a sentry on duty. Finding this reassuring, she closed her eyes and quickly drifted off to sleep.

A low, but persistent, growling aroused Freddie. She sat up quickly, her attention on Avatar. He was standing across the room, teeth bared and growling. Following his gaze, Freddie twisted her head to look toward the kitchen. She saw nothing.

Turning quickly back toward Avatar, she asked, "What's the matter?"

Almost before she finished her question, his growl escalated to a vicious snarl, and he took a step forward, ready to strike. She whirled around. There he was! Mr. Personality was standing, more or less, in her kitchen. Freddie screamed, but before she could even stand up, he was gone.

Being startled awake by a wolf growling in her living room and then the frightening apparition of Mr. Personality triggered a staccato rhythm to her heart beat. Her mind was careening wildly from one thought to another, each striking hard against the outer edges of her mind, trying to escape. She was unable to corral a single rational utterance.

Don't be frightened. He is gone for now, soothed Avatar.

Freddie finally spoke, the words tumbling out. "What does he want? Who is he? And why does he keep popping in and out?"

I can't answer all your questions. I know from my own encounter with him that he embodies the strongest force of evil my kind has seen in many,

many years. When I came across him in the woods, he almost destroyed me. For the few seconds when our life forces were linked, I had a strong vision of another. You.

I don't know why he chose you as a target. There was little information about you. Perhaps he wasn't even consciously aware of you then, but there was still a strong emotional connection to you. Sensing you would be in grave danger from him, I called out to the spirits of my brothers. They rescued my spirit from his grasp. Then it became my mission to warn you and guide you as much and as long as I am able.

"How would he know me?"

I don't know. Except for his negative energy surrounding you, only the trail of your essence was there, almost like a memory.

"Then why did you think you had to protect me," Freddie's confusion was increasing, "and how did you find me?"

The one overwhelming sense I gleaned about you from the trail of your essence was your inherent goodness. I knew this man would be compelled to challenge that in you, and it would ultimately make you his enemy.

"But how did you find me without any information?" Freddie's logical mind was desperately trying to fill in the gaps.

You know me as Avatar. I travel alone, but I am not alone. There are others who serve the cause of keeping evil from gaining ground in the Universe. They, too, are called Avatar. Remember when I told you that your thoughts were being sent out into the Universe? Well, when your encounters with him began, your fear and your cries for help were heard by all of us. It led me to you. As I watched you, I knew you were the one.

Freddie was struck by the irony of this situation. All her life she had struggled to maintain control, to do the right things, to not *rock the boat*, and now she was embroiled in the most bizarre, out of control situation she could ever have imagined. On top of that, Avatar was instructing her to let go of her precious control. Despite her experience at the cabin, letting go was not going to be easy. Even now she was experiencing remorse over how she had handled the situation with those two men.

Looking at the wolf, Freddie knew her fear was nudging her

toward putting herself in his hands, but her inner strength was telling her she must decide for herself what was best. Any decision she made now would be strictly emotional and probably reckless. What she needed was information. There was so much she didn't know about what was going on, and she sensed it was only a matter of time before she would have to face her demon.

Chapter 40

Day 14

*A*fter a restless night, Freddie drove to the library at Memphis State University. In the reference department she headed for the bank of local computers with databases listing materials available in the library even though she had no idea what topic to research. There were at least a million ways to approach the recent events. A natural place to start was the supernatural, but maybe she should consider Indian legends. Having seen Avatar with her own eyes, even *her* skeptical mind was ready to accept the possibility that Miya's tale wasn't just a legend. Something might even explain Mr. Personality.

By the time her turn came at one of the computers, she was wrangling with the idea of searching for good vs. evil. Miya and Avatar both asserted that this apparition of hers was an evil force she must engage and overcome. Even the experience with Cleland and Charlie... Freddie paused. The police had eagerly given her names to put to the faces of the two men, but it only made it more difficult to put behind her. Knowing their names made them seem too familiar. Still, the incident smacked of good against evil, assuming of course that trying not to be murdered put her in the category of *good*.

Her thoughts raised the question in her mind: *Is there really any such thing as evil or is it just a matter of perception? Is evil a reality that I can touch, that I can actually eliminate from my world?* These thoughts led her to type in "Does evil exist?" in the search box.

The results were immediate. Obviously she was not the only person wrestling with this concept. She wasn't surprised to see that Alexander Solzhenitsyn, the Russian author who was exiled from the Soviet Union six years earlier, had something to say about evil. "If only there were evil people somewhere, insidiously committing evil deeds, and it were necessary only to separate them from the rest of us and destroy them. But the line dividing good and evil cuts through the heart of every human being. And who is willing to destroy a piece of his own heart?"

Freddie was struck by his comment for she now knew that she could and did destroy two living souls.

Scrolling down through the search results, she noticed a great many references to Zen—so many that she felt strangely relieved. Perhaps it was an omen that answers awaited her. Writing down the call numbers for all the books related to Zen, she got in the elevator, checked the list on the wall showing which call numbers were filed on which floors, and pushed the button she needed.

The library was quiet, which was normal for a library, but as Freddie wandered through the stacks trying to find the books on her list, she became apprehensive. Finally she found the right section. Quickly grabbing them off the shelves, she hurried to the elevator without even glancing past their covers.

The elevator was empty, but as the doors closed, the hair on her neck stood up. Thankfully, it was a quick drop to the ground floor. When the doors opened, Freddie rushed out as if someone were after her. Involuntarily, she glanced over her shoulder to see if she had successfully escaped her invisible pursuer. Just before the doors closed, she saw the faint image of a man in the mirrored walls of the elevator,

Freddie stumbled and bumped into the opposite wall. It couldn't be! The elevator was empty when she got on. Control fled. She felt faint, and extended her arm toward the wall for support.

"Are you all right, Miss?" asked a man as he reached out to steady her, taking the stack of books she was carrying.

"What?!" Freddie couldn't collect her thoughts enough to comprehend what the man was saying.

"You look like you've seen a ghost," he replied, a look of genuine concern on his face.

"I did!" Freddie blurted out before she could stop herself. The man's presence alone was allaying her anxiety. She found it easier to breathe, and her control was returning.

"Pardon me?" he asked. Freddie raised her face to look for the contempt she expected to see but found genuine interest. "Are you sure?" he asked.

Now it was Freddie's turn. "Pardon me?" He laughed. She quickly added, "I mean, are you making fun of me?" Her brows furrowed, and her bottom lip stuck out in a pouty fashion. It was so cartoon-like that he laughed again. Freddie jerked around and tried to leave, but he caught her arm.

"I'm not making fun of you. Honest. The look on your face was just so delightfully impish that I couldn't help but laugh. Besides," he continued, "when you think about it, it's really your fault!"

"What?" Freddie put her hands on her hips in a challenging stance.

"See! There you go again!" he laughed. Before she could reply, he said, "Listen. Do you want to go to the cafeteria and have a cup of coffee? You look like you need a cup. I know I do."

Freddie reeled in her emotions. "Sure." She was actually relieved to have flesh-and-bone company, especially a good Samaritan. It didn't hurt that he was rather cute besides.

He paid for both cups of coffee despite Freddie's protest. Leading her to a table by the window, he pulled out a chair for her. Surprised that such graciousness existed in today's world, Freddie hesitated for just a moment before sitting down.

"Thank you," she said.

"You're very welcome." He smiled at Freddie as he seated himself in the chair next to hers. For some crazy, inexplicable reason, she was glad he hadn't sat across the table. While he was doctoring his coffee, Freddie took the opportunity to get a good look at him.

He reminded her of the stereotype professor from old movies on television. His dark brown hair was thick with soft, loose waves. It was long enough to curl under around the neckline. *An extremely charming look,* she thought. He wore navy blue corduroy pants and a light weight navy blue sweater with diamond patterns on it in beige, dark green, and burgundy, sort of like a large argyle sock. She couldn't suppress a giggle.

"What?" he inquired. Trying to imitate her earlier pouting expression, he asked, "Are you laughing at me?"

"No. Honest. I was just thinking that I have a pair of socks that match your sweater." Freddie was desperately trying to maintain a sober expression.

Looking even more hurt, if that was possible, he declared, "Ah-ha! You *are* laughing at me! Woman, do you not realize that this sweater represents the sum total of my value to this university? I can't believe you would belittle this symbol of my years of devotion to my craft."

"I have absolutely no idea what you're talking about!" she exclaimed, unable to restrain her laughter any longer.

He abandoned his injured look and sedately explained. "This sweater was my Christmas present last year from the department in lieu of traditional bonuses–budgetary constraints you know. It does match the new décor in the cafeteria rather well though. Don't you think?"

Freddie was uncertain if he was serious.

"Don't worry. I've gotten over the phase of my depression where I considered shooting up the cafeteria in order to make a point. Besides, they would just renovate the cafeteria and then probably repossess my sweater!"

Genuinely enjoying this man's company, Freddie said, "I don't even know who you are. I gather you're a professor, but otherwise, I'm having coffee with a perfect stranger!"

"At least our relationship is off to a good start. You've already realized that I'm perfect. With that out of the way, let me introduce myself. My name is Garrison, and no, I don't go by Gary. I prefer to embrace the full breadth of my given name. Besides," he added, "my last name is McCrary, and Gary McCrary sounds more like the makings of a limerick than the name of an illustrious college professor."

"Oh! Illustrious, are we?" remarked Freddie. She thought of Ryan. Both men possessed a playful quality, but with Ryan the strongest attraction was sexual, the kind of attraction you read about in romance novels. With Garrison, there was an easiness to their bantering that made her feel safe, protected, just sitting here talking to him.

"Hello-o-o! And who might you be?"

"I'm sorry. My name is Freddie Marsh, well actually, it's Fredrika, but I go by Freddie. I'm a technical analyst in commodities."

"Interesting collection of books for a technical analyst," he said as he examined the book titles. "Zen Mind, Beginner's Mind." He paused. "There seems to be a recurring theme here. Strange reading for someone with their feet firmly planted in the breakneck world of investment and speculation."

"It's a long story." Freddie was reluctant to tell him what was happening. She didn't want him to think she was a nutcase.

"I have lots of time. Let's start with what happened at the elevators. You said you saw a ghost?"

Freddie stared at him. Could it be possible that she'd run into someone by chance that might actually take her seriously? "Why are you interested? You don't know me. I might just be a head case or something."

"I'm interested because I saw your face. You couldn't fake a reaction like that. You actually saw something, and I believe in ghosts or at least in things that are beyond our normal experiences.

"Besides, I just have a gut feeling that you need help. These kinds of experiences aren't usually treated seriously by most people. Am I right?"

"Well, only two other people even know about it. If I told anyone else what is really going on, I'd spend the rest of my days locked up at Bolivar. That's why I'm not sure I want to tell you."

Ignoring her reluctance, Garrison asked, "Why are you checking out books on Zen?"

Glancing at the stack of books on the table, she wasn't sure how to answer his question. "I did a search with the question *Does evil exist?* and there were so many that had the word Zen in the description that I decided to go with the most prominent reference. Since I know nothing about all this, I thought it might at least point me in the right direction."

Garrison had placed his left elbow on the table and was supporting his chin with his hand, listening intently. "Do you think this ghost you saw was good or evil?"

Freddie was shocked by his question. Garrison had moved right to the heart of the matter despite the fact she had told him nothing so far. "I don't know for sure. I've been told he's evil. He definitely scares me, but that doesn't mean he's evil. Someone else who should know, however, says he is."

"Who's this someone else?" Freddie had been dreading this question. If she told him it was a wolf, he'd probably hotfoot it out of here, and she didn't want him to leave.

"I'm not sure I can tell you."

"Why not?"

"You would never believe me."

"You don't know that."

"Trust me on this one," she remarked assuredly.

"Maybe you need to trust me. It doesn't sound like you have too many people in your court you can count on. Maybe you need to improve the odds."

Freddie was strongly attracted to having this man in her court. She needed someone to talk with about what was happening. Maybe then she could scrape together some clarity about her current bewildered state.

Abruptly she started her tale. "It began when I went to Chicago to teach...." Freddie told him the truth about everything except Charlie and Cleland. She didn't have the stomach to admit she had killed two men. Nor did she want him to know *how* she killed them. She let him believe she overpowered them through the element of surprise and held them for the police.

When Freddie recounted her meeting with the wolf, minus its connection to Charlie and Cleland of course, she expected to see Garrison flinch, but he never even blinked.

"...so I decided to see if there was an alternative to trying to destroy this so-called evil. I'm having trouble with this battle of good vs. evil. I can't explain it except to say that I can't believe my life comes down to that."

Garrison sat quietly for a few minutes. Freddie was uncomfortable in the silence. Then he reached out and took her hand, placing both hands over hers.

"You've been through a great deal. First, let me say that I believe you, Freddie. Second, I would like to help you. I know quite a bit about the philosophies on good and evil as well as the folklore portraying it as an inevitable battle. As a full professor at the University, I also have access to just about any information we might need."

Looking straight into her eyes, he asked, "Would you be willing to let me help you?"

Freddie's eyes filled with tears, and she was unable to form an answer. So she just nodded. Garrison put his arm around her shoulder and pulled her head against his chest. She felt safe with this perfect stranger, and it was a remarkably good feeling.

Chapter 41

Days 14-15

*D*arian returned to the same ravine where he'd left Robyn six times over the next two days. Not all were as eager as Robyn, but in the end, they all served their purpose. That was the most important thing.

Some of the women Darian picked up on the street. Others he met in fast food joints. The third was a woman he saw walking down the sidewalk with a man. She kissed the man lightly on the lips and waved as he entered an office building on 3rd St. Darian followed her a couple of blocks. Then he pulled up beside her and rolled his window down. Leaning over the seat, he yelled, "Could you help me?"

She came over to the car and leaned down. "Are you lost?" she asked.

"It's these one-way streets," he replied, smiling at her. "I keep missing my turn. I need to go over to an address on the next block—uh, 4th St., but I always cut over too soon and then have to drive around the world again."

"What are you looking for?"

"There's supposed to be a lawyer's office on 4th, but I don't have the exact address." Fortunately, he had remembered seeing a sign for a lawyer the last time he drove down 4th.

"Oh, yeah. I know where you're talking about." she said. "What's the name of that street where you turn?" she mused aloud and then laughed. "I've lived here so long, I just go everywhere on autopilot."

"Would you mind showing me? I'll drive back around and drop

you wherever you were going."

She looked doubtful. Darian smiled at her. He could see her resolve weakening. "Hey, that's all right. I understand," he said as he put the car back into drive.

"Wait! That's all right. I'll show you. It's just around the corner. I'm not in a hurry anyway." She reached out and opened the car door.

As he started off, Darian asked, "What's your name?"

"Kathy. Kathy Briscoe."

"Why don't you let me buy you a cup of coffee, Kathy Briscoe? I'm not in that big a hurry either. I'm just a little dizzy from driving in circles!"

She laughed. "Okay."

Darian smiled because his excitement was already escalating.

After the addition of Kathy Briscoe to his energy reserves, Darian returned to his cabin to allow himself time to rest. His thoughts drifted to his newfound nemesis—Freddie. His mind was so finely tuned to her by this time that his intent was enough to open the vortex and whisk him to her location.

Emerging from the worm hole that connected his universe with Freddie's, Darian found himself standing behind Freddie in an elevator. Before he could even celebrate his good luck at finding her alone, the elevator doors opened, and Freddie rushed out of the elevator as if the hounds of hell were after her. He saw her collide with a man just as the doors closed. Totally frustrated, Darian allowed himself to hurtle through space to rejoin his body.

The most difficult task for any person to undertake is seeing through their buffers to the truth. It was no different for Darian. His obsessive seeking after personal power clouded his vision to many things, the most recent being the insidiousness of wanton sexual activity. The inevitable reaction of the powers of the Universe to such unleashed desire for sexual dominance or lust of any kind is destruction—an eating away of the pure substance which comprises one's life force.

Although a victim of his own desires, Darian was too self-important to notice. If he had, he would have made a connection between his three-day spree with Angela and how quickly he had wearied observing Freddie's encounter with Cleland and Charlie. But he did not. So, it's not surprising that he also failed to notice that the energy consumed from his seven victims over the last two days had not only failed to augment his life force, it did not even fully replenish it.

Chapter 42

Day 16

Sitting on the side of the bed, Darian was suffering from a hangover but not from the excesses of alcohol. His demon did not live in a bottle. His demon was power—most recently, the power of sex. He had slept for almost twelve hours, but a heaviness still clung to him. Running his fingers through his hair as he got up, he stood in the middle of the floor, completely oblivious to the reason he felt like crap.

Shaking his head, he went into the bathroom to clean up. He stood under the showerhead for twenty minutes, letting the warm water hit his shoulders before running down his body. Although he didn't understand why, he felt strangely safe like this. There was a familiarity to it that he could never quite put his finger on. Being surrounded by the warm water was addicting. He resisted turning off the water and stepping out of the shower. Only when the water began to cool down as the reserve in the hot water tank reached its limit was he motivated to leaving his sanctuary.

Drying off with a towel as he left the bathroom, Darian pulled clean clothes out of his closet and slipped them on. Remembering that he needed to shave, he went back into the bathroom. Stepping up to the sink, he was shocked to see how haggard and drawn he looked. The dark circles under his eyes made him look thinner. Looking down, he realized he had fastened his belt in a new hole without even realizing it.

Concern furrowed his brow. *This is Freddie's fault,* he thought, never considering for one moment that he might be to blame. *Of course it's her fault! She started this cat and mouse maneuvering. I've expended way too much energy playing her game.* He couldn't believe she'd been able to dupe him. Look at him! He'd tried to be nice, tried to include her in his quest, but what had happened? It had undermined his concentration, and he had nearly become her prey!

Pacing across the room, Darian fumed. He was now certain the little incident with the wolf last month was a trick to make him doubt his power, to start him on the path that would lead to her. All those times she had appeared frightened by him were just ploys. Well, she was in for a surprise. He had no intention of being destroyed by her!

Darian was once again fully focused on Freddie, and he no longer cared whether she willingly merged with him or not. As a matter of fact, thoughts of torturing her were starting to excite him. He envisioned what it would be like to kill her slowly, to tear her limb from limb. He would wait until the last moment to snatch her life force so he could inflict as much physical pain as possible. He wanted her to understand the extent of his power before he captured her forever.

Before he could give intention to find Freddie, Darian remembered the wolf. *That's what I have to do!* he thought. *If I destroy that vile creature she used against me, then she will have no one to help her!*

Brimming over with anger, the elixir of his power, he didn't hesitate. Immediately focusing on locating the wolf, he was teleported through the familiar vortex to Freddie's house. He did not reassemble. Instead he listened for Freddie's thoughts to see if she was in the house. She wasn't, but the wolf was. He had been growling from the instant Darian arrived. He stared at the wolf.

"Well, we meet again, little lamb!" Darian said as he surrounded the wolf with his energy particles. Avatar seemed to visibly shrink in size in an attempt to escape his touch, but there was no escape.

"What do you want?" Avatar did not need to see Darian's form to recognize him.

"Revenge." Darian's voice sounded inside Avatar's head.

"For what?" The wolf ceased moving. He knew he would not escape this time.

"For everything. She's sadly mistaken if she thinks she can get the best of me. I've spent my whole life preparing for my destiny."

"What did she do to you?" The wolf wondered what illusions fueled Darian's rage. It was very difficult even for Avatar to see clearly through the landscape of Darian's mind.

"She tried to trick me, to draw me into her trap."

"She set no trap."

"Don't lie to me," Darian shouted. His voice was reverberating inside Avatar's head like the aftermath of clanging cymbals. Darian only needed to listen to know that the wolf was not lying to him, but he was too far past rational now. He was losing control.

"You were the trap. She used you to trick me into searching for her. When I thought you alone had overpowered me, I had no choice."

The internal voice echoing in Avatar's head escalated to a roar. "I WILL NOT BE BEATEN!"

Pausing for a few seconds, he very calmly asked, *Do you understand?* The wolf did not reply. Perhaps to lend weight to the idea that he was still in control, he tightened his embrace and asked again. Wincing from pain, Avatar responded that he understood.

Do you also understand that you will not survive this? Darian was speaking to him as if explaining to a child why he was being punished.

Avatar nodded. In his heart he determined to survive long enough to warn Freddie, but he did not allow this feeling to form itself into a thought for his thoughts were no longer inviolable.

Anyone who stands in my way now will be destroyed. You, my little lamb, are only the first.

Darian's awareness of the sensuality of expressing his power over other people was brought to its original peak early when his power served only to satisfy his baser needs—like his revenge against Harry Beel and Ruth. After meeting Angela, the sensuality of his power was resurrected, flourishing in a new way in the abandoned lovers' lane.

Today he was not concerned about replenishing his energies or ascending to his rightful place. He was once again totally focused on a baser need—revenge.

His childhood experiences with the Beels did not even come close to the intensity of the next half hour for Darian. Totally engrossed in his torture of Avatar, he teased him by compressing the cocoon of his energy particles until the wolf could barely breathe. Then, laughing, he watched him struggle to remain conscious against the onslaught.

How does it feel to be powerless? Darian snarled. *You are nothing without Freddie.* Darian's buffers refused to acknowledge that Freddie was not present when the wolf overpowered him at the cabin. He increased the pressure on the wolf's hind legs. Both legs cracked simultaneously, and the wolf collapsed, but he did not fall. The only force holding him up was the energy field of particles surrounding him, which were at once supporting him and destroying him.

Who are you? the wolf thought. *Why do you want to hurt Freddie?* Taking a deep breath, the wolf struggled to remain calm. He knew he was on his own this time. Calling upon his brothers as he had done before was not appropriate now. He had already communicated the danger that he sensed in Darian that day at the cabin to Freddie. He could do no more than that really. Yet, Avatar could not let himself give in, refusing to allow his pain to distract him. Otherwise, he feared that his hope of warning Freddie might surface. Talking should suppress his thoughts. Perhaps it would help him understand what was driving this man to align himself so completely with evil.

The wolf's calm exterior encouraged Darian's frenzied behavior. He began breaking the wolf's bones one by one. *You're a real crack-up,* laughed Darian as another bone snapped. *This is almost as pleasurable as sex,* he thought. *I never realized there was such a smorgasbord of opportunities out in the world for me to taste!*

Avatar was in excruciating pain, but he struggled to stay awake. It might be the only way to retain his life force. Trying to keep up the dialogue, he asked, *What is your name?*

Don't play games with me. You know who I am.

Actually, I don't.

Looking at the wolf who lay in his grasp, Darian knew he was in control. This wolf was no match for him. He didn't really understand how Avatar had overwhelmed him before. Although not ceasing in his rhythmic bone-breaking, he decided to answer the wolf. *You're full of questions. Aren't you? Oh well, since it doesn't matter anymore, I'll humor you.*

Then, abruptly releasing his hold on Avatar, he assumed the pixilated version of himself and gave a mock bow. "Allow me to introduce myself. Darian Marsh at your service." Resuming his bone-breaking position as well as his mockingly serious tone, Darian continued. *Freddie, of course, is my twin.*

Avatar gasped in surprise. *If Freddie is your twin, why would you want to destroy her?*

I didn't in the beginning, he admitted. *I just wanted to share with her what the Master shared with me, but she wouldn't listen. If she had, we would be joined together now. With her life force, we could have skyrocketed to the ultimate Power together. Instead, she's been trying to manipulate me from the start.*

Darian tightened his grip on the wolf as his anger rose. Despite his rage, Avatar knew that Darian was not as strong as he was the first time he encountered him. With luck, he would survive long enough, but it was becoming increasingly difficult to breathe. All of his ribs were broken, and the pressure Darian was exerting on his body was damaging his internal organs as well.

Darian noticed his own energy level getting dangerously low. The pleasure he was getting from the slow torture of the wolf had enticed him into staying longer than he should have. He was running out of time. Looking at the wolf, he knew he wouldn't last much longer. Darian knew that he should have just taken his life force in the beginning. Now he didn't have the strength left to struggle with him. The fine silver cord connecting Darian to his body was weakening.

Like a child, Darian wanted to gloat over this latest victory. He wanted to smile mockingly at Freddie as she realized that she could not stand in his way. Nor could she stand in the way of her destiny to be a part of him. *Still, when she discovers the wolf,* he thought, *she will know her time is short.* Making his choice, Darian abandoned the wolf to die and focused once more on Freddie.

He arrived rather abruptly in the stairwell of a parking garage. He struggled to reassemble because he wanted Freddie to see him as clearly as possible. Doubtful that he could sustain his concentration much longer, he was rewarded with the vision of Freddie stepping onto the lower landing. She did not see him.

It's time. You can't stop it! Darian could barely control himself enough to put his thoughts together. Seeing her refusal to look at him, he said, *You can't hide.* Struggling, he continued, *You are part of me.*

Freddie screamed just as the door into the stairwell opened, revealing a man Darian didn't recognize. Before he could focus on the man's thoughts, his energy drained away, and he could no longer withstand the pull backward toward his body. He vanished into the vortex.

Upon emerging from the vortex, his body would not respond to his commands. His life force was too weak. His pulse was so shallow it was hardly noticeable. His breathing was ragged. He felt like he was floating in outer space without a tether and rapidly running out of oxygen. Mentally, he was flailing his arms, trying to push his way through space, trying to fully reconnect with his body.

It was like a bad dream. Fear closed in around him. Suddenly his thoughts catapulted him into a large room. It was the same room from his dream last week. Darian tried to run, but his feet were mush. Someone called his name again. It was Angela! *What is she doing here?* Relieved, he thought, *She'll help me.*

Turning toward the sound, he tried to move faster, but his legs were locked in slow motion. No matter how hard he tried, he could not gain any ground. Suddenly, out of the shadows, a woman emerged and called to him.

Angela? His fear wanted this to be a familiar face. As the shadows receded to reveal their gift to him, Darian froze. It was Freddie. But, how could that be? It was Angela's voice he heard. More frightened than he had ever been, Darian was painfully aware that he was in no position to defend himself. He could barely move.

What do you want? he demanded in an effort to maintain control.

Nothing at all.

What do you mean — nothing? You want to destroy me!

That's your choice. Not mine.

No-o-o-o! Get away from me. Why are you here?

You are part of me.

Hearing his own words turned back on him, Darian panicked. The harder he struggled, the more resistance his legs encountered and the slower his pace. He ran until he was so exhausted that he fell down on his knees, gasping for air.

Without warning, he was no longer in the great hall. He had fully reconnected with his body. It was several minutes before Darian could move his fingers or lift his arms, but even when he felt the strength of motion return to his limbs, he remained still.

Darian's outer calm gave no evidence to the turmoil taking place within him. He had never come so close to losing connection with his body. He still didn't know why his energy levels were so low. He had invested several days into building up power, preparing himself. Seven women had sacrificed themselves to his cause. Except for the pack of wild dogs he had consumed, this was the most energy he had ever consumed in such a short time. Why had this happened? It didn't make sense. If he couldn't determine what caused this problem, he knew he could never save himself if Freddie came for him.

Then there was that damn dream. *If it was a dream,* thought Darian. Was it real? Could Freddie insert herself into his dreams? Why had she sounded like Angela? Darian shook his head. It was too confusing, and he was too tired to sort it out. Closing his eyes, Darian knew he needed rest before he could do anything else. Lots of rest.

Chapter 43

Day 15

After their coffee date in the cafeteria, Garrison and Freddie spent the next two days together. First, Garrison explained why he didn't think the school of Buddhism called Zen was the only or even the best place to find the answers she sought, despite the books she had gathered in the library.

"Buddhism," he told her, "is among what most people refer to as eastern religions. However, there are many schools of thought in the western world that also embrace the idea of being mindful of your thoughts and actions and of seeking to develop wisdom and understanding as well as leading a moral life."

Garrison said, "Despite the fact that Buddhists follow the teachings of Siddhartha Gautama just as Christians follow the teachings of Jesus, there is only one Truth, one God, whatever you may call it.

"If you look closely enough, Freddie, you'll see the glow of Truth in all religions, but, it's the truth with a small letter "t" that causes all the confusion. That truth is man's interpretation of the real, capital "T" Truth, and believe me, it comes in all shapes and colors. It is the source of religions."

"I can believe that," remarked Freddie, remembering her own not-so-stellar experiences with church.

"A major difference between the mainstream eastern and western religions is that many eastern religions embrace the idea that all paths should be honored. On the other hand, in the west, Protestants especially feel compelled to believe there is only one path to enlightenment or salvation as they call it. So even though they can't agree among themselves on the exact nature of that one path, which, by the way, is why they have so many denominations, they still manage to band together as Protestants to claim superiority over the rest of the world.

"They mock those who are willing to allow everyone to find their own path to enlightenment. They ridicule those who follow the teachings of any but Jesus. They even mock those who follow Jesus' teachings but interpret them in a way that allows a person to actually honor the scriptures by following their creative birthright of being made in the *image and likeness.*"

Realizing that he was on his soapbox again, Garrison pleaded, "Sorry, excuse my preaching—"

"That's okay," Freddie said.

"So, the bottom line is that the main difference comes down to personal responsibility. Do you choose to embrace a philosophy that puts the onus for wrongdoing on some evil creature called Satan? Or would you rather embrace a philosophy that places the onus squarely on your own shoulders?"

Before Freddie could respond, Garrison continued. *Obviously he's on a roll,* she thought. "The latter philosophy recognizes the original intent of the words in the sacred writings. This is really important in your case."

"Why?" she asked, anxious to get a word in edgewise.

"Well, you're interested in the concept of evil, and knowing the actual meaning of the original word goes a long way toward understanding what the original authors of the sacred writings intended, regardless of whether you believe the words to be those of men or God."

Barely pausing for breath, he went on. "The word translated as *evil* actually means *immature* or *unripe*. When taken in context with the literal meanings and not our connotations of the words in these writings, it should be quite obvious, even to the most fanatical fundamentalist, that evil refers to your *level* of understanding of your true relationship to God. In other words, it merely defines the maturation level of your thoughts and emotions."

"So, are you saying that people who do evil things have sort of pinched off God from their lives?" she asked.

"Exactly! Our lack of understanding of our relationship to the Universe is why we make choices that aren't healthy. Choices that some specifically label as evil or bad. The whole point of this short journey we experience on the planet Earth is about learning to make better choices so that we move more into alignment with our true essence. Some of us who follow the teachings of Jesus call this true essence within each of us the Christ." Garrison paused to take a sip of coffee.

Taking a rare opportunity to speak, Freddie said, "Wow! You've really given this whole religion, mysticism, spirituality thing a lot of thought, haven't you?" She was amazed and impressed by what he knew and his passion about it.

"Well," he replied, looking a bit self-conscious as he caught his breath and realized he had talked nearly non-stop for the last ten minutes, "being a psychology professor for most of my colleagues is all about hard science, but I'm more interested in what goes on in people's heads. The stuff that arises from their connection to the spiritual realm. It doesn't make me very popular with my peers, but," he smiled defiantly, "I guess I don't really care!"

There was an easy familiarity developing between them that brought Freddie to his defense. "I like it when a person stakes a claim on what they want and refuses to be moved by popular opinion. I understand what you mean about your peers. Being odd man out is sort of a lonely life sometimes," she said.

"True." Steering the subject back to topic, Garrison asked, "Do you agree with the concept of evil I described?"

"It makes more sense than anything I've ever heard before." She paused to consider a few thoughts that arose when Garrison was talking. "Do you think then that the evil Avatar is seeking and the evil personified in Miya's legends is not really a separate and distinct entity?"

"I think that evil is the inevitable expression of anyone who doesn't have a mature enough understanding of God. I'm not talking about religious dogma. I mean an understanding of the attracting force called Love because that's the force that is God."

"So, are you saying that evil exists in all of us?"

"To one degree or another, depending on your level of maturity or understanding."

"So a person who is a vicious gossip is evil just like a person who murders someone?"

"Yeah," he shrugged. "Any expression you or I have that's not based on unconditional love is an immature expression. Now, most of us, because our society conditions us to do so, seek to restrain these less than desirable actions. However, there are people who aren't affected by social mores. These are the ones the rest of us usually point to and call *evil*. But the truth is that evil exists in all of us. It is not a separate entity. It just makes you feel better to blame it on something else when you slip up and let that part of yourself express for all to see."

Freddie nodded. "Then legends and fairy tales are just metaphors for what is going on within each of us?"

"Well, they are metaphors both for the nature of our psychology and the attempts we make to separate ourselves from what is unpleasant within us."

"So how does something like Avatar exist?"

"It's kind of complicated, but if enough people believe in something, their collective consciousness will create it just as each of us creates the nature of the experiences we have in life. For example, there's concern among a lot of people these days that the strong belief in Armageddon by fundamentalists is going to cause it to manifest. Fortunately, the balancing force of those who believe in personal responsibility for experiences is working hard to raise the consciousness. I guess we'll see in twenty years or so if they succeed."

"So, is Avatar real then? I mean I never thought about such a thing, and I certainly haven't seen it on the nightly news."

Garrison laughed. "Of course he's real. Manifestation doesn't require 100% agreement for something to happen, but when it happens, it's real to everyone. If you were required to lose all doubts before you could create what you desire in life, none of us would ever manage to achieve a single goal. We'd all be wallowing in the world of second best or third. Your existence is determined by your dominant beliefs just like the majority of electoral votes determines the next president whether you and I like him or not."

Getting into the rhythm of their discussion, Freddie posed question after question to Garrison. Together they searched the university database for any references to Avatar or any other legends that paralleled those of the wolf and the Great Chief. She wanted to find some information in the telling of those stories to give her a clue about the role of Mr. Personality. Freddie was hoping he was only an apparition, perhaps summoned by the Avatars who believed so strongly in the actual face of evil. If not, she knew that eventually she would have to deal with him literally face-to-face.

Chapter 44

Day 16

*T*he next evening, exhausted after two days of searching and discussing, they both slumped back in their chairs and moaned simultaneously. "Oh my god, we're in synchronized motion! Isn't that called entrainment or something? Should I be worried?" laughed Freddie.

Garrison grinned. "Depends on who's training whom."

The sun was setting, and the last rays of sunshine were casting strange shadows in the room as they filtered through the stacks of books on Garrison's desk and fell upon the wall and the floor. Idly, Freddie raised her hand until it intersected a ray of light. She formed the shape of a rabbit with her fingers. Her mind was numb. They had worked hard, and she'd learned a lot in the last two days, but it was also the best time she'd ever had. Garrison was so supportive. She still had trouble accepting he actually believed her especially since he'd never even seen proof that she wasn't crazy!

"A penny for your thoughts," offered Garrison.

Clearing her throat, Freddie said, "I'm really grateful to you for helping me. I don't think anyone has ever extended themselves for me like this before." Her emotions were rising and threatening to close down her throat, so she hushed.

Sensing how difficult it was for her to express her feelings, he replied, "You don't have to be grateful, Freddie. This is fascinating to me. Some people spend their whole lives hoping to see a UFO. My passion is studying the mysteries of life. I meant it when I said that I believe there's more to life than what the scientists try to corral into Petri dishes and onto microscope slides.

"Maslow warned us that if we lose our sense of the mysterious or the numinous that we will be diminished by that loss. I study the eastern philosophies because, as Aldous Huxley explained so eloquently, these philosophies don't deal with how well I adjust to society and others: They deal with how well I adjust to the nature of things which expresses in my mind-body and in the universe at large."

Freddie shook her head and laughed. "I'm sorry, but I was just thinking that it feels like I've completed a whole semester of college in the last two days!"

A little embarrassed by his didactic tendencies, Garrison apologized.

"No, no! It's been great!" she declared, still chuckling. "I wasn't criticizing you. It's just staggering how much you know about all this."

She realized how tired she was and how vulnerable as a result. So, she took the opportunity to steer away from any more emotionally-charged conversation by asking, "I do have another question though. The yin and yang. What did you call that drawing that represents them?"

"The Taiji."

"It seems to support this idea of the inclusion of opposites, such as good and evil in a person's psychology like you talked about."

"Yeah. It illustrates how every whole has within it both light and dark, good and evil. Even the black of the Yin has within it the white of the Yang. The Yang possesses a portion of the Yin as well. The Taiji portrays the unity of these opposites and how each supports the other. The reason it's such an important concept is because it's through the complementary expression of these opposing forces that manifestation occurs. Noumenally, they are equal forces in the Universe."

"Noumenally?" Freddie asked.

Without missing a stride, he replied, "It means intellectual intuition rather than something that's directly observable."

"Oh," Even though fascinated, Freddie was slightly intimidated by Garrison.

"In other words, it's only in the world of phenomena, the physical world, that one force becomes superior to the other. When this happens, it's nearly always inevitable that people start to believe it would be beneficial to rid themselves of the "inferior" force, hence, the battle of good vs. evil."

Garrison got up to get a drink. Watching Freddie sitting in her chair with her mouth pulled sideways as she chewed on the edge of her lip, Garrison wondered what she was thinking about.

Almost in answer to his ponderings, she spoke. "In a roundabout way, that's sort of what's bothering me about Mr. Personality."

"What?" Garrison was not following her logic.

"I don't even know this guy. Who am I to say that he's evil and I'm not? Am I right just because I'm me? I'm pretty sure he thinks he's doing the right thing. Avatar insists he's evil and has to be destroyed, but…" Her voice trailed off for a second. Before Garrison could reply, she continued. "Look, you just indicated that trying to rid ourselves of evil was wrong."

"Wait. I didn't mean to confuse you. I may have gone overboard trying to explain all this." Garrison did not want her to let her guard down.

"No, you didn't," she assured him. "I'm trying to understand concepts that I haven't spent any time at all thinking about before. I needed to hear the things you've told me. I'm just trying to apply it to what's going on."

Directing the conversation back to her point, Freddie said, "To be honest, I'm trying to figure out why I get to be called *good* and Mr. Personality is *evil*." Freddie was struggling with what had happened at the cabin, but she didn't want to reveal this to Garrison.

Garrison paused for a moment to consider the philosophical depths this conversation could take. "Let me give you an example that might help." Picking up his drink, he returned to his chair.

"Do you understand what happens when you decide to pick up a rock and throw it at a rat, digging its way into the wall of your house?"

"It flies through the air and hits the rat on the head."

"Does it?"

"Sure, it does."

"What if the rock weighs five pounds?"

Laughing, Freddie asked, "How far am I from this rat?"

"Too far to hit it with a five pound rock!" said Garrison, throwing a rolled up paper towel at her.

"Okay. Okay. What happens?"

"Well, there are two forces at work. The active or positive force is the action of your arm throwing the rock toward your target, the rat. The passive or negative force, also called the force of inertia, is the mass of the rock itself.

"These two forces exist independently of each other, but they also complement each other. The rock won't move without the active force of your arm. Yet the passive force of the rock, or its weight, determines how well you are able to achieve your goal of hitting the rat.

"If it's a perfect weight, you hit the rat square on the head. If it weighs too much, you miss the rat entirely and hit the lawn mower. The rock ricochets and makes a dent in the neighbor's Cadillac," he remarked playfully.

"Your point?" Freddie asked with a raised eyebrow.

"Whether you hit the rat or the Cadillac, both forces are at work. The bad thing happened when the size of the rock was too much for your throwing ability. It didn't matter that both times your goal was a constructive one.

"In the case of you and Mr. Personality, you could both have what you consider to be constructive goals. But, if your rock is too heavy—and in this case that refers to what we talked about yesterday: how capable you are of evil acts or the maturation level of your thoughts and emotions—then you will more than likely dent the Cadillac."

"Yeah. That's my point exactly. Mr. Personality may not intend to be evil. Maybe his rock is just too heavy!"

Garrison couldn't help laughing. "I take back what I said. You are a complete nut!"

"No. I'm serious," she insisted. "What if he thinks he's doing the right thing? What if he just doesn't understand enough to appreciate the impact it will have?"

"Freddie, do you think it's your responsibility to save him from himself?" Garrison was getting more worried by the minute about the direction the conversation was taking.

"No..." Freddie mechanically moved her fingers through the remaining rays of light to create shapes on the wall. Thinking about her encounter at Jodi's cabin, she added, "A jury of my peers would probably agree that Charlie and Cleland were evil, but it doesn't change the sick feeling I get when I think about hitting them over the head with that fireplace poker." She was sticking to her fabrication about what happened. "It didn't have to end the way it did."

Watching her face as she spoke, Garrison asked softly, "Are you afraid Mr. Personality is going to kill you?"

"Yes."

"Are you having visions of beating him to the punch? Is that what's bothering you?"

"There's a part of me that wants to annihilate him, but there's another part that doesn't. The kill, crush, and destroy part is easier to understand, that's all. I guess self-preservation is a pretty basic instinct." Freddie yawned and gracefully tried to cover it up by shifting in her chair.

"Hey," said Garrison, looking at his watch, "it's getting late! Maybe we ought to quit for the night." It was only seven o'clock, but they had been at it for ten hours. "Are you hungry?"

Freddie nodded.

"There's an all-you-can-eat Italian place around the corner on Highland. Care to try it?"

"Sure!" Freddie replied quickly. It had been two days since her last encounter with Mr. Personality, but she still didn't relish being alone.

After locking up his office, Garrison escorted Freddie across campus to the parking garage on Central. They entered through the side entrance because Garrison had parked his car near the stairwell on the third floor.

"Race you to the third floor!" Garrison shouted as he darted up the stairs.

"Are you crazy?" she shouted back. "I can barely walk upright!"

"Wimp!" he called back as he rounded the next flight of stairs, moving out of her sight. She ran to catch up with him. Just as she reached the door to the second level, she heard Garrison open the third floor door.

"Beat cha!" he shouted. "I'll start the car," he said just before she heard the door close.

"Cheater!" she shouted back even though she doubted that he could hear her. She slowed down to catch her breath. She was really out of shape. When she arrived on the last landing before the third floor exit, she paused, bending over with her hands on her knees to take a couple of deep breaths before starting up the final set of steps.

It's time! You can't stop it! The voice echoed in her head. She stayed bent over, afraid to look. Maybe if she didn't look, he would just go away.

You can't hide. You're a part of me.

Freddie screamed. It came from deep within her and was more like a plaintive howl. When she looked up, she saw Garrison standing in the doorway. He was slack-jawed, his eyes staring toward the space in front of him.

He can see it! I know he can see it! she thought. Then the image vanished. Freddie fell back against the stairwell wall and sobbed. Shaken out of his trance, Garrison rushed down the steps to her.

"It's okay," he said.

"You saw him. Tell me you did," she pleaded.

"Yes, I saw him," he confirmed.

"Could you hear him?"

"I didn't hear anything, but I had just opened the door when you started screaming. What did he say?"

"The same thing he's always said. Only this time he said that I couldn't hide from him because I was a part of him!" Freddie was shaking uncontrollably. Garrison put his arms around her and held her close. "I've never been as frightened as I am now."

"Did he say anything else?" Garrison asked.

"No. That was enough. I probably scared the hell out of him when I started screaming. I sounded like an animal in agony." A nervous laugh escaped.

"Listen. We don't have to go out to eat. We could go to your place or mine and fix a sandwich."

"I'd rather go to the restaurant. Maybe being around people will bring me back to earth. Right now I feel like I'm trapped in a nightmare zone, and I can't wake up." Freddie started walking across the parking lot. Garrison held the car door for her. Stepping forward to get into the car, she paused. "Thanks for being there."

Without a word, he leaned over and kissed her gently on the mouth. She responded without hesitation, and he pulled her to him. Feeling so safe for the first time in days, Freddie allowed herself to lose touch with her surroundings and melt into him. Then Garrison released her and pulled the car door open further for her to get in.

It was only a few blocks to the restaurant, and both were silent. It was a relaxed silence, an extension of their embrace. Garrison parked the car in front of the restaurant. Freddie got out and walked around the car to join Garrison. He put his arm around her and kissed her lightly on the cheek. It seemed as natural to her as breathing.

Over dessert, Garrison suggested they go back to Freddie's house. "That's different!" she exclaimed.

"What?"

"Usually the guy asks the girl back to *his* place."

Garrison laughed. "Well, we could, but I have an ulterior motive."

"Oh, this is getting interesting. Are you sure you don't have a wife at home you don't want me to see?" Freddie asked only half in jest.

"Actually I do." Garrison dropped his eyes. He sighed. Freddie felt the jarring thud of her heart as it fell into her stomach.

Looking across at her, he said, "When I asked you to my place earlier, I thought she'd gone to her mother's for a few days. I called home to check my messages when I went to the restroom and discovered that she'd come home early."

Freddie could not find any words. Her mouth dropped open slightly. At first she thought he was kidding, but when he looked at her, his expression was dead serious. Pushing back her chair before the tears could reach the surface, she said, "I think you ought to take me home."

Garrison reached across the table. "Wait!"

Jerking away, she said, "No! I want to go home now."

"Freddie, I was pulling your leg! You're such a tease that I thought I'd give you a dose of your own medicine. I didn't know it would upset you so much. I'm sorry. Really I am."

Freddie sat back down. She didn't know whether to slap him or laugh. She hoped he was telling her the truth.

"Go ahead," he said.

"Huh?"

"Go ahead and hit me. I know you want to."

"How do you know that?"

"I just put myself in your shoes. Why wouldn't you? Listen, I just didn't think. I assumed you believed me when I told you earlier that I wasn't married, but it's not your fault. These days it's the norm rather than the exception to be told lies by men." Freddie was sizing up his words as he spoke. "Forgive me?" he asked.

"Sure," she said, deciding to trust him. "By the way, what's the ulterior motive you mentioned for going to my place?"

"Oh, that. I want to meet Avatar. You were waiting for me on the sidewalk this morning, and I didn't get a chance."

"Can I ask you something?"

"Yeah."

"Do you *really* believe what I've told you? I mean, would you still believe me if you never saw the wolf?"

"Of course I believe you. What makes you think I don't?"

"Nothing in particular. It's—it's just that people usually have their own motives for doing things, and it's rare to find someone I can really trust."

"Listen. If you don't want me to see the wolf, that's the way it will be. I believe you, Freddie. I believed you before I saw Mr. Personality, and I don't need to see the wolf to convince me that you're not crazy." Garrison reached out and put his hand over hers.

They were silent for a few minutes. Then Freddie said simply, "Let's go."

When they arrived at the house, Freddie unlocked the front door and went in. She stepped aside to let Garrison into the foyer. "Let's go into the den, and I'll introduce you. Then I'll fix us a drink."

The wolf wasn't in the den. So Freddie headed for the kitchen. He wasn't there either. "Listen. I'm going to fix us a drink. Avatar's probably in the bedroom asleep. I'll go wake him in just a minute."

Garrison nodded as he sat down on the end of the sofa and faced the kitchen.

Freddie finished preparing the drinks and handed one to Garrison as she walked behind the sofa on the way to the bedroom.

"I'll be right back." Now that Garrison was here, she was excited about his meeting Avatar.

"I'll be right here," he replied.

Freddie walked down the hall. Her bedroom door was partially closed. Recent events having made her cautious, she tiptoed up to the bedroom door and eased it open. Peering into the room, she saw nothing wrong. *I wonder where he is?* she thought.

I am here.

Where? she asked, responding to the voice in her head.

In the study.

Freddie turned and headed back down the hall. She opened the study door. There on the floor was Avatar surrounded by all her papers and pictures. It looked like a tornado had spun out its fury within the walls of this room.

"Garrison!" she shouted as she ran to Avatar.

Garrison leaped to his feet and ran down the hall with his drink still in his hand. He found Freddie on her knees caressing the wolf along his shoulder as he lay on the floor. "What's going on?"

"I don't know," she replied. "I found him like this."

Is this Garrison?

"Yes, I am," replied Garrison, setting his drink on the bookcase just inside the door and dropping to his knees.

The wolf shifted his head slightly so he could look directly into Garrison's eyes, whose response had surprised him—and Freddie, for that matter.

"How—" began Freddie.

The wolf interrupted. *You must have very strong feelings for Freddie. Otherwise, you would never have picked up on the thoughts I directed to her.*

Freddie turned toward Garrison. He looked embarrassed as if his private thoughts had just been exposed for all to see.

I'm glad, said Avatar. *She is going to need someone who cares what happens to her.*

Startled by Avatar's words, Freddie demanded, "What do you mean? Are you leaving me? What happened to you?" Avatar was looking directly at Freddie, but she heard nothing. It frightened her. Then his words came into her mind.

Yes. I am leaving. My time on this Earth is done. My life force is very weak. I don't know why I'm still here except that his power was not as great as before. I was somehow able to withstand his efforts to consume my energies this time, but not soon enough to save my body.

"Mr. Personality was actually here? In my house? He did this to you?" Hysteria started to wash over her. If Avatar couldn't resist this maniac, how could she?

His body wasn't here, only his image.

In disbelief, Garrison spoke up. "His image did this much damage?" Looking around the room, he marveled at the awesome power it implied.

Avatar shifted slightly and whimpered. Freddie instinctively began petting him, thinking that somehow her affection for him would soothe him.

His name is Darian, and he is very powerful and very evil. He will strike out and kill anyone who stands in the way of what he wants. The wolf paused. Blood was trickling from his mouth, and his breathing had slowed to an erratic rhythm. *You, Garrison, may be in great danger.*

Frightened at the thought of losing anyone else, Freddie cried out, "Why? What does he want?"

He wants you, my child. You're part... Avatar's thoughts were fading. Freddie could barely hear them in her head.

"But why?" she pleaded. Her voice cracked with emotion. Fear was closing in on her. "Why?" she asked again. There was only silence.

Garrison reached down and placed his hand on Avatar's chest. "He's gone."

Freddie covered her face with her hands to hold back the onslaught of tears. Despite her best effort, she lost the battle. She trembled, making gasping noises as if she, too, were dying. Garrison reached out and pulled her to him. She laid her head on his chest and sobbed.

Chapter 45

Day 17

*T*he sun was coming up, but Garrison was already awake. Sitting on the sofa with Freddie's head in his lap, he gently stroked the hair along her face. She looked like an angel, he thought. Why was it necessary for her to endure so much pain? Freddie stirred. Afraid he was disturbing her sleep, he put his arm on the back of the sofa.

He sat quietly for the next twenty minutes, wondering what to say to her. He hadn't been totally honest with her, but he felt it was justified. If he'd told her the truth, she might have pushed him away. He didn't want that.

Without warning, Freddie sat up. She looked confused for a moment but adjusted quickly to finding herself sleeping on Garrison's lap. Rubbing her eyes, she asked, "Did you get any sleep?"

"A little," Garrison replied.

"You shouldn't have let me sleep like that all night."

"It's okay. I can doze off anywhere."

"No, I mean you shouldn't have let *me* sleep like that all night. I'm so stiff I can barely move!"

Laughing, he shoved her off the sofa onto the floor. "You selfish little wench! Here I was worrying about you, standing guard all night, getting very little sleep I might add, and what do you do? Bitch, bitch, bitch! Did you hear me complaining because my legs went numb hours ago from the weight?" Freddie swung at him playfully. "No-o-o! I did not complain, perfect martyr that I am!"

He reached down to help her up, and she pulled him toward her. Not being prepared, he rolled off the sofa and landed on top of her.

Both were laughing hysterically as Freddie tried to push him off of her. It was a welcome outlet for the stress of the previous night. Rolling over onto his side and propping himself on one elbow, Garrison said, "I can't take all this frivolity on an empty stomach!"

"Me either!" As she tried to get up, she banged his chin with her head, and he bit his lip.

"Foul!" he cried. "Ten yard penalty."

Seeing the drop of blood forming on his lower lip, Freddie touched her finger to the blood. Garrison took her hand in his, pulled her toward him, and kissed her gently. Garrison released her, but Freddie pulled him back, kissing him with such intensity that it startled them both. When she finally released her hold on him, he stood, holding out his hand to help her up.

As she let him pull her up, she was worried. Had she taken too much for granted because she felt vulnerable right now? Then Garrison bent over and lifted her feet off the floor and carried her to the bedroom. Dreams of knights in shining armor paled beside the feelings surging through her as he laid her gently on the bed.

It was the sweetest, most wonderful hour in her entire life. She'd never known she could feel that way. The genuine caring, the feeling of being truly joined with another human being. She had experienced some very highly charged sexual moments in the past, but this transcended the sexual act. It reached beyond the physical to that cage where her soul had been imprisoned for so long. Garrison had opened the latch and allowed her soul to once again soar through the vastness of the Universe. Only this time it was not alone. She wasn't sure how she felt. She only knew that she was not the same as she'd been three days ago or even an hour ago.

Garrison took her hand. "Do you think we ought to get up? We have a lot of things to do and not much time in which to do them."

Feeling a little guilty about taking up all his time, she said, "It just dawned on me that you and I have been together since I met you on Monday. This is Thursday, and you haven't worked all week. At least not at the University. I'm not going to be responsible for getting you fired, am I?"

"No. I don't have any regularly scheduled classes this semester."

Surprised, she asked, "Why not? Do they pay you not to teach?"

"There are those who would appreciate it if they did, but the truth is that I was awarded a research grant last year. So, I took a leave of absence from the University for one semester. I didn't really leave, as you can see, but it enables me to concentrate on my research without being distracted by classes. It also freed up the University from paying my salary for a while. They weren't too upset about it."

"Who's teaching your classes?"

"No one. The way it is these days, the University never offers all the classes every semester. Students often have to enroll for an extra semester in order to fulfill their course requirements because what they need is not being offered during what should have been their last semester. I feel sorry for them, but it's common, and this is only one semester."

"What about your research? Aren't you getting behind?"

He laughed. "You are a worrier, aren't you? No, things have gone very well. I could take a two week vacation and still be on schedule. So stop worrying. No one is going to give me demerits for being out of pocket."

"Okay. I just needed to know for sure," she replied, sitting up on the side of the bed.

"Get dressed, and we'll go out for breakfast."

"I can fix something here."

"No. I want to go out," he said, knowing he was going to have to tell her about himself, but dreading it.

"Now it comes out!" she declared, hitting him with her pillow. "You're afraid to eat my cooking."

"You'd better believe it. Whoever heard of a commodity analyst who could cook?" He kissed the top of her head and then pushed her in the direction of the shower.

An hour later they were getting into Garrison's car when Freddie spotted Jodi standing in her garage. Jodi didn't look in their direction. After Garrison backed out of the driveway, she reached over and honked the horn to get her attention, but she kept her back to the street. Freddie shrugged. She was probably engrossed in what she was doing. Jodi could be very intense. A twinge of regret passed through her. She hoped Jodi wasn't still afraid of her.

Garrison didn't know Jodi, but from all Freddie had told him, he assumed that's whom she was honking at. "What's wrong?" he asked, seeing the worried look on her face.

"I don't know," replied Freddie.

"She probably just didn't hear the horn."

"Maybe."

"What? What are you thinking?"

"Well, you didn't see her the other day at the cabin. She was really scared. Scared of me. I haven't seen her since I got back. I've been with you most of the time. So I don't know if she's still afraid of me or not. Maybe her feelings are hurt because I haven't called her. Think so?" Freddie looked at Garrison, hoping for reassurance.

"Look. Didn't you say she was your best friend?"

"Yeah, but—"

"But nothing. If she's your best friend, she'll get over whatever's bothering her. Just give her some time. Okay?"

"Okay," replied Freddie, but she wasn't so sure that time would take care of it.

Not having a destination in mind, Garrison tried to think of the best place to eat. He wanted to make sure they could talk without a time limit. He dreaded this conversation because he was sure that Freddie would think he had been using her.

"Do you mind if we just go to Mrs. Winner's?" he asked. "The breakfast crowd is gone, and it's too early for the lunch bunch. Plus, fast food joints don't care how long you stay."

"Are you that hungry?" she joked.

"No, silly, but it drives me crazy when I'm trying to talk, and the waitress keeps asking me if everything's okay. You know they just want you to free up their table." He added, "We need to draft a plan of some kind."

"You're right. We should decide what to do next. Besides, being in a fast food place with lots of windows feels safer to me somehow. I don't think my resident ghost will show up in a public place. Do you?" She was almost pleading for confirmation.

"Probably not," replied Garrison as he pulled into the parking lot of Mrs. Winner's. He had been right. The only customers were the drive-thru ones. They had the entire dining room to themselves. They each ordered a bacon, egg, and cheese biscuit, a cinnamon swirl, and coffee. Garrison led the way to a table near the front window.

"Wait here. I'll be right back," said Garrison. Freddie watched him go out to his car. Reaching into the back seat, he brought out his briefcase.

Settling down at the table, Garrison placed his briefcase on the chair beside him. "I thought we might need something to write on, and I always carry legal pads with me. Let's eat first though. I'm starving."

Garrison was killing time, trying to put off the inevitable. Finally they finished eating. He knew he had run out of excuses. He reached into his briefcase and pulled out a couple of legal pads.

"Let me clear off the table and get us some more coffee before we get started." Freddie jumped up, gathering all the paper and plastic forks onto a tray. "I just love their biscuits! They're sort of addictive."

"Well, if we stay long enough, maybe we can have biscuits for lunch!" Freddie just laughed at him as she headed to the courtesy counter for more coffee.

Garrison dressed up his coffee with cream and sugar, stirring it very carefully. He gave Freddie a pad and pencil. *Okay, this is it.* Taking a deep breath, he said, "Freddie, I know we're supposed to be working on a plan, but I need to talk to you first. It's really important."

It felt like someone kicked her in the stomach. *What are you trying to do, Garrison? Give me a heart attack?* She had no idea what to expect, but she couldn't help wondering if Garrison was too good to be true. Trying to calm herself, she asked as nonchalantly as she could manage, "What is it, Garrison?"

He reached across the table and placed his hand on hers. There was such worry and concern on his face that Freddie started to panic. *Omigod!* she thought, *He does have a wife!* It was the worst thing she could think of at the moment. Her stomach flopped like a fish on the beach.

"Freddie, I haven't been completely honest with you." Her heart was pounding so hard she could barely hear what he was saying. "Monday when you were in the library and you saw Mr. Personality in the elevator..." He paused.

Her mouth was so dry she could hardly gather up enough saliva to speak. "What about it?"

"Well, I didn't just happen along."

"Garrison! What are you talking about? You're scaring me. Just spit it out!"

"Don't be scared, Freddie. There's no reason to be scared." Looking at her face, he suddenly understood that she thought he had lied to her so they could make love, and now he was preparing her to be dumped.

"Freddie, for reasons I don't quite understand, I feel as if we were meant to be together. These last few days seem a little like a fairy tale and a nightmare all jumbled together."

"Which part am I?" asked Freddie, still hurting from what she had imagined he was about to say.

"You, Freddie, are the fairy tale. I think you know that," he replied. Freddie felt ashamed when she saw the distress in his face.

"So what *are* you saying?" she asked.

"I didn't just happen along," he repeated. "I knew that Darian, or Mr. Personality as you were calling him, was there." Freddie gaped at him, her mouth open. "I was there because I sensed his presence. That's why I wasn't taken aback when you said you'd seen a ghost."

"Wait a minute! Are you telling me that you know this fruit loop?" She was sickened by the thought.

"No! I don't know Darian. I just knew there was a presence nearby that was out of its body."

"How could you know that?" she demanded.

"That's what I want to tell you. It's a long story."

"Well, I certainly have plenty of time—at least until Mr. Per— excuse me, until Darian shows up again!" Freddie was angry that Garrison had not told her the truth. Whatever it was.

Seeing the anger flashing in her eyes, Garrison asked, "Will you promise to hear me out? To just let me tell you so you'll know that I really do want to help you?"

"Sure. Fire away." Freddie was using anger to stave off her hurt feelings and regain some control. She leaned back against the chair and looked him straight in the eyes.

"When I was a child—"

"Do we really have to go back that far?" she asked snidely.

"You promised to hear me out." Garrison hadn't realized how fragile Freddie was. He hoped they could survive this.

"Okay. Go ahead."

"When I was a child," he continued, "my father was an alcoholic and very abusive. He beat my mother when he was drinking, and when he was sober, he beat on me. It didn't take much to set him off. Just being who I was and where I was seemed to be enough. When I was smaller, he tended to hit me with the back of his hand. As I got older, he chased me around the house, swinging his belt. I often wished he'd chosen to beat me when he was drunk rather than sober. At least then, he wasn't as sure-footed. Anyway, it always ended the same. He'd catch me and hit me over and over again." Garrison paused. He had never told this story to anyone, and it was more difficult than he had imagined.

Although Freddie was still in the dark about her connection to all this, she was no longer angry. She ached to put her arms around him and hold him close to her, but she remained perfectly still.

He continued. "Probably the only reason no one reported him was because no one knew. I was too young for school. Mother was too scared. My family had no friends to notice the marks on either of us. During the time he was beating me, I began separating myself from my body. I was trying to escape the pain, and I suppose, just pretend it wasn't happening. I didn't have a lot of options at the time. I didn't even realize at the time that I was leaving my body.

"When I was five years old, my mother finally got up enough nerve to divorce my father. He moved to California, and we never heard from him again."

"Thank God!" Freddie said.

"For a few years everything went well, and I forgot all about being able to separate from my body. Then my mother started dating again. It seems she just had bad taste in men. She rarely brought any of her dates home. She did come home with bruises on her arms and occasionally a split lip." Freddie winced.

"She always had a story to go along with them, and being a kid, I wanted to believe her of course. But when I was ten, I heard her telling a friend that her date had gotten a little frisky, as she called it, and knocked her around. I wanted to kill him."

"What did you do?"

"You have to understand. My mother was all I had, and she was always kind to me. I didn't blame her for my father being a monster." He smiled. "She always came into my room at night to tuck me in. Sitting on the side of the bed, she'd tell me how lucky we were to have each other. Usually she'd run her hand slowly across my forehead to push my hair out of my eyes. The last thing every night, she'd lean down and press her cheek against mine and kiss my ear lobe. Then she'd whisper, *I love you, baby*. I can still remember the soft smell of

SECOND CHANCES

349

flowers that always lingered after she was gone."

A huge knot formed in Freddie's throat. She tried desperately not to cry, but the tears were slipping out anyway. Garrison didn't notice. He had been staring at his hands, clasped in front of him since he began telling his story.

"The thought that anyone was hurting her was more than I could stand. After I heard what she told her friend, I'd lie in bed at night thinking about it until it seemed the anger couldn't be contained inside me.

"Then one night it happened again. I separated from my body. When I was looking down at myself, all those other times when I was younger came back to me. I can't tell you how excited I was. Even as a ten-year-old, I knew this was not commonplace. I vowed to keep it a secret, even from my mother. Over the next two years, I practiced. I even discovered that I could move things with my mind. Telekinesis."

Garrison took a drink of his coffee and looked out the window. He knew there was no turning back. He had to tell her everything. Resuming his focus on his hands, he continued.

"When I was twelve, my mother was dating this guy named Lester Ballard. He seemed nice at first, and she started inviting him over for dinner. She'd never brought anyone home before so I thought maybe this was a good thing. After about two months, I noticed that Lester wasn't around so much. I wondered why, but I didn't say anything. Then one evening he shows up at the front door. Mother asked me to give them some privacy. I went to my room and turned on the radio.

"I got hungry after a while so I turned off the radio and went to fix myself a sandwich. I tiptoed out of my room because I thought she and Lester were still in the living room. When I didn't see them, I went to my mother's bedroom to ask her what happened to Lester. She wasn't there. I was alone in the house. I searched everywhere and couldn't find her. Our car was still in the driveway, but Lester's was gone. I couldn't believe she'd just leave without telling me, but I didn't get upset. I figured she'd be right back. I fixed a sandwich and went back to my room.

"I fell asleep and had the worst nightmare of my life. I saw Mother and Lester at the neighborhood park. They were just inside the woods on one of the walking trails. Lester was bellowing, and he had his hands around her throat. She was choking. Then I saw him throw her down on the ground. She didn't move.

"That's when I woke up screaming. I was in a total panic. I didn't know what to do, and there was no one I could call. Then it hit me. I'd go there myself. I would leave my body in my room and see for myself if it was real."

Tears crept out of the corners of Garrison's eyes. He covered his face with his left hand. Freddie saw his shoulders trembling. She wasn't used to men crying, but she reached out and touched his arm. He put his right hand over hers until he regained his composure.

"Garrison, you don't have to do this."

"Yes. Yes, I do." He raised her hand to his lips, kissed it gently, and then held it against his cheek for a few seconds. Taking a deep breath, he continued. "I was at the park in seconds. I saw my mother, lying on the ground. She had a look of bewilderment on her face. I knew she was dying.

"Freddie, I lost control. Lester was just standing there like the winner in a boxing match. I kept expecting him to raise his fists in the air and circle her body. I was just a kid, but I never felt as much hate before or since as I did at that moment.

"I lunged at him. I was so angry that I completely forgot that my body was still in my bedroom. He stumbled backwards, slapping his arms in the air. That was when I remembered he couldn't see me. I don't know if it was the anonymity, knowing that I could get away with it, or what it was. But, I started pushing and shoving him across the park grounds. He fell down several times, but I was relentless. Each time he managed to get up and run.

"By the time we reached the thoroughfare bordering the park, Lester was hysterical. He had no idea what was happening, but he must have thought it was Mother's ghost. Just as he reached the edge of the road, he shrieked, *Get away from me, bitch!* That was the last straw. My fury propelled me toward him. He fell backward onto the highway. Right into the path of a big truck. I just looked at him and turned away. I felt no remorse at all. He didn't die until the next morning I found out later.

"I went back to where my mother was lying on the ground. She smiled at me as she rose out of her body. I was so glad she could see me that I didn't realize what was happening at first. She smiled at me again, reached out toward me with her hand, and said, *I love you, baby.* Then she was gone beyond my reach."

By this time, Garrison was crying in earnest. Freddie went around to his side of the table and pulled up a chair. She put her arms around him and held him close. Tears flowed down her face as well, as much for her as for Garrison.

Thankfully, no one had come into the restaurant for lunch yet because it took Garrison nearly five minutes to control his emotions. Feeling very protective of him, Freddie went to the counter and got refills on coffee, a glass of water, and extra napkins.

"Are you all right, Miss?" the lady at the cash register asked.

"There was a death in the family," Freddie replied. "Sometimes it just hits you at the strangest times." It was sort of the truth, she thought.

The lady nodded. "I know what you mean. My husband died last year. I'm so sorry." Wanting to help but not knowing what to do, she said, "Here. Take these biscuits. Sometimes it helps to eat something." Freddie smiled at her, genuinely moved by her concern.

When she got back to the table, Garrison had stopped crying and was wiping his face with the corner of a napkin.

"Here. Use these. They're clean, and I got a glass of water to dip them in."

Looking up at her, he said, "I think you need these worse than I do."

Grabbing her mirror out of her purse, Freddie laughed when she saw her reflection. "We must look like a couple of escaped mental patients!"

Garrison chuckled. Then he drank some of his coffee and watched her straighten her make-up. For a few minutes things seemed normal, but it was an illusion he thought. Things would probably never be normal again.

Freddie broke the silence. "Why didn't you tell me?"

"I just couldn't. When I sensed Darian in the library, I was as frightened as you. I've never encountered another traveler. Then I saw you standing across from the elevator, scared out of your mind. The next thing I knew I was talking to you. Since then I've come to believe I was meant to be there."

"I'm glad you were." She squeezed his hand.

"You looked so innocent, and you were so scared. I was afraid that if I told you that I knew what was happening, you'd run away. As we became friends, I was terrified that if I told you the truth, that is, about killing Lester, you would hate me."

"Why would I hate you?"

"I killed a man for God's sake!" Garrison said.

"He deserved it." Freddie could feel the discomfort of her own secret starting to invade her composure.

"But, don't you see? You were in the same kind of situation, and you were strong enough to resist killing those two men." Freddie squirmed in her chair. "I've always struggled with what I did because I've never felt any sorrow about his death. On the other hand, I know there must be something wrong inside me that I could just kill him like that," said Garrison, shaking his head in disgust.

"Garrison, sometimes in our lives, we're confronted with situations which are beyond our understanding, and we deal with them the best way we know how. You were protecting your mother. I was protecting Jodi and myself. We're just human, Garrison. We are fraught with frailties and shortcomings. If we act with the best intentions and revenge bleeds into the mix a little, it's not always something we can control."

She paused, unable to maintain her pedagogic attitude. "There's something I need to share with you, too. I didn't just overpower those two men. I killed them. Not only that, I think I enjoyed the power I had when I did it."

Garrison looked at her in complete surprise. Choosing not to make a direct reference to her killing the two men, he asked, "Were you afraid I'd think less of you if you told me the truth?"

"My reason was the same as yours. I was ashamed to tell you. I have felt remorse, but I don't really think I would handle it differently if it happened now. That's what has bothered me the most. Hearing your story helps me accept that I can't relive the past, and I can't go forward if I don't let go of it. I did what I did. Maybe I'll handle it differently if there's ever a next time. Maybe not, but I can't just shut myself down because of it."

Sensing a need to take a breather, Freddie picked up a biscuit and took a bite. "Here," she said, handing one to Garrison. "The lady at the counter said it helps." Pausing to swallow, she asked, "I have a question. Why were you able to hear the wolf when he was talking to me?"

"I don't know for sure. I just know that I seem to be sensitive to the plane of existence where telepathy and out-of-body experiences occur. It's not really uncommon. There are lots of anecdotal accounts of similar experiences by others."

"Avatar seemed to think it was because you had feelings for me." Freddie knew she was fishing, but she didn't care.

"He may have been right. It's entirely plausible that an emotional bond between two people would make it easier. They'd be on the same wavelength, so to speak." Garrison knew what she wanted to hear. "*Are* we on the same wavelength?"

Freddie was startled by the adept manner with which he turned the tables on her. "I would like to think so."

"So would I."

By sharing some of the things that had been tearing at the fabric of their hearts, Garrison and Freddie reached a new plateau with each other. They trusted each other, at least as much as they trusted themselves.

Chapter 46

Garrison sat behind his desk scribbling notes and frowning. He and Freddie had decided that his office was the most untainted place to work. Going back to her house so soon after what had happened to Avatar hadn't felt quite right to Freddie. Garrison agreed, but he hoped that what happened to Avatar last night hadn't tainted her memories of their later lovemaking.

Garrison opened his mouth to speak several times as he scrutinized what had happened and what he knew about it but abruptly closed it. Finally, he said, "Look, Freddie, I'm going to suggest something that may not be all that appealing to you, but it may be necessary."

Sensing the seriousness of his mood, she abstained from her usual repartee. Instead she just waited for him to continue.

"I've been trying to approach this situation in a logical manner. The obvious approach, one a journalist would probably take, is the *who*, *what*, *when*, *where*, *why*, and *how* approach. "

"Okay," Freddie responded quickly, surprising Garrison. "Let's take each of those and form a specific question."

"Actually, I've been trying to do that. The first one's rather obvious. *Who* is Mr. Personality? We know his name is Darian, but other than that, I'm stumped. Second, *What* does he want and *What* is it that you can't stop? For the third one – *When* – my question concerns what he meant by "It's time.""

"You could ask *When* is this thing that I can't stop going to happen!" interjected Freddie.

"Yeah. That may be the most important question. Fourth, *Where* is he? I mean physically, of course. Fifth, *Why* is he after you specifically? Finally, *How* is he doing this? That's probably the only question I have an answer to considering my own experiences."

Warming up to this approach, Freddie jumped right in. "Let's start with *Who*. We know his name is Darian because Avatar told us. However, *Who* has to include more than just his first name. I want to know what his relationship is to me. I want a last name."

Stumped already, her enthusiasm started to wane for the logical approach. "Until we know these things, I don't see how we're going to answer any of the other questions."

"I agree with you, but I still think it's important we address each of the questions anyway. It may spark a memory or a connection for us."

"Okay." Freddie did not sound too optimistic.

"In addition to knowing his name, Avatar told us he is powerful and evil. That's sort of who he is and what he is, I guess," said Garrison

"What he did to Avatar is proof of that," she remarked, a slight tremor in her voice. Thinking about last night brought tears to her eyes. "What does he want?" she cried.

"You apparently."

"But WHY?!?!" Freddie clenched her fists in anger, striking the edge of the desk with them.

"Do you remember what you told me Darian said in the stairwell?"

"Of course!" she replied impatiently. "He said the same thing he always says! *It's time. You can't stop it.*"

"No, not that. The last thing he said."

Freddie did not answer. Garrison waited. Finally, she said, "He said, *You are a part of me.*" A shiver ran through her, and her shoulders jerked.

Leaning forward, Garrison put his hand on her shoulder. "Freddie, I know this isn't easy, but we have to do it. I don't think he's going to go away, and if we don't figure it out, he's going to win.

Frankly, I don't know what it means for him to win, but I shudder to think of the possibilities."

"But how could I be a part of him?" she whimpered. "Maybe I misunderstood him. You didn't hear what he said, and I was pretty freaked out."

Settling back into his chair, Garrison said, "No. You heard him right."

"How do you know that?" Now her voice had a combative edge.

As much as he hated to ask her to do it, he said, "Think back to last night before Avatar died. You asked him what Darian wanted. Do you remember?"

She nodded. "He said Darian wanted me, but I—"

"He also said something else," insisted Garrison.

"No, he didn't." Her voice got louder and more insistent. "Don't you remember? Those were the last words he said before he died. I asked him why, but he never answered."

"You're wrong, Freddie." Garrison was not enjoying this confrontation with her but knew it was unavoidable. "He said two more words before you asked him why the second time, but you were so emotional that you probably didn't hear him."

"What words? I don't remember anything else."

"He said, *You're part* but he never finished the sentence. His life slipped away, but he was confirming what Darian said to you in the stairwell. The point is, this idea that you are a part of him must be a primary element of his fixation on you."

Garrison waited for Freddie to reply, but there was only silence. While he was talking, she had turned to stare out of the window. Now she was like a statue chiseled from stone. Garrison couldn't even tell if she was breathing. He waited patiently, letting her assimilate all the troublesome events of the last couple of weeks.

Garrison's office faced the west. So the shadows of the evening seemed to linger far into the morning hours. The branches of the large oak tree in the courtyard protected this safe haven from the sun's rays, but now the sun had moved far enough into the sky that even the stately old tree could not forestall the inevitable. A stream of light fell on Freddie's face with the same suddenness that accompanies the setting of the sun.

At first, Freddie didn't move. Gradually, Garrison saw tiny movements of her fingers and then her shoulders shifted slightly. Finally she blinked and shifted her gaze toward the room. Garrison still did not speak. Although he had been patiently waiting for nearly half an hour, he knew it was better if *she* broke the spell she'd been under.

Freddie turned toward him finally but said nothing. A tear rolled down her cheek. Just one. She made no move to wipe it away. Garrison felt his insides being ripped apart. To him that one tear said more about Freddie than any words could have. It carried in it all the fear and sadness he knew she was carrying; yet it heralded the strength that was the core of who she was. She wasn't denying a weaker side, but she was refusing to allow it to control her, especially now.

"I've accepted that I am a part of Darian somehow," she said without warning, responding to Garrison's remarks a half hour earlier. "I assume that means he's kin to me. I don't know much about my family. My parents didn't seem to have any. It seems kind of ridiculous now, but when I was growing up, I never gave it much thought. I knew my grandparents were dead. So I never asked questions."

"Do you have any scrapbooks that belonged to your parents? Or maybe legal documents?"

"Yeah. There are some boxes I keep in the attic. I've never gone through them." Before he could reply, she hastened to add, "I know. That sounds crazy, too, but there was no reason to look through them. My parents didn't leave any money, and I knew they didn't have life insurance. The lady next door went over and boxed everything up for me. As far as I knew, she was the only friend my mother had.

"It seemed a little intrusive to rifle through their stuff. They never talked about anybody beyond our little family. I guess I was bound by a lifetime of secrecy. Anyway, their things are still in the attic, taped up and labeled."

"Then I think it's time to adjourn to your house," suggested Garrison, rising from his chair. He expected her to resist, but reluctantly Freddie gathered up her purse and her notes and followed him.

Chapter 47

Glancing toward Jodi's house as Garrison slowed to turn into her driveway, Freddie couldn't tell if Jodi was home. It made her sad to think she may have lost her best friend. Looking at her own house, she wondered if her feelings about this place would ever be the same again.

Last night they had buried Avatar in the back yard even though she knew it was against a city ordinance, but then, having a "pet" wolf probably was, too. This morning she'd actually forgotten for a while what had happened last night. While she and Garrison were making love, there seemed to be nothing else. Maybe it was *because* of everything else that their passion had been all-consuming. She wasn't sure, but she didn't intend to lose what they had. Even Avatar sensed a special connection between the two of them.

There was a palpable silence in the house. Without hesitating, Freddie threw her purse on the sofa and headed toward the stairs off the kitchen. The attic area was expandable so the stairs weren't retractable. Garrison followed her. At the top of the stairs she flicked a switch on the wall. When she turned the door knob, the door flew out of her grasp and slammed against the wall. Instinctively, Garrison ducked.

Laughing, Freddie said, "Sorry. I always forget to open the door *before* I turn on the attic fan, and it nearly jerks the door off its hinges!"

Garrison stepped into the attic room. His eyebrows raised when he saw the size of the fan mounted in the end gable of the house. It was at least four feet across.

Noting the look of disbelief on his face, Freddie explained. "The reason it's so large is that I use it to cool the house in the summer. I open all the windows, prop open the attic door, of course, and turn on the fan. It's sort of like living in a wind tunnel, but it keeps the heat and my electricity bill down."

"Uh huh," he said skeptically. "Do you think we'll be able to look through these papers up here?"

Thinking he was referring to the heat build-up, she replied, "Sure! It'll cool down in a few minutes."

"I'm more concerned about the papers being sucked up by the fan. I'm also a bit worried because I've lost some weight lately, and I'm sure I present a better lift to thrust ratio these days!"

"You-u-u!" she said, shoving him playfully.

"I'm serious. I can feel myself levitating at this very moment!" he said, grabbing hold of one of the wall studs.

"Move over here out of the path of the door, silly." Freddie had moved into the area of the attic framed for an extra bedroom. All the boxes were neatly placed in this skeleton room. "These are the boxes I was talking about."

Garrison noted that each of them was labeled either *clothes* or *papers*. Those labeled "papers" far outnumbered the others. This did not promise to be an easy task.

"Do you want to do this up here? There are an awful lot of boxes to go through. Maybe we ought to carry some of them downstairs. At least we could sit." Garrison didn't like the closed-in feeling of the attic.

"Do you mind? That's a lot of boxes to carry down the stairs."

"That's okay. Besides, there's more light to see by downstairs, and it's closer to the refrigerator." He grabbed two small boxes and started toward the door. Freddie grabbed one medium-sized box and followed him down.

Within fifteen minutes, all of the boxes marked *papers* were stacked in the den floor. Freddie carried one of the smaller boxes over to the breakfast room table and opened it, revealing a pile of pictures.

"What is it?" asked Garrison as he shut the refrigerator door and popped the top on a soda.

"Looks like a bunch of old pictures," she replied as she stuck her hand down into the box and lifted the contents on one side. Then she let her hand fan through them as they fell back into place.

"Let's empty them out on the table. Once you point out your parents for me, we can search through the pictures together. If we can find information on some people you don't know, there's a chance they could tell us more about your family."

"Okay." Freddie placed her hands against the inside edges of the box and gently tunneled her way to the bottom. "Pull on the box," she said.

Garrison removed the box from the contents, and they spilled across the table despite her efforts to contain them. She leaned against the table as she released her grip on the rest of the pictures, trying to keep them from tumbling to the floor.

Freddie plucked a picture from the top of the pile. "These are my parents," she announced, handing him a small snapshot.

Garrison looked carefully at the two people in the photograph, searching for traces of Freddie. Her mother, wearing a sweater and a full skirt, was of average height with shoulder-length, dark hair. She had pulled it back on the sides and fastened it in the back. Her husband's arm was around her waist. He was about four inches taller and had a "preppie" look about him with his v-neck, pull-over sweater and a dress shirt and necktie. Smiling broadly, they looked very comfortable together. They reminded him of college kids in old issues of the campus publication.

"They sure look young here," he commented.

"It's hard to tell. There's no date on yours, but this one," she said, picking up another small photo, "has 1957 written on it, and they look pretty much the same." She held it up for him to see. It was black and white. "They would have been 27 years old then, nearly my age. I was five years old then."

"Do you know these people?" Garrison was holding a photo of her parents and another couple. Turning it over, he said, "It says Arliss, Roy, Nancy, and Bret."

"Well, Arliss and Roy are my parents' names. Nancy and Bret. Hm-m-m. Let me see. It sounds familiar." Once again she was biting the corner of her bottom lip and frowning.

A tell if I ever saw one, thought Garrison.

"Oh, yeah! They lived next door to us when I was little. They lived in the same house as the lady who packed up the boxes for me when they died. It seems Mom said something about Bret dying. I don't know about Nancy. They moved away probably fifteen years ago. I'm trying to remember their last name, but I can't seem to dig it up."

"Did your parents always live there?"

"Well, not always, but it's the only place I remember."

The phone rang. Freddie jumped, knocking pictures onto the floor. "So much for having myself under control," she muttered as she walked toward the phone.

"Hello?"

"Is this Freddie? Freddie Marsh?"

"Yes, it is. Who's this?"

"My name is Angela. Angela Downing."

Freddie glanced at Garrison and shrugged, indicating she did not know the person on the other end of the line. "Should I know you?" she asked.

"No," responded Angela, "but I do know your cousin. Actually—"

Freddie interrupted. "My what?" She managed to control the tone of her voice, but Garrison guessed that the conversation was not a welcome one.

"Your cousin. Darian Marsh. As I was saying, that's actually who I'm looking for. Do you know where I can reach him?"

Freddie stiffened at the mention of Darian's name and turned away from Garrison so that she could focus. She felt her blood pulsing through the vein on her neck, but she managed to respond in a measured tone. She wanted to learn as much as she could from this woman who seemed to know his name and his relationship to her. "Should I?" she inquired politely.

"You mean you don't?" Angela knew Darian had intended to surprise Freddie, but it had been a week since she saw him last. She assumed he had gone to see Freddie. Afraid now that she'd spilled the beans, she pleaded with Freddie. "Please don't let him know I called when you do talk to him. He wanted it to be a surprise. Please?"

"Why would it be a surprise?" Freddie was trying to ask the right questions, but not knowing the plot of this play, she was only confusing Angela.

"Well, he said you had never met. I located you for him through databases available to the library where I work." That was sort of true she thought. "I just figured you didn't know about him either."

Without addressing her statement, Freddie asked, "Do you know why he wanted to find me?" By now Garrison was standing next to her. There was no doubt in his mind that the call was about Darian.

Angela was distressed. If Darian hadn't contacted Freddie by now, she had spoiled it for him. Still, she thought, it seemed that things were not quite the way Darian had told her. A tingle of apprehension passed through her. She felt like a fly caught in a spider's web. "Look. I've said too much already. I didn't mean to interfere. I should never have called. I just wanted to talk to Darian."

Sensing Angela's panic and not wanting to lose the only connection to this madman she had, she shifted her focus to Angela. "Have you known him for long?"

"Not really. I met him nearly three weeks ago, and he spent several days at my house last week. We sort of hit it off," she added as an explanation. Then her voice softened. "It was very special."

Freddie recognized the sound of infatuation. Unexpectedly she found herself worrying about Angela. How could Angela, who sounded like a sweet young woman, be infatuated with the same monster who had killed Avatar and maybe Joyce? Despite her concerns, Freddie couldn't help being excited. This meant Angela knew what he really looked like and maybe where he lived.

Angela continued, "I haven't seen him in nearly a week, and I don't know how to reach him. I just thought he'd gone to see you. At least I was hoping he had." Her voice trailed off.

"Why did you hope that?" Freddie disguised her disappointment that Angela didn't know how to reach him.

"I thought maybe I'd done something wrong. I mean, those three days—well, they were really nice, but I haven't seen or heard from him since."

I have, thought Freddie.

Despite Angela's obvious attraction to Darian, Freddie sensed that it was more than his failure to call her that was bothering Angela. She had to know what it was. This woman was her only link to stopping him. Sure that Angela would be reluctant to point a finger at Darian, she played on her emotions. "Do you think something might have happened to him?"

"Yeah. Well, no...maybe." The hesitancy in her voice sparked excitement in Freddie akin to reaching the final lap in a long distance race with no one ahead of you. Maybe they'd finally found a way to stop this maniac!

"What does that mean?" she asked. "Has someone else been hurt? Someone he knew?" Freddie's instincts pointed toward violence where he was concerned, but she didn't want to put Angela on the defensive. So she continued to show concern for him.

Angela started to cry. "I don't know."

Between sobs, Freddie gently beseeched her. "You can tell me, Angela. I need to know, and you're the only one who can help me."

Imploring Angela's help was the ticket. Her concerns flooded out of her in a nearly incoherent fashion. She was on the verge of hysteria, and Freddie was having to constantly soothe her just to get the details straight.

Seven women's bodies had been found the night before in a ravine outside of the neighboring town. The media had refrained from describing their bodies, but the gossipmongers in town had called it *unholy*.

"What does this have to do with you? Or Darian?" Freddie asked.

"I know it's silly, and I shouldn't be saying this to you—you being his cousin and all—but one of the girls worked at a restaurant where Darian and I went on our first date. I saw the way she looked at him. I also know he was flirting with her. On our way out of the dining room, I saw his reflection in the glass. He put his hand under her chin and made a kissing gesture toward her. After we got to the car, he went back in. He said the cashier gave him too much money. I believed him, but today I'm not so sure." There was a short silence. "I'm probably just imagining things," she said.

Freddie didn't want to lose her at this point. "Something else is upsetting you besides this one incident, Angela. Tell me what it is."

"This is really silly. You probably think I'm a head case."

"I know that you're upset, but that doesn't make you a head case. Talking can only help, and I'm willing to listen. Nothing you say is going to upset me. So get it off your chest. What else is bothering you?"

Angela didn't need any more prodding. "One of the other women was friends with a woman where I work. She described a guy who was supposedly seen talking to her friend the day she disappeared. It sounded like—" Angela stopped cold. She couldn't bring herself to say his name.

"It sounded like Darian?" Freddie tried to help her along.

"Yes," she whispered. "What should I do?"

"Have you talked to the police?" Freddie asked. Not wanting her to know that she didn't know where Darian lived, she quickly added, "Which police department is handling the investigation?"

"The bodies were found near Lowell Park outside Dixon. I don't think the park is inside the city limits. So it could be the Dixon police or the Lee County Sheriff's Department." Freddie didn't want to ask her the name of the state, and she didn't have to. "It might even be the Illinois State Police because I think Lowell Park is a state park."

Freddie sighed. "You're going to have to make your own decision about getting involved with the police, but I will tell you this. If you truly believe that Darian's involved, I'd stay away from him if I were you. Don't try to reach him, and if you hear from him, don't let on that you suspect anything.

"I mean it, Angela. If he is involved, you don't want to be number eight. Will you promise me that?" Freddie couldn't stand the thought of one more person dying, and in her gut she knew Darian wouldn't hesitate to kill this sweet woman whose only flaw was that she cared about him.

"You're probably right," she agreed. "I don't really know him that well, and you don't sound so sure about him yourself." There was silence. Then very calmly and deliberately, she asked, "If you find out something definite, will you let me know? I really *need* to know."

Freddie frowned. She trusted her instincts, and they were shouting that there was something else Angela wasn't telling her. "Sure. How do I get in touch with you?" She grabbed a pen and began to write, repeating it aloud. "8-1-5-5-2-6..." Writing down the last four digits, she said, "Got it! Listen, Angela, If you need anything, call me. It doesn't matter what. Just call me or call the police. Okay?"

"I will. Thanks," she replied. "You're a real angel."

Hanging up the phone, Freddie turned toward Garrison, but before she could speak, he was firing off questions.

"What did you mean when you asked if someone else had been hurt? What police? Who's Angela? What's—"

"Whoa! I'll explain everything, but I need to start at the beginning." In a few minutes she wound up her recounting of the phone conversation.

"So you think then that Darian is your cousin? That means we were right in assuming he's part of your family."

"At least according to what he told Angela. Come on. We need to finish going through these papers."

"What do you expect to find? You know who he is and where he lives, more or less."

"Something. Anything. I don't just want to prove that he's my cousin. I want to know what's motivating him. I mean, if he's really my cousin, did my Dad have a brother that he screwed over, and his son is out for revenge? More important, did my Dad even have a brother? I don't know of one."

"Why does it have to be your Dad? Couldn't it be your Mother's side of the family"

"Angela said his name was Marsh, which means my Dad's family. He would have to be the son of my Dad's brother or maybe an unwed sister. If I can at least find out if my Dad had any siblings, we might have a place to start." She picked up a box filled with papers instead of photos and began to sort.

Resting his elbows on the table, Garrison stared at the picture in his hand. His eyes glazed over as he focused inward on his thoughts. When his attention returned to the breakfast room, his torso fell back against the chair.

"What is it?" asked Freddie, who had been watching him for the last few minutes, wondering where his mind was taking him.

"There is one other possibility."

"What do you mean *one other possibility*?" she asked, perplexed by his statement.

Garrison looked at her. "Do you remember telling me about your visions? The one in the restaurant and then the one at Miya's?"

Freddie looked blank. "Yeah, but I don't see what that has to do with this."

"You said you felt like you were in your mother's womb, and you saw another child, a male child. Then at Miya's you saw a third hand in your lap." Garrison hesitated because he was hoping that Freddie would reason it out for herself. She only stared at him.

"Don't you see, Freddie? It all fits. Your mother's womb, what the wolf and Darian both said about your being a part of him. Even seeing a third hand in your lap. It all points toward their being an intimate connection between the two of you."

"What the hell are you talking about?" Freddie cried as she stood up. Her irritation was obvious. "I've never heard of him before. How could there possibly be an intimate connection between us?"

Afraid to continue but more afraid not to, Garrison said, "Freddie, you need to quit fighting this. There's a part of you that knows the truth and has known it all along. Let it out." He reached out to take her hand, but she jerked away from him.

"I don't know anything! Do you understand what I'm saying? If I knew, I wouldn't be sitting here rummaging through my dead parents' papers like some kind of scavenger!" she shouted.

There was silence. Garrison looked at her without expression until finally, he made the decision to force it out into the open. "Freddie, Darian is your brother, probably your twin brother. There's no other explanation that makes any sense."

"NO!!" she screamed. Whirling around, she grabbed the vase from the end table and flung it across the room. The crash was followed by a mournful wail that emerged from her as she sank to her knees on the den floor.

Garrison knelt down and put his arms around her. With his face resting against her back, he rocked gently back and forth. He felt the anguish as her body jerked with pain, but she made no other sound after her hair-raising cry. When her tears fell on his arm clasped across her chest, he let his own flow freely.

Chapter 48

*A*ngela's hand lingered over the telephone receiver. She had no proof that Darian was involved in these horrible murders. Jackie's description of the man she'd seen with Sharon the same day she'd disappeared was surely Darian. This was a small town, and there weren't that many "drop-dead good-looking" guys around. The irony of the description did not escape her. What she'd *not* found when she tried to find some background on Darian at the library added to the uncertainty she'd picked up from Freddie. She convinced herself to call the Sterling Police Department.

Larry Boelke, the detective on duty, answered her call. "This is Detective Boelke, Sterling Police Department. How may I help you?"

"I don't know," she replied. It had seemed like a simple act when she dialed the number. That was before it was answered by someone she knew.

"Do you wish to report a crime?" Detective Boelke was being very patient. His years of experience in a small town had taught him that the lack of anonymity often kept people from reporting crimes.

"Larry?" Angela asked, forging ahead.

"With whom am I speaking?" he inquired, still being formal. The voice was familiar, but he couldn't quite place it.

"This is Angela Downing."

"Angela! I haven't talked to you since…since a long time! How have you been?" Although he was glad to hear her voice, he did not lose sight of the fact that she had probably not called the station to talk with him.

"Not so good," Angela replied.

"Are you hurt?" he asked. He didn't know why he responded that way. Perhaps the recent murders over in Dixon really had gotten under his skin.

"I'm not, but I'm afraid others were."

Larry straightened up in his chair. She had his full attention now. "Why don't you tell me what's on your mind?"

Feeling a little less threatened, but still frightened, Angela said, "I met a man several weeks ago at the library. I helped him locate a missing relative." A little embarrassed, she said, "He was really handsome, and I liked him. The next week he asked me out. We went to Donovan's to eat. Afterward he dropped me off at the house. I didn't invite him in."

Larry wondered where this was going, but he said nothing.

"The next night he showed up at my house. He stayed until Saturday morning. I haven't seen him since." She paused, trying to decide how to express her suspicions.

Leaning back in his chair, Larry relaxed. It was obvious this had nothing to do with the recent murders. "Did he steal something from you, Angela? What exactly are you concerned about?"

Reluctantly, she continued. "The night we went to Donovan's, he was flirting with a girl named Robyn. Today a person at work said her best friend Sharon was last seen with a guy fitting Darian's description just before she disappeared."

Larry sat up so quickly, the arms of his chair slammed against the desk. "Robyn? Sharon? Are you telling me that you think this Darian killed those women?"

Hearing it put to her in the form of a question by a policeman eliminated any doubts that remained. "Yes, Larry. I think so, but I can't tell you why."

"Did he say anything to indicate his involvement?"

"No. Remember, I saw him last on Saturday morning. The murders took place after that. I kept thinking I would hear from him."

Trying to gather as much salient information as possible, he asked, "Why do you believe he's the murderer?"

"Larry, I can't prove that he murdered anybody. It's just a hell of a coincidence that he knew both of those girls when he said he was new to the area." Sighing, she said, "Yes, we had an affair, and no, I don't know that much about him. He was a perfect gentleman with me, but if there's the slightest chance it's him, I'm afraid not to speak up."

"Do you know his full name and where he lives?"

"His name is Darian Marsh. He lives northwest of here in the country. That's all I know except that he drives a blue Pontiac with gray interior. It's not new, maybe ten years old."

"What about this relative you helped him find? Can you get in touch with him?"

Angela didn't correct his use of the masculine pronoun. For some reason she didn't quite understand, she didn't want to involve Freddie. She shook her head. "I just showed Darian the search results, and I can't remember the person's name."

"That's too bad," Larry remarked, silently noting that his job would be a lot easier if people were more observant.

"There is one more thing, Larry."

"And what's that?" Detective Boelke was straddling the fence between excitement and aggravation. Having a lead on a high profile case was exciting, but Angela's lack of detail was aggravating.

"I looked him up in the databases at the library. I couldn't find anything on a Darian Marsh, at least not in the United States. He doesn't seem to have a telephone listing. He did tell me his parents were dead, and I know he's 27 years old. Other than that, which he told me himself, I found nothing to confirm that anyone by that name actually exists."

"Great." This was getting worse by the minute.

"I don't have access to the Motor Vehicles database, but you do. You could run the description of his car because I know it had Illinois plates."

"I don't suppose—"

"No," she interrupted, "I don't remember the number." Angela felt she was creating more problems than she was solving. Then she had an idea. "You might contact the real estate agents here in town. How many rural properties could have been sold to a male out-of-towner in his twenties in the last year or so? Besides, Larry, if it was a female agent, trust me, she will remember him."

Larry's spirits were improving. Angela's idea was pretty solid. He would check out the car, and with a little help from his team, it wouldn't take long to check out the twelve or so real estate agencies in town.

Chapter 49

$\mathcal{A}$ faint, musty smell, usually associated with old clothes or memorabilia, pervaded the den and breakfast room where all the contents of the boxes from the attic had been scattered. Freddie stood and began to gather everything into neat piles, placing the piles into any box that would hold them. Garrison followed her lead. He was reluctant to break the fragile silence. It seemed that Freddie had always been a part of his life, but the truth was she hadn't been. Less than a week's acquaintance did not qualify him to judge her present mental state. He was depending on her to guide him.

Reaching down, Garrison picked up a document that looked official. It was a certified copy of Freddie's birth certificate. *How odd,* he thought, *that her birth certificate would choose to surface at this moment among all these papers!* He began to read. A baby girl was born to Arliss and Roy Marsh at 12:12 AM on April 6, 1952, in Peoria, Illinois. She weighed 7 lbs. and 5 ounces. There was no indication if it was a single or multiple birth.

Noticing Garrison's interest in the page, Freddie cocked her head to one side so she could read the heading. Without a word, she took the certificate from him. She raised her eyes to his. "Do you suppose they would indicate on your birth certificate if you were a twin?" There was a hopeful tone to her question.

"I don't know," replied Garrison. "Since the purpose of the document is simply to certify that a particular person was born, it might not be considered necessary to state if he or she was a twin. However, I would think there is some documentation somewhere."

"Perhaps I could..." Freddie stopped mid-sentence. At that moment she realized she could analyze the situation to death, but nothing was going to change. She was only delaying the inevitable under the guise of being rational. For a moment she said nothing. "I'm going to have to deal with him face-to-face, aren't I?" she concluded.

"Yes," Garrison answered. The very thought of it terrified him. Not for himself but for Freddie, who was not nearly as tough as she pretended. Darian, as far as Garrison was concerned, could not be saved even by the best of intentions, but he was afraid Freddie's soft heart would be her undoing.

"It doesn't really matter if he's my brother or not because I'm not going to be able to avoid this." Garrison nodded in agreement. "Yet, for some reason, I need to know. Do you think I'm crazy?" she asked. Before he could answer, she continued. "If he's not my brother, it seems more palatable. It sort of freaks me out to think I actually have a brother, but then to think he wants me dead..." Unable to ignore her own insight, she admitted, "but I'm probably just trying to delay the inevitable." She emitted a deep sigh, the drone of submission strong.

"We could make some phone calls to Springfield, Illinois. Usually there's some government department responsible for vital statistics. If we find out that being a twin is noted on birth certificates, then we'll know that he's not your brother. We might be able to get the hospital to tell us something—that is if they still have access to those records. It could take weeks." Seeing the look on her face, he added, "Look, I'm willing to do whatever you want to do. Heck, we'll drive to Peoria if we have to!"

"There's one positive aspect to all this," Freddie said.

"There is?" asked Garrison. He tried not to grimace as the burning sensation in his throat brought on by anxiety and the lack of food since the biscuit feast at Mrs. Winner's reached a peak.

"Yes. If all this hadn't happened, I'd never have met you. Maybe there is truth to the idea that all things work together for good."

"Without a doubt," Garrison replied, squeezing her hand. "Where do you want to start?"

"Let's call information and see if we can get a number for the department that handles birth certificates."

A low grumbling sound caught her attention. "What was that?" she asked anxiously, suspicious of any unfamiliar sound.

"A warning," replied Garrison ominously. "A warning that I'm going to pass out from hunger if we don't get something to eat soon."

"My God!" she exclaimed. "I completely forgot about eating."

Part of her pictured the two of them at a nice restaurant, sipping a glass of wine, having a nice, quiet meal without a single thought of Darian to spoil the moment. The tug of reality was too strong, however, and with a sigh of regret over her lost fantasy, she asked, "Pizza delivery okay with you?"

Half an hour later Garrison and Freddie cleared off the table in anticipation of the pizza. "Well, the information from the lady at Vital Statistics didn't eliminate your being a twin."

"No, it didn't. I think it's odd that such an important piece of information would be left off a birth certificate. I mean, what good does it do to make a note of it on a part of the form that's not retrievable later?"

"Who knows? When have you ever known a government agency to do anything that smacks of common sense?"

Sighing, Freddie said, "Well, that leaves us with the hospital, but I kind of doubt they'll be able to access files that old quickly. Don't you?"

"Yeah," Garrison replied. "Hey! Didn't you say that Angela looked you up on a database for Darian?"

"Yeah. At the library where she works, but she thinks I'm his cousin."

"Maybe you are. Still, she's got to know something about him, don't you think? You didn't ask her any specifics really."

"You could be right." A loud buzz interrupted their conversation. With hardly a pause, it sounded again.

"Pizza!" declared Garrison, jumping up from the chair. Don't get in my way," he warned, "unless you have no fear!"

Startled, Freddie burst out laughing at Garrison's antics. *It feels good to laugh,* she thought. She wondered if she would still be able to laugh when this was all over.

Garrison entered the kitchen with the pizza held out before him like a trophy. "I've got mine. What are you going to eat?" he inquired innocently.

Slapping his shoulder, she grabbed the corner of the pizza box and tugged. "The question is what are *you* going to eat?"

Pulling and grunting loudly as if it were a contest between titans, the two of them slipped away from their fears, returning to a place where only the bond between them mattered. A place where nothing existed beyond the focus of their immediate desires. A place and a time where only the id ruled the day. No ego. No concerns for the matters of other men. No worries about intellectual pursuits. Only for matters of the heart.

With the abruptness that often accompanies an adult's meanderings into this almost forgotten place and time, the tug-of-war ceased, leaving behind a faint awkwardness.

Garrison recovered first. "I'll get us something to drink. You tear the lid off the box. Do you have any napkins?"

"Sure. They're hanging right over there," said Freddie, pointing at the roll of paper towels under the kitchen cupboard.

""Cute!" he replied, rolling his eyes.

A short while later, one sad-looking slice of pizza remained in the box on the breakfast room table. Only a few scraps of topping were left on it. Freddie had picked off the cheese and the hamburger meat, leaving the olives, mushrooms, and onions for Garrison.

"Su-ure!" said Garrison. "Now I know how much I count around here. You take all the prime pieces and leave me the scraps!"

"And you want me to—?" she asked, tongue-in-cheek.

"I want you to...I want you to..." Garrison's expression changed. "I want you to be with me forever."

"Excuse me?" Freddie couldn't believe he had said what it sounded like. It sounded a lot like a marriage proposal, at least the ones she'd seen in the movies, but it couldn't be. They had only known each other— Her thoughts came to an abrupt halt. *They had only known each other a few days.* Saying it to herself shattered the illusion she had known him forever, but it certainly seemed like she had.

"I want you to be with me forever."

Confused by the contrast between the facts and her feelings, she tried to mask her confusion by being funny. "At what salary?" she asked.

"I'm serious, Freddie. I can't believe it myself, but I know we were meant to be together, and I don't care if that sounds like a cliché! What we have goes beyond a conventional relationship. As silly as it might sound to you, I feel like I've known you all my life. How can that happen in a few days?"

"Maybe it's just the emotional nature of what's been going on." Freddie's mind was hard at work trying to carve out a rational box to put her feelings in.

"Maybe. Or just maybe there's some truth to the theory of reincarnation. Hell, I don't know. It doesn't matter what it is. I just know that I haven't felt like this with anyone before. From the first moment I saw you at the elevator, I felt a connection I couldn't explain then and still can't. I thought it would dissipate, but it's done just the opposite."

Thinking of Angela and Darian, Freddie said, "Maybe you're just infatuated with the weird."

Knowing she was playing devil's advocate, Garrison said, "No. Let me ask you. Have you ever read a book and then years later picked it up to read, not remembering that you'd read it before?"

"Yeah."

"Do you recall how it gradually became familiar, but you still couldn't remember what happened, so you had to keep reading? That's the way it's been for me with you. Somewhere in the recesses of my mind, there's a memory of you. A few years ago people were talking a lot about soul mates. I never put any stock into the idea, but now I'm not so sure."

"So what are you saying?" Freddie was still not brave enough to make the quantum leap from his circuitous remarks to a marriage proposal.

"I'm asking you," he said, pausing to get down on one knee, "I'm asking you to marry me, Freddie, when this is all over."

"Do you really think it will ever be over?"

"Yes, and then I want you to marry me."

Freddie stared at him in silence. She had never expected a marriage proposal, and she wasn't sure at this moment if she was going to survive long enough to get married.

Nervously, Garrison asked, "Should I take your silence as a *no* or just a state of shock?" He wasn't sure this had been the best time, but it was too late now.

"The latter," she replied. "I just wasn't expecting it."

"Well?" he insisted. "The suspense is giving me heartburn!"

"Yes," she said. "Yes, I will marry you!"

Letting out a rebel yell, Garrison jumped up from the floor and scooped her out of the chair. He whirled around and around with her in his arms.

Breathless, she cried out, "Stop! You're making me dizzy!"

"*You're* dizzy? *I'm* dizzy—dizzy with excitement! This is the most wonderful moment of my life!" he exclaimed as he lowered her to the floor. He pulled her toward him and kissed her gently. Their surroundings faded into the background as they lost themselves in each other's embrace.

Garrison stiffened as he became aware of an intrusion into their momentary bliss. Noticing the tenseness in his body, Freddie reluctantly tore herself away from the euphoria of the last few minutes. Aware of her need to be alert, she listened intently. Then she heard it—a faint, buzzing noise. It set off alarms in her, but she didn't instantly know why. As her mind was trying to access associations that might trigger answers, there was a loud crash. Then darkness.

When the threads that run through your life come together in harmony,
the pattern that results can right wrongs and create indescribable joy,
but this pattern is not static. It is not yours alone.
Its threads are bound to the past, present, and future
of all who reside in the Universe.
- The Book of Metanoia

Fredrika and Darian: A New Pattern Begins

Chapter 50

Day 17—Memphis

Shaking her head to regain her senses, Freddie realized she was in the back yard. Looking toward the house, she saw the shattered breakfast room window. Large shards of glass were sticking out of its frame. *Garrison!* Turning, she saw him lying on the grass three feet beyond her. Struggling to get up, she stumbled over to him. There was blood everywhere! Falling down on her knees, she screamed, "No!! This can't be happening!" Frantic, she looked around her but saw no one. She slapped Garrison's face lightly to awaken him. He moaned and struggled to open his eyes. Blood was running down his forehead into his left eye. Freddie reached over and wiped her hand across his forehead, pushing his hair out of the way.

Trying to sit up, he croaked, "What the hell?"

"Don't!" she cried. "Your leg is pretty badly cut." Undoing the brooch on her sweater that held the ends of her scarf together, she pulled the scarf loose. Then she wrapped it around his leg like a tourniquet.

"I don't think we were unconscious long, but you've bled quite a lot." Looking up from her handiwork, she saw Garrison's eyes roll dangerously toward his eyebrows and knew he was going to faint.

Seeing him like this brought on a wave of nausea. "Lie down, Garrison. You're hurt, and I am NOT going to let you die on me. Do you hear me, Garrison McCrary?" She was shouting at him, as much from fear as from an attempt to keep him awake.

Garrison uttered something so softly that Freddie couldn't hear him. Leaning closer, she asked, "What did you say?"

"Darian," he whispered.

"What about him?"

"The buzzing. It was Darian. I remember now. That's what I heard at the library. I didn't realize what had sparked the feeling that he was there until now."

In an instant the past few weeks rushed through Freddie's head. *Of course*, she thought. *The buzzing. I've been hearing it all along. I just didn't make the connection.* She'd heard it in the garage at the airport before she saw Darian in the terminal and again on the plane and at the hotel. Even that day at the cabin before she faced those two horrid men, she'd heard the buzzing. She hadn't made the connection then because she'd been so distracted. It was his calling card, and she'd missed it!

Looking around her, she wondered where Darian was. She wasn't picking up on his presence. If there was a buzzing sound, it was being carried away by the briskly-blowing, evening wind.

Darian had not reassembled. He was inside the house, but from where his life force floated, he could easily watch the two of them. Since his nightmare yesterday, he had tried to rest, but instead he'd spent hours trying to understand why Angela and Freddie appeared to him as the same person in his dream. Was he misjudging one of them? Which one? No matter how many different ways he approached it, his thoughts always drifted back to the wolf.

The wolf could only have been a trap—a trap set by Freddie. How else could it have beaten him that day in the woods? If the wolf was a trap, then Freddie *must* be his enemy. Nothing else made sense. He was certain he had not misjudged her intentions. She had just used Angela's voice to confuse him. No, he was certain. There was no connection between the two. Angela was just the devious means Freddie had used to creep into his dreams.

Such arguments had raged in his head all last evening. He had no sure answers, but the battle had given him a renewed strength and determination to destroy his adversary.

As he watched Freddie lying on the grass unconscious, he knew he could end it without a ripple of resistance, but he didn't just want victory. He wanted to savor his win. He wanted to feel its lusciousness in the same way you swirl a soft, chocolate crème around in your mouth from cheek to cheek, tasting bursts of flavor as the chocolate melts, leaving its mark on everything it touches.

He had watched Freddie tying her scarf around the man's leg. Now she was looking around. Searching for him. It was time! Moving quickly out into the yard, he simultaneously reassembled, allowing his image to hover two feet above the ground.

"Behind you!" Garrison shouted at Freddie, but it only emerged as a croaking whisper.

Whirling around, Freddie lost her balance and fell onto her backside. Looking up at the grinning apparition, Freddie was afraid. Turning toward Garrison, she said nothing, but the look in her eyes told him everything.

"You have to go, Freddie," Garrison told her.

"But—"

"Go! Leave your body. You have to fight him on the same plane so that the playing field is level."

"I can't! You have to help me," she pleaded.

"No, I'm too weak to focus, and my body is too weak. Too much blood lost. It's your fight now, darling. You can do it. I believe you've done..." His voice trailed off as he lost consciousness.

Seeing him lying there helpless, she remembered Avatar saying that Garrison might be in great danger because he cared about her. The fear of losing him ignited years of anger that her insatiable need for control had compressed into a very tightly-packed layer of white-hot emotions—emotions that had no focus, no target on which to center their fiery attention. Until now.

Without even thinking about it, she rose up from her body and faced Darian. *It's over!* she said to the twin apparition.

It's only beginning, he laughed.

You're right about that because your pain is only beginning! She lunged at him, forcing him backward through the gaping hole left when she and Garrison were hurled into the yard.

Darian quickly recovered and started spreading himself out like a net as he had done with the pack of wild dogs. Garrison's words of encouragement to Freddie had let Darian know she wasn't as experienced as he was on this plane, and he intended to use it to his advantage.

The moment she saw his particles start dispersing into a lattice-like structure, she realized his intent. With the concentrated force of a cannon ball, she burst through an open space to her right, knocking the television onto the floor. The screen shattered, sending pieces of glass in all directions.

Enraged, Darian pulled his particles together and rushed Freddie, but she thrust herself to one side. His lunge splintered the wall studs between the den and the bedroom, but the wall did not collapse. Taking advantage of his miscalculation, Freddie tried to mimic him by expanding the surface of her astral body to use it as a net, but she was not quick enough.

Out in the yard Garrison regained consciousness. Sitting up, he saw Freddie's body lying on the grass. At first he thought she was dead, but before his mind could wrap itself around the idea, he heard the commotion in the house. He crawled toward the house, dragging his wounded leg. Grimacing as tiny bits of glass pricked his legs and hands, he pulled himself up to the window sill, which was about all that was left of the window. He saw two separate images, but they were no longer in recognizable form. They were simply glowing particles. Although most people on the planet would not be able to see them, Garrison could, and it was the only thing that mattered to him at the moment.

A stream of particles flowed into a ball and shot toward the kitchen like a comet with its tail leaving a trail of light behind it. Instinctively, he knew it was Darian. He turned toward the cloud of particles from which the comet had escaped. His head was filled with loud, dissonant noises. It was like having his head tuned to a station that was off the air.

"Freddie?!" he cried. Suddenly, as if an unknown hand had made a tuning adjustment to the universe, his head filled with thoughts. It was just like when he was out of his body. For the briefest of moments he forgot the danger in face of the amazing sensation the experience was evoking.

Able to hear Garrison's thoughts as well, Darian saw a golden opportunity to destroy a part of Freddie. *Aren't you dead yet?* he asked Garrison through his thoughts.

Garrison was gripped by fear. He couldn't really fight Darian in physical form, and his body was too weak to withstand the trauma of his pulling his life force from it. There was nothing he could do. Turning toward Freddie, his emotions expressed his desire to see her in her body, to touch her and hold her one more time.

Paralyzed by the desolation driving Garrison's feelings, Freddie felt she was standing alone on the edge of a great abyss with nothing but emptiness ahead. Standing there with formless tears filling her up, time stood still.

In the distance a figure approached out of the emptiness, but she was unable to move. As the figure drew closer, she recognized it. It was herself but another self—the one who always had everything under control. Astonished, she saw figures approaching from all sides. Each was different, but each was Freddie. She was surprised that she recognized them all. One loved to play, loved getting the chance to be vulnerable when she was with Garrison. One walked slowly but confidently and knew she could do anything she set her mind to do. Each of them walked toward her until at last she embraced them all.

That can be easily remedied! Darian's thought was as loud as the report of a handgun. It sent a vibration through the air, reinstating the passage of time and bringing Freddie back into the dimension where Darian was threatening the life of the one she loved.

She felt a strange new strength, a new unity, as she declared, *Leave him alone! This is between me and you, Darian, and it is over!*

You're wrong. His death is your fault. You should never have gotten him involved in— No-o-o!

Chapter 51

Day 17—Illinois

The sirens were silent, but the lights were flashing atop the six police cars. There were two cars from each jurisdiction—Sterling, Dixon, and the state of Illinois. Detective Boelke's car led the convoy down the country road. He had located the Pontiac Bonneville much quicker than he'd expected. He knew it was the right one. The owner was listed as Darian Beel. Too much of a coincidence. Besides, Angela hadn't been able to locate a Darian Marsh, and using fake last names was a common ruse for criminals.

Once he knew the right name, it was a simple matter of tracking down the real estate he had purchased. Within two hours the three law enforcement agencies left the Sterling Police Department and headed out LeFevre Road. They waited until they were outside the city limits to start their flashing lights. No point in having a line of nosy citizens following them. There was no telling what was going to happen. Of course, the residents of Sterling had rarely seen such a processional of cop cars, even without their lights flashing, and word soon spread that something was going down.

As Detective Boelke's vehicle approached the turnoff to Darian's property, he picked up his radio mike. "Listen, men. I'm about to turn onto the gravel road. It's still another three miles to the cabin according to the real estate agent. She said no one else lives down this road anymore. So, we don't have to worry about evacuating anyone. However, I want all of you to be on alert.

"The cabin is situated in a small clearing in the woods. The only way in is this narrow gravel road, and we have no way of knowing what to expect. Does everyone understand?"

The other officers replied affirmatively. Boelke made the turn and drove a little over two miles before picking up his mike again. Clutching the button on its side, he was about to tell the teams to park their cars about a mile from the cabin and spread out so the suspect couldn't escape.

"What the—?!" Boelke slammed on his brakes. The other cars followed suit, sliding to a halt and spewing gravel everywhere. Throwing his car into park, Boelke threw open his car door and stood on his left leg, his right foot still resting on the floorboard of his car. The other officers got out of their vehicles and moved forward until they were clustered around Boelke's car.

"What the hell happened here? A fire?" Bart, one of the state policemen, asked.

"Have you ever seen a fire do anything like this?" Boelke muttered. "Besides, those trees aren't burned. They're—they're just dead."

"It's not just the trees. Everything is dead. This is creeping me out," said the lieutenant from Dixon.

"Listen. Do you hear something?" Bart, who had suggested a fire as the cause of the devastation facing them, had his hand cupped over his right ear. His question brought to their attention the overwhelming silence that surrounded them. Feeling ill-prepared for what lay in front of them, they welcomed the opportunity to follow anybody else's lead. They each cupped a hand around an ear.

"Yeah. I hear it," said one of the officers.

"Whadd'ya think it is?"

"Sounds a little like animals, but I sure don't see any," said an officer from Dixon, looking around as he spoke.

Detective Boelke heard it, too. Looking at the cabin, which was still about a half mile ahead of them but clearly visible through the barren woods, he decided to stick to his original plan. "Okay, men, let's spread out through this dead area and form a perimeter around the cabin. You all have your radios?" he asked.

Everyone nodded.

"Okay. I'm going to stay at this point until the rest of you are in position and close the circle. Harold, you head around the south side of the circle until you're back of the cabin. Then let me know. Jim, you lead the way around the north side and stop short of the back of the cabin. Buster, you and Bob follow behind Jim on the south. Bart, you go in behind Harold. Everybody ready?"

The men nodded, and the two groups started off in different directions. It only took about ten minutes for all of the men to be in position.

Using the portable radio, Larry said, "Let's move in slowly. Everyone stay alert. If we get within thirty feet of the cabin without any sign of the suspect, Bart and Bob will move toward the front of the cabin with me. Harold, Jim, and Buster, I want you to cover the rear exit if there is one. Understood?"

No one emerged from the cabin as the officers approached the front entrance. When they regrouped, Bart, who had noticed what sounded like animals earlier, turned to Boelke and said, "I can hear it even louder now than before."

"Me, too!" said Bob. Boelke nodded in agreement as he pointed toward the cabin. Pressing the button on his radio, he quietly instructed the men in the back of the cabin to hold firm while his team entered the front door. If the suspect tried to escape through the back, they'd be ready for him. Boelke wanted him alive. So he activated the radio again. "Do not shoot to kill. Repeat. Do not shoot to kill."

As they were climbing the steps, Boelke noticed that one of the windows was broken. He kept his eye on it as they approached. When the three of them reached the porch, Bart raised his leg to kick in the door and quickly step out of the way. Boelke and Bob were backed up against the wall on either side of the door frame, ready to enter with guns drawn.

Just as Bart's foot made contact with the wooden door, the thud of his foot was accompanied by a loud, scurrying noise. The door creaked but did not succumb to the attack. The other two men, guns poised and heads turned toward the door, hesitated. The sounds in the cabin struck fear into their hearts. It felt like the balance had shifted. More than just a single man was behind that door.

Crack! The sound of the rusty hinge finally giving way caused Boelke and Bob to jump out from the wall and turn, prepared to enter the cabin. The door was still standing upright. They stood, looking at the door, frozen in place by the incongruity of the moment. The door slowly tilted backward. Then with a sudden shift in tempo, it fell to the floor, causing all three men to jump in alarm. Later, Boelke compared it to watching a movie in slow motion. Boelke stepped into the room, followed by Bob, and finally, Bart. They were unprepared for what they saw.

On the edge of what was left of the woods stood a wolf. He had watched the men enter the cabin. He knew they wouldn't understand what had happened, but he knew that justice as he understood it had been served. Another like himself, an Avatar, had died last night at the hands of this man, and the torch had passed to him to rid the world of this evil.

He had entered the circle of death not long before the humans arrived. Expecting to immediately be forced to fight for his own life as had his predecessor, he instead found nothing. He felt nothing. Cautiously, he moved forward until he reached the steps of the cabin. Sniffing, he sensed the physical presence of a human in the cabin, but for some reason the man had not detected his presence. Warily, he climbed the steps until he stood on the porch. Still nothing.

He eased toward the window and peeked in. The man was sitting in a chair. He looked dead. Deciding to take a chance and hoping for the element of surprise, the wolf leaped through the window. Glass flew in every direction, stopping just short of the chair in which the man sat. Yet, the man did not move.

Moving cautiously forward, the wolf was struck by a sudden flash of insight. The man was not dead. His spirit had simply left his body as he had done when he killed his brother Avatar. Fearing his return, the wolf struck without hesitation. His teeth tore into the neck, ripping the artery into shreds. Blood gushed from the wound.

Standing silently beside the chair, the Avatar wondered if this man's powers were great enough to revive his body. Having never encountered anyone quite like Darian before, this young Avatar was uncertain. One thing he did know for sure. Every spirit requires a body to interact in the physical world. If their body is destroyed, they cannot forcibly take another. They may be able to steal a life force while outside their own body, but they cannot steal a physical body. *That was the answer*, he thought. *Destroy the body.*

Before he could put his plan into action, the wolf heard noises outside the cabin. Walking to the window, he saw animals approaching the cabin in much the same way they probably lined up to board Noah's ark, except this time there was only one of every kind. The wolf understood. He leaped out the window and walked away. His part was over. The rest was up to them. It was sweet justice for all.

At first the three police officers just stood there inside the door with their mouths open. Finally, Bart spoke, "Looks like roadkill to me!"

They heard the others entering through the back porch door just as Harold shouted, "Look out! Run!" A gun went off. Boelke, followed by Bart and Bob, rushed toward the back of the house with their guns drawn. They reached the back door and stepped out just in time to see a bizarre herd of animals running through the dead forest.

"Well, I'll be damned! I've never seen anything like that in my life."

"What the hell were they doing in the cabin?" asked Harold, a little embarrassed that he had panicked.

"Making adjustments to the food chain. The predator became the prey," said Bart.

Chapter 52

Day 17—Memphis

No!! Darian's panicked thoughts reverberated throughout the room. The hair on Garrison's neck stood up as a shiver involuntarily passed through him like a tidal wave. Freddie's newfound strength had not prepared her for such a reaction from Darian. Her particles lingered in the air, making no move toward her nemesis.

My body... Darian's thought faded into nothingness.

"Look!" Garrison pointed toward Darian. The glowing particles that were his life force were dimming as though someone had adjusted the rheostat controlling the current of his life force.

What is it?

"His body! Someone has destroyed his body!" By this time Garrison was no longer thinking. He was shouting as loud as his throat would allow.

Directing his attention toward Darian, he taunted him. "You realize you're trapped, don't you? You can't go on, and you can't come back. You don't have a connection to the physical world anymore because your body is gone. The cord was cut!" An almost deranged burst of laughter erupted from Garrison.

Filled with horror, Freddie declared. *It's not funny! Now he has carte blanche to wander around and kill whomever he pleases. He'll only get stronger and stronger!*

"No, no! You don't understand!" Garrison's reply was filled with urgency because he didn't want to lose precious moments that would allow Freddie to finish off this evil force one and for all. "His hold on his body was diminished before he even came here today. That's the only explanation for why he didn't notice what was happening. Why? I don't know. It could be a lot of reasons. The one that comes to my mind is what happened in Illinois. He must have done more than kill those women. He must have sexually assaulted them. Investing your life force, your energy, into promiscuity is a misuse of sexual energy, and it diminishes your own life force.

"Anyway, now he's in a no-man's land. His spirit didn't enter the other side," said Garrison, obviously on fire with enthusiasm for the change of events. "The door opened, and no one was home! He's trapped. Don't you see, darling? Unlike Scrooge's partner, Jacob Marley, Darian can no longer effect either good or evil. He's essentially impotent!

"Leave him be, Freddie," he pleaded. "He's a hoarder of life forces. Why do you think he killed those women? Why do you think he's after you?"

Freddie's mind released no thoughts. She was still numbed by what was happening.

"Freddie!" Garrison shouted at her. "Darian only wants power. It's his drug of choice. Let him be. It's sweet justice after his ruthless seeking after power that he spend eternity as powerless as it's possible to be!"

Freddie knew that Garrison was only worried about her safety even though he sounded like a bloodthirsty fanatic at the moment. Turning her attention to Darian, she was overwhelmed by the flood of sadness coming from him. A sadness that was as impossible to escape as the mugginess of a humid New Orleans afternoon.

Everything about him was open for inspection. The barriers he'd been able to sustain before had fallen. She saw his past from the time of their births to the orphanage to the Beels. She felt his pain as she watched his memories of what Harry Beel had done to him. She felt the anger that was born out of fear—the fear that became his master. The rest of Darian's life with its carnage and misguided vision rolled out before her—from Ruth to the seven women in Illinois.

Shaken by what she'd seen, Freddie remained still. Darian stayed where he was. He was like a swarm of fireflies frozen in time with their warm glow flickering out one by one.

"Freddie!" Garrison shouted at her again. "Freddie, come back to your body. Leave him! He can't do any more harm."

Freddie made no move to comply.

"He was a totally worthless soul, Freddie—a throw-away, a reject. There's nothing you can do for him now. He never had any value. Come back to me!" A sobbing sound escaped his throat.

Finally, Freddie responded to Garrison's appeals. *He does have value, Garrison, but he never had guidance.*

Garrison interrupted. "It doesn't matter what battles are raging inside a person, Freddie. You always have a choice, and he made the wrong ones!"

From the moment of his birth, he's been rejected. Our parents gave him away. People adopted him that cared nothing for him. He's never had anything or anyone in his life he could count on. He simply took his path of least resistance.

"What?!" Garrison wasn't following her train of thought. His fear for her was overriding his own ability to think rationally.

Avatar said power is an ambiguous thing. If I attempt to control it by directing its path with my human will, I will always chose the least desirable path." She paused before continuing. *"I didn't really understand him at the time. How could it be that I would always choose the wrong path? Now I can see how Avatar was right, but how he was also wrong.*

It's true, Garrison, that we always find ourselves on a path of least resistance. I can't change that fact. What I know now is that the path itself can be changed. That's what Avatar failed to acknowledge. If I use the power that's within me to change my underlying structures, such as the uncompromising way I look at things, instead of using it to forcibly change the things around me, I'll still find myself on a path that offers me the least resistance, but it will no longer be the same path. Hopefully, it will be a better one.

Darian never understood love. How could he? His life was filled to capacity with abuses. Is it any wonder that his path of least resistance was the desire to wield more power than those who abused him? Can you blame him for wanting to use his power to change the world he knew?

"Freddie, we talked about this before. You can't change him."

No, I can't, but I can address my relationship to him. Why did the two of us come together after all this time? Was it just to destroy each other and maybe you?

Freddie sensed the fear emanating from Garrison and knew it was fear for her and his own fear of losing her. *Darling, I have to resolve this in my own way. I can't live with the polarized belief that I'm right and Darian's wrong. I know that assigning the label of good and evil is inaccurate because I, too, have killed.*

"But—"

Freddie hastened to cut off his protests. *Garrison, as long as I allow Darian and myself to remain in these opposing categories, nothing will ever change in my life. I can never love you the way I want to. Another force has to be brought to bear on what has happened. There has to be a new solution, a new way of thinking. The solution can't be one or the other. It has to contain both, transformed into something different and better.*

Freddie spread out her empyreal arms in conclusion to her remarks. Like a child welcoming his mother's forgiving love, Darian came to her. She closed her arms around him and held him until they were no longer two. They were one. The glow of their joined particles increased, and Freddie returned to her physical body.

Once they were seated back inside the house, Garrison asked, "Why?" After everything Darian had put them through, he desperately needed answers. He wasn't sure what had just happened.

"There's good in everyone, Garrison."

"How can you see good in him?" he interrupted. "He was ready to kill you *and* me to get what he wanted."

"Remember the rock?" she asked calmly.

"The what?"

"The rock. You know—good and evil? The active force of

throwing the rock, its interaction with the passive force or the weight of the rock?"

"Yeah, but—"

"There's no *but*, Garrison. You said that both attempts, the success *and* the failure, had a constructive goal originally. The outcome was only different because of the strength of the passive force or in your example, the weight of the rock." Suddenly their roles were reversed. Freddie was now the teacher.

"But—I know, *no buts*—but this is different! Darian was pure evil." He was not prepared to accept her sacrificing philosophy.

"No, it isn't. Darian had all the same desires and ambitions you and I have. He wanted his life to have meaning."

"As what?" asked Garrison snidely. He was getting frustrated with her, but Freddie just ignored it because she knew what he feared.

"When you were a child, did you want first of all to be *somebody* who counted? Someone others admired? Or did you always—from that first moment you thought about your future—know you were going to choose to make your life count by being a teacher?"

"Of course not! How could I have known that? I didn't realize until I went to school and saw what teachers did that it was the path I would take. That's why we expose kids to different careers—so they have more things to choose from."

"Exactly! Darian was just like you." She hurried on before he could protest. "He wanted to count, but his experiences didn't produce positive role models or ideals. Every experience with the world outside himself was a painful betrayal." Freddie paused as she recalled some of what she had witnessed through Darian's still powerful memories.

"He used that pain, which was all he knew, to propel himself toward safety. Power was his only safe haven in the world he knew, Garrison. It was the weapon others used to abuse him. In time he forgot why he desired power in the first place. He lost sight of that hurt little boy because safety was no longer an issue.

"The quest for power became his path of least resistance. It supported his feelings about nearly all the experiences he'd ever had. He's not so different than some of those who have lots of money. The more power he acquired, the more he thought of himself as special, even god-like. He fooled himself into thinking his life was better, that he was evolving."

Freddie paused as she noticed that the wound on Garrison's leg was starting to drip blood. She carefully untied the scarf, repositioned it, and tied it again. Then taking his hand, she continued, "Garrison, Darian and I started life together. We were in the same womb. There were no differences in that protected space. Yet, the choices our parents made took us down totally different paths."

"But he still had choices, Freddie. He could have chosen differently."

"I know that. I'm not excusing his choices or his actions, but it does not change the fact that his intentions were originally good. He just wasn't strong enough to overcome the weight of his life. Nothing he was ever exposed to produced enough positive experiences or people to sustain him or help him make better choices."

Taking both his hands in hers, she said, "You and I were. You had a loving mother. I had loving parents. Despite that, I know that it could have been me as well as Darian who took a destructive path."

Snorting in disgust, Garrison replied, "I don't think so!"

"I do. There have been many times in my life when I've agonized over what to do. Most of the time my decisions were directly related to my relationships with family, friends, or work. There were many times when the *wrong* thing would have been the easiest, and I admit to being tempted, which means I could have made that choice. Fortunately, my environment convinced me to do otherwise. How can I sit in judgment when I've come so close to the edge myself?"

Realizing that her arguments were not convincing Garrison, she knew that he might never understand. The one thing she was sure about was his love for her. She could feel it in every molecule of her body.

As tears filled her eyes, she said, "He never knew he had a family until the last few weeks, and he never even had a single friend, Garrison. When his control waned toward the last, I could see and feel his pain. It tore my heart in two. I just couldn't leave him there alone."

Sobbing now, she said, "When he came to me, stripped of his malignant power, there was such love! I've never felt anything like it. I didn't overpower him, Garrison. He came freely. There were no longer any distorted or misguided emotions. He was like a newborn. As I held him, we joined in spirit."

She knew that was what Garrison had been waiting to hear. He was afraid that he had lost her in those few seconds he had witnessed. Wiping her face, she looked at Garrison, expecting to see disapproval.

"You're not afraid that his nature will affect your actions?" asked Garrison hesitantly.

"No. There was nothing wrong with his intrinsic qualities, but like seeds, they required nourishment in order to flourish. Without it, the weeds took over. He's part of me now, and I intend to love and cherish his spirit. Together, we will be something better than we could ever have been apart."

Taking Garrison's hands in hers, she looked into his eyes. "Darian deserves a second chance, my love. We all do."

Garrison leaned over and kissed her gently. "What do you think about calling an ambulance for me?" he asked.

Chapter 53

Three Months Later

The crickets chirped loudly as Freddie and Garrison cuddled next to each other on the patio glider, holding hands. The moon's light illuminated the back yard, and the summer's insects were gathering in the glow of the porch light. Freddie's thoughts drifted back over the last three months. It was difficult to remember the terror now, but she knew it had been real. It was more real than anything had ever been up to that point in her life.

Things were different now. She and Garrison had gotten married six weeks ago. Jodi was her maid of honor. Although she had wondered if she and Jodi would ever be best friends again, Jodi was at the house before the paramedics could unload their equipment when the ambulance came for Garrison after the battle with Darian. Freddie knew then that things were back to normal.

These weren't the changes that Freddie's thoughts were focused on, however. It was Freddie who had changed the most. The Freddie who was too scared to trust herself, too scared to trust anyone, was gone. The love she'd experienced the last three months had changed her life forever.

Of course, Garrison loved her. He was always there for her. He was her closest friend, and she had never trusted another living soul the way she trusted and loved Garrison. But, the love that had thrown back the doors of her heart had been born when she embraced Darian's spirit that day.

She would never be able to describe what she'd felt when it happened. The only word that ever came to mind was *love*, but it seemed so inadequate. She'd felt the presence of other souls who had gone before. As these souls seemed to mingle with hers and Darian's, the love being shared was multiplied again and again. She felt no separation between any of them.

Perhaps, she thought, *oneness is a better word.* It didn't really matter. The Freddie who would once have agonized over it until she had analyzed it from stem to stern was no longer at the helm of her life. She had definitely changed and was changing still.

A ringing sound inside the house broke into her reverie. She got up to answer the phone.

"Hello?"

"Hi! This is Angela Downing. Do you remember me?"

"Of course I do. Garrison and I have been trying to reach you. I wanted to let you know that everything is all right."

Not quite understanding how anything could ever be all right again, Angela said, "I'm in Wyoming with my Uncle Tom right now."

"Oh?"

"I've had some news, and I wanted to share it with you considering—well, you were really nice to me."

"Great! What is it?" Freddie had a special feeling for Angela because she knew Darian had cared about her.

"I'm going to have a baby. Darian's baby."

For a moment, Freddie was silent. She wasn't sure she'd heard Angela correctly.

"Freddie? Are you there?"

"Yes! I think that's wonderful, Angela."

"Do you? Do you *really?*"

"Yes, of course I do!" *It really is wonderful,* she thought.

"I thought perhaps—"

"What's the matter, Angela? Are you afraid because of what Darian became?"

Angela hesitated. She was very confused. In the last three months she'd had plenty of time to think. She'd gone over and over the days she'd spent with Darian. She'd convinced herself that he had *not* loved her, but she couldn't understand why he spent four nights with her and didn't kill her. Instead, he had been very amorous. She wanted to believe that somewhere deep inside him, there had been a tiny spark of feeling for her, but there had obviously been a monster in Darian. What if her child—?

"Yes," she finally replied.

"Do you want this child, Angela? Forget what Darian did. Do you want *this* child?"

Without hesitation, she replied, "Yes."

"Then that's all that matters. If you love and care for this child, it will have a better chance than Darian ever did." Freddie could hear Angela sniffling as she spoke.

"Freddie, I haven't told anyone this because I didn't think they'd understand, but I want you to know. Most people only see a monster when they think of him now. I've tried to hate him for what he did, and I do hate *what* he did, but I can't bring myself to hate him. Can you understand that?"

"Yes, I understand completely." Freddie knew that she'd have to stretch the facts a little, but she intended to tell Angela what she needed to hear. She knew for a fact how Darian felt even if she couldn't tell Angela exactly how she knew.

"I never got a chance to tell you this, but Darian and I did talk before he was killed."

"Really?" Angela was surprised because she assumed that he'd never made it to Memphis since they found his mutilated body at his cabin.

"Yeah. I—uh—never saw him in the flesh, but he did tell me about you. He said you were the only person who had ever been kind to him without wanting something in return. He loved you, Angela, in the best way he knew how. It wasn't an emotion he'd experienced much in his life."

Angela was sobbing. So Freddie sat quietly, waiting for her to finish. "I needed to hear that. It matters to me, regardless of what everyone else thinks about him." Pausing, she took a deep breath. "There's one more thing."

"Yes?"

"Would you be my baby's godmother?"

"Well, I don't know—"

"I'm sorry," Angela butted in. "I know it's asking a lot after everything that has happened."

"No! That's not it. I was just wondering," Freddie paused deliberately for effect, "if aunts can be godmothers."

"What?" Angela had no idea what Freddie was talking about. "You'd be the baby's second cousin or something, not its aunt."

"There's one other piece of news you don't know, Angela. Darian wasn't my cousin. He was my twin brother."

Astonished, Angela gasped, "Your *twin* brother? How could you not know you had a twin?"

"My parents put him up for adoption at birth because he had medical problems, and they couldn't afford to pay for the medical costs. They thought the system would take care of it. I didn't know about him, but obviously he had found out about me. Even when he came to you the first time, he knew."

"Why didn't he just tell me?"

"Paranoia, I guess," replied Freddie, not wanting to reveal all Darian's secrets to her. "But it doesn't matter because he and I made peace. I love him, too, Angela, and this child is a second chance for him. A chance to leave a legacy of good."

After getting Angela to promise to keep in touch and to come for a visit, Freddie walked back out on the patio where Garrison was stretched out on the glider gazing at the moon.

"Who was that?" he asked.

"Angela."

"Oh?"

"She's having Darian's child. Isn't that wonderful?"

Garrison looked up at her and smiled, thinking of the news Freddie had given him only that morning. He was going to be a father. Sensing his thoughts, Freddie leaned over and kissed him.

"What was that for?" he asked.

"For being you," she replied as she sat down and put his head in her lap. Looking up at the moon, she smiled. Darian would live on in more ways than one.

About The Author:

I hope you enjoyed *Second Chances*. If you haven't read my other novels, be sure to check them out at this URL: www.amazon.com/Dannye-Williamsen/e/B004KEAFE8 or at the URLs below.

www.DannyeWilliamsen.com, www.SassyScribblers.com www.WilliamsenPublications.com

Fiction:

Second Chances:

http://www.amazon.com/Second-Chances-Dannye-Williamsen/dp/097260586X

The Threads That Bind:

http://www.amazon.com/Threads-That-Bind-Dannye-Williamsen/dp/0972605878

Center Stage:

http://www.amazon.com/Center-Stage-Dannye-Williamsen/dp/0972605835

Brita Madison series:

Book 1 – Chasing Shadows

http://www.amazon.com/Chasing-Shadows-Madison-Paranormal-Mysteries/dp/1507743491

Book 2 - Shattered Hearts

https://www.amazon.com/Shattered-Hearts-Madison-Paranormal-Mystery/dp/1542366259

Book 3 - Unraveling memories

https://www.amazon.com/Unraveling-Memories-Madison-Paranormal-Mysteries-ebook/dp/B07T91CWHC

Circles of Freedom:

https://www.amazon.com/Circles-Freedom-Dannye-Williamsen/dp/1719178305

When the Walls Come Tumbling Down:

https://www.amazon.com/When-Walls-Come-Tumbling-Down/dp/B08LNJL1PH

The Elyrian Emergence:

https://www.amazon.com/Elyrian-Emergence-Dannye-Williamsen-ebook/dp/B092P8XQXR

Invisible Shadows:

https://www.amazon.com/Invisible-Shadows-Dannye-Williamsen-ebook/dp/B0B1VV87TT

Nonfiction:

12-Step Business Plan for the Solopreneur

http://www.amazon.com/12-Step-Business-Plan-Solopreneur/dp/1453611223

The Seasons of My Soul – A Poetic Diary

http://www.amazon.com/The-Seasons-My-Soul-Poetic/dp/0972605843

The Creative Model for the Solopreneur – Making the Creative Process Work for You

http://www.amazon.com/The-Creative-Model-Solopreneur-Process/dp/1466262079

Metaphysical Minute – Philosophy on the Run

http://www.williamsenpublications.com/store/p3/_Metaphysical_Minute_-_Philosophy_on_the_Run.html

Life Untwisted - Targeting Your Potential With A Fearless Attitude

http://www.amazon.com/Life-Untwisted-Targeting-Potential-Fearless/dp/0972605851/

MindSlap! - Shifting Your Perspective From Conditioned Reactions To Conscious Choices

http://www.amazon.com/MindSlap-Perspective-Conditioned-Reactions-Conscious/dp/1516815041/

Where Do I Go from Here?

https://www.amazon.com/Where-Do-Go-Here-Consider/dp/1542692520

Book of Metanoia

http://www.amazon.com/Book-Metanoia-Wisdom-Facilitate-Journey-ebook/dp/B00VPJG06I/

A Weary Traveler

https://www.amazon.com/dp/B07T7VGJFQ/

Descriptions of My Fiction Books

Second Chances – Paranormal Suspense

Second Chances is the evolutionary journey of Fredrika, whose life has been defined by her fear of an unspoken power within her and her need to suppress it by controlling herself and the world around her. Everything is brought into question by the appearance of a ghostly stalker, who disrupts her ordered existence and kills her assistant, leaving her clueless how to get rid of the chaos that has taken over her life.

When she is forced to step outside the rational confines of her life to accept the help of a wolf named Avatar, who seems to know more about what's going on than she does, the first step in her evolution begins.

The Threads That Bind – Paranormal Suspense

Thirty-nine years after *Second Chances*, the threads that bind the generations begin to reconnect for the final battle in *The Threads That Bind*. By quirk of fate, Mandy Gray, whose last and best friend was Fredrika Marsh, leaves her secluded profession as a research psychologist in 2019 to take a position as a guidance counselor at Briarton Academy where the orphaned and wealthy Jillian Missildine is a student. They become fast friends, but it is four years before they discover the thread that connects them.

Once this connection is made, all the others — those connected to the past through Freddie and her nemesis — flow swiftly toward each other. The patterns of their lives become tangled and knotted, and the decision has to be made about who will survive.

Center Stage –Romance with a Paranormal Twist

April Saunders is a woman after the brass ring and willing to do whatever it takes to feel it within her grasp. In her quest to be center stage, she barely even notices the trail of victims she leaves in her wake. Eventually her husband and daughter join all the others left behind.

Now the tide has turned. She has been left behind. No power. No options. No family. No friends. No hope.

Then a mysterious and seemingly magical woman named Grace appears at her door. Despondent, April is so weak-willed at this point she allows Grace to take charge, unaware that her life is about to take a turn few ever get to experience. As she takes a preternatural journey into her past, will her ambition continue to rule her heart? *Can there be salvation for one who has betrayed so many?*

Brita Madison Paranormal Mysteries Series

"Only the living are so persistent. The dead seem to understand that time is no longer an issue for them."

<u>Chasing Shadows [Book 1]</u>

Brita Madison is at best a reluctant psychic, and Chief of Police James Weston is the "poster boy for conservative." *Can he accept the unimaginable?*

Brita has found a sanctuary in Williams, Arizona, a refuge from the multitude of visions and voices that have chased her all her life. Then one vision touches her soul, and she finds herself embroiled in the middle of a missing person's case with a woman's life at stake. Little does she know that this is only the beginning.

Brita's visions uncover a trail of murders centered around the historic Route 66. As Brita steps deeper into the world she has been trying to escape, she and Weston are in a race against time to identify the serial killer. This journey threatens to tear apart their lives as well as those closest to them.

<u>Shattered Hearts [Book 2]</u>

In *Shattered Hearts* Brita Madison's newfound courage is pushed to the limits. A ghost boy she encounters in Phoenix while at a gathering of her new writing clients, who all possess and write about paranormal abilities, ignites an adventure that drags everyone in her world into the dark underbelly of a pedophile ring. Trying to rescue the children puts all of them in the cross-hairs, including her boyfriend Sam and her unofficial partner, James Weston. Many hearts will be shattered before this case is put to rest.

<u>Unraveling Memories [Book 3]</u>

Brita Madison has come a long way since she first met James Weston five years ago. After nearly being killed twice and losing her best friend James at the hand of an evil pedophile, she appreciates the slower pace of her interactions with the spirit world since moving to Phoenix with her new husband, Sam Jenkins. All that comes crashing down when the past returns with a vengeance, threatening her family and friends.

As if to make up for lost time, spirits begin showing up whose muddled memories test the resolve of Brita and her friends, old and new, to meet the challenges from the past and the present.

Circles of Freedom – Contemporary Thriller

When Brandon Boehle creates the Circles of Freedom blogs to strike a blow for truth, he has no idea of the loss, the love, and, the chaos it will set in motion. When the dominoes start to topple, there's a race to survive for friend and foe alike.

Brandon never imagines that a mercenary hired by the President of the United States would be out to kill not only him, but his assistant, Alise Winston, and the professionals who are writing the blogs. What started out as a simple, though carefully safeguarded, effort to get the truth out there has put all of them in the crosshairs. He quickly realizes that his expectations of the United States government have been naïve.

The contract put out on Circles of Freedom turns out to be the least of the worries for the country. A nefarious plot is uncovered to overthrow the government, and the players believe themselves to be untouchable. Circumstances draw Brandon and Alise and all those closest to them into this dark plot. Their only hope lies in a twist of fate.

When the Walls Come Tumbling Down – Women's Fiction

When the Walls Come Tumbling Down is a touching, page-turning novel of triumph over fears and sorrows. As it unfolds, it reminds us that when a crack appears in our walls and widens, something new has a chance to appear.

Two generations apart, Ashley Stanford and Claire Montoya have very little in common until their universes collide. Each has built walls in their life to survive. Ashley, however, has a head start of nearly six decades over Claire as a brick mason of the psyche. Tragedy has brought them together.

For well over a decade, Ashley has been the caregiver for her husband, who now lives in a nursing home. Trying to rediscover her life, she meets Claire, who is homeless and being stalked by a local drug dealer for reporting him to the police. Ashley takes her in and soon discovers there is much more to her story than she could have imagined.

After committing to helping Claire, Ashley is faced with her husband's passing. To help her occupy her mind in her grief, Ashley joins Claire on a journey that could turn both their lives upside down.

The Elyrian Emergence – Science Fiction

Elyria is the only country on the planet of Galen which is located in the Andromeda Galaxy. Galen meaning *calm* and Elyria meaning *blessed place* demonstrate the principles upon which this civilization was founded many centuries ago. Escaping from their ancient planet before it imploded as the result of their destructive policies, the mission of the Founders, those who orchestrated the means of escape, was to develop a civilization based on the philosophy of Self-Emergence.

On the surface, it seems to be working until the Karons, the sensitives who monitor the global energies, detect a negative shift in consciousness. The Karons' visions wake those in charge from their complacency and send them scrambling to curb the decline engineered by someone with an inordinate amount of power.

The questions this team of people find themselves asking are these: *Can we stop this before it's too late? How could we have not seen how vulnerable we are?*

The ultimate question is whether Elyria will wake up and realize that Self-Emergence is a forever journey, one where fear of the mistakes made by the ancient planet have no place if they are going to survive.

Invisible Shadows – Contemporary Thriller

Marriage, even dating, is not on Allegra Harris' list of goals until she meets Harper Frost during a land deal negotiation. A top-notch negotiator, Allegra is justifiably proud of having reached the position of Senior Vice-President of Security Land Investments. Harper's deal falls through, so she's startled when Harper keeps asking her out even though she has no time for relationships. Harper turns out to be as career-focused as she, and the two of them fall into an easy rhythm and ultimately marriage.

Having felt alone most of her life, Allegra doesn't recognize the superficiality of their marriage. She feels content because neither makes demands on the other's time, that is, until Allegra discovers she is pregnant. For the first time, she experiences a love that actively competes for the attention she's always reserved for her work. Chloe's birth shines a new light on hers and Harper's lives and creates a shift in their marriage, but she still believes she loves Harper. Still, the earlier loss of her nest egg to shore up his business lingers in the back of her mind as her need to protect her daughter's future grows.

Everything moves along routinely until the day Allegra receives a phone call from the NTSB. It seems Harper is presumed dead in a plane crash in the Atlantic Ocean while on a flight to Nassau. With no body found, Allegra's life is turned upside down. Trying to handle his affairs, she discovers she did not know her husband at all. The more she tries to tie up loose ends, the more stray threads she discovers. Threads that lead to more questions: Did Harper Frost ever really exist? Is he still alive? Is he dangerous?

Descriptions of My Nonfiction Books

MindSlap!

Is your life making you miserable? Make the move to a better life by learning how to make the creative process work for you! *You need a method that works no matter what your goal.*

Just because an approach worked for someone else doesn't mean it's going to work for you! You are unique! Your background, your relationships, your education, your experiences all contribute to a wonderfully unique YOU. They influence your thinking and the way you approach the systems that are supposed to make you successful. Most important, however, you need *a system that allows you to master your intentions.*

Why is it so important to master your intentions? Your Life Intentions are those intentions that are in harmony with your vibration in this life experience. Your Life Intentions are the basis for all that makes you unique.

When you create goals in your life that are expressions of your life intentions, you not only experience greater joy and greater prosperity, but you are taking a path that will bring you full circle to the understanding of how unique you REALLY ARE! Who are you behind all those erroneous thoughts about yourself? You are a powerful, creative being! To use this power for its greatest purpose, you have to be aware of your creations. *You cannot discover your life's purpose without becoming a conscious creator.*

This brings us back to finding the best method for doing this. You're not looking for a Life Method. You need a method that is spiritually based and allows you to work effectively with your inner psychology.

You need a method that is the driving force behind the Law of Attraction. In *MindSlap!* we offer you a process that is outlined in sacred texts back to ancient times. However, the messages, such as those in the parables, are esoteric or hidden beneath the surface circumstances. It was given this way for those who are ready to dig deeper and take on the mantle of Spirit. *The 7-Step creative process in this book is the esoteric engine that will move your dreams forward!*

This is the process that enables you to work on letting go of all that isn't serving you. It helps you manifest the goals that express your Life Intentions. Every time you use it, you hone your skills and enhance your inherent abilities – all of which takes you closer and closer to your ultimate goal:

- being at one with the understanding that you and God are One
- accepting your creative birthright and mastering your Life Intentions
- consciously co-creating with God.

Please be aware that *MindSlap!* is the paperback version of a 5 CD audiobook titled *It's Your Move! Transform Your Dreams from Wishful Thinking to Reality*. It was a Bronze Award Winner in ForeWord Magazine's 2004 Book of the Year Awards. There is a very limited supply remaining, but as long as they last, you can contact me at dannyewilliamsen@gmail.com to order for a reduced price: $20 + shipping (US only).

Metaphysical Minute – Philosophy on the Run

Metaphysical Minute is a breath of fresh air in the saturated field of personal evolution. Clarity, insight, and passion punctuate these powerful essays on the concepts that form the foundation for everyone's journey toward spiritual understanding.

Metaphysics is simply an approach to self-knowledge that reaches beyond the belief that it is what we do that is important. It searches always for the path that creates healing within one's soul.

Here are a few of the comments by readers:

"My "Chicken Soup" for Spiritual and Personal Growth. Metaphysical Minute - Philosophy on the Run by Dannye Williamsen is a wonderful tool if you are looking for personal and spiritual growth. This book contains a collection of essays that are not, by any means, a fast, easy read, but an intensely deep, thought provoking look at the way we, as people, look at situations surrounding us and the way we deal with them. I highly recommend reading one essay at a time and then taking time to ponder on the message within it." – S. Wolters

"Metaphysical Minute is a deep, spiritual, and insightful collection of essays that will make you think and define how to live your life to the fullest. I absolutely love it!" – Katia Lord

"I love your book. It feels like my heart's talking!" – Amber Zain

Where Do I Go From Here?

Does it feel like life has let you down? It can be so discouraging when you have worked hard and seen no real return. Your life can begin to cycle between hope and disappointment until you feel that nothing works for you. You see those around you prospering, and you can't understand it. Why not me? you ask.

Then you wake up one morning and ask an age-old question: Where do I go from here? You thought you were on your right path, expressing your passion, but it seems to have fallen on deaf ears.

Whether you're young, old, or somewhere in-between, this moment is when you can make the greatest decision of your life. Stop looking to life for your answers. Clean the lens through which you view life. Examine your inner world as you move forward.

Life Untwisted – Targeting Your Potential with a Fearless Attitude

In trying to live our lives, we inadvertently get things twisted around. We lose sight of what is important for our spiritual growth and what is inconsequential.

Of course, nothing is really inconsequential because lessons are there to be learned regardless. However, it is still important for us to prioritize the people, the actions, the feelings, the thoughts in our lives because most of us tend to turn our worlds upside down. We make the least important the most important and vice versa. We carry the residue of experiences around with us that we should have released long ago and let them rule our lives.

In order to live a happier life, we must learn how to develop a fearless attitude and how to target our potential. Each of these undertakings involves certain areas of work. To develop a fearless attitude, we must work on building a foundation, healing, and strategies, each of which also include many areas of focus. To target our potential, we must understand the creative process, develop visions for our life and business as well as learn how to create better relationships.

A Weary Traveler

Yes, I am a weary traveler at seven decades into my life. I am still searching, and it may seem from the words that flow from me that there is a lack of faith. There isn't. It is just the weariness that can come from traveling the paths we choose for ourselves even though we say we don't want to be on them. Yet, here they are. Some paths are personal. Some are part of the groups of humans with which we identify.

My words sometimes reflect a personal venting; other times an awareness of truth that holds for all of us; and sometimes simply personal observations of the world around me. I can only continue to search for a higher understanding because growing is not an option for me.

The Book of Metanoia

I have consciously been on my spiritual journey for over 40 years. Since the turn of the century, I have been expressing myself through writing. These bits of wisdom came out of my own experiences at different times over these years. I am thrilled to share them with you. If you read my first two novels, you will recognize a few of them that I included there and attributed to the Book of Metanoia, which was only a work in progress at the time.

The Seasons of My Soul – a Poetic Diary

I won't pretend these poems have any value to the literary world because I'm quite sure they don't. They were simply my way of expressing the emotions that were overtaking me at different times in my life and yet filling me with wonder at other times.

I won't apologize if their structure falls short because these "poems" were my safety valve—the outlet that let me release my unproductive emotions. They were also the way I was able to express my personal growth when those around me did not see things the same way I did. So, I bless them. . .warts and all!

As you read the poems, you will notice that I have given you the date each was actually written, beginning in 1963 when I was 14 years old. I also shared the event or attitude that sparked the poem. After I discovered these expressions of mine tucked in-between the boxes and boxes of paper I had accumulated over the years, I instinctively put them in chronological order. That was when I realized it was an order that defined my spiritual journey with all its ups and downs, lessons ignored, and lessons learned. So, at the top of each poem, you will see a running commentary. It is psychological in nature. With hindsight and hopefully greater wisdom, I have tried to present an inner perspective, showing my true journey from 1963 through the poem I wrote when I reached fifty.

Friends who have read my compilation have uniformly told me that even though I had different experiences than some of them, they still recognized the emotions behind the different poems. They said that some evoked memories while others stirred up emotions they thought they had resolved.

Whatever their effect on you, please know that I lay no claim to being a poet. I do believe, however, that we are all one, struggling to express ourselves and experiencing the same emotions with differing circumstances. If my journey helps you in any way, I am simply grateful.

Excerpt: The Threads That Bind

(Sequel by Dannye Williamsen)

Prologue: 2002

*T*he air was crisp when Freddie and Garrison McCrary arrived in Bettles, Alaska. They had flown in from Nome via Fairbanks. Just being in Alaska was a dream come true for Freddie, but their last night in Nome was an experience she wasn't likely to forget. The sky lit up with a burst of lights in shades of green and blue. Then a brilliant, red hue mingled among them, almost overwhelming the emerald greens and azure blues. As the intensity of the geomagnetic storm decreased, the aggressiveness of the red lights gave way to the greens and blues until nothing remained but the night sky.

Garrison was looking forward to today's adventure. They had chartered a Cessna 185 to do some flight-seeing. They were in agreement that viewing the Brooks Range of mountains from the air was going to be a spiritual experience. Just being here without civilization and thousands of cars was like stepping back in time. In the entire town of Bettles there were only about 40 people, one lodge, and two charter services. The service Garrison chose advertised a Cessna 185. As a small plane pilot himself, he was familiar with this model and knew that having a backup pilot was always a prudent plan.

Settling in at the Bettles Lodge was quick, and it wasn't long before Freddie and Garrison were in the air. Just before boarding the Cessna, Freddie nudged Garrison and whispered, "What if our pilot is a real stick in the mud?"

"I doubt that he is. After all, he'd probably die from boredom if he sat in silence the whole trip day after day. What worries me," said Garrison, "is that we're going to be shut up in a space the size of a water closet with this guy. I just hope he used deodorant this morning!"

"Sh-h-h!" Freddie hissed, trying to keep from laughing as the pilot approached them.

"Are you folks ready to take off?" Jeff asked with a grin.

"Absolutely!" they declared simultaneously.

"Then let's get this trip started." By arrangement with the air service, they were getting an extended tour of the Brooks Range.

"It's so quiet," whispered Freddie. "I feel like I'm in church, and if I talk too loudly, I'll disturb God."

Chuckling, Garrison replied, "It certainly relieves you of all the distractions in life. I understand why people fall in love with the majesty of this wilderness. It's like we slipped through a time warp and are viewing God's unspoiled creation before man's footprint ever soiled the ground."

"I've heard quite a few descriptions in my time, but that's a different one," said Jeff, looking back over his shoulder, "but, I have to agree with you. After flying out here for the last several years, I think I would die if I moved back to San Francisco."

Holding tightly to Garrison's arm, Freddie replied, "I wish that I could live in this moment forever, but," she sighed, "that would be impossible!"

After admiring the scenery for a while, Garrison noticed that Jeff kept glancing over his left shoulder. He turned to see what was catching Jeff's attention and saw another small plane behind them. From this distance he couldn't tell what it was. "Jeff, are you worried about that plane? I've noticed you keeping an eye on it."

"Yeah."

"It's a fairly safe distance away—don't you think?"

"It's not that. I'm not aware of any other charters up here today, and I don't recognize the plane."

"Maybe it's a private plane." Garrison wasn't particularly worried. The skies were clear, and he knew that the chances of a collision were nearly nil.

Jeff frowned. "I've changed course a couple of times so that you folks could see some areas I think are spectacular, and every time that plane has kept pace with us. It keeps the same distance and the same course."

"Why don't you try to reach them on the radio?" asked Garrison, concern starting to surface.

Jeff nodded. He had been trying to convince himself that he was overreacting, but Garrison's suggestion gave him an excuse to act. Picking up the mike, he tried several times to contact the mysterious plane, but there was no answer.

"Okay," said Jeff, "I'm going to make a drastic course change. If he follows, I'm going to head back to base. I don't want to get caught up in these mountains and run out of gas trying to evade this creep."

"Why don't you turn your course toward him? It would make him have to change course to avoid a collision, which I'm sure he would do. I doubt he's on a suicide mission. If he corrects his course so that he can continue to follow us at a distance, then I say, let's get the hell out of here!" Garrison declared.

"Sounds good to me," said Jeff, turning the plane to his left.

Frightened, Freddie peered out the window, able to see the other plane clearly for the first time. When it turned to the right to avoid their paths crossing, Freddie breathed a sigh of relief.

"He's probably like those drivers on the freeway. They settle in behind the lead car and let them make all the decisions so they can relax," said Freddie hopefully.

Garrison wasn't so sure. He kept pressing his face against the window to see where the plane went.

"Do you see anything?" asked Freddie.

"No," replied Garrison. "How about you, Jeff?"

"Not so far."

Not wanting to ignore any possibilities, Freddie pressed her face to the window on her side. "Omigod!" she cried.

"What is it?" Garrison shouted.

"There it is! It's behind us on my side. I can just barely see it."

Getting nervous, Garrison touched Jeff on the shoulder. "I think I'm ready to head back. What about you?"

"You got it! I'm not interested in playing war games up here with some nut-ball."

Suddenly the plane lurched. Freddie screamed. Garrison shouted at Jeff, "What's happening?" The plane dipped, quickly losing altitude.

Pulling on the controls, Jeff shouted, "I don't know. The plane isn't responding. It acts like it has a mind of its own."

Freddie looked down. All she could see were white-capped mountains and cerulean pools reflecting the mountain peaks. Her thoughts turned to her daughter, Alicia. At that moment she knew her ill-spoken wish was coming true. She would live in this moment forever because these primeval mountains would be the last things she ever saw.

The plane seemed to stop in mid-air, as impossible as that was. The sides of the plane bowed inward as if some invisible machine was crushing it between its jaws. The windows broke free of the frame as the body of the aircraft crumpled. Garrison unsnapped their seat belts and pulled Freddie to him.

"I love you," he whispered in her ear, tears flowing down his face.

Freddie turned and kissed him. "I love you, too." She laid her face against his, their tears merging, as she sensed the impossibly slow downward movement of the plane begin. "What's happening to us? Do you think it's possible that it has something to do with—"

Her words were cut off as the plane, looking more like a crumpled wad of paper, slipped into one of the cerulean pools Freddie had admired, hidden from curious eyes forever.

http://www.amazon.com/Threads-That-Bind-Dannye-Williamsen/dp/0972605878

www.ingramcontent.com/pod-product-compliance
Lightning Source LLC
Chambersburg PA
CBHW051436260626
47162CB00001B/126